EM

"What's on?" *Guide.* She was a bit nervous now that dinner was over. They settled on a salute to George Gershwin, and the rich chords of the "American in Paris" suite filled the room. But Dorrie could not sit still.

The fourth time she rose from the couch, Travis took hold of her wrist. "What now?" he asked.

"My plants. I forgot to water them."

"They'll live through the night." He stood and took her other hand. "Dance with me, Dorrie."

She felt her body loosen as they danced to the sweet old songs: "Embraceable You," "How Long Has This Been Going On?" and, at last, "I've Got a Crush on You." Travis was a much better dancer than George had been.

As the song ended, Travis tightened his arms around her, laid her head into his neck, and stroked her hair. "Dorrie?" he whispered. He lifted her chin and looked into her eyes. "I'd like to kiss you," he said. "May I do that?"

The kiss, gentle and searching, surprised her. She hadn't had a kiss like that since she was a girl, and it stirred long-lost memories. "Mercy!" she breathed, and he laughed softly. "You're some kisser, you are!"

He gave her another, this one more intense. She responded with an unexpected hunger, then found herself kissing him back, tightening her arms around him.

Dorrie felt like a block of ice set out in a tropic sun.

CATCH A RISING STAR!

ROBIN ST. THOMAS

MAYBE LATER, LOVE

CLAIRE BOCARDO

ZEBRA BOOKS
KENSINGTON PUBLISHING CORP.

This book is for:

My mother, Rita Crothers,
who always knew I could;

My great-aunt, Nelle Thrift,
who always knew I would; and

My husband Larry, who said,
"Do what makes you happy."

ZEBRA BOOKS

are published by

Kensington Publishing Corp.
475 Park Avenue South
New York, NY 10016

First printing: September, 1992

Printed in the United States of America

One

Every day since her husband's death, Dorrie Hunter Greene had learned something new and surprising about herself. Last week it had been that she conducted private monologues. Aloud.

"Quit mumbling, Mother!" Marcie had called from the kitchen. "Who're you talking to, anyhow?"

Dorrie, brushing out her thick salt-and-pepper hair, had been startled and embarrassed.

"Nobody, honey," she'd said. "Only myself."

Since then, she'd caught herself at it times beyond counting. "Thinking out loud," she called it, fearing its possible implications. Bad enough to be widowed, without being crazy too.

Now, hunched over the black-bound double-entry accounting books in the back of the jewelry store George had left her, she was discovering how angry she could be at a defenseless dead man.

5

"How could you, George!" she protested. "You never taught me one thing about business! How am I supposed to run the store when I can't even do books!"

Dorrie had been in this stockroom as a little girl, when her father owned the store; as a young woman, when her husband became her father's partner; and in middle age, in name half-owner but in fact as much a decorative piece as any cut-glass flower bowl on the shelf. Now she was its full owner, still as unaware of the way the store ran as she'd been in the beginning.

"Damnation!" she muttered, pushing her glasses up the bridge of her nose. "Sent your daughter to the University of Texas for an MBA and kept your wife as ignorant as a child!" She threw her pencil across the stockroom. It bounced off the green shade of the single bulb that hung from the rafters and clattered to the ground, and George's eyebrow rose in the back-most corner of her mind. Eyes burning with unshed tears, Dorrie got up and walked back among the shelves of fine china and crystal to retrieve the pencil. Her glasses fell off when she bent over, and she put them in her pocket.

"I'll just have to ask Marcie and her fancy degree to teach me bookkeeping, that's all," she muttered, folding her glasses and slipping them into their needlepoint case. As if she didn't have enough on her mind.

Dorrie blew her nose, picked up her jacket, and walked through the store. She unlocked the door and let herself out, then turned back and locked the door, walked a few steps away, and returned to try the door as George had taught her.

A few cars moved up and down the wide, brightly lit street. The shops had been closed for hours. Dorrie checked her watch—eight-thirty—and debated whether to walk home or down to the cafeteria on the corner to eat. Eating won. Not because she was hungry; she was seldom hungry anymore. Only because she was not ready to face the house alone. It had been nearly two months since she'd wakened to find George dead beside her, but entering that empty house was no easier than it had been the first week. Thank goodness for her cat. Still, sweet and intuitive as he was, Domino was no replacement for a husband.

"I just can't keep up with it," she protested. "Here it is the middle of November, and I haven't even unpacked the Christmas decorations!" She looked back over her shoulder, feeling like one of those crazy ladies who prowled the downtown streets talking to themselves and digging in garbage cans.

George would not mind about the decorations. He'd been the lone holdout, a stubborn traditionalist refusing to decorate for Christmas until Thanksgiving had passed. She could do it next

7

week, Dorrie thought, reaching into her pocket for another tissue. Maybe Marcie and George II would help her decorate.

Of course if Two helped, his sweet little wife would insist on helping too. Dorrie winced and shook her head. If Susan helped, the place would look like a dimestore. Susan would drag out every tricked-up gimcrack made since the Year One to produce an angel-and-Santa stew—Rudolph lying in the Virgin Mary's lap—and then she'd call it "cute."

"I'd rather ruin it with my own hand," Dorrie said aloud. "Thank you all the same."

She'd had another of those odd dreams again last night, one she couldn't remember except for the lost feeling it had left behind. She'd been dreaming a lot recently, strange dreams. The first one had been unusually vivid. In it, a lovely young woman who looked like Princess Ozma had led her to the ornate double doors of a grand ballroom. The doors swung open, and she heard Benny Goodman's clarinet playing the wistful notes of "Goodbye." Semitransparent figures swirled about her, the men in tuxedos and the women in full-skirted ball gowns like those of Dorrie's girlhood. Watching them, she noticed a widening hole in the center of the parquet floor; then, piece by piece, the parquetry fell through until Dorrie stood upon bare rafters, looking down at bright sunlight streaming through the building's frame. She had felt no fear, only wonder as the rafters had become a cloud of pale, yellow butterflies and she'd realized she was standing in midair.

"And you died as I lay dreaming," she told George now, "and I've been in midair ever since."

The cafeteria was a short walk down University. The stores on this street backed up onto houses fifty and more years old, frame-and-brick bungalows with deep verandas and dormers in the roofs. Between Hunter & Greene's Jewelry and the cafeteria stood a Walgreen's with one of the few remaining soda fountains in Dallas; a sporting goods store that catered to the college kids; a camera store with its own small photo lab; and Jeannine's Beauty Shoppe, whose window had held the same white latticework wound with the same pink plastic flowers for as long as Dorrie could remember. Jeannine had done Dorrie's hair every Thursday morning since 1973.

A flash of heavy, cream-colored paper sticking out of her purse caught Dorrie's eye, and she smiled. All day long, she'd been saving the letter from Charmaine to read over dinner: her dessert.

Charmaine Stubbs (it was her maiden name; Dorrie'd quit trying to keep up with her married ones) had popped in and out of Dorrie's life at odd intervals ever since they'd been girls together in school. Mr. Hunter, Dorrie'd understood much later, had sent his daughters to Miss Pickerel's

9

Private Academy to protect them from contamination by the common run of children. Dorrie smiled now, remembering: he had not counted on Charmaine, whose newly oil-rich parents had sent her from a small west Texas town to Miss Pickerel in the vain hope of giving her some "culture."

Scared, gangly, and rough as a cob, Charmaine had taken to Dorrie immediately. And, never having met anyone remotely like Charmaine Stubbs, Dorrie had been fascinated. They were eleven when Charmaine had offered Dorrie her first cigarette. When Dorrie'd said, "No, thank you. I don't smoke," Charmaine had been incredulous.

"What?" she'd demanded. "Even when you won't get caught?"

"I swear to God," Charmaine used to say, "you have no sense of adventure *at* all!" But she'd made it clear to the others that anybody who wanted to mess with Dorrie would have to get past Charmaine Stubbs first. Not many tried. Even Barbara, Dorrie's older sister, had treated her with respect when Charmaine was around.

Light from the cafeteria's windows warmed the street, and the odors of fried chicken and hot bread filled Dorrie's head. She pushed through the double doors and entered into warmth and quiet. The dark-haired woman behind the salad counter waved as she approached.

"Hi, Miz Greene. You almost missed us; we

10

close in a few minutes. I thought you weren't coming."

"I worked a little later than usual at the store." Dorrie shrugged and offered a small, self-deprecating smile. "I've got a lot to learn about business, Gracie. I'm afraid there'll be a lot of late nights."

"You'll make it," Gracie said. "How 'bout some of this Waldorf salad now? Made it fresh this afternoon."

"Thanks." Dorrie accepted the salad and picked up a slab of white fish with a glutinous, pale yellow sauce on top and a dish of unnaturally green broccoli. After ordering chamomile tea, she sat down, put on her glasses, and removed the letter from her purse. It had a Peruvian stamp and was addressed in an impetuous scrawl. Smoothing the folds from the stiff paper, she began to read:

Dorrie—
  I'm so sorry. Darren, my oldest one, clipped George's obit from the *Morning News* and mailed it in September, and it's been following me for two months. It caught up with me on this mountaintop just yesterday. I don't know what to say. My longest marriage only lasted twelve years, and I wanted out bad, and it was *still* unshirted hell to be alone afterward! And it's been so

long since I saw you—three years, I think—
but you're always in my mind and I hate that
you're hurting. George and I never did understand each other worth a damn, but I
knew you loved him and he treated you
right, and that was good enough for me.

I was thinking about coming home next
week (the 20th) anyway. This settles it; call
you when I get there. I'm alone too, now—
this trip was to celebrate the divorce—so
maybe we can spend some time together and
catch up.

You'll make it through whatever comes;
you're tougher than you look. But if you
want somebody to talk with, or just *be* with,
I'm on my way.

All my love (as ever),
Charmaine

P.S. After Feather and Lovett and Sweet,
I'm back to Stubbs. This time, I won't even
have to change the monograms—and this
time, it really *is* Forever After! See you next
week.

Smiling, Dorrie poked a bit of the tasteless
whitefish into her mouth and chewed absently,
thinking of Charmaine in her wedding dress (the
first one), her unruly orange hair battling the veil
as she kicked her train behind her to start down
the aisle; Max Feather, the slender, dark-haired

groom, pale with anticipation; Dorrie waiting across from him in sea green taffeta. Forever After. It had lasted into their middle thirties.

Charmaine had married again at forty-two—another doctor, Forever After—and divorced within a year, just before she went to Tibet. She'd come back by way of India, where for a while she'd lived (how closely, Dorrie had preferred not to know) with a guru.

"Do you know, that sneaky little sumbitch wanted me to sign over my *income* to him?" she'd said later. "Can you believe it? 'No, sir!' I told him. 'Buddha is Buddha, and bidness is bidness!' " She'd grinned. "Little shit threw me out of the ashram for lack of faith. I couldn't pack fast enough!"

But through some form of magic, Charmaine had always seemed to know when Dorrie needed her. She'd cut short a vacation in the Bahamas to appear the day after Dorrie miscarried her second child. She'd been with Dorrie when she got the phone call saying Mama'd died, and she'd held Dorrie's hand through the funeral; George hadn't liked it, but he'd put up with it. When Dorrie was so worried about Marcie's friends and sex and dope, Charmaine had "borrowed" Marcie for a weekend at Disneyland ("I need a kid," she'd said. "You can't go to Disneyland without a kid.") and the problem had simply evaporated. When Dorrie'd been wading through the Slough

13

of Despond in her early forties, Charmaine had appeared out of nowhere (actually, out of India, but it had seemed no less miraculous for all that) to make her laugh again.

The lights blinked. Dorrie stacked her dishes on the tray and stood up. So she's coming back, she thought, slipping into her coat. From Peru. She'll have flying saucer stories to tell . . . goodness knows what.

Later, as she fell asleep, she thought of the letter again and smiled. That night she dreamed.

She is in the hall of a large, labyrinthine school. She is too old to be in this school, and she's embarrassed not to have finished her work here, but she has one more class to complete before she graduates. She and Charmaine signed up for the class together a long time ago, but Dorrie got sidetracked and has never been able to find the classroom.

The halls are full of students, laughing and shoving, slamming locker doors and shouting to one another, but when she tries to ask them about her class they laugh at her: "How can you not know what class you're in?"

"Shoot, lady," a tall boy says, grinning, "if you haven't found it by now, you might as well hang it up. It's almost time for finals!"

The hall monitor says disdainfully, "There

14

must be some mistake: you're looking for room 302 in a building that has only two floors."

Students surge through the halls like schools of fish, and Dorrie is caught in a flood of youngsters climbing the stairs to the top floor. They disappear into their classrooms, and she is left standing alone. She moves from door to door, listening for the teachers' words, trying to recognize what the classes are about, but all the doors are shut: she can hear only the buzz of interested voices, occasional laughter. Even if she could hear, she thinks, it would not help: she cannot remember her teacher's name or the subject of her class.

Still, Dorrie knows she will be held responsible for the course material. She wanders the halls in the wan hope of finding her classroom, knowing that she will not. If only she could hear Charmaine's voice . . .

Two

Dorrie woke up cross and tearful, angry without reason. Two and Susan and the children would be there in an hour to take her to church. She didn't want to go to church, but she knew she'd end up there anyway because she hadn't the strength to argue. Before George's death, she hadn't been there for fifteen years; since, she'd gone only to keep peace with her son. And dear, conventional Two would be appalled that she was not eager to hear the pastor's sermon on Why We Should All Be Thankful.

"I am *not* thankful!" she told him, glaring into the mirror as she rinsed out her toothbrush. "You go ahead; be as thankful as you please, but I'm simply not in the mood!" Of course, she could never say such a thing to her son. He was too much like his father; he would not understand. And as to Susan . . . Susan would be horrified. Susan often misquoted Robert Louis Stevenson:

16

"The world is so full of such marvelous things, I'm sure we should all be as happy as kings!" A few months ago Dorrie would not have argued, but now her world view was less sanguine.

She poured a cup of coffee and sat on the back steps in the morning sun. The garden had been her salvation after the funeral, accepting in patient silence her tears, her protests, her bewildered rage at having been left to rattle around alone in this big house. God was present in the soil when she could find Him nowhere else. The smell of fresh earth as she'd dug tulip bulbs to winter in the storm cellar had comforted her. Clumps of daylilies in their second bloom had given her hope for her own recovery.

"Your Michaelmas daisies sure are pretty this year. They're always the last to bloom, and they make such a show."

Dorrie turned to see Jessie Buynum step through the gap in the hedge that separated their yards. They'd been neighbors more than twenty years, and suffering through their kids' teens together had wrought an unbreakable bond between them. Jessie, in worn bluejeans and a plaid shirt, sipped from a coffee mug.

" 'Morning Jess," Dorrie said. "They do, don't they." The plants looked like weeds through most of the year, but in late October they repaid her patience with great clouds of fine-petaled, pale-blue flowers.

17

"What've you been up to?" Jessie crossed the yard and plumped herself down on the steps next to Dorrie. "We've hardly seen you for weeks."

"Been spending a lot of time at the store, I guess."

Jessie reached up to pat Dorrie's knee.

"Feel closer to him there, do you?"

"No closer than anyplace else. I just can't stay here all by myself. I used to fuss about how quiet George was—how hard it was to get a word out of him and how you could be in the same room with him for an hour before you even knew he was there—but believe me, Jess, I know the difference now. At least at the store there are real, live people to talk to."

"You know you can come over anytime. I'm always there, and Reese don't care. He's as happy to see you as I am."

"Thanks, Jessie. I know."

Dorrie could imagine how happy Reese would be to see her. George hadn't been cold in his grave before Reese had come sniffing after her like a dog after a bitch. One Saturday afternoon when Jess had gone to visit her mother in the nursing home, he'd come over to sit on the porch with her just like this. She'd gone inside to pour iced tea for him, and he'd followed her into the kitchen. Instead of sitting at the table, Reese had backed her up against the refrigerator door and tried to kiss her.

Dorrie had planted her palms against his broad chest and given him a shove so hard he'd cracked his back against the bar four feet away.

"What do you think you're doing?" she'd demanded.

"Just offering a little comfort," he'd said, rubbing his back. "You don't seem real grateful for it, I must say."

"Grateful!" Too shocked to do anything but splutter, she'd watched him back around the bar and make for the door. With his hand on the knob, he'd turned back.

"That's okay, Dorrie. I'm a real forgivin' man. You'll think better of it soon, and then just remember: I'm right next door." He displayed a horrid leer. "I'm a real good handyman, you know. I'd be happy to drive your screws any time."

When the screen slammed behind him, Dorrie sagged against the fridge and wondered what she'd done to lead him on. Nothing, she knew, but it had taken several days to move past guilt into indignation.

Now she looked at his wife—plain, kindly, sensible Jessie—and wondered if she knew the sort of man she'd been married to all these years. One thing was sure: Dorrie'd never tell her.

"You coming to garden club Wednesday week?" Jessie asked. "We've got a real good speaker lined up, the head gardener at the Arboreturn. And it's at Nonie's house. you know what good refreshments she always puts out!"

"Sure," Dorrie said. "I'll be there. Maybe she'll make that New Orleans chocolate cake again. I could eat the whole thing myself."

"Well, everybody'll be real glad to see you. You missed September and October both, and you never miss a meeting. We've all been worried about you."

Maybe, Dorrie thought. She certainly hadn't been swamped with calls, though two or three of the women had been by the store.

They finished their coffee in companionable silence, and Jessie stood up.

"Reese'll have my head if I don't get over there and get dressed for church," she said. "He must have a crush on the preacher's wife or something. We can't miss a service." She bent to pat Dorrie's shoulder and started across the yard.

"Don't be a stranger, now," she called, and disappeared through the hedge.

Dorrie went inside to dress. Poking through her closet for something to wear made her cross all over again, dissatisfied with herself and her appearance. Her clothes looked limp as dishrags, and her skin sallow. She of the naturally pink cheeks, who hardly ever wore makeup, spent thirty minutes on her face and still didn't like it. She ended up washing off everything she'd put on and making do with a little powder and blush.

The children arrived promptly at ten.

"Where's your hat, Mother?" Susan asked as they started out the door. "You always wear a hat to church."

"I forgot it. Trey, dear, will you get my black hat from the hall closet shelf?"

George III, a tall twelve-year-old, found the hat. Dorrie jammed it onto her head without the aid of a mirror and turned to Susan.

"Will I do now?" she snapped, and stalked to the car without waiting for an answer, still angry and now ashamed of herself besides. Susan couldn't help being Susan, she told herself. She was perfect for Two; the last thing he needed was a wife with a brain in her head. Lord *God,* I'm being hateful! she thought, and felt tears burning her eyes. What's the matter with me?

In church, she dabbed angrily at her eyes when they sang George's favorite hymn: "Abide with me, fast falls the eventide. The darkness deepens; Lord, with me abide." He had not. He'd gone off somewhere behind the clouds, and she would never see his face again. Wendy, Trey's little sister, squeezed her grandma's hand surreptitiously and made Dorrie feel even worse. What right had she to impose her grief on a ten-year-old? She shut her eyes during the sermon, her whole body rejecting the message. When it was over, she rose from her aisle seat and rushed out the door to wait for the family at the car.

Later, she helped Wendy and Trey set the table at the grand, new, energy-efficient house Two and Susan had just bought on a creek lot in Carrollton. It had been Two's proof — as much to himself as to the world — that his practice was doing well: five bedrooms, three and a half baths, two living areas (one with a cathedral ceiling and one for children), a separate library, and a large, sunny, island kitchen with not just the microwave, but also a food processor built in.

On Susan's second-best lace tablecloth, they laid out the Towle silverplate and Franciscanware she and George had given the children for their wedding. Susan set out a holiday centerpiece she'd made of fancy gourds, dried wheat, and red corn in its husks, tied with a large, orange-satin bow. Three plastic geese of descending sizes — Papa, Mama, and Baby, Dorrie guessed — marched in a row beside it.

"That's pretty, Susan," Dorrie said, by way of apology for her earlier rudeness. "You made it?" At Susan's nod, she added, "You did a nice job."

"Thank you, Mother. I found the pattern in *Woman's Day*. They always have beautiful craft projects." Susan adjusted a gourd. "The geese were my own idea," she added modestly. "I'd be happy to make one for you, if you like."

"Thank you, dear, but I probably wouldn't use it. I don't decorate much at home anymore."

"Oh, but you should!" Susan exclaimed. "It's

just as important to have the house pretty for yourself as for somebody else, don't you think?"

"I suppose so. I just forget."

"Well," Susan said, her voice full of doubt, "whatever you say. Let me know if you change your mind."

In all the years Dorrie'd known her, Susan had never learned to relax into the family's bosom. Her need to please could be suffocating. Anyone would think a runner-up in the Miss Texas pageant would have a little self-confidence, but there was nothing of the spoiled beauty in Susan. The only thing beauty had spoiled for Susan, Dorrie thought, was her ability to believe that she could be loved for anything else. It was the Marilyn Monroe Syndrome at work: no matter how sweet, how kind, how generous, how talented she might be, Susan's day could be ruined by a hair out of place or a spot on her blouse. And Dorrie'd discovered that rejecting Susan's help in however small a task was tantamount to rejecting Susan herself.

"Maybe you can teach me how one day," Dorrie said. "For now, I already have more than I can use."

After dinner, when the children had gone out to play, Dorrie offered to help with the dishes.

"That's all right, Mother," Susan said. "You just go sit down with George. This won't take me a minute."

23

Dorrie went into the library where her son was playing a Bach concerto on his stereo. Though rather small, the library was Two's favorite room. The end wall was lined with books: histories, biographies, and political tomes—Susan kept her romance novels in the den shelves. Crown molding in a repeating spiral pattern set off pale peach walls, milk-washed woodwork, and a soft blue carpet.

"Two," she said, sitting in the smaller of the blue leather wing chairs that flanked the front window, "I seem to have developed an allergy. My nose has been running for weeks, and my eyes water all the time. Can you do anything for me?"

"Of course," he said. "I've noticed it, and it's been worrying me." He paused before adding seriously. "You know, Mother, the medical community has been discovering more and more links between physical and emotional states. I wonder if your 'allergy' isn't caused by depression—unshed tears, so to speak, demanding their way out. You haven't been the same since Dad died."

"You can't expect me to recover overnight."

"I know. But even if you alleviate these symptoms, you'll still have to deal with the causes: Dad's death, the store, being alone. . . . Of course Susan and I are always here and Kurt and Marcie only live a few miles away . . ." He cleared his throat with the same "harrumph" her

24

father had used. "Your social life has dropped to zero. It's not healthy."

Poor Two, Dorrie thought, exasperation mixing with her pity. He never had been able to handle emotional issues. Like his father, he always went stiff when feelings were deep. She stood up and crossed the room, her back to him, bringing her voice into control.

"It's not the same without your dad," she said.

"I understand that. If something happened to Susan . . . Well, I can't even think about it. But I just finished a course in this, Mother. I'm doing a lot of geriatrics these days, and yours is not an uncommon problem among the aging."

Rage welled up and squeezed off Dorrie's windpipe as Two reached under the end table for his pipe. He opened the walnut humidor at his elbow (a gift from Susan, it was a terrier with inlaid mother-of-pearl eyes and each hair carved precisely in place), and filled the pipe. Concentrating his gaze on his hands, Two carefully tamped the tobacco into its bowl as he went on speaking.

"I have this friend who does counseling," he said. "He could help you sort out your feelings and get back on your feet. Will you think about it, please?" Dorrie's son the doctor got up and crossed to the desk from which he took a card. "Here's his name and address. He's usually booked pretty solid, but if you tell him you're my mother he'll make time for you."

"Thank you," Dorrie said, slipping the card into her pocket. She wanted to smack him. Geriatrics, indeed! She was only fifty-five years old, a strong and healthy woman!

"Would you mind taking me home now?" she asked, her voice deliberately feeble. "Suddenly I'm very tired."

Three

Dorrie walked up the steps of her comfortable, 1920s style, brick-and-frame bungalow, conscious of Two's eyes on her back. He was always careful to see a lady safely into the house before he drove away, she thought. It was an old-fashioned courtesy that had become a modern necessity. She crossed the deep, roofed porch, turned the key in the lock, and waved as she let herself in.

The house was a large square, divided by a wide central hall and staircase and wrapped three sides round with an old-time "settin' porch." To the left of the entry, folding double doors opened to a long living room and, behind it, what had once been a screened sleeping porch. To the right, through a wide arch, was the dining room, with the kitchen behind. The other end of the hall opened into a large back porch. Dorrie had converted it to a laundry room and added a lavatory

27

and shower when the children were small, and—because it was the clean-up station on the way into the house—the kids had dubbed it the Mud Room.

To fight her way out of the desperate years she'd waded through in her early forties—her "Slough of Despond"—Dorrie had remodeled much of the lower story. It had started when she'd entered her dark kitchen one gloomy morning and immediately retreated to her bed at the mere sight of its stained counters and worn linoleum.

That day she went out and bought a metal tape measure, graph paper, drawing pencils and eraser, and an architect's rule. When she came back, she measured the walls and windows, marked the location of the plumbing, and designed a new kitchen with an efficient U-shaped work space, floor-to-ceiling cabinets on the long inner wall, and built-in appliances.

At the rear she added a sunny dinette with deep plant ledges behind its upholstered half-hexagon banquette and greenhouse-style windows to bring the sunshine in. Dorrie had the old linoleum ripped out and the original oak flooring restored, and she put thick, bright rugs in the work area. In the dinette, she'd laid a round rag rug and set upon it a pecan table she'd found in a used-furniture shop on McKinney Avenue. The painters had put three coats of white enamel on her cupboards, and on their doors Dorrie stenciled Old World hearts and flowers in brilliant oil paints.

Her kitchen had become the most cheerful room in the house, and the most her own. Though she'd been unable to use it for weeks and the house had been full of strangers, the room satisfied her in a way she could not explain. She was hooked.

The next project had been the sleeping porch. Since the children were in college and George wouldn't dine there, the screened porch had lost its usefulness. Dorrie had it glassed in and installed more plant ledges along the two window walls, which were on the north and east sides. She removed the laundry-room door so its steam could humidify the porch, and her African violets thrived. Two gave her four orchid plants—a catteleya, a phaleanopsis, and two cymbidiums— and a book about orchid growing the next Mother's Day, and Dorrie's sun room became an orchid room. Once she'd brought in her mother's cushy old rose-velvet sofa, a small coffee table, and a reading lamp, the orchid room became her retreat.

Dorrie had only redecorated, not remodeled, the living room. That was George's retreat, and she'd done it to his taste: white walls, floral damask drapes over ecru sheers at the front picture window and the two tall side windows, patterned area rugs in shades of tan and maroon on the dark oak floors, and cream woodwork, including the fireplace frame and mantelpiece and the bookshelves on either side.

Upstairs were four bedrooms and a big, old-fashioned bath. Dorrie had saved the enormous, old, footed bathtub and added a glassed-in shower. In a burst of self-will, she had pink marble countertops installed. George would have preferred beige or white, but he was so distressed at her long spell of gloom that he didn't argue.

"Suit yourself," he'd said. "It doesn't matter to me."

Their bedroom was furnished with Dorrie's grandmother's carved oak four-poster and chifforobe, an almost-matching pair of nightstands she'd found in an antique store, and a tall pier glass. A spidery, off-white spread that had taken her a year to crochet, mounted on a length of blue satin, covered the bed. The nine-by-twelve carpet of Wedgwood blue left an eighteen-inch border on all sides, and floral-patterned curtains hung at the windows.

As Dorrie entered the house, Domino greeted her with a yowl expressing his resentment at being shut in on a Sunday afternoon.

"I know," she told him, "but you were hiding when I left. It's your own fault for being such a scaredy-cat. All Wendy and Trey ever wanted was to love you."

Domino rubbed up against her legs while she

refilled his dish, and then Dorrie went into the living room. George's leather recliner sat abandoned at the far end of the room with a rack of outdated *Time, U.S. News and World Report,* and *Business Week* magazines beside it. She kept forgetting to throw them out.

Dorrie took the card Two had given her from her sweater pocket and set it on the mantel, leaning it up against the only picture of George she'd kept out. It showed him in 1952, just before they were married, leaning up against the front fender of his brand-new Oldsmobile. The car, which had been tan, looked as big as an ocean liner. George was wearing a pinstriped suit with wide lapels that, she remembered, had been brown. His fedora had also been brown, like his figured silk tie, his eyes, and his hair.

George had been a tall man, taller than six feet, and thin; he was thirty before she met him and still as spindly as an adolescent. As a girl, she'd been intimidated by his age and height. His skinny body had made him seem vulnerable, as had the sober, earnest expression that he wore in the picture and had worn all his life, right into his coffin.

"See what you've done?" she demanded. "Your son thinks I need my head examined! And isn't it just like him to pawn me off on a psychologist instead of giving me a hug!"

Two certainly was his father's on, just as Dorrie had been her father's daughter. She'd learned early to curb her impulses, restrain her emotions and her wilder instincts toward self-expression, and channel them into permissible behaviors. Daddy'd never laid a hand on her in discipline; it was not his way. He just withdrew when she stepped out of line and didn't return to her until she stepped back in again. Dorrie'd read somewhere that girls married men like their fathers, and she guessed it was true.

George had come into the store as watchmaker when Dorrie was sixteen, and he watched her grow up: attended her graduation from the Academy, ate Sunday dinners at the house, squired her to dances and the like when she came home from Stofford. She understood Stofford had become a respectable college since, but in those days it had been more of a finishing school. Daddy and George had formed an understanding while Dorrie was there that when she returned she would become George's wife, and once she'd figured it out it had seemed as safe a fate as any. It kept Daddy from worrying about leaving his business to her—there had been no son and never any question of leaving it to Barbara, who had married unsuitably—and she had liked George well enough.

"You were a good husband to me, too," she told him now, gazing at her hands. Her rings picked up the light and twinkled back at her.

"Thoughtful, generous . . . Not the most romantic man, but a girl can't have everything."

Her engagement ring had been the occasion for the only really romantic thing George ever said to her. When he'd put it on her hand, she'd been surprised to see that two emerald baguettes flanked its central diamond.

"But I thought emeralds were unlucky!" she'd said. "Why emeralds?"

George had leaned forward to touch her cheek.

"That's just to remind you," he'd said, "always to stay a little Greene."

"I could have done with a tad less protection," she said now. "Truly, George! Wouldn't it have been kinder to let me learn what I need to know?" He'd hated having to let her help out on the sales floor during Christmas, though she'd enjoyed it and sold more than even his most experienced salespeople.

"You don't have to work," he'd said over and over. And she'd always argued: "I like it, sweetheart. And if it's me helping out, the money stays in the family." He'd never paid her a salary, of course. Everything he had was hers. It would have been foolish.

Dorrie turned her back on the photograph and blotted her nose. Two had pressed a pill upon her before he brought her home and, firmly urging her to see his friend, had left the bottle. The pill had done her little good, and she doubted that the friend would either. Still, Two would nag—gently but interminably—until she went. It was the only way he knew to show his love.

She might as well get it over and done with. She'd call tomorrow.

Wondering why it doesn't bloom, Dorrie takes her orchid plant off its hanger and carries it to the sink. Maybe something is eating at it, she thinks, or it's not getting enough warmth. She turned it out of its pot and sees the roots like desiccated white worms, inextricably tangled among themselves. They are so crowded they have no room to grow.

Poor thing, she thinks, searching out a larger pot and filling it with fresh bark. No wonder it's in such a sad condition.

She separates the roots carefully, spreading them over the bark and staking the plant. There, she thinks: that's better. The plant settles into its new pot with an almost audible sigh. It has not flowered in so long that she's forgotten what its flower looks like, but now it begins to grow before her eyes. A sheath appears in the fold of its dark and leathery leaf, and Dorrie can hardly wait to see it bloom again.

Four

"Mrs. Greene? You may go in now."

"Thank you." Dorrie laid down the magazine she'd been pretending to read while she pondered the irony of Dr. Wisemann's name, wondering whether he'd chosen it to fit his career or been forced into the career to defend the name. Following the pretty girl's gesture through a large, blond-oak door, she entered an office that resembled a small living room. On a slate blue carpet before sheer, lemon yellow drapes stood a crushed-velvet couch the color of Michaelmas daisies. At right angles to it was a square-armed chair upholstered in a royal blue and yellow stripe. The walls were the same shade of yellow as the pages of George's accounting books.

She did not see the doctor until he rose from a seat behind the massive oak desk at her right and trundled around its end to greet her, his fleshy palm extended.

"Hi, there, Dorothy! It's so good to meet you!" Dr. Wisemann's voice was incongruously reedy. A man so large, Dorrie thought, should be a basso, not a tenor. Only Dorrie's father had ever called her "Dorothy."

"How do you do," she murmured, taking his hand. His flesh was so warm that she glanced up to see if his face was fever flushed. It was not, though above his chins the mouth was round and red as a cherry Life Saver.

"Won't you sit down?" Dr. Wisemann gestured toward the sumptuous couch and Dorrie sat at its front edge, her spine straight, and folded her hands in her lap. The doctor lowered himself into the chair and leaned forward, elbows on his knees, to stare at her from behind round, wire-rimmed glasses.

"What seems to be troubling you, Dorothy?" he asked. His voice was like warmed maple syrup.

"I feel foolish taking up your time," Dorrie said, "but young George insisted. His father died two months ago, and he's worried about me."

"I understand. No one is ever really prepared to lose a loved one. It must have been a terrible shock."

"It was." Amazing insight, she thought. Dr. Wisemann continued staring into her eyes, waiting for her to go on.

"He left me a business I don't know how to run," she explained. "It's difficult."

"It must be hard, being forced by your husband's death into a situation you're not sure you can cope with."

So Two had sent her to a parrot. She would have to speak to him.

"I'll learn to cope," she said. "It's just hard right now, with everything so changed. I have a lot of practical problems to solve."

"Does that make you angry?"

"Sometimes." She shrugged. "It can't be helped. The work still needs doing."

"Of course."

Dorrie leaned forward and reached for her purse.

"Dr. Wisemann," she said, "it's kind of you to see me like this, but my biggest problem right now is running the store, and I can't expect you to tell me how to do that. There's no need for me to waste any more of your time."

"Are you sure you're not displacing your anxieties onto the business, Dorothy?" he asked. "Grief is hard on anyone, and especially someone who's been married as long as you had. You must miss him very badly. How many years was it?"

"Thirty-five and a little."

"A long time. Did you get along well?"

"I don't remember any serious quarrels. It was a good match. My father's only piece of advice worked out well."

"And what was that?"

"He told me, 'Always be at least as polite to your husband as you would to a complete stranger.'"

Wisemann's right eyebrow formed a barely perceptible arc.

"That sounds a little cold."

"He was talking about respect. It's important to have respect between two people who live together."

"What about love?"

Dorrie couldn't help smiling.

"My father didn't speak of such things. I believe he assumed it."

"And did he love you, your father?"

"I think so. He wasn't a demonstrative man, but he took good care of me. And he saw to it that I married a man who would care for me as well as he had." She straightened, folding her hands in her lap. "Yes, my father loved me."

"Interesting," Dr. Wisemann murmured. He was silent for a moment, gazing at her, but she said no more. At last the doctor spoke.

"Tell me about your marriage."

"There's not much to tell. We were married when I was twenty, had a son and a daughter, raised them into respectable adults, and lived peaceably together until my husband died two months ago."

"Peaceably," he echoed. "What about passion? Deep feeling?"

Dorrie felt her face grow warm.

"George was not a passionate man, and I was taught self-control at an early age. We lived quietly, and we were content."

Dr. Wisemann continued to stare at her, the eyebrow slightly more elevated, making his expression quizzical. Irritation sharpened Dorrie's voice.

"I realize that's terribly old-fashioned," she said, "but it satisfied us. It was enough."

"And now he's gone, is it still enough?"

Dorrie shook her head, annoyed with his thickness.

"Now he's gone, it's too late to worry about it. We had what we had, and now I don't even have that."

"You sound angry."

"I suppose I am. He left me alone with a job he hadn't taught me to do because of his pride: he was afraid someone would think I 'had to work.' I have a right to be angry!"

"No one suggested anything else, Dorothy. You always have a right to your feelings."

"Do I!" she said. "Well, Dr. Wisemann, suppose you tell that to my son. Maybe then he'll leave me alone to work out my own problems, and I won't need to waste any more of your time." Dorrie stood abruptly.

"Thank you for your trouble," she said. "Please report that I can manage on my own." As the doctor rose, she wheeled toward the door and was gone.

She was still indignant when she went to bed. Tomorrow, she thought, she would speak to Two about his meddling. Love was not excuse enough for invading her privacy.

Dorrie stands at the back of a church, her hand on her father's arm. He is wearing a cutaway coat with striped pants: his shirt front is stiff as an icebox door. As the wedding march begins, Dorrie looks down at herself and sees not a white gown, but silk pajamas with wide stripes of black and white. She marches sedately down the aisle toward her tuxedoed husband-to-be, staring at her surroundings.

White lilies of cloying sweetness are tied at the end of every pew. Mama, dressed in a silvery gown, dabs at her eyes with a scrap of white lace as Dorrie passes. George's back, straight and narrow, is before her.

"Who gives this woman to this man?" the minister asks, and Dorrie's father places her hand in George's. She hears "love, honor, and obey," and George clamps a wide emerald bracelet around her wrist.

"With this ring I thee wed," he says, "and with all my worldly goods I thee endow."

The bracelet is as heavy as iron, but Dorrie

does not complain. It would be worse than un-
gracious to find fault with such a beautiful and
costly gift. George would be hurt, and her father
would be furious.

She woke feeling like a child whose birthday
has been ignored. Thanksgiving would be two
days after tomorrow, and she had not heard from
Charmaine.

That evening, tired of the cafeteria's menu, she
came home to fix her own supper of scrambled
eggs and toast. Fixing for one was hardly worth
the effort unless she got frozen dinners, and
those tasted like cardboard.

I really must get myself organized enough to
eat properly, she thought. Depression was natural
in her circumstances, but she mustn't let it destroy her health. She was too young to follow
George so soon. Of course she'd known all her
life, when she'd let herself think about it, that he
would go before her; but his death had been so
out of character: George never did anything suddenly. She'd expected to have time to prepare herself to be alone, but now here she was. . . . She
ate absently and then drifted into the orchid
room, where she plunked herself down on the
comfortable old rose-velvet sofa.

"It's just you and me now, Domino," she said, scratching the puff of white hair below the cat's black ear. He butted his head into her hand, purring loudly. Wide, unblinking, green eyes stared up at her from the white mask that had given him his name. "What do you think we should do for fun?"

The cat jumped down off the sofa and stalked over to the bookcase's bottom shelf where Dorrie kept her old photo albums.

"Again?" Dorrie said. "Well, all right."

She pulled out the thick red album that held pictures of her teen years and opened it to a picture of Miss Pickerel's eighth-grade class of 1948. There she was in that plain old uniform—navy jumper and tie, white blouse, white bobby sox and brown oxfords—standing next to Charmaine. Charmaine could add panache to even that outfit, Dorrie thought fondly.

Opposite was a photo of the two girls at church camp, standing outside the tent they'd slept in with Annie Zirkle, Maribelle Gooding, and Georgia Click. Georgia'd become Dr. Georgia Nelling, a gynecologist, and Maribelle had married a corporate executive and been dragged from pillar to post for twenty years before he'd run away with a twenty-five-year-old secretary named Debbie. Annie Zirkle had died in an auto accident the year they were seniors, but Charmaine had survived. Always survived.

All those years together, Dorrie thought wonderingly. When they were girls, Mama used to invite Charmaine home for weekends. Daddy would say, "What? That hoyden again?" and Mama would answer, "How's she ever going to learn to behave if she doesn't spend time with civilized people?"

But nobody'd ever really civilized Charmaine; they'd only taught her to pretend. It was part of her charm, Dorrie thought, never having let anybody change what she was inside. She'd gone her own way in life, fortified by inherited oil millions invested in futuristic technology—bought IBM stock in 1960 and that alone was enough to keep her in style forever. Charmaine referred to Dallas as "home base" and traipsed all over the world, returning as the fancy struck her.

George had never been comfortable with her. Charmaine's unpredictability had driven him crazy, but Dorrie thought it made her interesting. Though she'd never known what she'd do with Charmaine's freedom if she had it, Dorrie had always envied her friend's courage and her unfettered ways.

Charmaine had needed courage; her life hadn't been as easy as she wanted people to think. Ever since she'd lost custody of her sons in that terrible court battle the year after her first divorce, Charmaine had never been able to settle in one place for more than a few months. It was as if no place could keep her happy for long.

Max had talked the court into declaring her an unfit mother. Not that she was one, Dorrie thought; she'd been a marvelous, if somewhat exotic, mother. But it had been only a few years after the Kennedy assassination, and the whole town had been still in shock, afraid it would be blamed. Already a bastion of conservatism, Dallas had reverted to a reactionary and iron-clad rectitude.

Like a lot of other people in other parts of the country — if not in Dallas — Charmaine had spent the Sixties in a state of rebellion. She'd been living unconventionally, and with nine-hundred-ninety-nine-year sentences being handed down for possession of marijuana, even her millions had not made her immune to judgment. The family court judge had been severe. He had not just taken her children away and put visitation rights at their father's discretion, but delivered a hellfire-and-brimstone sermon that would have made a parson blush.

Charmaine had been angry for a long time, a deep-down anger that would not forgive and could accept no comfort. But she'd kept the house, and she'd visited the children as often as Max would allow, dropping in on Dorrie whenever she was in town. Dorrie had ached for her pain, but there had been nothing she could do beyond listening and loving her.

She wondered how their friendship would have developed if Charmaine had stuck around, married more successfully, obeyed the conventions enough to be accepted. God knew, money bought a lot of tolerance in Texas. Dorrie shook her head.

"I can't see it," she told Domino. "Money or no, she just never let anybody hold her back. The only voice she ever listened to was her own." She stroked his hair, black as burnt wood, and it crackled under her hand. "I just wish I'd had her backbone."

The cat looked deeply into her eyes and then placed one white paw gently over her lips. Dorrie chuckled.

"You've been listening to George," she said.

Five

Late Tuesday afternoon Angie, the college girl who helped out part time at the store, called Dorrie from the back of the store.

"Miz Greene? There's this lady on the phone for you? Says to tell you she's your long-lost friend?"

"I'm coming." Dorrie set down the Windex and rag she was using to clean the top of the display case and half-ran to take the phone.

"Charmaine?"

"No, it's Madame Pompadour! You're harder'n hell to lay hands on, girl. I been trying all afternoon! Finally called your son's house, and his wife said call you at the store. You working up there these days?"

"Working at it, anyhow. Where are you?"

"Home. Got in late last night and slept the day away. When do you get off there?"

"Whenever. The store closes at six, but Zada can lock up. I don't have to stay."

"S'pose I come pick you up, then. Hell, it'll take me two hours just to put myself together—takes longer every year. It's almost three now: five o'clock?"

"All right. See you then."

Charmaine still carried herself like the Queen of the World, Dorrie noted when she arrived. She'd gained weight, but she'd needed that. She always had been skinny as a stick, but now she was a solid presence. Her hair had darkened from flame to a rich auburn—almost certainly chemically enhanced—and she wore it braided into a corona with little paper daisies poked into it at random intervals. Dorrie noted the details of her outfit: a hand-worked silver necklace with great chunks of amethyst; a white blouse embroidered in navy geometrics; a heavy skirt made of hand-woven Guatemalan cloth, navy, with stylized white eagles worked into the fabric; and fawn-colored, high-heeled Frye boots.

"Dorrie!" Charmaine cried. "My god, girl, what's happened to you? You're gray as a ghost!"

Dorrie's hand rose to her hair.

"Gee, thanks. I really needed to hear that, Charmaine!"

"Never mind." Charmaine wrapped her in a

47

strong hug. "I still love you just the same. Want to go have a drink?"

"I suppose. Just let me get my jacket. Zada, you'll lock up?"

"Of course," Zada said. "You go on. Have a nice time."

Stepping into Charmaine's bright red Porsche, Dorrie grinned.

"This is some car," she said.

"Ain't it? There's something to be said for taking a boy to raise, even when it doesn't work out. Gives you a whole new set of toys." The motor roared, and Charmaine looked over her shoulder and jumped into the stream of traffic. "That place down on Greenville still open? Ado Annie's?"

"So far as I know. I haven't been there since the last time we went."

Dorrie was quiet on the way, allowing Charmaine to entertain her with tales of the Andes: the Indian woman who'd made a place in her hut for the American *turista,* the trek on donkey-back up the side of the mountain, the air so thin you couldn't keep a fire burning. As they turned into the restaurant's parking lot, Charmaine glanced across the seat at Dorrie.

"You're not saying an awful lot," she complained. "You okay?"

"Just tired," Dorrie said. "I can't seem to get over being tired."

48

"Uh-huh. Well, come on. You'll feel better after you've had something to eat."

Ado Annie's had slipped into fern-bar decor since they'd been there last, but Dorrie and Charmaine had beaten the after-work crowd. A slim young man in black pants, a pleated white shirt, and a red bow tie seated them and went to fetch white wine spritzers while they studied the menu.

"Nice little buns," Charmaine said as he walked away. "Wouldn't you like to just reach out and grab some?"

"This is nice," Dorrie said, tasting her drink. "Cool."

"White wine spritzer's about all I ever drink anymore, excepting Kahlua. I do love Kahlua, but I'm afraid my carousing days are all but past."

Dorrie was glad to hear it. She didn't feel like carousing, but saying no to Charmaine had never been easy.

They ate lightly. Charmaine kept trying to draw Dorrie into conversation, studying her friend more closely each time her efforts failed. At last Dorrie pushed away her half-full plate and leaned back into the corner of the booth.

"No appetite, either?" Charmaine said. "And you've hardly said a word in two hours, and we used to talk like a house afire. What is it, Dorrie?"

49

"I don't know. Maybe I'm just getting old."

"Old, my ass! You're six months younger'n me! Come on, Dorrie, what's the matter?"

"I'm all right. Considering."

"Well, being a new widow can't be much fun, I'll grant you that. Tell me about it."

Dorrie shrugged apologetically.

"It's been hard. I got to thinking about it a while back, and it's the first time in my entire life I've ever lived alone." Her voice was low and soft. "The first week — well, to begin with, I was just stunned. Numb. It was a good thing, really — got me through the week of the funeral. But it was a little like undergoing major surgery with a local anaesthetic: you know what's going on but you can't really feel it. And then when the anaesthetic starts to wear off, it hurts so much that first you're afraid you'll die, and then you're afraid you won't." She looked down at her hands. "I'm sorry. I don't need to burden you with this."

"The hell you don't. Tell me."

"The thing is," Dorrie said softly, "I don't know who I am anymore. I spent all those years being George Greene's Lovely Wife, and now he's gone I don't know how to be anything else."

"That's a rough one. I went through something like it after my first divorce, though not as bad, of course — I wasn't as set in the role. I was completely whacko for a while, remember?

50

Went on a three-month sex binge and then joined a women's commune. It took me about a year to straighten myself out."

Dorrie gave her a wan smile.

"I can't quite see myself doing either of those things."

"No. Not your style. But honey, you got to do something. You can't just sit here and drive yourself crazy."

Dorrie leaned forward, her expression painfully earnest.

"It's not just that my whole adult life has been a lie," she said, "though heaven knows that's bad enough. It's this: first of all, if I'm not what I've always thought I was, what am I? And second, how could I have been such a fool as to confuse what I was doing with what I was? I feel like such an idiot!"

"Sounds like a full-blown existential crisis to me," Charmaine said. Her voice was sober, but her eyes crinkled.

Dorrie laughed.

" 'Existential crisis'! Mercy! And I thought I was only losing my mind!"

"Always happy to help out. Well, you've identified the question, and that's half of answering it. And you've got a leg up on it: I didn't have anybody, but you've got me."

The waiter appeared at Charmaine's elbow.

"May I bring you ladies some dessert?" he

asked. "We've got some great mud pie in the kitchen. Or would you rather have a drink?"

"Just the check, thanks," Charmaine said. She turned back to Dorrie. "Let's get out of here. We'll go collect your nightie, and you can sleep over at my house. It'll be like old times."

Six

At about noon on Thanksgiving Day, Dorrie heard the kitchen door open.

"Mom?" It was Kurt, Marcie's husband.

"Here I am, dear."

Kurt stuck his head through the living-room arch as Dorrie rose from the couch. Marcie'd done well in choosing Kurt, Dorrie thought every time she saw him. They'd met at college, where he was a grad student in music, and they fit like two pieces of a jigsaw puzzle: opposites making a perfect match. She was dark, he blond; she brisk and practical, he gentle and dreamy; she slim and muscular, he broad and soft-bodied. Of all the children, Kurt was the only one who never failed to kiss Dorrie hello and goodbye.

"You about ready?" he asked. "Marcie's waiting in the car. Where's your sweater?"

"Here it is." She turned her face up for his kiss as he helped her into it, and then followed him out. Marcie sat in her brand-new, silver-gray BMW in the driveway, the motor running.

A classic shirtwaist of jade silk, a teal sweater, and a chunky, Art-Deco-style necklace of lapis lazuli set in silver showed off her fair skin to perfection. Black hair, smooth as a cap, curved around a face as precise as Marcie's mind.

"You look lovely, dear," Dorrie greeted her. "I never cease to marvel that I'm the mother of such a stylish woman."

"Thanks, Mom, but I had to get it from somewhere. Take a little credit, will you?"

Dorrie laughed.

"Caught again!"

Marcie turned onto University and accelerated through a yellow light before she spoke again.

"I guess Susan's got a real do planned," Marcie drawled once they were underway. "She's been saving up fancy plans as long as she's been married, waiting for the day she could be in charge of holiday dinners."

"Anybody'd think you were jealous, dear. As far as I'm concerned, she's welcome to it. I'd have let her take over years ago if your father and brother had been willing."

"Well, God knows I never wanted to do it! All those adorable little ruffled aprons and the fruit bowls you don't dare touch and the accordion-pleated turkey centerpiece . . . Just cook it and set it out is my way!"

"That's why I do our cooking," Kurt said, smiling. "I think if Marcie had it to do, we'd live on frozen entrees."

"Well, then, the one who wants to do Thanksgiving finally gets to do it, so we can all be happy." Dorrie leaned forward and laid her hand on Marcie's shoulder. "Please, honey, don't pick on your brother and Susan today. Everything's going to be strange anyway, with Dad gone. I can't stand it if you-all fuss besides."

"All right, Mama, I'll be good if Twoie will." Marcie grinned. "I'll play real nice and mind my manners, and Kurt and I'll be good as can be."

"It's not Kurt I worry about."

"Do you know who else is coming?" Kurt asked.

"I believe Susan invited my cousin Myrtle Todd and hers," Dorrie said. "How many of them will come, I don't know. I haven't seen Myrtle since Dad died, her living so far out, and you know how it was then — we didn't have time to talk."

"She's alone now too, isn't she?" Marcie asked. "I remember when Uncle John died, her kids were going to have her move in, but she turned them all down. Aunt Myrtle's nobody's fool." She wheeled the car smartly around a corner.

"I never did blame her," Dorrie said. "When a woman's kept her own house for so many years, it would be hard to move into somebody else's no matter how much they loved you."

55

Marcie glanced shrewdly over her shoulder at Dorrie.

"My brother and his sweet little wife trying to talk you into coming to their house to live?"

"They've thought of it. I haven't given them a chance to ask. Susan would think I don't love her, and the only way I could make your brother understand would be to lie—tell him I'm sentimental about the house or something."

"You're not?" Kurt asked.

"Not really. I suppose I should be—I've lived in it for thirty years, brought up my children there, all that—but honestly, no. It's a good, comfortable house and I like where it is—but the main fact is, I put a lot of time and effort into getting it just the way I want it. I'd hate to have to start all over somewhere else—especially someplace that wasn't mine."

"There's nothing like your own home." Marcie turned down Two's street. "You remember Daddy when I came home from college? There I was, twenty-five years old, holding an M.B.A., wearing my pinstriped suits and bow-necked blouses to work in a big-time investment firm in the canyons of downtown Dallas, and my Daddy trying to talk me into coming back to my little pink ruffled bed in his house! Never could understand why I wouldn't do it. Imagine how he'd have felt if I'd brought Kurt home for the night!"

Dorrie laughed.

"He felt much better when you were safely married," she said. "He always hoped you'd give him another grandchild. He loved his grandchildren."

"Well, stranger things have happened, but I wouldn't count on that one anytime soon."

"It's a shame I can't do it for her," Kurt said. "We'd have half a dozen. It's not so hard on a musician's career, having babies."

"There'll be plenty of time for that later; I'm only twenty-eight. Right now, I'm establishing a career; pregnancy is not an option." She coughed. "Anyhow, I don't know that I have the patience for it."

They pulled up in front of Two's house, and Marcie said, "You ready for this mess now?"

The children, playing on the porch, ran to the car to greet them. Dorrie reached for her door handle.

"Ready as I'll ever be, I reckon," she said.

"Now, Mother, you just go sit with George in the living room," Susan said when Dorrie offered to help in the kitchen. She was the only woman Dorrie'd known since her mother who actually wore an apron to cook in, and a fancy one at that: two rows of ruffles, and geese appliqued all over it. "I've got everything in hand here; it's cooking all by itself, and the table's even set. Would you like to see it? It's so pretty!"

Susan had laid her best damask cloth, with dark yellow lace covering it, and used the dishes she'd had the store special-order for her clear back in September. The china was brown on white, the plates having turkey gobblers in their centers and an elaborate design of fruits and flowers around the raised, fluted edges. Cranberry glass goblets stood at each place. The centerpiece was a scarlet ceramic cornucopia with wax fruits and vegetables spilling from it, lying on a bed of straw.

"What happened to your paper turkey?" Marcie asked. Dorrie shot her a warning look.

"I thought I'd try something different this year, what with the company and all," Susan said. "Do you like it?"

"It's very pretty," Dorrie said. If she had done it, she thought, the cornucopia would be of wicker and the fruits real—but of course, it had not been hers to do this year, and she wasn't sorry. "The new dishes are nice, and I really like that glassware."

"Thank you," Susan said. "I just like making things pretty. It's not like it was work."

"Aunt Myrtle's here," Two called. "Come on, you kids; get out there and greet your cousins."

Myrtle had brought her oldest girl, Marilu, and the family: Marilu's husband Lynwood and their three teenaged children, Duane, Tammy, and Robert. Marilu was fifteen years younger than Dorrie, and they'd never been close. She'd been a tacky little girl, Dorrie remembered, always one-upping everybody and rude to her elders. Now, with hair the color and texture of straw, she was outsized and florid in a print dress of polyester georgette and shiny black pumps with needle-slim, three-inch heels. Marilu in heels, Dorrie thought, gave one a whole new understanding of the phrase "piano legs."

Lynwood had always reminded Dorrie of a bear, even when he was young. Now he was plain fat, his broad belt with its massive gold-and-silver buckle acting as a sling for the pumpkin belly that preceded him. Of the two, Dorrie preferred Lynwood. He was at least not shrill.

The children, expensively dressed in appalling taste, were just what Marilu deserved, Dorrie thought. Duane, the eldest, had shaved one whole side of his head except for a large, block-style *D* that he'd let grow and dyed black. His sister was no less bizarre with orange hair spiked around her head like the Statue of Liberty's crown and eyelids so weighted down with silver shadow that the lids stayed half-shut, as if she could not be bothered to lift them. Robert's only dash was in the red high-topped basketball shoes that flopped, untied, around his ankles. Well, give him time, Dorrie thought; he's only thirteen.

Marcie nudged her.

"And you thought I dressed funny in my teens!" she muttered. "Get a load of that crew!"

"Oh, Marcie! I forgot to tell you," Dorrie said. "Guess who's back in town? Charmaine Stubbs!"

"You're kidding! What's she been up to lately?" She turned to Kurt. "Charmaine Stubbs is a hoot. You've got to meet her, hon; she's a real trip."

"Well," Dorrie said, "she's just back from Peru, celebrating her third divorce. He wasn't much older than you. Billed himself as 'Life Counsellor to the Stars' and did all that touchy-feely stuff out on the West Coast. You should hear her tell it: she made me laugh till the tears came."

"I can imagine. I remember when she used to come to the house — only when Daddy was away," she explained to Kurt. "Charmaine and Daddy got along about like two strange cats. She used to dress like an overage hippy with bangles, and love beads, and feathers in her hair. Really bizarre. I think Dad was afraid she'd lead Mother astray. My God, Mother, she must have done everything there was to do in the Sixties and Seventies! A sociologist could have a field day!"

"A constant source of entertainment," Dorrie agreed. "Anyhow, we went out to dinner the night before last, and I ended up spending the night at her house. I didn't realize how much I'd missed her."

"Well, I'm glad she's back," Marcie said. "You could do with a little fun, and I can't wait to see her myself."

Later, when they all sat down to eat, Two offered the blessing.

"Father, we thank You for bringing us all together at this Thanksgiving board," he intoned. "We have much to thank You for: our health, our family members both present and absent, the home You have so graciously given us, and of course the food before us." Duane stared at the ceiling, and Dorrie saw Marilu's arm twitch as she smacked him under the table. "And we remember too those who are less generously provided for. Father, may they share in Your blessings today. Give them grace to be thankful for what they have, and remind them of Your constant care." Marcie's eyes rolled, and Dorrie hoped Two would finish soon.

"We also ask Your special blessings on our departed father George," he droned, "seated at Your Heavenly table, and on our mother Dorothy, here beside me. Keep her ever mindful of her many blessings, and help her to recover her old spirit."

Dorrie winced. More than anything, she hated being prayed over; there was no defense against what people said about you to God. Kurt took her hand under the table, and Dorrie made her own quick prayer — *Make him stop!* — but he went relentlessly on.

"God grant that she may live with us in patience and mildness, supported by our loving care for many more years to come, for You have said 'Blessed are the meek.' And we pray that You, Father, give us all the strength to overcome our present sorrow. Bless this food, that they who eat it may gain the power and the wisdom to know and to do Thy holy will. In Jesus' name we ask these things. Amen."

As the "amen" rolled around the table, Dorrie looked up and met Myrtle's eyes. The lid of the left closed slowly and then opened again.

"You did that right well, Two," Myrtle said. "Your mama must be proud."

If he said another word, Dorrie thought, she would rise up and smite him where he sat. *Then* Myrtle would have something to wink at!

Dorrie accepted a healthy serving of meat and dressing and added a spoonful of candied yams, one of green beans with bacon, and cranberry sauce. The table talk slid around her like water around a sunken stump. Reports on Duane's football team and its chances for a statewide victory, gossip about other members of the family, polite questions about Kurt's work with the symphony and Marcie's at the brokerage — it all flowed past, leaving no impression.

At last Two pushed his chair from the table, leaned back, and sighed.

"Come on, you kids," Susan called, rising from her chair. "Let's clear off this table and make room for desert." Robert, Trey, and Wendy followed; the older children made no move to help. Marilu looked across the table at Dorrie.

"You didn't eat much," she observed. "Hardly enough to feed a bird."

"I wasn't very hungry."

"You lost weight since I seen you last," Lynwood said. "You got to eat, you know. Got to keep up your strength."

"I've tried to tell her, been trying for months," Two said. "She won't listen. Ever since Dad died, she's not the same: doesn't get enough sleep, stays down at the store all the time like an employee. . . . Skimpy eating's not the half of it!"

It would serve him right if she left the table, Dorrie thought, but she couldn't embarrass Susan in front of the family. She looked down at her plump middle and forced a laugh.

"Mercy! I'm about to waste away to a mere cartload!"

"You've never been fat, Mother," Two reproved her, "and you must've lost fifteen pounds since Dad passed on. I know you don't take me seriously, but I am a physician; I really do know what I'm talking about!"

Dorrie shut her eyes and touched her fingertips two by two, thumbs through pinkies, to her thighs. It was a trick she'd learned as a child to calm herself.

"If I'd lost fifteen pounds in August," she said, "you'd all be congratulating me. I do wish you'd stop worrying, Two. I'm not planning to starve myself to death any time soon."

"I beg your pardon, but I *do* worry. Constantly! You're not young. You insist on living alone. You won't let us take care of you, won't accept any help or advice from anybody — I thought it was just me, but you even walked out on the doctor I sent you to! Of course I worry!"

"Oh, for pity's sake, Two! Cut her some slack!" Marcie said. She looked ready to explode. "She's a grown woman — old enough to be your mother, if I remember rightly. Let her live her own life!"

Two turned on her, quick as a whip.

"Of course *you* don't worry about her — you're too wrapped up in your precious career! But some of us are still aware of our filial responsibilities. Susan and I *care!*"

"My God, you are a pompous ass!" Marcie started to say more, but Dorrie interrupted.

"Fight nicely, children," she said, her voice dry. "And if you don't mind, do it somewhere else. Being prayed for and worried about is burden enough; I don't need to be fought over as well." She laid her napkin on the table, pushed her

64

chair back, and stood up. "If you all will excuse me now, I believe I'll go and powder my nose before Susan serves the dessert."

As she left the room, she heard Marilu's avid voice.

"What doctor? Is Dorrie sick?"

She wandered down the hall and into the guest bath, locking the door behind her. George would have been appalled, she thought as she ran cold water over her hands. And after she had especially asked Marcie not to start anything! But holiday dinners had been tense ever since the children grew up.

When they were little, Dorrie recalled, Two and Marcie had got along beautifully. She'd looked up to him, and he was her protector and teacher. But in her teens, Marcie'd become more independent and they had begun to bicker. Though she'd grown less stridently feminist since marrying Kurt—Dorrie guessed he served as living proof that not all men were chauvinists—Two seemed never to have recovered from Marcie's rejection.

To make matters worse, Marcie enjoyed pulling her brother's strings; like a child, she would outrage him at every opportunity just to hear him holler. The continual power struggle wore Dorrie out.

Dorrie reached into her sweater pocket for a lipstick and dabbed it on her mouth. Poor Susan. Well, they would all get through it somehow, she supposed. One way or another, the day would have to end. But she would certainly be glad to go home.

"Once more into the breach," she told George, unlocking the bathroom door. "At least their voices sound civilized now."

Seven

Driving home later, Marcie tried to talk about the incident, but Dorrie cut her off. Now, alone in her house, she was angry all over again.

"Did you see, George?" she demanded of his photograph. "Your grandchildren, with their eyes as big as dinner plates? Marilu drinking it all in, so happy to see that my children weren't any better mannered than her own? And poor little Susan, almost in tears with her lovely dinner party falling around her head! How could they? I wanted to smack them both!"

She and Barbara had never been permitted to be so ugly to one another, she remembered. When their father caught them quarrelling, he would send them both to their rooms until they were "ready to live with the family." She'd never heard her father raise his voice in anger, and when Mother did, he'd walk away.

"It used to drive her crazy," Dorrie told George

now. "She'd be ready to go to the mat, and he'd just disappear. But I never thought it was the right thing to do; I tried to teach ours to work things out, not bottle them up." She turned away. "I grew up so frightened of contention—never could say a word until I was so angry I didn't dare speak. I don't know, George: did I do right?"

He didn't answer, but that was nothing new. George had always known a rhetorical question when he heard one.

Dorrie plunked herself down on the couch and turned on the TV. The networks were still showing football, but the arts channel had a dance group on. The dancers, in skintight suits with stripes up the arms and legs, tangled themselves by pairs and groups into impossible positions to create living puzzles, comic and tragic by turns. She had no idea what they meant by their contortions, but she could not look away.

The other night, when she and Charmaine had been talking, Dorrie had had a crying jag over George. Charmaine had held her through the worst of it and kept silent until Dorrie'd begun to quiet.

"People don't really die, you know," she'd said then. "They just wear out their bodies and leave them behind. He's still alive somewhere."

"I know." Dorrie blew her nose. "I've had . . . experiences before this."

"Tell me."

"Well, you remember my Grandma Rose. I was pregnant when she died, the year after I miscarried. . . . They didn't want to worry me, so Mama hadn't even told me Grandma was sick. On the night she died—just at the same hour—I was standing in the rose garden admiring the sunset. It was beautiful, with the sky all streaked with salmon and mauve and sunlight gliding the undersides of the clouds. A little breeze sprung up and lifted the hair on the back of my neck, and then, suddenly . . . you know how everybody has his own distinct smell?"

Charmaine nodded.

"Well, suddenly I was surrounded by my grandmother's smell, an acrid-sweet blend of sweat and Cashmere Bouquet. And I just stood there for a minute with my head raised, waiting . . . attentive, wondering why I should smell that."

"And then what happened?"

Dorrie smiled, remembering.

"Nothing, really. I just had this intense feeling of . . . blessing, I suppose you'd call it. Palpable love, flowing all over and through me, and then it was gone." She looked up. "They called me the next day to say she'd died. Just then."

"She came to tell you goodbye?"

"Something like that. For a long time, I used to feel her presence. I even talked to her." Dorrie was silent for a moment, and then added quietly, "I do the same with George. I know he's there; I just can't see or touch him." She'd raised her head to look into Charmaine's face. "Is that crazy?"

"No. I wouldn't tell it to just any old body, but it's not crazy. Not a bit."

But it wasn't much comfort, either, Dorrie thought now. He was just as gone either way, and here she sat alone.

What had brought her to this point? All her adult life she'd been a proper wife and mother, as if that were what she'd been born to, but look at her now: children grown, husband gone, and no more need of all she'd learned by doing than an ant had of galoshes. Why did she have to keep on living when all her work was done? George was dead, the children could not be civil to one another, and she herself was of no use to anybody . . .

Too depressed to cry, Dorrie leaned her head back against the cushions wishing she need never wake up again.

The young woman, the one Dorrie dreams of so often, is leading Dorrie sorrowfully through an aged and abandoned, lightless house that threatens to collapse around her. Dorrie knows this house: she has been here before and thinks it once belonged to her, though she cannot remember. The house is full of trash: worn-out furni-

ture, broken toys, dead things. Spiders creep upon the walls, and their webs hang from the ceilings. At the head of the stairs, the young woman points to Dorrie's right. There, framed and standing upon the desk she owned as a girl, is Dorrie's notice of acceptance to the University of Texas. The glass is fractured and the paper stained with age and tears. Dorrie stops to look at it, remembering the drama scholarship her father forbade her to accept.

Turning a corner into a small room, Dorrie stops and stifles a cry of horror.

She has bumped into a doll's crib in which lies an infant dying of neglect. It is naked, lying in its own waste and covered with sores. The baby's belly is distended, its limbs like sticks, and its fingers mere twigs. Dorrie had forgotten all about this baby, but now she remembers that it is her own. It has been waiting here while she went about her business, and she is afraid the infant is too weak, too severely damaged by her neglect, to save. Desolate, she picks up the baby and stumbles, weeping, from the house.

When the store closed at six on Friday, Charmaine was waiting.

"I've been having the best time!" she said. "Found this place called Olla Podrita where they

71

have all kinds of crafts and handmades, and just looked all afternoon!"

"You did more than look," Dorrie said. "You're loaded down!"

"I didn't do too bad. Only bought half of what I wanted to, and I'll find uses for it. Anyhow, don't hassle me. I'm going to fix your dinner."

"Will I survive it?"

Charmaine laughed.

"Even with your delicate stomach! I learned how to make this fabulous fish in Peru — you won't believe it!"

"I already don't. I never saw you turn a hand in the kitchen in your whole life."

"Shoot! I got a *fund* of talents you don't know, Dorrie Greene! Just you wait!"

Charmaine still lived in the same red-brick house in Highland Park out of which she'd thrown her first husband. Dorrie, in soft wool slacks and an old gray sweater, watched her friend roll orange roughy in seasoned cornstarch, fry it, and cover it in a tomato sauce made with green peppers, onions, several cloves of garlic, and an orange powder from a packet with a Spanish name.

"Here," Charmaine said, tossing her a head of lettuce. "Tear this up for the salad while I fry these plantains."

When the meal was ready, it was almost too pretty to eat.

"You do have untold talents," Dorrie said. "This is delicious!"

"Just because I trot all over the globe, that doesn't mean I can't put a meal together!" Grinning, Charmaine leaned back in her chair and sighed. "I'll have you know, I've just satisfied one of my life's ambitions: got your admiration for doing something useful!"

Dorrie laughed. "I've always wanted yours for doing something exciting but I never had the courage to pull it off."

"Well, it's never too late to start. We'll think of something. That's a promise."

After supper, Charmaine left the table and returned with a small, carved, wooden box in her hands.

"Tell you what," she said, setting it on the table and raising its hinged lid. She removed a packet wrapped in an embroidered scarf of purple silk. "Why don't you let me read your cards."

She unfolded the scarf, which was covered with strange symbols. Inside was a Tarot pack.

"When did you learn to read the Tarot?" Dorrie asked.

"I don't know—just something I picked up in my travels. You know me: if it's there, I'll pick it up and look at it."

Dorrie grinned. "Problem with that is, you never know where it's been."

73

"Christ, you sound just like your daddy! He never did know what to do with me."

"I know. Daddy wasn't very tolerant of individual differences. I remember one time, he said, 'Why does she have to *cultivate* her eccentricities?' "

"Shoot, they're what's interesting!" Charmaine shoved the silken wrapper into her pocket and started shuffling. "So is there anything special you'd like to know about?"

Dorrie laughed ruefully. "Life and better things yet," she said. "Right now, my whole existence is a question." She had never had her fortune told before, never believed in fortune-telling. Still, what else did she have to do this evening?

"Well, we'll just see then."

Having set the Queen of Cups in the center of the table, Charmaine started laying out cards in the form of a cross.

"This covers her, this crosses her," she muttered, "this beneath her, this behind her, this crowns her. This before her . . ." She paused, looking at the card. "Not bad," she said, and went on: "This her fears, this her friends, this her hope, this the outcome."

Dorrie waited as her friend studied her future. The cards were full of brilliant colors, the drawings on them grotesquely fascinating: dogs like jackals; a horned, goat-legged devil with a pitch-

74

fork across his knees; a youth in motley walking away with his worldly belongings tied on a stick over his shoulder.

"All right," Charmaine said at last. "Death covers you. Not necessarily a real death, though of course George's is probably part of it. It's like a door, with one side an end and the other a beginning. That's the immediate influence. And crossing him is the Fool: see him, happy as if he had good sense, out to seek his fortune and about to walk over a cliff? He shows you're facing a choice you're not prepared to make. Ring any bells?"

"Several."

"You're not going to make it easy, are you! Well, you always were close-mouthed; I don't know why you'd be any different now."

Dorrie pointed at the card at the bottom of the cross. It showed a tower being struck by lightning. A man and a woman were falling headlong from its burning windows as dogs leapt up to bite them.

"Charming," she said. "What's this?"

"The foundation of your present troubles," Charmaine told her. "The Tower represents some sudden, usually shocking occurrence that brings your life crashing down around your ears." She looked up. "I'd say being widowed meets the description, wouldn't you?"

"In spades." She was tired of thinking about it,

so sudden and so terrible. She still woke at night and reached toward his side of the bed, and it was always a shock to find the sheets smooth and cold. "So then what?"

"Behind you—the influence just now passing out of your life—is the Hierophant. He represents convention: observing all the ceremonies, relying on authority to run your life—giving a damn what people think. He's the absolute opposite of anything I've ever been or done. When he turns up in my cards, he's always standing on his head."

"I can well imagine." Dorrie grinned. "So what does he mean here?"

"You've always lived very conventionally—you haven't had a helluva lot of choice in that, given the marriage you chose. But the card's position says that influence is passing out of your life. You don't have to do that any more unless you just want to."

"I wasn't always crazy about it," Dorrie admitted, "but it kept the peace. Now Two's picking up where his father and grandfather left off, wants to retire me to my rocker. He's sending me *off* my rocker, if you want to know! Last week he had the gall to remind me that he's studied geriatrics, for pity's sake, by way of convincing me I need psychiatric help!"

"Bless his pointy little head! Did you go for it?"

76

"Well . . ." Dorrie grinned. "I did go to the doctor . . . but I lost my temper and walked out on him."

"Did you really! Great galloping ghosts, Dorrie! There may be hope for you yet!"

Dorrie reached for the pot and refilled their cups with Red Zinger.

"Go on with the cards," she said. "This is getting interesting."

"Well, the next one's the Hermit: advice and teaching, maybe a mentor. That's a possible; the card that crowns you may or may not appear in your future. But the card before you, the next one, is definite: the Chariot shows victory, with you in the driver's seat. It says you'll take over the reins of your own life and succeed at it. It's a warning, too, not to run over anybody on the way, but I can't see you doing that."

"Hooray for our side," Dorrie murmured. In her whole life, she had never held the reins. They had gone from Daddy's hands to George's. Now they hung limp, and it was all she could do to keep Two from grabbing them. "When does this start?"

"Sounds to me like it already has. I never saw you so smart-mouthed."

"Thank you, Charmaine. It's your influence, you know. My daddy always did say you'd be the ruination of me." Dorrie grinned, looking at the four remaining cards. "Well, get on with it: what next?"

"The card at the bottom of this row is for your fears, and it's the Devil: sex, drugs, and rock 'n' roll." Charmaine chuckled, shaking her head. "How predictable of you! Well, you're right to fear temptation if I'm going to be hanging around here—that's what I do best. Look here, this next one is for your friends; usually that position shows what your friends think about your situation, but the Empress is 'my' card. It means I'm back in your life for a while."

"That's good. I could do with some comic relief." She was afraid to think about how much she was counting on Charmaine's strength and humor. Heart as big as the world, and permanently itchy feet. Like Mary Poppins, Charmaine would be gone when the wind changed.

"You could do with a little more than that, girl, if you ask me! The Star is for your hopes, and it represents the Gifts of the Spirit: hope, love, and courage. . . . It also shows you receiving unselfish help."

"Well, I can use all of that I can get. What about the last card? The outcome?" The card, called the High Priestess, showed a young woman seated between two pillars, one dark, one light. A crescent moon curved up around her feet, and she wore a cross on her chest.

Charmaine stared at the card for a moment and then looked up at Dorrie with a Cheshire-cat grin.

"I can't tell you," she said.

"You *what?*" Dorrie demanded. "You went through all that, and now you won't even tell me how it's going to come out? I'd do better with Madame LaZonga down on Harry Hines Boulevard!"

Charmaine laughed.

"Not won't: can't. The High Priestess is the Great Mystery, the unrevealed future. All I can tell you is, the choice you make back here with the Fool is going to make the difference. Just pay attention, and choose right."

"Shoot, Charmaine! Tell me something I don't know! Why did I let you talk me into this anyhow? It doesn't mean a thing!"

"Maybe it does, and maybe it doesn't," Charmaine said, "but the fact remains, I haven't seen this much life in you since I came home. You're almost like yourself again!"

Eight

On Saturday, Dorrie arrived at the store to find a world turned upside down. Angie was late to work; Willis, the salesclerk, had called in sick; and Zada, who had opened for her, seemed to be feeling poorly too. It had rained during the night, and water had blown under the door; Dorrie walked in to find Zada mopping.

Zada Strait had been in charge of the china and crystal for more years than Dorrie could remember and had taken charge of the store since George's death. She was a large, erect woman with hair that had been the color of stainless steel for at least twenty years and a voice deeper than George's. Childless, she had come to work at the store after a divorce; Dorrie knew no more than that about her personal life, but Zada was an excellent saleswoman and a model of efficiency. Even at less than her best, Zada was worth any two others Dorrie'd ever seen.

Customers wandered in and out in sixes and

sevens — high-school kids and middle-aged women, mostly. There were no fewer than half a dozen at any given time all day long, and the cash register chimed regularly. Dorrie had just reflected that she'd be a long time ringing the receipts tonight when the phone rang at the back of the store. Angie was giggling with her friends, showing them dangly earrings, and Zada had a customer. Dorrie half-ran to the back and picked up the phone on the fourth ring.

"Hunter and Greene," she answered. "May I help you?"

"Morris Stein. May I speak to George Greene?"

No one had asked for George for weeks, and Dorrie was surprised at the pain it caused her.

"I'm sorry. Mr. Greene passed away in September. This is Mrs. Greene."

The man — he sounded young, Dorrie thought — babbled a few phrases of confused sympathy.

"You're very kind, thank you," she said. "What can I do for you?"

"Well, I'm with Bijoux. I was working with John Savage — do you know him? — and your husband on the purchase of Greene's, and he — your husband, I mean — was to call us back earlier this month to iron out the final wrinkles . . . I . . . uh . . . Do you know what he intended to do?"

Dorrie felt as if she were on an elevator that had dropped twenty floors in as many seconds, leaving her stomach behind. She straightened her spine and took a deep breath.

"Sell the store?" she said. "To Bijoux?" It was one of the largest chains in the country. She could not believe . . . "George *hated* chains!"

"We entered negotiations with him in July, Mrs. Greene. He approached us. We had all but a few minor differences worked out, and we wanted to close in January." The man sounded irritated. Dorrie didn't answer him.

"Do you mean you didn't know about this? He didn't discuss it with you?"

"My husband always felt that a man ought not to burden his wife with business decisions, Mr. . . ." She had forgotten his name, and he showed no disposition to repeat it. "He usually worked things out to his own satisfaction and discussed them with me afterward." Even to her own ears, Dorrie sounded like a ninny. What must this man think?

"But you were half owner! He must have said something!"

"He'd been talking about retirement, but I wasn't aware that he meant right away. I mean, he wasn't the sort . . ." None of this man's business. "We hadn't discussed it," she said.

"I wonder if I might come by the store and talk

with you tomorrow, Mrs. Greene," the young man said. He sounded fully recovered from his earlier embarrassment, sternly businesslike. "I could fill you in on everything that's been done to date, and then you'd be ready to meet with Mr. Savage when he's in town the week of the tenth. I have a proposal from our legal department to resolve the remaining differences." Dorrie did not speak, and his voice took on a worried tone. "Of course, with Mr. Greene out of the picture, it's a whole new . . . I mean, you may have other plans . . . But our offer is still open. We want that store, Mrs. Greene, and we'll be happy to work with you toward a sales agreement."

"I couldn't possibly tomorrow, Mr. . . ."

"Stein."

"Mr. Stein. Saturday will be much too busy for me to consider taking any time out. Perhaps next week . . ."

"Monday? Suppose I pick you up for lunch on Monday, and we can talk about it then. Would that be satisfactory?"

It would give her the weekend to think about it, and she supposed she ought at least to find out what Bijoux had in mind.

"All right," she said. "Monday at noon."

The wheels in her brain slowed to half speed for the rest of the day, burdened by the question of selling the store. George had been distracted all through August. Dorrie'd been aware that something was on his mind, but each time she asked, he'd said, "Nothing," and changed the subject. Whatever it was, was business; knowing that, she also knew that there was no point in badgering him. He would speak when he was ready.

But to sell the store! Deciding how many diamonds of what quality to buy was one thing, but to sell the store without consulting her . . .

"Oh, Dorrie, I was so sorry to hear about George!"

Vera Adler, an old customer, was at her elbow. Dorrie had belonged to Vera's bridge club a few years ago until she got so bored she'd had to quit. Vera was still at it.

"Thank you, Vera."

"I'd just been in the day before and bought the loveliest amethyst necklace, so Victorian — seed pearls and all — and then to hear the very next day. . . . It was such a shock!"

"It was very sudden. We were all shocked."

"What will you do now?" Vera's dark eyes, magnified behind thick glasses, reminded Dorrie unpleasantly of an owl's. "I suppose you'll be selling the store. Wasn't George the businessman of the family?"

"I haven't decided, Vera. But what can I do for you today? Are you looking for some little thing for Herbert's Christmas?"

Twenty minutes later, she was putting a pair of

sapphire cufflinks and matching studs in a satin-lined box and ringing up the sale.

Vera leaned over the counter to whisper.

"I don't suppose you know what he's giving me?"

"No. He hasn't been in." Dorrie smiled as she handed Vera the package. "And if he had, you know perfectly well I wouldn't tell you. That's one reason Herbert shops here!"

"Well, you can't blame a gal for trying!" Vera dropped the package in her enormous Vuitton bag and started for the door.

"Come back, now," Dorrie called after her. "It's always good to see you."

Dorrie returned to the back of the store and tried to call Walt Longstreet, George's lawyer. If anybody'd know about this, she thought, Walt would. His service told her that he was out of town and would be back in the office Monday morning. Wonderful! Dorrie thought. What ever happened to, "If there's ever anything you need . . ." Maybe she could catch him at home Sunday evening. He could at least go with her to meet young Mr. Stein.

Angie left at five, and Zada brought Dorrie a hamburger when she came back from supper. Traffic through the store had slowed, but Dorrie let the burger lie on her desk until it turned to stone and then quietly dropped it in the trash. It had been kind of Zada to bring it, she thought, but she could not eat.

As they were locking up, Zada offered her a ride home. In the car, the women talked about business until they were within a block of Dorrie's house.

"May I ask you something?" Zada said then.

"Yes, of course. What is it?"

"I just wanted to know . . . It's been two months since Mr. Greene passed away, and I wonder what your plans are. For the store, I mean. I . . ." She looked away. "I'm not ready to retire, and it's really hard for a woman my age to find a job this good. I've put in a lot of years here."

"I know you have," Dorrie said with quick sympathy, "and they've been good years. You've been such an enormous help to me since George . . ." Dorrie's coat weighed uncomfortably around her neck, and she shrugged it loose. "I don't know, Zada. I've had an offer, but I haven't had time to think about it, and I just don't know what I'm going to do."

"I see. Thank you. I appreciate your frankness." Vera turned the car into Dorrie's drive. Her face was bleak. "Will you let me know when you decide?"

"Of course. And Zada? If I do sell, I'll make your job a condition. I'll see that you can work there as long as you want to."

Thank you," Zada said. She was silent another moment, and then laid her hand tentatively on Dorrie's arm. It was the first time she'd ever touched her boss's wife. "I hope you don't sell, though," she said. "I'd rather work for Hunter and Greene."

The next morning, reminiscing over the breakfast table at a nearby coffee shop, Charmaine said George's name and Dorrie interrupted.

"You know, I had the strangest call yesterday; I've been puzzling about it ever since. A man from Bijoux called and said he and George had been working out an agreement. . . . George was going to sell the store!"

"And he hadn't said anything to you?"

"Not a word! That's what was so strange about it: you'd think he'd have said *some*thing!"

"Hell, yes! It was half yours, wasn't it? When do you suppose he planned to tell you?"

Dorrie shrugged.

"Probably after he got it all worked out, and then it would have been, 'Sign here, sweetheart.' George never wanted me to bother my pretty head about business."

Charmaine snorted. "I hate to speak ill of the dead, Dorrie, but that man was an absolute dinosaur! How did you ever stand it?"

Dorrie smiled. "Living with George had its

compensations. He was old-fashioned about a lot of things, but then so am I. And you always forget: he was fifteen years older than we are. George would have been seventy in January."

"What do you suppose he had in mind?"

"Retirement, I suppose. He'd been talking about it for years, but he was a man who needed to work. George wouldn't have known what to do with himself without the store. I do wish he'd talked to me about it. He was always so afraid I'd worry, but I worried more about not knowing."

"So what're you going to do now?"

"I don't know. I'll have to talk to the children. It is a family business, even if neither of them does seem interested."

"Well, the cards don't lie; maybe this is your choice. What do you want, Dorrie?"

Dorrie smiled.

"Just to keep everybody happy, mainly. It's what I always have wanted."

Charlene's eyes rolled a full circle. "Tell me!" she said. "Sometimes I've absolutely despaired of getting an opinion from you that hadn't been chewed through four other mouths before yours. Honey, listen: George is gone. Two and Marcie don't give a sweet damn about the store; she just wants you to be happy, and he just wants you to behave. The only one with anything to gain or lose by this decision is Dorothy Hunter Greene. *Please,* Dorrie, please yourself on this one!"

Dorrie leaned across the table and touched Charmaine's hand. "Thanks," she said. "You always did look out for me, and I do appreciate it. After I've heard their say, I'll decide for myself. Promise."

As Dorrie lay in bed that night, her mind returned to the Tarot reading. An end and a beginning, Charmaine had said, and an uninformed choice. Well, endings always did turn into beginnings if you lived through them. As to the choice, that had been truer than either of them knew — pure luck, Dorrie guessed. But life was full of choices; this one was more pressing than most, but she'd have to make it soon, whether or not.

The High Priestess had been a cheat, she thought, smiling softly. Either you could tell the future or you couldn't; Charmaine couldn't have it both ways. It had been fun, though, more fun than she'd had in a long time. She would forgive Charmaine the High Priestess, if only the Empress turned out to be true. Yawning, she shut her eyes.

Dorrie feels wind whipping her hair, whistling past her ears. Something is cutting her hands, and she looks down to see leather thongs bound around them, stretching forward to the necks of two horses, one dark and one light. She is in a Roman-style chariot, out of control; the road runs along the top of a cliff with an angry sea below. The black horse pulls against the white. "Whoa!" she cries, yanking on the reins. The horses rear, screaming. "Stop!" Dorrie screams. The horses race faster, veer closer to the edge, and she knows she is about to tumble down the bluff, horses, chariot, and all, into the dark and troubled water.

Nine

Dorrie called her children to a family conference on Sunday evening, and they responded as Charmaine had predicted.

"Sell," Two said. "You know that's what Dad wanted. He was arranging the sale so you wouldn't have to run the store. John Young, that cardiologist I sent him to, told me after Dad died that he'd diagnosed arterial sclerosis. Dad knew, and he was trying to protect you."

"I wish he'd told me," Dorrie said. "We might have planned better. But he's gone now, and I'm the one who has to live with the decision."

"Well, if you want my advice—"

Marcie interrupted. "She didn't ask for your advice; she asked for your opinion, and you've given it to her. Now why don't you shut up and let her make her own decision."

"Thank you, Gloria Steinem," Two said.

"Mother knows what Dad wanted. I think she ought to do it."

"Thank you, dear," Dorrie said. "I'll consider that carefully. Marcie, how do you feel about it?"

"I feel like you ought to do what you can live with best. At this point what would help most is looking at the probable impact of your choices. What are they?"

"To sell or not to sell, I guess—that is the question, isn't it?"

"Right. What are the advantages of selling?"

"Assuming they make me a decent offer—and I wouldn't know one if I met it on the street—the main one's financial security. I already have that, don't I?"

"Dad's accountant could evaluate the offer for you," Two said.

"Stop interrupting," Marcie told him. She turned back to Dorrie. "Don't worry about that. I can evaluate the offer for you. What are the disadvantages?"

"Oh, Marcie! Where shall I start? I can never remember not having the store. It was my grandfather's, and then my father's, and if I'd been a boy it would have been mine. It would be like losing an arm! And then, I can't bear the thought of becoming one of those bored, lonesome old women who drive their children up the walls for lack of anything better to do. I don't know what I'd do with myself if I didn't have the store!"

"You could do what you've always done," Two said. "Keep house, visit friends, enjoy your grandchildren . . ."

"Next you'll have her tatting doilies!" Marcie said. "For God's sake, Two, she's got nobody to keep house *for!* Why shouldn't Mother work if she wants to?"

"One nice thing about being a grandmother," Dorrie said dryly, "is that when the children start to squabble you can send them home. It's harder with your own."

"Sorry," Marcie said. "Go on, Mom."

"The thing is, I hate to give up the store, but I don't know how to run it. If I hang onto it, I'm afraid I'll run it right into the ground."

"What about hiring a manager to teach you the business?" Marcie asked. "That puts you in a better bargaining position if you want to sell later."

"Where would I find one? You can't just put an ad in the newspaper for something like that — you have to know somebody."

"Have you talked to Walt about this?" Two asked. "He must know something about it. Or Dad's accountant — what's his name, Burton? Have you talked to Burton?"

"Walt's out of town; he's supposed to call me Monday morning," Dorrie said. "I didn't try Mr. Burton, but his number must be in Dad's book down at the store. I'll call him Monday." She turned to Marcie. "Honey, if I can't get either of them to come, will you go to that meeting with me? Mr. Stein's picking me up at the store for lunch tomorrow, and I don't know what to say to him."

"Two women against a shark like they're going to send?" Two protested. "Let me go!"

"You're in surgery Mondays," Dorrie said, adding a silent "Thank God." The less confident Two was about what he was doing, the more impossibly he behaved, and he'd never wanted to know squat about the store. Without even thinking about it, he'd find forty ways to offend a potential buyer. "I don't want to interfere with your work, I just don't want to go alone."

"Well, you call me when you get back, then, hear?" Two lowered his chin and gave Dorrie a severe look over the tops of his glasses. "And try to get some sleep tonight, will you, Mother? You look a wreck."

"Thank you, dear," Dorrie said. "I'll do my best."

When they'd gone, Dorrie made herself a cup of tea and curled up on the rose couch. Domino jumped up into her lap and started to sing a deep, throaty song of content. Dorrie's favorite orchid, the Bc. Bellefleur that hung from the ceiling, caught her eye and she looked up to see the tip of a bud sheath emerging from the fold of one of its fat, emerald leaves.

"Look at that, Domino," she said. "It's going

to bloom at last."

"Prrrowt," Domino said.

"Don't you dare eat it," she warned. "It's my favorite, and it hasn't flowered for more than a year. I was afraid it was dying, but see? It's budding after all."

The cat yawned with exaggerated disdain and shut his eyes.

"I know," Dorrie said. "But I care. You just leave it alone, now, hear?"

She picked up a novel Marcie had recommended about a fortyish divorcee who wrote Country and Western songs. As she read, she chuckled at the woman's lyrics and marveled at the number of beds she bounced on, grateful to have been safely married before the Sexual Revolution took place. Equal pay for equal work was long overdue, she thought, but turning women into roués was another matter altogether.

She'd packed her own sexuality away for safekeeping years ago, never thinking that at some future date it might be necessary to unpack it and dust off the moth crystals. Not now, she thought. Not yet. Still, she was only fifty-five, not an old woman yet. Her mouth twisted in a rueful half-smile. Old enough to know better but not yet old enough to care.

At last her eyes grew sandy, and she laid the book aside. Insulted at being dumped from her lap, Domino complained all the way up the stairs

95

as he followed her to bed.

Dorrie walks along the beach of a small, deserted island. The sand is gritty under her bare feet, and a cold wind whips the rags that cover her. She wraps her arms tightly around herself and looks out to sea at the upturned keel of a capsized luxury yacht. The others were all swept away, but Dorrie was washed ashore with the other flotsam.

She stubs her toe on a mound in the sand and drops to her knees to uncover it. After digging for several minutes, she discovers the round top of a wooden trunk whose iron bands have rusted away.

Lifting its lid, she sees a pirate's treasure; pieces of eight, rubies like pigeon's eggs, chains wrought of gold and heavily tarnished silver, a mirror whose gold-and-silver back depicts a sorrowing woman. She turns it over to see the glass shattered, fragmenting her reflection. As she picks up a string of pearls, its cord snaps and the pearls scatter on the sand.

Dorrie empties the trunk and spreads the treasure out upon the sand. Her heart is bitter. If she were not shipwrecked, marooned here all alone, these baubles would be beyond price. Here they are useless. They will not shelter her, clothe her, feed her, protect her from the blazing sun. Except for its irony, the treasure is not even amusing.

Walt Longstreet called Monday morning and pled ignorance of the proposed sale. Dorrie called Travis Burton, George's accountant, who at least knew what she was talking about.

"So they're back," he said. "They must want it real bad. I thought George had priced himself right out of the market."

"I didn't know anything about it, Mr. Burton. It came as a complete shock. Their Mr. Stein is taking me to lunch today to talk about it. I don't suppose you could meet us?"

"Not today, I'm afraid. I have another appointment. Find out what he's offering, and I'll drop by the store tomorrow afternoon to look it over, okay?"

"All right, then. My daughter's coming along to translate. I'm not that fluent in financialese."

Burton laughed.

"That's okay; that's what I'm for. I'll see you tomorrow, then."

Mr. Stein strolled into the store about ten minutes before noon and stood near the front, checking out the diamond case and the display of Italian and German crèches Charmaine had set up Sunday when she'd helped Dorrie decorate the store. He looked more like a salesman than a buyer, Dorrie thought: custom-tailored gray silk suit, sparkling white batiste shirt, silk tie, Italian shoes shined to a high gloss. . . . Masses of golden hair waved above his high forehead. Gorgeous diamond stickpin, she noticed, listening to her customer dither over a decision between two pairs of inexpensive earrings for her nieces. Square cut. Must be a carat and a half.

"I don't know which one to give which girl," the customer moaned. "Whatever I decide, there'll be jealousy . . ."

"Why don't you take them both and get their mother to make the choice?" Dorrie suggested.

Zada approached the man, and Dorrie saw her turn away after a brief exchange. He looked back at Dorrie, smiled, and nodded. As her customer was leaving with the earrings, he approached her with his hand outstretched.

"Mrs. Greene? I'm Morris Stein. I didn't realize it was you—I was looking for a much older woman."

"How do you do, Mr. Stein. It's nice to meet you." His hand was cold and a little on the limp side. "I hope you don't mind: I've invited my daughter to come along. She should be here any minute."

"Not at all! I look forward to meeting her."

Dorrie saw Marcie's car slip neatly into a parking space in front of the store.

"Here she is," she said. "If you'll excuse me, I'll just get my coat . . ."

A half-hour later she looked around the dining room at the Adolphus Hotel. Crystal chandeliers hung from a ceiling as high as Heaven itself. Crystal, silver, and brilliant white napery sparkled on the tables, and a pianist played Mozart on a mahogany baby grand in an alcove to her left. A bud vase holding a single, fresh, yellow rose with sprigs of fern and baby's breath decorated their table.

This wasn't just lunch, Dorrie realized; it was an attempt at seduction. And Morris Stein seemed less like a shark than an eel.

The business part of their meeting had lasted all of five minutes. Dorrie'd explained that she was not ready to commit to the sale but had agreed to consider his offer. He'd handed her a packet of papers with his business card and offered to answer any questions she might have, and that had been that. Now, ordering a *crème brûlée,* he was doing all he could to charm her. His smile showed teeth so perfect that Dorrie winced for the hours he'd spent in dentists' chairs.

Marcie laid her hand on her mother's.

"If you-all will excuse me," she said, "I've really got to run. I have a one-thirty meeting. Mom, Kurt and I'll drop by the house this evening to talk if you like. Shall I call you?"

"Do, honey. No need to call — I'll be home after the store closes."

"I wish you wouldn't put in such long days. Twelve hours gets old in a hurry. It's not good for you."

"Don't coddle, dear. I'll see you tonight, okay?"

"If she decides to go through with the sale," Stein said, "she'll have all the time off she can handle."

"I think that's what she's afraid of," Marcie said. "Nice to have met you, Morris. See you later, Mom."

"Nice lunch?" Zada asked after Stein left the store.

"Lovely," Dorrie said. "More than I could eat, but it was beautifully served."

She wondered how much Zada knew about the sale. If George had been that closed-mouthed with his own wife, Dorrie doubted he'd said anything to his help. Poor thing, she seemed worried, though . . .

Dorrie carried the papers Morris Stein had given her back to George's office to read, but could make only partial sense of them. She couldn't relate to the numbers: more than a million dollars for the building itself, which her grandfather had built in 1923; tens of thousands for the fixtures; an open figure for the stock, which would have to be inventoried. By the time they were through, she realized, it would come to more money than she could imagine. What would she do with all that money if she accepted it?

She'd always wanted to travel, but with George gone there was nobody to travel with. She already owned all the things she could ever imagine wanting. Two kept talking about security, as his father had done, but it was hard to get excited about security when she lived in a house she owned and had never gone hungry except by choice.

Marcie'd already invested the insurance money, and its income would keep her in minor luxury for another fifty years if she never saw another dime. She could increase her gifts to the Arts Council and the Children's Foundation, establish a scholarship in George's name at the University, even build and staff a shelter for the homeless, though she'd probably be as inept at that as she was in the store. Giving it away might be fun, but of course that would create a whole new set of problems. So what did she need with all that money?

Dorrie folded up the papers without reading the Terms and Conditions. Here she was, she thought, being offered all the money in the world, and what was the good of it? How unimaginative she'd become! She couldn't think of a thing to do with a million dollars except give it away, and if she did that her son would have her locked up!

"Well, George, what do you think?" she asked his picture that night. "Should I sell it or keep it? Do you think I can make a go of it?"

He made no answer, but she knew what he wanted. Hadn't he tried to accomplish the sale before he died, so she'd never "have to work"? As if she had never turned a hand at home. True, she'd always had a housekeeper until the children left, but she'd been the one who managed the household money, hired and fired the help, cooked and sewed and mothered her life away. What had he thought that was, if not work? She'd just never had a paycheck, unless you counted the household money; that had been deposited to her account every month, as regularly as clockwork. He'd never put it in her hands himself. George liked to think her hands were too dainty to be sullied with anything as crass as money.

Men could be so foolish, she thought. All he'd succeeded in doing was preventing her from learning what would enable her now to make a sensible decision.

The problem followed her up the stairs and

into bed, and she drifted off to sleep with it still in her mind.

Dorrie is driving George's 1968 Buick Roadmaster down a country road when suddenly she finds a barricade with a detour sign blocking her way. She pulls off into a wooded roadside park and gets out of the car.

The tops of all the trees have been sheared off; they are as flat-topped as African plane trees. Dorrie wanders through, looking at them, and sees a little concrete-block house beside the paved walk. It was a window, and an old man with a beard is seated inside. She wants to ask him what has happened to the trees, but he has not invited her in and she must not impose on him.

Who would do such a terrible thing, she wonders, and why? This is not ordinary pruning; no loving gardener would treat the trees so harshly. She waits for the old man to come outside and explain, but he ignores her. At last she returns to the car where she weeps for the trees' mutilation.

Ten

Tuesday afternoon, Travis Burton came in. He was a medium-tall, thick man with graying hair, wearing a navy pinstriped suit, a red tie, and rose-tinted aviator glasses.

"It's a good deal," he said after looking over the papers. "George must've really held their feet to the fire. Financially speaking, it's a magnificent deal!"

"I suppose," Dorrie said. "It's an awful lot of money. I just have this feeling . . ."

"What feeling?"

"I can't even tell you. Just hate to let it go, I guess."

"Sentimental about it?"

"Mr. Burton, I feel foolish saying this—selling is so obviously the thing to do. 'Take the money and run,' isn't that what they say? And I don't even know what I'll do if I turn it down. Goodness knows, I don't know how to run it!"

He was staring at her hands, and Dorrie realized that she was twisting her wedding ring around and around her finger. The emeralds mocked her. Is this green enough for you, George? she thought. She folded her hands and went on.

"It's just that I've been in this store all my life. It's like home to me, and I almost feel as if I'm being thrown out!"

Burton smiled.

"Well, Dorrie—May I call you Dorrie? It's odd: I probably know as much about you as your best friend, and we've barely met. George was so protective."

"He never liked me to be involved with the store," Dorrie said, "except for entertaining an occasional out-of-town sales rep. George was old-fashioned about that. Yes, please, do call me Dorrie."

"Thank you." His smile was wide and generous; it made him look kind. "And you'll call me Travis, I hope. Of course, George never intended for you to feel like that. He just wanted to save you the worry, free you to enjoy yourself. There are a world of things to do besides this: travel, volunteer work, school. Maybe you'd like to learn to write or to paint. Lots of women return to school when their children are grown. What would you like to do?"

Dorrie shook her head.

"Traveling's no fun alone. If George had lived . . . but there's the irony, you see: if he'd lived, I could never have pried him out of here for so much as a month's travel."

"Volunteer work?"

She shrugged. "Young George would like that. It suits his ideas of how aging widows ought to occupy their time, but my experience with it hasn't been all that rewarding. All those women with more dollars than sense throwing charity balls to feed the hungry, when the cost of their decorations alone would feed thousands."

"So that's out." Travis paused, assessing George's pretty, lost-looking widow, noticing with interest the intelligence in her eyes. "What did you do before George passed away?"

"Read a lot. Gardened. Cooked. PTA when the children were small; I was glad when I could let that go. I helped out at the store when there was a real pinch, though George hated that." She smiled, remembering. "I always did enjoy the sales floor, though; it was fun. Of course, George did the real work. What I did was more like entertaining guests."

"I'm sure you're an excellent salesperson, Dorrie. You're a charming woman."

"Thank you." Startled, Dorrie looked up into his face. He smiled again, and she dropped her gaze to the desktop. "The fact is, Mr. . . . Travis, I don't really know what I want. My son wants me to sell because George wanted it, but the problem with that is, once I sell, it's gone. I can't change my mind."

"Do you need more time to consider it?"

She shook her head.

"I've been over all the things people suggest you do with money," she said, "and they don't appeal to me. I was brought up to make myself useful. I don't want to just play away the rest of my life. I don't need the money—George took care of that, God bless him—but I do need something to do. The store is something to do."

"I see your point. Still, the world is full of things to do, and a million plus is a great deal of money to pass up."

Dorrie gave him a wry smile.

"Contrary to popular opinion, there is such a thing as 'enough.' George was heavily insured; money's not what I need right now." Her face, reflected in his glasses, looked embarrassingly earnest. "The truth is, Travis, I'd like to see if I can be a businesswoman. If I keep the store and hire somebody to teach me to run it, would you teach me to keep the books and manage my financial affairs? I'd ask my daughter, but she has enough on her plate just now."

"I'd be glad to help you, Dorrie. I've been doing it for your husband for years."

"I don't know anything about business, you understand. You'll have to teach me a lot. I may be a trial to you at first."

Travis Burton smiled and removed his glasses, and she noticed for the first time that his eyes were a blazing shade of blue.

"We'll work it out," he said. "Just let me know what you want to do, and I'll do what I can to help."

Dorrie heard herself humming later that afternoon and realized that the feeling of heaviness that had sat upon her for weeks was gone. She moved so lightly that even Zada noticed.

"You sure seem cheerful," she said. "Everything go all right with your meeting?"

"Fine." The store was empty for the moment, and Dorrie was bursting with her decision. Standing by the front cash register, she patted the stool beside her. "Come here, Zada. Sit down. I've got some really good news."

Zada perched on the stool, her face stiff with anxiety.

"I'm not selling the store," Dorrie told her. "I'm going to keep it and run it myself, if you'll help. Zada, would you accept the position of manager and teach me this business?"

Zada's eyes widened, and her hand flew to cover a gasp.

"Oh, Mrs. Greene! I . . . I never expected . . ." Zada's face reddened, and her eyes grew wide. "Of course, I helped Mr. Greene all along—*Manager!* I was just so sure you'd sell . . ." She shook her head, and Dorrie saw that her hands were trembling. "Are you sure? Is that really what you want?"

"I'm sure. Why hire a stranger when you've been here all these years? You've been managing the store for months without the name or the wage. I do hope you'll accept."

"Well, if you're sure . . . Of course I will."

"It will mean teaching me how, of course. If I'm going to keep the store, I need to learn to operate it."

"I know just how Mr. Greene did everything, Mrs. Greene. All the suppliers and the billing and his customers—everything! There's a lot of detail," the lines between Zada's eyes, which had been deep with tension, softened slightly, "but there's no hurry now, is there? I can teach it to you bit by bit."

"I hope so. George never would teach me. I believe he thought it wasn't ladylike to have ideas about anything more serious than flower arranging." She paused and looked soberly at Zada. "There is one condition, you understand."

All the light went out from behind Zada's face. Her eyes narrowed, and her mouth turned down.

"What is it?" she asked.

"You'll have to call me 'Dorrie.' As closely as we'll be working together, 'Mrs. Greene' won't do."

"I left the papers at the store," Dorrie told Marcie later that night. She'd come to the house while Kurt was at rehearsal to talk over the sale. "Mr. Burton told me it was a wonderful deal, but I've decided I don't want to sell."

"I can't say I'm surprised," Marcie said. "But have you decided what you'll do now?"

"That's the great part: this afternoon, I made Zada my manager. She's going to teach me the business!"

"Really! What made you offer her the job? I sort of expected you'd hire a professional manager."

Dorrie could almost see the wheels turning behind Marcie's eyes.

"It was the most impulsive thing I've ever done in my life," she said, "but think about it: she knows the store inside out. She's been our china buyer forever, built that department up till we're one of the best in Dallas . . ." Dorrie's voice trailed off into uncertainty, but she forced determination back into it. "I think she'll be wonderful."

"Zada is pretty sharp, if you can get past that Great Stone Face act," Marcie said thoughtfully. "And she's been there nearly all my life. I didn't even think about Zada." She thought again, and then said, "Do you think she'll be as loyal to you as she was to Dad?"

"Why wouldn't she be?" Dorrie said. "She loves the store! Her loyalty's a given, and I can't imagine Zada doing anything even mildly dishonest. She's the most upright woman I've ever met."

"You're right, of course. You can't fault her experience; nobody knows Hunter & Greene's like Zada does." She smiled. "Even so, it'll be interesting. She's as odd a duck as I ever met."

"Zada and I get along fine," Dorrie said. "And Travis Burton has agreed to teach me about the financial end. That was one of my biggest worries, you know. Your dad never let me balance so much as a checkbook in his life."

"Come on, Mom! I showed you how to do that myself! Balancing books is nothing to worry about—numbers are one of the few things in life you can really count on!"

"But they're so implacable, dear. I've always hated them."

Marcie smiled. "Well, you still ought to learn the basics, just to keep the help honest."

"I'm not worried about the help; just my own ignorance." Dorrie laughed, embarrassed. "But

111

you know, I feel just like Judy Garland in that movie: 'Hey, kids! We can put on a show!'"

She'd call Mr. Stein in the morning, she thought on her way to bed, and then she'd have to call Two. She should have called him already—he must be beside himself by now. His favorite position, she thought, and was instantly ashamed of herself.

She wished he wouldn't worry so, but Two had been born worried. All his life he'd spent so much time ensuring his safety that he'd never had time for fun.

She wondered what had ever happened to make him so unsure. She'd spent the first twenty years of his life trying to build his confidence, but every time she told him he was good at something—even when she said she loved him—he'd given her that look: "Of course you'd say that; you're my mother." Instead of believing in himself, he'd questioned her judgment. It was as if he'd been born knowing he could never be good enough and had struggled against the knowledge all his life.

His father hadn't been any help, either, she thought. Orphaned at four and raised by an uncaring aunt, George had never been able to believe that anyone who professed to love him would stick around. Grandma Rose used to tell her, "There's not enough love in the whole world for an orphaned child, Dorrie; you'll just have to be patient with him." She had been, too, but he'd never been convinced she wouldn't finally leave or die on him.

It had shown in the way he was with the children: afraid to give himself, especially once they'd outgrown their babyhood and could walk away.

Poor George, she thought. Poor Two. I wish I'd known what to do for them.

Walking through a dark forest, Dorrie sees the flickering light of a bonfire and hears chanting. She sneaks up on the campsite where she finds a group of white-robed men standing off to one side. Suspended from a huge tripod over the fire is a wicker cage with a man huddled in it.

Dorrie climbs a tree, praying that the chanting men won't see her. She inches out on a limb to a spot from which she can see the cage. The man in it cowers in a fetal position, arms pressed closely to his sides, head on his knees. His hands are closed around a living object—a bird?

"Pss-sst!" she hisses. "Pss-sst! I'm here! Let me help you!"

Warily the man looks up. It is George.

"George! It's me! Let me help you!"

"Go away!" he moans. "The limb is weak; it will break. If they find you, they'll kill you."

"They're not paying any attention to me," she insists. A long pole appears in her hands, and she pushes it out toward his cage. "Grab on, I'll set you free."

Slowly George opens his hands. The fluttering object he has been hiding is his naked heart.

Eleven

The next day, Dorrie sat down with Travis and went over the books to get an idea of the store's salaries, expenses, and income.

"Is that all Zada earns?" she asked, shocked. "It's not very much, is it?"

"Well, now that she's your manager she should be due for a raise."

"I should think! What's the going rate for managing a store of this size, Travis?"

He named a figure that was more than twice Zada's present salary.

"Can the store afford that?"

"I think so. George was . . . unnecessarily conservative in the matter of wages, and especially for women. And of course, he never paid a manager's salary. He was his own manager."

Dorrie thought for a moment.

"Tell you what," she said. "Suppose I double

her salary and offer her a percentage of the profits at year's end. What do you think?"

"I think that's both generous and creative. The bonus will be tied directly to her performance; that's the best kind."

"So that's a good business decision."

Travis smiled. "Yes. But don't forget about yourself, Dorrie. You're working full time now. You should have a salary too."

"A salary!" She laughed. "Think of that!"

"It makes the bookkeeping easier. One of the quickest ways to ruin a business is to skim the profits off the top. A thousand a week would be a reasonable figure, don't you think?"

"A thousand a week! I don't need that!"

Travis laughed.

"Well, you'll be earning it, and it's a lot less than George took out. Save what you don't spend for your old age."

It would be a lot different from living on a household allowance, Dorrie thought. A thousand dollars a week earned by her own work! Never again would she have to feel guilty about indulging herself in a new set of encyclopedia, a rare orchid plant, a weekend getaway. It would take some getting used to, but she was ready to try.

Later that afternoon, Dorrie asked Zada, "Do you suppose it would be all right to make Thursdays my regular day off? I have a standing appointment with Jeannine down the street on Thursday mornings."

Zada looked—for Zada—amused. "You can take any day you want. Take two! It's your store, Dorrie!"

"I know. I just wanted to know if it was okay."

For the next few weeks, her attention was so closely focused on the store that everything outside it became a blur. Every day she woke at eight, ate a light breakfast, and left without even a cup of coffee to be at the store by nine. Once there, she put the coffee on, tidied up, and let the help in before she opened the store. Business was good; the store always had several customers, and not just lookers, either; they seemed to be buying the high-end merchandise this year. Travis dropped by every week to talk things over, and she made it a point to be businesslike with him. It was important to her new professional image.

Dorrie discovered that Willis was a rock collector; he'd been studying gemstones ever since he was a boy. With Zada's and Travis's agreement, she put him on commission and moved him into fine jewelry while she concentrated on learning the costume stock. Gem sales, which had been slow since George's death, picked up so noticeably that she put Angie on commission too. Really, Dorrie thought, it was shocking how little George had paid his help. How could they have lived all these years?

Working in the store, Dorrie often felt closer to George than she had when he was alive. She might be alone in the back room, rearranging the displays out front, or adding up the day's receipts after the store was closed; wherever, he was there.

"Well, what do you think?" she asked him one night. The numbers had added up right the first time through, and she was feeling sassy. "I don't know why in the world you ever made such a mystery of this. It's not that different from running a household when you think about it."

And it wasn't. She had three employees instead of one, but "employee relations" were just like working with the housekeepers, repairmen, and yard workers she'd had over the years. "Buying" meant merchandise instead of furniture, appliances, or clothing for the family, but salesmen were salesmen. And customers . . . well, customers were like guests, to be treated graciously even when they were obnoxious. At worst, it was like dealing with fractious children; she just had to sift through the chatter to find out what they really wanted, and then help them find it.

The books were like budgeting: this much money would go this far, and if she spent it on one thing, she didn't have it to spend on another. The difference was, the excess she used to squeeze out for gifts and indulgences was now called "profit." Actually, it was a little boring. How could George have stayed excited about this for nearly fifty years?

"Dorrie?" Jessie Bynum's voice called. Dorrie padded across the kitchen to let her neighbor in.

"Lord, girl, where have you been? In hibernation? You haven't answered the door or the phone for weeks!"

"I've taken over the store, Jess. I'm trying to learn to run it."

"Good for you. Reese thought you'd sell it, get out of there, and be a merry widow. So how's it feel to be a PWG?"

"PWG?"

"Poor Working Girl. That's what my mom used to call me when I worked at the dimestore before I got married."

Dorrie laughed. "It's okay. Zada Strait's managing the store and teaching me the ropes. Have a cup of coffee? How're your kids?"

"They're doin' good, doin' good. Wayne's wife Chrissy's pregnant again, due in the spring."

"Their fourth?" Dorrie asked, setting two cups on the sun-washed breakfast table. "Sit down, Jessie."

"Yeah. Two years apart, just like clockwork." Jessie settled herself into a ladder-backed chair and wrapped her hand around the warm cup. "They say this one's the last."

"Four children, in this decade! When we were young, everybody wanted big families, but for the past twenty years it seems nobody's wanted more than the regulation two point five." Dorrie smiled. "I think it's great. I'd have had a dozen if George'd been willing."

Jessie laughed.

"I always envied you with only two, and such good ones. Mine were into everything. Used to worry myself sick over them, especially the girls, but they turned out all right in the end."

Jessie's Sally, Dorrie remembered, had been a real problem. Somewhere in her middle teens Sally'd decided she'd had all she could take of being good, and she'd gone right off the rails. She and Marcie'd been close, and it had scared Dorrie. That was when Charmaine had come along and taken Marcie to Disneyland—flown her halfway across the country just for a weekend and bought her a "California" outfit of purple tie-dyed bell-bottoms, a rose-pink shirt, and huaraches—and Marcie had veered in the other direction afterward. It had taken Sally ten years, a bad marriage, and single motherhood to straighten herself out.

"How's Sally these days?" Dorrie asked.

"She's doing fine. Got a promotion recently, so she's making more money. Her little Brittany started school this fall, and she loves it."

Jessie stayed for nearly an hour, talking over old times, until Reese telephoned for her.

"I swear, that man treats me like a combination daughter and house slave," she said, laughing. "Well, Dorrie, don't be a stranger. Come and see me sometimes on your day off."

Maybe, Dorrie thought. She'd always enjoyed Jessie, but she'd as soon stay away from Reese.

Susan and Two expected her for Christmas, and of course she would go. Marcie and Kurt would be out of town. They'd been saving for nearly a year for a Caribbean cruise, and Dorrie envied them the trip.

"Why don't you come with us, Mom?" Kurt asked. "It's not too late to buy tickets."

"Oh, honey, don't tempt me!" Dorrie said. "I'd love nothing better—the beaches, that blue ocean, all that color—but I couldn't do it to Zada. She needs me here." She smiled. "It's not bad, you know, to be needed again."

"Come on, Mom," Marcie said. "How long

has it been since you did something just for fun? You can take the time off!"

"Not this year," Dorrie said. "Lord, I'm just now beginning to figure out what I'm doing! I've got enough on my plate for now."

"I wish you'd reconsider. You know, Two's not the only one who worries. I try not to hassle you, but I can see what you're going through. Don't bury yourself in the store, Mom; that was Dad's life, but it's not yours. You've got years and years ahead of you, and I'd like to see them happy ones."

Dorrie took her hand and held it.

"Thank you, honey. I do appreciate it. I'm going through a rough spot right now, but things will straighten out soon. The store helps, honestly. It gives me something else to think about."

"Well, if you're sure . . ." Marcie grinned. "I guess Two would disown you, anyhow. It's bad enough you're not home baking cookies; if you didn't show up on Christmas morning, he'd have a fit! He was so sure you'd retire to your rocker like a proper grandma." She laughed. "Poor old Two gave up on me a long time ago, but he never has quit hoping you'd grow up to be Maribelle Morgan."

Dorrie laughed with her. "I know," she said. "Poor Two. I'm so glad he has Susan."

* * *

For the first time, Dorrie did not set up a Christmas tree at home, nor even hang a wreath on the door. She told herself she was all decorated out from doing the store and that she wouldn't have time to enjoy it, but at bottom she didn't want a tree. Without George to argue Scotch pine versus balsam and to string the lights, it would only make her sad.

But the Saturday before Christmas, she came home after nine at night and entered the orchid room to find a three-foot tree covered with tinsel and twinkling lights sitting on top of the coffee table.

"Oh, my," she said. It would be Susan's work, of course. Dorrie had declined her help with a tree earlier in the week, but here it was. She crossed the room to stare at the Renaissance angel on its top, its rosy papier-maché skirt in crisp folds. Her eyes filled. George had brought the angel home from the store twenty years ago, and it had topped their tree every year since.

"Oh, dear," she murmured. Susan's motives were pure; all she wanted was everybody to be sweet and happy all the time. Blessed are the meek, Dorrie thought. Now she would have to appear grateful for a "kindness" she had neither asked nor wanted.

She took off her coat and turned on the living room light. Crossing to the mantel, she picked up George's picture, then wandered to the couch and plopped down, the picture in her hand.

"Do you remember that time Trey felt so sad about losing his puppy," she said, "and she told him to 'put on a happy face,' and I said only fools are happy all the time — how hurt she was? And puzzled, as if I'd attacked her. Poor Susan just can't face the fact that life's not all sunshine." Dorrie shook her head. "I hope for her sake that Two outlives her. I don't know how she'd deal with his death."

Dorrie bent to take off her shoes and was surprised to see water drop onto her skirt. A tear.

"Who said you could leave me?" she whispered, staring at George's face. "Who gave you permission to check out and leave me here alone? No one to cook for, no one to dress up for, no one to sit with in the evening or lie down with at night . . ." She raised her head and looked at the picture. "It's not fair, George! You had no right!"

He didn't want to hear it, she decided. Never had wanted to know when she felt shortchanged, and especially not about love. One time she'd complained that he never told her he loved her, and he'd been indignant.

"I married you, didn't I?" he'd said. And George had been nearly as strait-laced as her father. Intimacy had been hard for him, and she — a child of the Forties, when sex had been

124

truly unmentionable—had been embarrassed to tell him she liked it.

But it was more than simple Puritanism. Each time she got pregnant, George entered a state of panic that lasted until the baby was safely born. He'd been so upset after her miscarriage that he'd never wanted her to try again, and when she told him Marcie was coming he'd been so distraught that he'd had a vasectomy. She had signed the papers in anger, thinking bitterly that a man who didn't want children didn't deserve to have them.

After that, even though pregnancy was no longer an issue, their sex life had all but stopped. George had seemed to feel that sex was messy and uncontrollable at best, an unfair demand his body made upon him and one he satisfied as seldom and as efficiently as he could. She had wept an ocean, thinking it was her fault, until at last she'd figured out that she could have been Sophia Loren in black lace and he still wouldn't have wanted her. It was not she, but sex itself that put him off. Once she'd figured that out and stopped blaming herself, it had been easier.

So she had not complained when, as he got older, his body demanded it less. You take the bad with the good, was what she'd always been taught, and there was plenty of good about being married to George even if they did disagree on that question.

Dorrie had been taught from infancy to despise self-pity, and she saw no sense now in crying about things that couldn't be helped. She blew her nose, climbed the stairs, crawled into her icy bed, and pulled the down comforter close around her neck. It took her a long time to get warm enough to sleep.

Dorrie is cooking a gourmet dinner for George, humming as she stuffs the patty shells with creamed lobster, smiling as she beats the hollandaise for fresh asparagus, dancing around the kitchen as she whips cream for the out-of-season strawberries that were so hard to find. Imported coffee is brewing, and the smell fills the kitchen as she waits. He will be home in a few minutes. She has set the table with her best china and the sterling and sent the children to her mother's for the night.

When George comes in and climbs the stairs to change his clothes, her anticipation mounts. At last he comes back downstairs, and she takes his hand to lead him into the dining room. She sets the beautiful, fragrant dishes on the table and waits for his approval.

"Here, sweetheart, try this," Dorrie says, placing a patty shell on his plate.

George picks silently at his food. He takes a

piece of plain bread and bites into it, and then shoves a spear of asparagus across his plate with the King Francis fork.

"Perhaps another time," he says. "This is too rich for me. My stomach's been upset all day." He rises from his chair, pats the top of her head, and leaves the dining room.

Dorrie clears the table and scrapes the food down the grinder. Maybe tomorrow, she thinks. A nice pot roast with carrots and potatoes.

Twelve

Dorrie woke up feeling rotten and could not force herself out of bed. At last she rolled over and dialed Zada's number.

"Will you open up for me this morning?" she asked.

"Of course. Is anything wrong?"

"I don't know . . . I just can't seem to get it in gear."

"Well, you've only been working six twelve-hour days a week for the past month. Do you reckon a day off would destroy your health?"

Dorrie laughed. "Probably not. Are you sure, though? It's been so busy—"

"We'll handle it. You just rest, and we'll see you tomorrow."

"Well, all right, then . . ." Dorrie hesitated, torn between arguing further and going back to sleep. "Zada? Thanks."

She slept until the phone woke her at half-past ten.

128

"Dorrie?" Charmaine's rough voice demanded. "You sick or just lazy?"

"I don't know for sure. I woke up feeling awful, and Zada said stay home."

"Did I wake you?"

"I should have been up hours ago."

"Well, you don't sound good. I'm coming over, and we'll just see."

Dorrie put on George's old brown-flannel robe, found her fuzzy slippers, and stumbled down the hall to the bathroom. Her face looked gray in the wall mirror, and she opened the medicine cabinet and dumped a pair of aspirins into her hand, hoping she'd feel better after a shower.

By the time Charmaine arrived, Dorrie was dressed in gray flannel slacks and a ticking-striped shirt with its tails hanging. Her hair was still wet, and she hadn't bothered with makeup. The smell of coffee perking was helping to revive her, but guilt still nagged.

"You're looking pretty peaked, girl," Charmaine told her. "If I were you, I'd let it rest a day or two. Anyhow, you been shut up in that damned store night and day for weeks. You need a day off."

"I suppose. Even Zada gets one of those." Dorrie yawned. "I could sleep for a week, if I could just stop dreaming."

"Nightmares?"

"Some. Mostly just really strange dreams. Disturbing."

"Tell me about them. I love dreams."

Dorrie smiled ruefully. "Too bad I can't remember any. They'd give you a fit." She didn't want to talk about it: dead babies, chariots racing out of control . . . "One time I dreamed Two was my father. I'd had an argument with some man, and he was scolding me . . . very Victorian."

"Your father, was he! Maybe it was a memory, not just a dream."

The coffee gurgled in the last throes of percolation, and Dorrie got up to pour it.

"That's goofy, Charmaine. How could I 'remember' my son as my father?"

"From a former life. They say people tend to stick together till they get things worked out."

"Reincarnation always sounded like wishful thinking to me," Dorrie said. "Endless opportunity to correct your mistakes? It sounds a little too good to be true."

"And white robes, heavenly choirs, and streets of gold don't? Not to mention your enemies burning in hell for all eternity. Talk about a revenge fantasy!"

Dorrie set a cup in front of Charmaine and sat down.

"You may have something there," she said. "Well, nobody can prove any of it, can they."

"I just take it for granted," Charmaine told her. She downed the last of her coffee. "Tell you what," she said, "I know what you need: let's have some breakfast and go shopping."

It was less an invitation, Dorrie knew, than a summons. Charmaine had a whim of iron.

"I don't need to go shopping. I've had all my Christmas presents bought and wrapped since August."

"You would. That's not what I'm talking about. We're going to get you out of those rusty old clothes and into something snazzy. No wonder you feel bad: you look like hell!"

"Thank you," Dorrie said. She hated buying clothes. The sight of her body in the dressing-room mirror, proof of the malignant powers of age and gravity, always got her down. "Do I have to?"

"Go put on your face while I make a phone call," Charmaine said. "Bacon and eggs first, and then we're going to make you gorgeous."

By noon Dorrie's tatty old clothes and flat-heeled shoes were in a Neiman Marcus bag, and she was in a fuchsia-colored silk blouse with a long, full, grape wool skirt and high suede boots.

"I look so washed out," she complained.

"That's what I've been saying!" Charmaine

took her elbow. "Come on, that's next. I have a special treat for you. Made an appointment when you weren't looking."

She hustled Dorrie out to the car and drove to a shopping center on the northern edge of Dallas, humming all the way and refusing to tell Dorrie where they were going. When they arrived, festoons of golden tinsel hung everywhere and Santas, sleighs, and cartoon characters opening gaily wrapped red-and-green packages filled every corner of the mall.

"You're going to love this!" Charmaine said. "Pure luxury, nothing less!" She led Dorrie into a shop with a mannequin's head of plain white porcelain in its single small window. A soft-faced, silvery lady greeted them.

"I brought my friend in for a complete facial. The works, including makeup," Charmaine told her. "Made the appointment this morning. It's her Christmas present."

"How nice!" the lady said. "Do you want to stay with her?"

"No, thanks; I've got shopping to do. When will she be done?"

The lady looked at her book. "Jon's next appointment is at two," she said. "Mrs. Greene should be ready by then."

Charmaine strode out of the store, and the lady led Dorrie to the back, wrapped her in a pink surplice, and sat her in a puffy pink chair before calling a slim young man to "do" her. He tilted Dorrie's face up and touched her cheek.

"Lovely skin," he said. "What do you use on it?"

"Soap and water."

"Oh, my dear! You'll dry it to a crust!" He dipped his slender fingers into a pink pot and started smoothing lotion onto her face.

"There, now, doesn't that feel good? I can see your skin just drinking it up!"

Dorrie was unused to having her face stroked, but she could not deny the pleasure of it. Relaxing into his touch, she smiled and murmured, "Just wake me when it's over."

Jon massaged her face for several minutes and then wiped off the excess with a tissue and reached for a pink bottle.

"Oatmeal masque, I think," he said, more to himself than to her. "Get out all that deep-down dirt, now that we've softened up the surface; pull off all that old, dead skin. And then a moisturizer to keep it fresh . . ." The masque felt cold and gooey on her skin. "You don't wear much makeup, do you?" he asked.

"My husband preferred the natural look," Dorrie said. Her face was already beginning to stiffen under the paste he'd applied, and she could feel her skin drawing up.

"Just lie back and rest now," he said. "I'll be

back in fifteen minutes to peel you. You'll feel like a new woman."

Really? Dorrie thought. I wonder who she might be!

When Jon came back and peeled off the masque, Dorrie felt like a snake shedding its skin. He wiped her face with cotton balls dipped in astringent and then smoothed on more creams and lotions, talking all the while. He glanced at the slip of paper pinned up over the mirror.

"Full makeup, too," he said. "What a friend!"

"We've known each other forever," Dorrie said, but Jon was already thinking about colors.

"Peach-beige foundation, I think, and this soft pink for your cheeks . . . Mauve shadow and navy liner to bring out the blue in your eyes. You really ought to do more with your eyes. They're your best feature."

Dorrie watched carefully as Jon made up her face. He muttered to himself as he smoothed blush on her cheeks, painted her mouth with a liquid rose color, stroked the powdery mauve shadow on her eyelids, and finished her off with a dusting of translucent powder just as Charmaine arrived.

"Now that's more like it!" she said. "You're starting to look like a woman again!"

"Thank you, Charmaine. I've always admired your tact." It would take some getting used to,

134

but she did look nice: like herself, only prettier.

Leaving the mall, Charmaine looked like the cat that got the cream. "We're not through yet, you know," she said. "We've still got a big day ahead of us."

"What now?" Dorrie asked.

"Now we buy a great big box of garbage bags and go home and strip your closet. You're not a housewife anymore, Dorrie. You need to get rid of all those old rags and outfit yourself from scratch."

"Charmaine! When am I going to shop? I've got a store to run—ought to be there right now!"

"I'll shop for you—get stuff on approval and bring it home to try. Don't knock it, girl; you'd have to pay a shopping service fifty dollars an hour for what I'm going to do for the sheer satisfaction of it! Every stitch you own is black or gray or navy. You look like you're trying to hide, and I'll bet your underwear's a disgrace."

"I'm in mourning, Charmaine."

"Bullshit. People haven't worn mourning past the funeral for thirty years. You're just scared somebody will notice you."

They spent the rest of the day sorting through Dorrie's clothes. In the end, Dorrie's wardrobe was reduced to one black suit old enough to be back in fashion, one good dress, three wool skirts, and a few silk blouses in pastel tones, plus the gardening shirt and slacks she'd stuffed under a cushion when Charmaine wasn't looking. Charmaine carried six big bags of castoffs out to her car and locked them in the trunk.

"They won't go to waste," she promised. "I got this friend runs a shelter for women. She'll be tickled silly to get these, and just you wait: you'll be tickled you got rid of them."

While she would never have admitted it to Charmaine, Dorrie felt light almost to giddiness that night looking into her empty closet. All those musty old clothes, the rags of her former life, gone! Room in her closet for fashionable, pretty clothes in the intense colors George had called gaudy: scarlet and purple and teal, electric blue and hot pink and jade. She would buy a fashion magazine tomorrow and look at the new lines. Women were wearing shoulder pads again and waist darts . . . Lying in bed, she looked around the bedroom. Maybe she'd redecorate too. She'd bought these curtains when Two graduated from high school, and she never had liked that painting . . .

Dorrie's house is full of carpenters and painters. A sawhorse blocks the staircase, and she hears hammering and the whine of an electric saw. She enters the living room to find the drapes torn down and the carpet ripped up. Someone is knocking out the front wall.

"What are you doing?" she asks.

"Got to let some light in here," the worker answers. "Room's so dark and stuffy, I don't know how you've stood it."

She climbs over the sawhorse and up the stairs, where she finds utter chaos. All the furniture has been moved out of her bedroom, and the wallpaper hangs in strips. The room itself has been moved to the southeast corner of the house, and its two new windows stand wide open. She can find no place to rest; even the closet doors have been removed from their hinges.

Dorrie wanders back down the steps, through the hall, and into the cellar. It is too messy and full of cobwebs to stay in, but at least it offers privacy. Tying a scarf around her head, Dorrie begins to sweep.

The following Thursday morning, Dorrie had Jeannine perm her hair and color it a soft, gingery blonde. Two would have a fit, she knew, but he'd survive it. It was her head, after all.

The garden club met that afternoon, and Dorrie attended for the first time since August. She'd joined in 1967, her mother's legacy, and she remained among its youngest members. The club kept its roster to fifteen, of whom ten to twelve attended every meeting. They often joked that in order for a new member to join, an old one had to die or leave town.

Even when the friendships forged in such a group were not close, Dorrie thought, their sheer longevity created unbreakable bonds. However the members' outside lives might change, the life of the club was constant; you couldn't just stop knowing people you'd known for twenty-five years. Even so, now that they were growing older, the women were falling into two subgroups: the still-married and the widowed, divorced, or never-married. Dorrie realized with a start that having to change groups was one reason she'd put off coming back.

"How are you, Dorrie?" Grace Imbry greeted her. Grace was the most recent newcomer to Group Two. Her husband, an accountant, had succumbed to a bleeding ulcer last spring, just at tax time.

"I'm doing fine, thanks." Grace had been the first one on her doorstep with a covered dish in September, beating even Jessie Buynum. The dish — a green-bean, mushroom-soup, and french-fried-onion casserole — had moved George's death out of the realm of nightmare and into reality. The house had been so full of droppers-by that day that Dorrie'd never had time to thank Grace properly.

"Well, it gets lonesome sometimes," Grace said. Her voice dropped. "It's easier for us widows to keep up with each other, without husbands to think of. You know you can always call on me."

"I know, Grace. Thanks." She glanced around the room, feeling cornered. "If you'll excuse me, I need to speak to Ola Mae."

Ola Mae Zucker, a still-married and this month's hostess, held out her generous arms as Dorrie approached.

"I'm so glad to see you," she said. "We've been worried."

"Well, I'll be making the meetings more regularly now," Dorrie told her, accepting her embrace. One nice thing about Ola Mae, when she hugged or kissed you, it was a real hug and kiss; none of this smacking the air by your ear. "I'm taking Thursdays off so I'll be free to come. I've missed you too."

"Good. Maybe one of these Thursdays we can have lunch together. I could use an occasional day off myself." She held Dorrie at arm's length and looked her over. "I love your hair, Dorrie. It's a real pleasure to see you looking so good."

"Thanks, Ola Mae. I just had it done this morning." She put her hand up to touch its soft curls. "You're sure it's okay? It's a big change."

"It's as pretty as can be. You'll get used to it soon and wonder why you waited so long."

The women began taking their seats, and Dorrie sat between Jessie and Nell Shifflet. Nell was the group's only never-married, now retired from the job at City Hall she'd had from the age of eighteen. Nell had loved the same "gentleman friend" for thirty years, but even after his invalid wife had died and he'd proposed to her, she'd turned him down.

"All I need at my age," she'd told Dorrie, "is to start picking up some man's socks." That had been fifteen years ago, and so far as Dorrie knew the man was still hanging around.

Dorrie listened with only half an ear to the program on african violet culture. Her african violets had always been the envy of her friends, growing and blooming in wild profusion despite her benign neglect. Sometimes, she thought, things did better if you just let them be. Harassing her plants with bug spray and fertilizers, moving them around from light to shade and back again, usually did them more harm than good. All she'd ever done for her african violets was love them, and they did just fine.

She reached up and touched her hair. Still, change was inevitable. Better to choose your changes than have them thrust upon you, if you could.

"I know you hated artificial color," she told

140

George later that evening, "but be honest, now: don't you think it's pretty?"

She touched her hair again — she'd been doing it all day, amazed at how soft it felt — and smiled.

"Okay, so you don't like it. But I like it, and I love my new clothes. The colors are so bright and pretty, it makes me feel better just to wear them. You wouldn't begrudge me that, would you?"

She sat on the sofa across from him and read for an hour or two until she was sleepy, and then folded the book shut and climbed the stairs. She was going to bed later and later these days. George had never been much company in bed, but at least he'd been there. She hated sleeping alone.

Dorrie is decorating a Christmas tree with beautiful gold and silver balls. As she works, standing back periodically to admire what she's done, she sees that each ball has somebody's name on it: Patience, Faith, Grace, Hope, Prudence, Joy. One has the name Love, another Forgiveness, and a third Courage. What odd names, she thinks, and then realizes that each ball is a Gift of the Spirit to be used during the coming year. She wonders who has sent them, but finds no signature on the box they came in.

Now it is Christmas morning. She is all alone, but not unhappy: the children will be over later, and she looks forward to seeing them. She takes the lovely balls off the tree and sets them around the house where she will be able to see them all year long.

Thirteen

On the Sunday before Christmas, Dorrie held a little after-hours party for the crew and gave them all gifts: a pale blue cardigan for Zada, dangly earrings for Angie, and a packet of stone-setting tools for Willis. She'd invited Willis's family and let Angie bring her boyfriend Tony, but that had turned out to be a mistake.

"Lord, George," she told him when she finally got home, "I'm glad you weren't there; you would've had a fit. Willis's boy flirted with Angie all night, and Tony got jealous and spiked the punch with Everclear—I found the bottle in the trash later—and Willis's younger kids were sword fighting with gift-paper rolls, and all three of the older kids were crocked to the eyeballs before the rest of us knew what was going on . . ."

She dropped into a chair and kicked off her shoes.

"What finally tipped us was, Tony leaned up against the back door, flashed this beatific smile, and slid down the door like a sack of potatoes. Willis was livid — stood over him with his jaws tight and his fists clenched — and Zada got a pitcher of ice water and poured it over the kid's head. Boy, did he come to in a hurry!"

Dorrie had been nearly as angry as Willis, and Angie had cried, afraid she was going to be fired. After reading all three kids the riot act, Dorrie'd had Willis help her pour Tony into the back of her car and put Angie in the front, and she'd driven them back to their dorms herself.

"I'm just glad he didn't throw up," she told George. "I know you would have canned her on the spot, but it wasn't her fault; she didn't bring the liquor." She giggled. "It was terrible, but I can't help laughing about it now. He looked like something in a cartoon!"

She leaned back in the chair, still looking at George. "Except for that, it was a pretty sad little party, with us all remembering past Christmases when you were there. Maybe I should've skipped it this year, but you always did it, and I thought they deserved it." Still, she would have to be more careful. "Next year it'll be family members only," she said.

She must be getting hysterical in her old age, Dorrie thought, trudging up to bed. Drunken

144

kids are not funny. She giggled again. It was the expression on Tony's face, she decided, and the way he slid down the wall. She'd never seen anything like it.

Christmas Day was all Dorrie had dreaded, with Susan determined that everyone be happy and everyone missing George. Wendy cried, and when Two sent her to her room Dorrie wondered what he'd do if his mother burst into tears too. Instead, she wandered coatless into the frigid back yard and stood there shivering until she'd brought herself under control. After dinner she asked Two to take her home.

"I hate for you to be alone tonight, Mother," Susan fretted as they approached the house.

"I'll be all right," Dorrie said. "Charmaine's coming over later, anyhow."

Two gave her a sharp look over his glasses rims.

"So that's it," he said. "What's she up to these days?"

"Nothing much, I guess. I think she's just sort of settling between trips; she's just back from Peru."

"How interesting!" Susan said. "What did she do there?"

"Probably took a cruise in a flying saucer,"

145

Two said. "Really, Mother, I've never understood the connection between you two. What do you see in that woman?"

"Why does anybody love anybody? I've never found it much use to puzzle out those mysteries."

"She the one talked you into dyeing your hair? You don't look much like a grieving widow, I must say!"

"Must you?" Dorrie said, her voice sharp. "Why?"

"I'm your son!"

"I'm not convinced that's reason enough to be rude to me, dear. When you were sixteen and had hair halfway to your waist, I remember being very careful not to judge you."

Two grimaced. "You should've made me cut it off. I still don't know why Dad didn't haul me to a barbershop. Can't imagine I ever did anything that dumb."

"He wanted to, and I wouldn't have it. I thought you deserved the chance to figure out who you were." If he'd let it grow to his knees and kept up with his guitar, he might not be such a stick now. "I have a business to run, Two, and you of all people should appreciate the value of appearances. Feeling bad is no excuse for looking awful."

"Maybe not, but *red hair!*" He pulled into her driveway.

"Please, sweetheart, not now," Susan said. "It's Christmas Day!"

Getting out of the car, Dorrie leaned to kiss her upturned cheek.

"Thanks for having me, dear," she said. "It was a beautiful dinner."

It was past eight when Charmaine arrived with a wrapped package in her hand. She'd spent the day with her older son, Darren, and his wife Lou.

"Merry Christmas," Dorrie said. "I'm glad to see you."

"Rough?" Charmaine asked. "It's not my favorite season, either." She shrugged off her coat, headed for the kitchen, and draped it over the back of a chair.

"Whoosh!" she said, dropping into the banquette. "I'm glad that's over. How was yours?"

"No worse than you'd expect of the first Christmas with George gone. Kurt and Marcie had the right idea; they left town for the holidays. Trying to have the same old Christmas with George gone . . . well, it wasn't merry."

Dorrie busied herself at the stove, setting water to boil for tea.

"I used to envy you at Christmas time," Charmaine said. "You had your whole family together — parents and children, even grandparents, for a long time — and Max never would let me come near the kids on Christmas Day. I

147

always had to see them some other time, make a crummy 'little Christmas' at my house. The first few times, I set up great, whopping Christmas trees and hung greens, decorated myself into a snit, piled up presents under the tree . . . but then all the boys wanted to do was collect their loot and go home. Max spent a lot of time poisoning their minds against me, and I wasn't with them enough to counter it. And then he married that little twit of a nurse and she set up this cozy little Father-Knows-Best household just like he'd always wanted."

"I felt real bad about that, Charmaine. I could see it happening, and there wasn't anything I could do." For the first few years, she'd made it a point to invite Charmaine's boys to play with Two, but that hadn't lasted either. They'd gotten into football in junior high school and cared about nothing else, and Two'd never cared a flip about football.

"I used to think about you at Christmas time," Dorrie said, "wondering where you were and what you were doing. You'd be in India or Africa or South America, having these wonderful adventures, while I was up to my eyebrows in piecrust and turkey dressing, preparing to feed a small army of kin that never did like each other that much. Aunt Mabel would pinch the children's cheeks, and they hated it. Uncle Joe Barley always brought a bottle, and then George

148

would spend the whole day worrying that he'd get drunk in front of the kids. I can remember wishing I were in Zambia with you!"

"No, you didn't. I just went as far away from Dallas as I could get, trying to find a place they didn't celebrate Christmas." She laughed abruptly. "There aren't many, you know."

Dorrie toyed with the ribbons on her present.

"Here, what am I thinking of?" she said. "Let me get yours!"

She went into the orchid room and took the package from beneath Susan's tree.

"Here," she said, "open it. I hope you like it."

The rustle of paper filled the room, and Charmaine lifted the lid off the large box Dorrie had given her and unfolded the tissue surrounding her gift.

"Oh, Dorrie!" she said, lifting out a mohair shawl, soft as a cloud, in mingled shades of purple, green, and blue. "It's lovely!"

Dorrie lifted the lid from her box and gasped. Inside, beneath a book called *Life After Life*, were six pairs of lace-trimmed silk panties and three lace bras.

"My lord!" she breathed. "Charmaine, they're perfectly beautiful, but what in the world ever got into you? I've never worn anything like this in my life!"

"Well, it's time you started. I've seen the state of your underwear, and sooner or later you're going to wish you had something pretty."

Dorrie blushed. "Later, I think. Much later. But thank you, Charmaine."

After Charmaine left, Domino followed Dorrie up the stairs and watched her lay the silks away in a dresser drawer. They glowed like jewels.

"What do you think, Domino?" she said, smiling. "Do I look like the sort of woman who wears emerald silk step-ins, or were these meant for somebody else?"

Domino jumped to the top of the dresser and considered the question. Dorrie held up a pair to admire the lace, and the cat reached out a paw and slapped at them.

"Don't do that," Dorrie said. "I'm warning you: tear these and I'll wear you out!"

Fourteen

Travis called the store the following Tuesday morning.

"I hoped I'd find you there," he said. "How's it coming?"

"Pretty well, I guess. Did you have a nice Christmas?"

"Yes, thank you. Went to Austin to see my grandbabies. Yourself?"

"I survived. They say the first one's always the hardest. What do I need to do about the books before the year ends?"

"I thought if you were free, we could talk about it over lunch."

"I don't usually leave the store . . ." Dorrie looked toward the front. Willis was polishing the diamond case, and Angie was stargazing. Only Zada had a customer. "Well, we're not that busy. What time?"

"Pick you up at noon," Travis said.

He took her to a little Highland Park café whose only decoration was bright green plants hanging against stark, white walls.

"I like this," Dorrie said, examining a flourishing aspidistra next to their table. "It seems so fresh. Like spring, almost."

"I eat here whenever I'm out this way. They make wonderful soups."

Dorrie fumbled in her large purse for a moment, and then looked stricken.

"What is it?" Travis asked.

"I forgot my notebook."

"Never mind. Let's just talk. Tell me, how are you liking business?"

"Well, it's certainly kept me busy. It's a challenge, having your life turned upside down like that: one day a pampered housewife, and almost the next a businesswoman." She laughed softly. "Thank Heaven for you and Zada Strait, is all I can say!"

"You don't seem to feel it's got the better of you."

"I'm hanging on—just barely, but so far, so good. It's nowhere near as hard as I imagined."

"I didn't realize you were so scared."

Dorrie laughed. "Neither did I, till it was too late! I get tired, of course—quit wearing high-heeled shoes the first week, and I even broke down and took a day off the week before Christmas."

"You've had your hair done," Travis said, studying her face. "I like it a lot."

"Thank you." Dorrie's hand lifted to touch it. "My son hates it. You don't think it looks . . . inappropriate in a woman my age?"

"It takes fifteen years off you. I'm surprised you didn't do it before."

Dorrie smiled and shook her head.

"George would've had a fit."

Travis laughed softly.

"You're right, and I wouldn't blame him. You'd have looked like his daughter." He studied her face for a moment, smiling slightly. "George went to great lengths to keep you out of sight, you know. Now I'm beginning to understand why."

The waitress brought their food, saving Dorrie from having to answer. What a peculiar thing to say, she thought. What was wrong with her, that George would have wanted to hide her?

Now that Christmas was over, Dorrie felt as if the whole world had come to a halt. Though she'd delayed putting them up, taking down the store decorations made her unreasonably sad, as if a party had ended. Angie went back to Saturdays, and Dorrie missed her giddiness during the week. Zada was even more taciturn than usual and Willis as quiet as ever. Marcie and

Kurt were still in Bermuda. Only Charmaine was left to cheer her, and she spent more and more time at her friend's house.

"What've you got good to read?" she asked Charmaine one night, standing in front of the bookcase. Charmaine's taste surely was eclectic, she thought: everything from anthropology to Zen.

"What do you like?" Charmaine asked. "Did you like that book I gave you for Christmas?"

"Yes, I did, a lot. Thanks. It's on my bed table, and I dip into it before I go to sleep at night. It's interesting, all those stories of people who've returned from the dead and what they think they found there."

Charmaine ran her finger across a string of titles. "You were talking about dreams a while back. Want to try this?" She pulled a small blue-bound book. "A psychologist writing about the most recent dream research. It's in the 'Truth is Stranger Than Fiction' area, but she's a serious scientist, a Ph.D."

Dorrie turned the book over in her hands. A pleasant-faced woman of about her own age smiled reassuringly back at her from the cover, and the jacket notes took her attention right away. "Defeat your greatest fears as you sleep," they promised. "Dream the answers to your most perplexing problems."

"I'll try it," she said, dropping the book into

the huge pocket of her skirt. "It'll be entertaining, anyhow."

"If you go on any great dream adventures," Charmaine warned, "don't you dare leave me behind!"

"I'll try to remember."

Dorrie read the book clear through that same night, starting after supper with Charmaine sitting across the room reading a book of her own and finishing in the small hours propped up in Charmaine's guest bed.

"Well, so what do you think?" Charmaine asked over breakfast. "How do you like the book?"

"It's very interesting," Dorrie said. "That stuff about the Philippine tribe that lives by its dreams—it never occurred to me that you could make a dream do what you wanted it to. Can you do that?"

"I haven't learned yet," Charmaine said. "Sometimes I know I'm dreaming, but I've never got to the point where I could change it. I guess I'd rather just watch and see where it takes me."

"I've never had a choice in the matter," Dorrie said dryly.

"I thought it was interesting what she said about dream friends. I wish I had one."

Dorrie hesitated. It was the part of the book that had seemed the farthest out, and remembering the young blond woman in her dreams had made her feel strange. She wanted no truck with spirit guides, and the "dream friend" sounded too close for comfort — none of which altered the fact that the young woman kept turning up in her dreams.

"If you buy the concept, I might," she said slowly. "She fits the description, anyhow. Reminds me of Princess Ozma, and she keeps showing me things. Gets me into all kinds of trouble."

"What kinds of things?"

Dorrie shot her a rueful grin. "Mostly the kind your best friend won't tell you. One night she took me into a haunted house and showed me a dead baby."

"How awful! I'll bet Jung would've had a picnic with it, though. Has she told you yet that you need time off from the store?"

"No. I think she got me into that in the first place."

Dorrie wandered into the living room and replaced the book. Near it on the shelf were books on reincarnation, and Dorrie dropped a couple into her purse.

A few nights later, she called Charmaine.

"Do you believe this stuff?" she demanded.

"Believe what? For God's sake, what time is

it?" Dorrie heard Charmaine fumbling with the phone, heard the click of a light, and then heard Charmaine yawn mightily. "Girl, it is half-past two in the morning! Why aren't you sleeping?"

"Your books won't let me. What about these children who remember houses in other cities and families and know their way around when they're taken there. Is that real?"

"I knew a nine-days' wonder like that once. Heard her prattling about hiding a silver bracelet her daddy'd made her in a cranny in some rocks, and then falling down a well and drowning. Even reported her funeral. And then they took this little blond seven-year-old back up into the Zuni reservation and found the place, and the little girl found the bracelet she'd described and pointed out the well. It'd been boarded up for fifty years, ever since the other child drowned in it." She yawned again. "Pretty convincing at the time."

"And nobody'd coached her, and she'd never been there before?"

"I knew the parents. They were horrified at the very idea — thought she was possessed of a devil. And no, she'd never been in that part of the country. So far as I know, neither had her folks."

"So how did they find it?"

"Landmarks, some she told them beforehand

and some she recognized. Once they got in the neighborhood, she went right to it."

"So you believe it."

"Let's put it this way: it's high on my list. Ninety percent of all I know is in a big bin marked 'IIP' for 'Interesting if Proved,' and it's arranged in order of likelihood. Reincarnation's right up there next to the idea that the spirit survives after death. What else can I tell you?"

"Go back to sleep, Charmaine. I'll talk to you tomorrow," Dorrie replied.

Dorrie spent the afternoon of New Year's Eve puttering with her orchids. At about four o'clock, she heard a knock at the back door.

"Dorrie?" Jessie's voice called.

"Come on in, Jess. I'm in here with the orchids."

Jessie backed through the door with a covered plate in her hands.

"I just brought you these cookies," she said. "The recipe makes so many, and Reese just eats them if I leave them lying around, and he don't need them anymore than I do." She laughed. "I just get a craving every now and again, and I remembered how you love chocolate."

"Oh, Jessie, Toll House! Bless your heart! I haven't made cookies in I don't know how long."

"This is the first year since we've lived here you haven't brought over a box of homemade

158

cookies for Christmas. We missed them. Of course I've seen how busy you are, gone all the time at the store. We do understand, only now you've got to give me all the recipes."

"I know. Lord, I used to bake for a solid week getting all those boxes ready! Neighbors, friends, the kids, the crew at the store . . . It was fun, too, but you're right; something had to go, and that was it."

Jessie peered into the hanging pot over the end of the couch.

"Gonna have some flowers on this one, huh. Which one is this?"

"It's the Bc. Bellefleur, that pretty one with the ruffled red lip. The sheath just started coming out a few weeks ago."

"Two didn't know what he was getting you into with those first four plants, did he? My lord, you must have a dozen now!"

"Fifteen. They've become my vice. Come on into the kitchen, Jess, and I'll make us some coffee. Did you-all have a nice Christmas? I saw the children in the yard in the morning."

"It was a zoo, but we had a real good time. Lord, Wayne's three and Sally's little boy, and Buddy came from Austin with his two—six kids between two and eleven, plus all their parents! The only one couldn't make it was SueAnn. She and Gerald are in Virginia. He's working at the Pentagon."

They talked about their children and grand-children while the coffee dripped, and then Dorrie poured them each a cup and sat back down at the table.

"Well, I hope this year'll be better for you than last year," Jessie said. "I worry about you, you know. Reese isn't God incarnate, even if he would like me to think so, but he's mine and he's there. I don't know how I'd manage alone."

"Oh, Jessie, you'd manage just like you always have. You do what you have to, that's all. I still have some bad times, but it's getting easier."

"You must stay down at that store till all hours. Sometimes you don't even come home till we've already gone to bed."

Jessie always had paid close attention to the comings and goings of the neighbors. She was the neighborhood house-sitter, picking up people's mail and newspapers when they were gone. Everybody knew she was better at keeping an eye on a place than even the police.

"Remember my friend Charmaine? She's back in town, and I've been seeing a lot of her. Even spent the night at her house a couple of times since Thanksgiving."

"Well, I'm glad of it if it makes you happy. She was a wild woman, no mistake about it, but I always liked her. She has a lot of grit, and she's funny besides. What ever happened to her boys? I remember when she lost custody, it almost killed her."

"Well, they're grown now, of course, but she spent Christmas with the older one. He still lives here in Dallas. I believe he's a corporate attorney."

"Her younger one was Buddy's age; they used to play together when he was over here visiting your boy. He sure was one sweet little boy. It broke his heart when his mama and daddy split up."

"I know. Hers, too. Losing those boys was the worst thing that ever happened to her, and her mother's never let her forget it. I love Charmaine's mom, but she blamed Charmaine and things've never been the same between them since."

Jessie nodded soberly.

"That'd be rough. Bad enough to lose your kids that way, without having your folks down on you about it. He couldn't have taken them from her these days as easily as he did then. We women've had to pay a terrible cost for the right to be ourselves."

Fifteen

Since business was slow, Dorrie busied herself cleaning out the office.

"Is there some excellent reason to keep all these old records?" she asked Zada. "I've found stuff dating clear back to 1947, when my father had the store. George always was a packrat, even at home—he was always sure he'd need whatever it was the very next day if I dumped it. But 1947!"

"I suppose not," Zada said slowly. "He always made up fresh files every January . . ."

"I just feel so stifled. Wouldn't it be nice to have some open space back here, free of all this dust and ancient history? I don't know about you, but I could use a little breathing room!"

"It's your store, Dorrie. Do what you want with it." Zada's voice was surprisingly sharp.

"Well, you're the manager, and I know

George had his reasons. But if all these papers are only here because he never got around to throwing them out, I'd as soon archive them."

"I'll find you a box," Zada snapped. She was gone before Dorrie could say any more.

"Why should she get mad about that?" Dorrie asked George. "My goodness, was there something you didn't tell me? The way she takes on, anybody'd think she was in love with the boss!"

Dorrie boxed up all the records, leaving only the previous year's in the file cabinet, and stacked them in the stockroom. The boxes were in the way, and Zada scowled every time she looked at them. After a day or two, Dorrie called Travis.

"I don't know what to do with this mess," she told him. "Will you come by and take a look at it?"

The next morning, Travis walked around the pile shaking his head.

"I used to compliment George on the thoroughness of his record-keeping," he said. "I had no idea."

"I don't think he was convinced that you can't take it with you," Dorrie said. "He was preparing for another jewelry store in a future life."

Travis's head jerked up to look at her. "I beg your pardon?"

163

"Nothing," Dorrie said. "It was just a joke." She paused, and then added, "I've been reading my friend's books. She has some unusual ideas."

He smiled. "Sounds interesting." He sounded more polite than interested. "I'm glad you're not alone, anyway. That was the hardest thing for me after my wife died, being alone."

"I didn't know you were a widower, Travis. How long?"

"Five years now. Our youngest child had started college that year, and Janie was really lonesome and sort of at loose ends. She kept talking beforehand about how her work was done, and there was nothing left for her to do." He crouched to study the label on a box, and then looked back up at Dorrie. "She just got sick one weekend, and by Monday morning she was gone. Flu, if you can believe it."

"That must have been hard. I didn't have any warning, either. George died in his sleep, beside me."

"I heard. I was real sorry about it. I know just how you must have felt."

"Well," Dorrie shook her head and deliberately made her voice bright, "at least I've been busy: he left all this behind to figure out. What do you think?"

"I think we ought to go to lunch and talk about something more pleasant, and then we can come back here and carry it all up to the attic."

Dallas was experiencing a warm spell; the sun was shining and the air was still as they walked down the street to the cafeteria.

"Makes you think of spring," Travis said. "Winter's not my favorite time of year."

"I like an occasional snowstorm," Dorrie confessed, "but the best thing about them is, they don't last. My daddy always said you could tell a Yankee by the way he'd shovel snow off the walk; if he'd just wait a day, it would melt all by itself."

Travis laughed. "I come from the upper Midwest. Took me a while to learn that."

In the cafeteria line, Dorrie chose a salad and a piece of baked chicken and watched Travis load his tray with pork chops, buttered new potatoes, and green beans with bacon.

"Have a dessert," he suggested, reaching for a slab of apple pie.

"The chocolate cake looks good. I'm a fool for chocolate."

He slid the plate onto her tray, smiling. "I'll remember," he said.

What for? she wanted to ask, but she let it lie. She wished he wouldn't look at her so often or so closely; it made her so self-conscious she could hardly keep track of the conversation.

"Well, what do you think?" Kurt asked. His hands were covered with cracker dust from the veal cutlets he was breading. Dorrie sat on the other side of the bar kibitzing as they waited for Marcie to arrive from her office.

"I love your new place, honey. My goodness, the twentieth floor! You-all are really moving up in the world!" Kurt looked wounded, and she laughed. "Anyhow, I never saw Dallas from so high up. What a view!"

"That's really what we bought it for, and with the park across the street we can plan on keeping it for a while. Believe you me, Marcie did her homework on this one: researched the hell out of it. Investment value, zoning restrictions, neighborhood ownership, the works."

Dorrie smiled. "She's like that: careful, like her dad. It's boring sometimes, but every family needs one."

"God knows I do." Kurt laid the last cutlet on a wire rack and reached into the refrigerator for a head of cauliflower, a handful of baby carrots, and a stalk of broccoli.

"Can I help with that?" Dorrie asked.

"No, just keep me company. We've hardly seen you since we got back. How's your life these days, Mom? Better?"

"Getting there." Dorrie brought him up to date as she watched his large, dexterous hands cut the cauliflower into tiny florets and sliver the bright orange carrots.

"Who's this Travis?" he asked. "He a nice guy?"

"He's been very kind, a big help. But he's the accountant and I'm the client, that's all. It's just business."

Kurt grinned. "You never know, Mom. Those guys can be tricky. How old is he? Married?"

Dorrie smiled at his teasing.

"About my age—maybe younger. And he's a widower."

"Good-looking?"

"I guess. I will say, he's about as different from George as a man can be. Short enough that I can look him in the eye without craning my neck. Thick as an oak, but muscular, not fat. And he has the bluest eyes you ever saw."

"Who has?" Marcie asked.

"Where did you come from, honey?" Kurt said. "Come give me a kiss. We didn't hear you come in."

Marcie stepped around the end of the counter, and Kurt wrapped her in a rocking hug. She melted briefly and then pulled away.

"Come on, we'll embarrass my mother."

"Don't mind me," Dorrie said. "I think it's lovely that you're still necking in the kitchen after six years."

Kurt grinned. "Just wait till she tastes the

sauce on this veal," he said. "Necking won't be the half of it!"

"Quit, now!" Marcie said, laughing. "You'll embarrass *me!*"

The sauce was all Kurt had promised, and the rest of the meal lived up to it. The dining-room table was next to a wall of glass overlooking the city, and Marcie and Kurt recounted tales from their trip as they ate. Dorrie and Marcie cleared the table afterward, and Kurt got out the photos they'd taken in the Caribbean.

"You know, it was strange," he mused, handing Dorrie a snapshot of a sandy beach backed by lush jungle. A small thatched house stood between the two, and several dark-skinned children in vividly colored rags played on the sand near it. "I've never lived near the sea, but those islands felt just like going home. I've never been so relaxed anywhere."

"Charmaine would say you were happy there in another life," Dorrie told him.

"Another incarnation? I've toyed with the idea," Kurt said. "I mean, look at me: I'm the first musician in the history of my family, and I'm soloing in one of the better symphonies in the country. I didn't inherit musical talent, but I never wanted to do another thing but play. And the way Marcie and I got together . . . First time we ever laid eyes on each other, it was like we'd known each other all our lives. No explanations, no need to get acquainted; it was more like catching up, like old friends who haven't seen each other in years."

"It's true," Marcie said. "In our romantic youth, we used to recite that old verse to each other: 'When you were a tadpole and I was a fish/in the paleozöoic time . . .'"

"Have you ever looked into the subject?" Dorrie asked.

"Oh, a little. Here and there," Marcie said. "Any more, so many people are talking about it that you can't help hearing. My God, look at the splash Shirley MacLaine's made!"

"Well, but that's Hollywood. What about real people?"

Kurt laughed. "I see what you mean. But you know, a lot of my friends are into metaphysics, and some of them are 'real people.' I don't know how much of it's true, but it's probably worth looking at."

"I don't know, honey. Charmaine's into it too, and I've been reading some of her books. I can accept parts of it, but some of the ideas make my head swim."

"Like what?" Marcie asked.

"Well, like simultaneous time."

"Simultaneous time?" Kurt asked. "As in, everything happens at once? I've felt that way sometimes!"

"Something like that. There's this theory that

time's not serial, the way we look at it; that our idea of time and events is actually like watching a parade through a knothole in a fence: it's all there on the other side, but we can only see it bit by bit."

Marcie shrugged. "Einstein said something like that—that time's a dimension just like space, but we know how to move through it in only one direction and we can't control that."

"But if you combine that with reincarnation . . ."

"Wow!" Kurt said. "Simultaneous incarnations! You could be a Roman centurion and a jongleur in Medieval France and a Russian peasant all at once!"

"And a Zulu warrior and a friend of Confucious. What if you ran into yourself? How would you know?"

"Oh, Mom!" Marcie laughed. "That's just too weird!"

"For me, too," Dorrie said.

"Well," Kurt said, smiling, "if it's true, it's true whether we believe it or not. And if it's false, it doesn't matter. It's still something to think about."

Several days later, Dorrie sat at George's desk with Travis beside her, going over the books. She'd made fresh coffee, and while they drank it they spoke of things they used to do when they were married. Dorrie blushed, remembering Kurt's teasing. How silly he'd been!

"Do you know what I miss? The theater," she said.

"We used to love it, too, but I haven't gone since Janie passed away. We had season tickets, but I let them all lapse." He took a sip of coffee. "Nobody to go with."

"I know. George and I had tickets, too, and I've missed three plays since September. I took my friend Charmaine to one and gave the other tickets to the kids. . . . I was supposed to go this Thursday, but everybody's busy."

She took a deep breath, astounded at the idea that had just occurred to her.

"I've got an extra ticket. Would you like it?"

Travis studied her face, his own showing uncertainty.

"I read the reviews last week," he said slowly. "It's a musical. Sounded good. May I pay you for the tickets?"

"Oh, no! They'd only go to waste . . ." She looked down at her hands. She was twisting her ring again, and the flash of the emeralds made her feel as unsure of herself as the girl George had given it to. "Of course you understand, it's right next to my seat, but you're under no obligation . . ."

"I'll enjoy seeing it with you. Suppose I take

you to dinner first. There's a nice little Italian restaurant right across the patio in the Quadrangle."

Dorrie blushed. "You don't have to do that, Travis. I just don't want to waste the ticket."

"I'd really like to, unless you'd rather not. Would you prefer to eat somewhere else?"

"No, that's fine, if you're sure. But you don't owe it to me. It doesn't have to be a . . . date."

"I understand. What time shall I pick you up?"

Sixteen

That Sunday, Two and Susan dropped by the house after church and let themselves in the front door. Dorrie was still in her robe, reading the paper at the kitchen table.

"Hi, Mom," Two said, bending to drop an awkward kiss on her upturned cheek. "Any good news today?"

"I can't tell you. You know all I read is the book section, the features, and Ann Landers. What are you-all up to this morning?"

"I was just wondering if I could borrow some of Dad's tools. The circular saw and the router."

"Sweetheart, you can *have* Dad's tools. I meant to give them to you all along; I just never think about it when you're here. You know where they are. Go on and get what you want."

Two stepped out the back door and crossed

the yard to the garage, and Susan poured a cup of coffee and sat down with Dorrie.

"What's on his mind?" Dorrie asked.

"He's going to put some shelves in my laundry room. How're things with you, Mom?"

"All right. Busier than I've been in a long time, but there's nothing wrong with that."

Susan watched Two cross the back yard and then leaned forward confidentially.

"I just wanted to tell you how much I admire your decision about the store. That was so courageous of you!"

Dorrie looked up, startled at Susan's intensity, and smiled.

"Why, thank you, Susan! But I couldn't let it go. It meant . . . well, I just couldn't. Losing Dad was hard enough. I couldn't let go of the store too."

"Well, most women in your position would be scared to take on a challenge like that." Susan looked down at her hands, embarrassed. "I just wanted to tell you how I felt."

"I appreciate it, dear. Goodness knows, your husband wasn't thrilled."

"He was just worried it would be too much for you. I mean, with Dad gone, and you never had any experience . . ."

"I'm making up for it now, and I do have help. Zada Strait might look like a dragon, but she's been an angel."

Susan reached across the table to take Dorrie's hand. "Mom, if you need anything, will you ask? Down there or here at the house, either one. I could bring my maid down to clean once a week, if that would help."

"Thanks, honey, but there just isn't that much cleaning for one person. I'm getting along. Maybe next spring I'll take a day, and you and I and the maid can turn the place out." She squeezed Susan's hand. "It's thoughtful of you to offer. If I need anything, I'll let you know."

Dorrie heard the screen door slam behind her.

"What're you two conspiring about?" Two asked.

"Nothing, dear." Dorrie looked up and smiled. "Did you find what you needed?"

"I put a few things in the car. Thanks."

"Don't thank me. I'm glad to see them put to use."

Two poured himself a cup of coffee and stood at the bar. His face wore the same earnest expression as George's.

"Mom, what did you ever do with Dad's personal things? His clothes and his jewelry and books?"

Dorrie sighed.

"I never did anything, honey. His clothes are still upstairs in his closet. I couldn't throw them away, and I couldn't sort through them either. I just shut the door and left them, waiting for you kids to help me decide what to do with them. I expect Kurt would like a few things to remember him by, but most of them will be yours."

"Would you like me to do it for you?"

"I'd be grateful. Why don't we call Marcie and Kurt and let them help?"

Two looked impatient.

"It wouldn't be right not to," Susan said. "Do you want to do it this afternoon, honey?"

"I suppose. Go ahead and call. I'll be upstairs."

Marcie and Kurt arrived within half an hour, and the family went up to the bedroom. Two was standing next to the closest door, his head against the jamb and his shoulders slumped.

"Honey?" Susan said, and put her hand on his back. When he turned to face them, his eyes were red.

"Are you okay, Two?" Marcie asked. Her voice held the same concern for him that Dorrie remembered from their childhood.

"I'm all right." His voice was thick.

"Take it easy, man," Kurt said softly. "We all miss him. We know what you're feeling."

Two gave himself a slight shake and straightened his shoulders. "Well," he said, "I guess we'd better get to it. You want to start with the clothes?"

"Go ahead," Kurt said. "The only thing of Dad's that would fit me is his ties, and you can have first pick of those."

"Except for this one," Marcie said, removing a red-and-gray stripe from the tie rack. "I want this one."

She walked back into the closet and touched her father's suits.

"They still smell of his aftershave," she marveled.

Dorrie knew. The first few weeks, she'd gone into the closet often for just that reason. She'd quit because it made her cry.

Marcie came out wearing George's black wool topcoat and his gray fedora.

"Very fetching, sweetheart," Kurt said, amused.

"May I have it, Mom? I'll get the sleeves shortened and wear it when I go up north on business."

"You look like a four-year-old playing dress-up," Two said.

"Do you want it?"

"No."

"Then keep your snide remarks to yourself. I like it."

"Cut it out, you two," Kurt said.

Two sorted the rest of his father's clothing

177

into two piles, a small one for himself and a large one for Good Will, while Kurt and Marcie went through the ties. When they were through, Dorrie opened the wall safe and brought out a tray of jewelry.

"Dad always meant for you to have this, Two," she said, holding out a heavy gold ring set with a square-cut emerald. "He was partial to emeralds. And the Masonic pieces should be yours; Kurt can't use them."

"I remember that ring," Marcie said, her voice soft. "He used to wear it all the time when I was little. I always thought it was so handsome."

"I wondered what had happened to it." Two slid the ring on his right hand. "He always said he'd give it to me when I became his partner . . ." His voice deepened, and he paused for a moment. "I hated to disappoint him that way, Mom. You know I did. I just wasn't cut out for business."

"He knew. He got over it, Two. Don't punish yourself."

"And I *was* cut out for it, but he never did offer me a place in the store." Marcie's voice was edged with bitterness. "I was a girl. Girls don't understand business."

"It's not too late," Dorrie said. "The store is mine now. I can offer you a place in it."

"It is too late. I'm doing something else

now. Anyway, it wouldn't be the same."

"I'm sorry, honey. He was very proud of you, you know."

"It would have been nice of him to say so." Marcie shrugged. "Never mind. He's gone. It's over."

It wasn't over, Dorrie thought, but she didn't know what more to say about it.

"Don't you wear french cuffs sometimes, Kurt?" Susan asked, her voice overbright. "There's a whole collection of matching studs and cufflinks here. Mom, are these blue topaz or spinel?"

"Sapphires, dear. They're just unusually light. They belonged to my father. Would you like them, Kurt?"

"I'd be proud to wear them. Thanks, Mom."

They sorted through the rest of the tray, with Dorrie dividing things as equally as she could among the children. A fire opal stickpin went to Marcie, a diamond one to Susan; Kurt accepted several sets of semiprecious studs and cufflinks, along with a cat's-eye ring, and Dorrie gave her grandfather's gold pocket watch and chain to Two.

Each object became a talisman as one or another of the children touched it; each seemed to carry with it a little of George. Marcie was stonily silent through most of the process, but Two showed more emotion than Dorrie'd

179

seen him display since he was a child.

By mid-afternoon, they were exhausted.

"It's been a long day," Kurt said. "What say you-all flake out on the couches, and I'll fix dinner? Come on, Susan, let's go to the store."

"The couch sounds wonderful," Marcie said when they'd gone. "I don't know what I'm so tired from. All I'm doing is standing here."

"It's wearing," Dorrie said. "But there's just one more room. Let's go downstairs. The living room's full of your dad's things, and then we'll be done."

Standing in the arch at the bottom of the stairs, Marcie swept the living room with a glance.

"There's only one thing in this room I want," she said. "Two can have everything here but the *Books of Knowledge*. Those are mine."

"I want the *Books of Knowledge!*" Two protested. "They're mine!"

"Look," Marcie said, "I didn't argue with you about one thing upstairs; whatever you wanted, you got. But I want those books."

"But they're mine! They were always mine!"

"They were ours. Now I want them. The only attention my father ever paid me was helping me read the *Books of Knowledge* and talking about what was in them. You were his son; what attention he had to give, you got. Now give me the books."

180

"I don't believe this! Those are *kids'* books! I'm the one with kids—I should have them!"

"Right. You're the son; you're the one who gave him grandchildren; you're the one he loved. I never blamed you for it. You didn't ask to be the boy or the firstborn; you couldn't help it that I was a girl and he never liked girls. But I paid for it all my life, and now I want something back. The books are mine, brother."

Two threw his hands in the air. "Take the damned books! I hope you choke on them!"

"Thank you." Marcie turned on her heel and stalked back to the orchid room. Dorrie, too shocked to speak, followed.

She found Marcie curled up on the couch with her fist over her mouth, looking like a child with a stomachache. Her eyes were big and dark.

"I never knew you felt that way," Dorrie said. "Darling, I'm so sorry."

Marcie stared at her without moving, her pain making her look fragile as a Dresden shepherdess.

"Your father did love you, Marcie. He just never did know how to show his love. It scared him, extending himself to anybody." She paused in the face of Marcie's silence and then added, "If it's any comfort, he was that way with me too, honey. And I know

181

he loved me. It was never your fault."

"He did the best he could, Mom. I know that. It just wasn't good enough." She barked a short laugh. "Sometimes I think it'd be easier if he hadn't. Then I could blame him."

"Oh, Marcie!" Dorrie sat beside her daughter and wrapped her in her arms. Marcie wept.

Seventeen

Travis arrived at six on Thursday evening, and Dorrie invited him in while she got her coat.

"What a pretty dress!" he said.

"Thank you. George always liked it. I've had it for years."

She felt awkward riding downtown beside him and found it hard to make conversation. At last, noticing that Travis was intent on driving, she simply sat with her hands in her lap, saying nothing.

During dinner, he poured wine and told her about the reviews he'd read. One of Dorrie's favorite performers, a tall, blond, angular young woman who did heart-rendingly funny "nervous females," was appearing in the revue, and Dorrie recalled the actress's previous performances for him. She was relieved when they sat in their theater seats and the lights went down.

Had she known what the show was about, Dorrie thought after the third sketch, she wouldn't have brought Travis. He laughed beside her at the trials of singles living in a society built for two, but Dorrie was mortified. How much more than an evening at the theater must he think she was inviting him to share?

"I know just what they're talking about," he said at intermission. "Those personal ads in the newspaper—have you ever read the *Dallas Observer?* It makes you wonder, but I've been almost frustrated enough to answer them myself a time or two."

"Have you really?" Dorrie's voice was soft. "I haven't even thought about that. George hasn't been gone long enough for me to start hunting a replacement." She blushed. "I can't even think about it, we were married so long. I was just a girl."

"It's rough," Travis agreed. "When Janie passed away, I'd been out of circulation for twenty-seven years—and what years! She wasn't in the ground before her friends started trying to fix me up with other women. It was embarrassing to say the least."

Dorrie shuddered. "It would be like being put up for sale, humiliating. I'd as soon walk naked down the middle of University Avenue."

Travis laughed. "Well, it was strange. All the rules had changed, and reading about it in *Newsweek* was no preparation. It was quite a shock, I don't mind telling you."

"Well," Dorrie said, "I have my hands full without it. I'm in no hurry."

Afterward, when Travis offered her a drink, she declined. Tomorrow was a work day, she reminded him, and they would both have to get up early.

But once home, she did not sleep. Instead, she propped herself up on the couch and read until her eyes glazed over and she could no longer focus on the page.

It didn't take long. The book was advancing the theory that all souls are fragments of One Soul, all connected to one another like cells in a living body.

"What do you think, Domino?" she asked, rubbing his favorite spot behind his ear. "Are you and I and the orchids all part of the same spirit? Is that why we get along so well?"

The cat stared inscrutably at her for a moment and finally yawned.

"I think so too," she said. "Let's go to bed."

Somewhere in the Bible, Dorrie recalled as she waited for sleep, Jesus had said, "I am in the Father and the Father in me." She'd always thought it meant God was like the air, in and around us all the time. But to consider being an actual part of God . . . It was just too much to think about at half-past three in the morning.

Dorrie is in a laboratory surrounded by glowing Bunsen burners, jars of brilliant liquids, petrie dishes growing cultures in glittering agar jelly. The young woman, dressed in a lab coat, is showing her around. She points to a microscope.

"Look there," she says.

Dorrie leans over, shutting one eye to peer down the scope, but the lens is out of focus: she sees only an iridescent smear of colors.

"I can't see anything," she says.

"You've got to focus," the young woman tells her. She places Dorrie's fingers on the knob. "Just keep looking at it till you see it clearly."

"What am I looking at?" Dorrie asks, dutifully twiddling the knob. "What is this?"

"A tissue sample. Cells of our body."

The lens clears and Dorrie sees not cells, but more people than she can count. She raises her head to ask, and the young woman nods encouragement.

"Look, now."

Dorrie peers at the unlikeliest congregation she can imagine. Here is a Chinese nun, there an Ashanti warrior; here a Roman senator, there a toreador in a full suit of lights. She watches a young mother nursing a baby, and identifies with both. There is a Kentucky farmer crumbling a clod of earth as he stares at the sky, and there a nurse tending an ancient crone in a wheelchair.

Four shaggy-haired, sweet-faced young men are making music. One has a prominent nose, and one wears tinted granny glasses . . . "I am you as you are me and we are us together," they sing. "I am the Walrus. Coo coo ca-choo."

The slide becomes a living tapestry, with each person moving independently but all together forming a growing, ever-changing, overall pattern. Fascinated, she watches for what seems hours, half aware that she is dreaming and hoping the dream will not end too soon.

Dorrie woke remembering only patches of the dream. The phrase "cells of our body" revolved in her mind as the faces faded. Still half asleep, she wandered into the bathroom and stared into the mirror.

"So I am the walrus," she told her reflection. "Coo coo ca-choo."

Eighteen

"How's business?" Charmaine greeted Dorrie the following Tuesday, the last in January, when she picked her up after work. They were planning to go to supper and then to an evening seminar on "Making Your Own Reality." Good luck! Dorrie'd thought on hearing the title.

"Slow," Dorrie said. "It always is in January, I guess. Then it picks up a little for Valentine's Day and drops off again till summer graduations and weddings."

"I've got a terrific idea," Charmaine said. "This artist friend of mine in California — does record jackets for New Age albums and stuff — is having a show the first of February in another friend's gallery. He called last night and wants me to come. Asked me to stay in his house. Why don't you come along?"

"I can't do that!"

"Why not? Give me one good reason!"

"For starters, he didn't invite me. I can't impose on a stranger that way."

"No problem. His little old twenty-room shack will hold one more, easy. I'll just tell him you're coming."

"You might give him a chance to say no," Dorrie said. "Anyway, what about the store? I can't just drop everything and go skylarking off to California!"

"Bullshit. You just told me it's going to be slow for months. Zada can handle it for a week; that's what she's for."

Dorrie sighed. Charmaine's iron whims again, she thought.

"No, Charmaine. Just no. I won't do it. Now let's talk about something else."

The temperature was twenty-eight when they flew out of Dallas on Thursday morning. They landed in Long Beach on a seventy-five degree afternoon, and Dorrie knew the clothes she'd brought were all wrong.

Their host met them at the airport. He looked more like a longshoreman than an artist, Dorrie thought: long-haired and stocky, stubble-chinned and graying, he wore tight, faded Levis and a striped gondolier's shirt snug enough to show every muscle in his well developed chest.

He was half a head shorter than Charmaine, who bent to embrace him.

"This is the friend I told you about," she said. "Dorrie Greene, Abbot Fisher."

"Glad you could make it, Dorrie," Abbot said, offering his hand. His handshake was firm, and his eyes took in every inch of her.

"Thanks for letting me come," Dorrie said.

"You're more than welcome. Any friend of Charmaine's . . ." He smiled and shrugged. "Let's go find your luggage and get out of here. I hate airports—all the pushing. Bad vibes." He went ahead of them.

"Bad vibes?" Dorrie repeated to Charmaine.

Charmaine laughed.

"You'll hear a lot of that kind of talk out here. Go home with a whole new vocabulary."

Driving through the city, Dorrie was spellbound just looking out the car windows. It had snowed in Dallas; here the beaches, the flowers, the tall palms lining the roads were almost too much to take in. Abbot and Charmaine talked about his show and the people he'd invited to the opening. Every time a new name was mentioned one of them would turn to explain it to Dorrie, but she was too busy looking to listen. With its bright sky overhead and brilliant colors rushing past, Los Angeles felt like another world, the product of vivid, multiple imaginations.

"I've invited a few people over for dinner this evening," she heard Abbot say. "I hope that's all right."

"Great," Charmaine said. "I've missed my old pals. Who-all's coming?"

Abbot laughed. "Only a few hundred of your most intimate friends. With you and Dorrie, I have ten houseguests this weekend." He made a face. "They're not all your pets, pet. Some were obligatory. Dorrie will get to meet your pet Object of Scorn."

"Lizzie V?"

He nodded.

"Well, Dorrie," Charmaine said, "prepare yourself. We're not in Kansas any more, Toto."

In the hills above the city, Dorrie caught occasional glimpses of enormous houses in every style from English Tudor to ultra-modern glass and redwood. Most were well-hidden behind high fences or flaming oleander hedges. Lacelike pepper trees with gnarled trunks, exuberant orange trumpet vines, shaggy-barked eucalyptus, and pungent camphor trees were everywhere.

Abbot stopped the car before a tall wrought-iron gate. It opened, and they entered a long uphill drive through wide, rolling lawns. As they crested the hill, Dorrie looked down at an enormous, white-stucco building with a walled courtyard, red-tiled roof, and several outbuildings.

"Well, here we are," Abbot said. "Home at last." He tooted his horn and a small, dark man came from behind the garage to take their bags. "Thanks, Hector," Abbot said. "Come on in, ladies, and I'll fix you a drink."

The house, its back to the road, was built to the ancient Roman design: three sides surrounding a courtyard, with a high wall closing the square. They entered an arched gate, and Dorrie saw a Moorish-looking arcade on the three sides of the house surrounding the patio. Abbot led them through the courtyard, past two swimming pools—one large, one small—and across a multileveled, paved patio the size of Dorrie's back yard.

He opened a glass door and the women followed him into a room with a dark-red tiled floor, white walls, and a two-story turquoise ceiling painted with clouds and white doves. Arched, tile-framed front windows overlooked a canyon; beyond it lay the city and a strip of light-colored beach outlining the metallic-looking, gray-blue ocean. The room's back wall was dominated by a fireplace that Dorrie thought must be big enough to roast an ox. Whole. At each end were stairs that led to skylit lofts with couches, easy chairs, and end walls of books.

"Come on," Abbot said, "let me show you the

rest of the house. I've made a lot of changes since you were here last, Charmaine."

"Abbot had just started the restoration when I left two years ago," Charmaine told Dorrie. "The house was built by an early movie mogul to entertain his Hollywood friends. Somebody'd made a nursing home out of it before Abbot rescued it."

Why not a hotel? Dorrie thought, following Abbot through the house. It reminded her of pictures she'd seen of San Simeon, but this place made William Randolph Hearst look like an unimaginative clod. Her head swam at the sheer scale of it, never mind the luxury.

After the tour, Abbot installed Dorrie and Charmaine in adjoining bedrooms with a separate entrance off the patio, apologizing because they had to share a bathroom.

"Don't give it another thought," Dorrie said. "We're used to roughing it."

The bathroom they were to share was all pink marble, gilt, and mirrors, featuring a whirlpool bath that, Dorrie thought, would hold a small party. The free-standing sink at the center was supported by a blushing marble nymph, her arms upraised to hold the basin.

"If he ever falls on hard times," Dorrie told Charmaine, "he can rent this out to a Middle-Eastern potentate. My lord, have you ever seen such a place?"

"You should have seen it two years ago. The room you're in had grape-colored walls, and until we got the vines cut away from the windows, we thought they were chocolate. And that beautiful living room was painted battleship gray, floor to ceiling. We decided the previous owner'd had an 'in' with the Navy Surplus."

"It's beautiful now. I've never seen anything like it; it's like being in a museum."

"Feeling a little intimidated, there?" Charmaine laughed. "Never mind. You'll be surprised how quick you get used to it. How about a swim before dinner?"

"In February?"

"The pool's heated. Water's probably warmer than the air."

Dorrie looked at the alabaster satin puff on her acre of bed.

"Not just now, thanks. If it's all the same to you, I want to unpack. Then I think I could do with a little liedown."

Nineteen

She hadn't expected to sleep; she'd only wanted time to acclimate herself and prepare to meet the rest of the houseguests. Abbot had said the party would be complete by about six o'clock, when cocktails would be served. When Dorrie opened her eyes, the ormolu clock beside her bed read half-past five. She lay listening for a moment, but could hear nothing but her own breathing and the tick of the clock. Either the others had not yet arrived, or the foot-thick adobe walls were insulating her from the party's sounds.

Bath, she thought. She stripped and put on the thick, lavender, terry-cloth robe she found hanging on the back of her door, and the marble nymph in the bathroom smiled sweetly as she stepped into the steaming shower. Dorrie dried herself on a lavender towel that defined the term "bath blanket," hung it carefully over a rack, and returned to her room to dress.

Stepping onto the patio, she paused to orient herself. Colored lanterns glowed in the arches around the courtyard, and the steam rising from the pools picked up their light to form low, iridescent clouds, misty as a Hollywood dream.

A silver-haired gentleman with a miniature orchid in his lapel sat reading near the smaller of the two pools. He looked up, smiled, and returned to his book. On a patch of grass to Dorrie's right, a man with thick, curly, gray hair tumbling to his shoulders and a pretty brown-haired girl, both in white robes, sat facing one another, their hands clasped, staring into each other's eyes and humming "Oohhmm-mm-mm-mm" to the limits of their breath. Their faces were as sober as if they were preparing Communion.

As Dorrie stepped into the living room, she heard Charmaine's voice. Looking up into the loft at the other end of the room, she saw her friend seated at a table. Several others sat nearby, and they seemed to be playing a game.

"There she is!" Charmaine called. "Come on up, Dorrie!"

Charmaine sat with a black-haired woman at a small table that held a Ouija board. Dorrie hadn't seen one of those since she was a girl. A friend's mother had caught them playing with it one day and, scolding about the Devil and all his works, had burned board, pointer, box, and all. Seated on a low, puffy chair nearby was a tall young man who might have been the son of Charmaine's partner; he looked bored, but the creamy-skinned red-headed girl at his feet who gazed up into his face seemed entranced.

On a couch to Dorrie's right was another couple; the woman, straw-haired and fat, reminded Dorrie of her cousin Marilu. Even in his brand-new Levis, the man looked like the miniature groom on a wedding cake. Next to Charmaine on a large ottoman, her feet tucked under her, was a grandmotherly woman with waxy pink flowers in her hair. Their fragrance surrounded her like a miniature force field. The woman set her feet on the floor and patted the place next to her.

"Sit down," she invited Dorrie.

"Everybody, this is my friend Dorrie Greene of Dallas," Charmaine said. "We grew up together. Dorrie, this is everybody—they'll tell you their names in a minute. We've just been trying out this board, but it's not doing anything good. Why don't you watch?"

Dorrie nodded and sat next to the gray-haired woman. "Thanks," she whispered.

"Welcome," the woman said softly. "I'm Dovie Freebird. It's a pleasure to meet you."

Dorrie was reminded of her favorite great-aunt, Rose's sister Phoebe. The family used to joke that Aunt Phoebe's true home was in some other world, and they quoted her non-sequiturs to prove it. But even though Phoebe had operated on her own logic, Dorrie'd always thought she was wiser than most, sweet to the bone, and plain as bread.

"Whoops! There it goes!" Charmaine hollered. "What's it saying? God damn, it's going so fast I can't keep up!" She lifted her hands. "Slow down, you!" she told the board. "Give me that again."

"M-E-S-S-A-G-E F-O-R- D-O-R-R-I-E, D-U-M-M-Y," the board spelled.

"Smart-ass," Charmaine said. "Dorrie, come here! It's talking to you!"

Dorrie stood up to see better as the pointer raced across the board. It moved so fast she could hardly keep up to spell out, "L-E-T D-O-R-I-E S-I-T.' "

"Sounds like it wants your friend," the dark-haired woman said. She removed her fingers from the pointer and stood up. "Here, take my place."

"How do I do it?" Dorrie asked, sitting down. Charmaine showed her how to rest her fingers on the pointer, barely touching it, and the others crowded around to watch.

"Somebody take this down," Charmaine called. Her fingers hovered over the pointer, exerting no pressure. At Dorrie's touch, it came to life and almost scooted from under her hands, racing in large circles like the warmup exercises she remembered from third-grade penmanship classes. A voice behind her said, "Look, joy circles." Then the pointer began to move in vigorous, purposeful, straight lines toward the letters.

"I AM ROSE," it spelled out. "I LOVE YOU, DORRIE. GEORGE IS HERE RESTING. HE WATCHES YOU AS I DO. TRUST CHARMAINE. SHE HAS LOVED YOU ALWAYS. FEAR NOTHING. YOU ARE STRONGER THAN YOU KNOW."

The pointer shot to "GOODBYE" and stopped. Dorrie nudged it curiously, but whatever force had made it move was gone. Taking a deep breath, she realized that she had hardly breathed in all the time the pointer was moving.

"Mercy!" she said softly.

Dovie, now standing behind her, patted Dorrie's shoulder as Charmaine laughed.

"I told you to be prepared," Charmaine said. "Surprised you, huh!"

"I should say it did." Dorrie's insides felt like jelly.

"Oh, grow up!" The voice was pinched and sharp. Dorrie turned to see the big blonde, now standing behind her. A heavily embroidered purple gown draped her enormous body, a faceted crystal pendant hung between her cantaloupe breasts, and a petulant expression soured her face.

"When people are channeling messages of Universal Love to lead us into the New Age," the woman said, "how important can a little message like that be? 'Trust Charmaine' my eye—Charmaine had her hands on the pointer!"

" 'I love you' is always important, Elizabeth," Dovie said quietly.

"Your buddy Gaz may preach love to the wide world, Liz old girl, but he hasn't improved your attitude a scrap!" Charmaine's eyes blazed, and Dorrie reached across the table to touch her hand.

As she did so, Elizabeth gasped and went pale; she shuddered, and her eyes rolled back so that only the whites showed. Wobbling backward like a dirigible set loose from its moorings, she began a series of convulsive jerks. The little man who'd been sitting with her rushed up behind to support her, but her flailing arm knocked him aside. Then, seeming to catch herself, she stood upright, planted her feet on the thick, Oriental carpet, and folded her arms across her chest. Her face set in a severe expression, eyes narrowed and mouth turned down.

"Thou art correct." A deep, commanding voice issued from Elizabeth's mouth. "Gasm El Cid does not approve of such arrogance to an expanding soul."

Dorrie looked at the other faces around her. Charmaine's bore a look of cynical disbelief; the others' expressions ranged from amusement to outright awe.

"Glad you agree, Gaz," Charmaine said. "Now why don't you see what you can do to shape that broad up?"

"Thou hast little room to criticize her manners," the voice said sternly. "First remove the log from thine own eyes, that thou might see to remove the mote from hers."

"That ain't no mote—it's a goddam Sequoia! You just get your girl off Dorrie's back, fella. I'll believe her 'Universal Love' when I see a little in action at the one-on-one level!"

"Gasm El Cid will not be spoken to in this way," the voice intoned, and then Elizabeth shuddered again. Her color returned, her arms relaxed to hang at her sides, and after a moment she teetered backward again and collapsed heavily into the couch.

"What happened?" she asked. "Was it my spirit guide?"

"Yes, sweetheart," the little man said. "Just relax now. Rest. You know how he exhausts you."

"He said you've got lousy manners," Charmaine told her, "and I agree. I think you owe my friend an apology."

Elizabeth stiffened and glared at Charmaine.

Then, sighing heavily, she shut her eyes, rested her head on a cushion, and laid the back of a pudgy hand across her brow.

"Please, Charmaine!" Her voice was weary. "You know how channeling drains me! At least have the courtesy to let me recover before you attack."

"About as much courtesy as you had for Dorrie. Come off it, Lizzy baby. You're not fooling anybody!"

Elizabeth rolled her eyes extravagantly, sighed again, and, clasping her hands as if for prayer, turned to Dorrie.

"I don't know what came over me," she said, her voice artificially humble. "I do beg your pardon . . . Dorrie, is it? Of course your little message was important!"

"It's all right," Dorrie said. "I didn't even know what was going on."

"Bitch!" she heard Charmaine mutter as Elizabeth sauntered away on her blue-jeaned bridegroom's arm.

"What was *that!*" Dorrie asked.

"Lizzy or Gasm El Cid?"

"Either . . . both . . . What do I know?"

Charmaine laughed.

"Elizabeth Van Hartesveldt is an East-Coast society dame who got bored with the Junior League and found out trance mediumship got her more attention. Gasm El Cid's the spirit she channels, claims to be an Egyptian from the time of the Pharoahs. At first, I hear she was the straight goods; that is, she let herself go and the spirits or her subconscious or whatever took over and gave serious messages. Her husband Robin—that little wart that was holding her up—thinks she's a marvel. But ever since old Gaz took over, Lizzy's been all self-promotion and money-grubbing. She holds these five-hundred-dollar-a-head seminars all over the country to spout metaphysical platitudes in a man's voice—in King James English, no less!" She shook her head. "Excuse my cynicism, but why an ancient Egyptian would use King James English . . ."

"It's so authoritative," a dry voice said behind Dorrie. She turned to see the bored young man.

"But why that outburst?" Dorrie asked.

"You were on her turf, getting messages from the Great Beyond. What's worse, you were the center of attention. That old cow flat couldn't stand it!"

Charmaine grinned. "By the way, how's your Grandma Rose?"

Dorrie laughed. "All right, I guess. She still loves me, anyway."

Twenty

When dinner was called, the orchid gentle-man approached Dorrie.

"You must be Dorrie Greene, Charmaine's friend," he said. "I'm Corbin Fox, your dinner partner." He offered his arm. "May I take you in?"

"Thank you," she said, resting her hand lightly on his arm as she had been taught at Stofford. She glanced at Charmaine, who was talking with a tubby young man in a silvery monk's robe tied with a golden cord. A soft leather bag hung from the belt, and he kept dipping his fingers into it.

"I'd give something pretty for that robe," Dorrie said. "I never saw anything look so soft."

"Mohair," Corbin said. "A bit affected, but it is handsome."

"Who is he?"

"Hugh Llewellyn. The bag is full of hand-made crystal runestones. He's never without it."

"Runestones?"

"A form of divination used by the ancient Celtic peoples." He pronounced the *C* as a *K*. "There's a great deal of lore connected with it, both Germanic and Druidic."

"I see." God would forgive her the lie.

Corbin seated her between himself and a hawk-faced man of indeterminate age. With his silvery hair and pale skin, Dorrie thought, he looked just like the hood ornament on her father's old Pontiac. Corbin took the end seat on their side of the table, next to Charmaine, who sat at its foot talking with a large and intense, black-haired man on the other side. Dovie smiled across the table over an arrangement of white and purple orchids as Dorrie sat down.

"Excuse me, Walter," Charmaine said. "Let me introduce you to my friend: Dorrie, this is Walter Friml. Walter wrote one of the books you read."

"Really? Which one?" Walter asked. Dorrie heard "vich von."

"I think it was the one called *Your Former Lives*." Dorrie said.

"And how did you like it?"

"It was quite . . . extraordinary," Dorrie said. "That was the first serious thing I'd ever read about reincarnation."

Walter chuckled. "Sometimes ve forget that this ancient idea can still surprise. Tell me, did I confince you?"

Dorrie smiled an apology. "You convinced me that it's worth looking into."

The hood ornament laughed. "What a gracious denial!" he said. "Congratulations, Dorrie! Walter likes to think his logic is irresistible."

"The argument was excellent," Dorrie said, "but I was taught to avoid snap decisions." She wished the subject had not come up. After Elizabeth's display, Dorrie'd had all the attention she wanted for one evening.

"For a student of metaphysics," the hawk-faced man said, "that's an extremely useful attitude. A tolerance for uncertainty helps too."

"I'm finding that out," she said.

"I'm Hermes Mason," he said. "Happy to meet you."

"Thank you. The soup is lovely, don't you think? I wonder how it's seasoned."

Hermes nodded, his eyes crinkling slightly. "It is indeed. Perhaps you can ask the cook tomorrow." He looked across the table. "Walter, don't you have a new book coming out soon?"

Dorrie darted a brief "thank you" look at Hermes and tried to pay attention as Walter expounded on the book, but between its unfamiliar ideas and his heavy accent, her mind soon began to wander. She was trying to identify the vegetables in her salad when Hermes spoke again.

"What do you do, Dorrie?"

"I'm a housewife. That is, I was until recently. My husband died in September and left me a store to run, so I guess I'm a merchant now."

"I'm sorry for your loss," he said. "That must be quite a change, and especially hard under the circumstances."

"I'm doing all right, I guess. Charmaine's been a big help."

"A long friendship?"

"Since we were girls."

"You seem very different."

Dorrie smiled. "My daddy always said Charmaine was 'different.' I'm pretty much the same as anybody."

"You underestimate yourself. What do you think, Corbin? An interesting chart?"

Corbin nodded. "A Taurus sun, I'd guess. Lots of Venus, anyway: beauty and charm."

"Chart?" Dorrie asked, embarrassed at the

compliment.

"Horoscope. Corbin is an astrologer. He's been writing teaching articles for *American Horoscope* for nearly thirty years."

"I've always been curious about astrology," Dorrie said, "but I never learned much more than my family's signs. You're right, though, Corbin; my birthday's in the middle of May. How did you know?"

"Coloring. Body build. Facial structure. Each of the signs has its own look about it," Corbin said. "Astrology gets a little more respect these days than it used to. It's a little like psychology, you know: as much art as science." He looked toward the head of the table. "The young woman at our host's right is also an astrologer and a numerologist as well. The two work together."

Dorrie looked down the table at a vivacious, curly-haired brunette with enormous gray eyes. She was wearing a lavender gown of Grecian cut, set off with a necklace of amethysts and pearls.

"I thought she must be a movie star."

Both men laughed.

"I guess she's as close as you can get without actually appearing on the screen," Hermes said. "Renata Dare. Bills herself as 'Astrologer to the Stars' and appears on at least one talk show a month. Corbin, here, is too shy for that."

"And too plain," Corbin added.

"What about the others? That gray-haired man next to her and the brown-haired girl I saw him with earlier?"

"Lonnie and Liana Chance. He's built an empire on metaphysics: seminars, self-help tapes, subliminals, books. He has homes in Kauai and Arizona and a big bookstore down on the beach. Married Liana about two years ago. I believe she was a college student."

A maid took Dorrie's salad plate away and replaced it with a plate of fish and stir-fried vegetables. The steam rising off the plate smelled delicious.

"Who is that rather remote young man next to her?" Dorrie asked. "I met him earlier, but I've forgotten his name. What does he do?"

"That's Darius Fogg. He works for Lonnie. New Age music."

"Published a book last year, too," Corbin said, "or rather, Lonnie published it for him. Interesting work, about the vibratory correspondences among colors, musical tones, and the chakras."

Dorrie tried to remember what chakras were and shook her head.

"What about Dovie?" she asked. "What

does Dovie do?" She regretted the question before it had left her mouth; if Dovie "did" anything, Dorrie didn't want to know.

"Dovie's an interesting case," Hermes said. "She was a perfectly ordinary woman — Abbot's housekeeper, actually — until about three years ago. Then one day she didn't come to work, and he went to her house and found her with a high fever, delirious. Of course he had her taken to the hospital. She alternated between delirium and coma for weeks, and the doctors said the fever had cooked her brain."

"Oh, no!" Dorrie said. "She seems such a sweet person."

Hermes smiled. "The story doesn't end there. When she started to recover, Dovie realized that she knew things about almost everyone she met, and that they were true things: family problems, coming dangers and opportunities, illnesses, the locations of lost items . . ."

Dorrie stopped chewing to listen.

"She thought she'd gone crazy at first," Hermes said. "Scared her half out of her mind. But Abbot brought her home and cared for her, introduced her to people who could help her understand her new abilities. She's remarkably accurate, and there isn't a phony bone in her body."

Dorrie looked across the wide table. Dovie smiled at her and waggled her fingers just as Aunt Phoebe used to do, and Dorrie smiled back. How terrible to know so much about people, she thought. The world was full of such awful secrets.

"What about you, Hermes?" she asked. "You seem so . . . real."

Hermes laughed. "We're all real." He looked down the table, and Dorrie saw his eyes pause at Elizabeth before returning to her. "On second thought," he said dryly, "perhaps some of us are a little more real than others. But the only phony thing about me is my name: I was born 'Herman' and hated it. I'm clairvoyant and I do psychometry—picking up impressions from objects or clothing. I do a lot of missing persons work and help the police out when I can."

"Aren't you working on that starlet's case?" Corbin asked. "The one they found in the dumpster behind Sunshine Studios?"

Hermes nodded. "She wasn't killed there, of course. It was a party, and she'd been knocked around some and then shot full of drugs. OD'd. She was dead for hours before anybody noticed, and then they panicked."

Dorrie stared at him, her mind frozen.

"Police about to catch up with them?" Corbin asked.

"One's left the country, but they'll get the other guy in a day or two. We know where he is."

By the time dinner ended Dorrie's head was spinning, and soon afterward it began to ache. Feeling the tightening between her eyes that foretold a major headache, she found a quiet nook on the patio and sat down.

"Are you all right?" a soft voice asked. Dorrie looked up. Liana Chance stood beside her.

"It's just a headache," she said. "It's been a long day."

"Let me help you," Liana said. "Here, lay your head back against the cushion, and I'll rub it away."

This kind of headache didn't rub away; it required sleep, but the girl looked so concerned that Dorrie didn't want to tell her so. She leaned her head back, and Liana set her fingers along Dorrie's jawline and her thumbs above the bridge of her nose.

"There?" she asked, and Dorrie said, "That's it."

"Take a few really deep breaths," Liana told her. "You're all tense." She rubbed with her thumbs, at first gently and then harder. "Relax, now," she said, her voice low and gentle. "Leave a little space between your teeth. Imagine a bowl of relaxation pouring over your skull, dripping down over your face."

As Liana continued the massage, Dorrie felt her tension draining away.

"Thank you," she said. "I'm Dorrie Greene. Aren't you Liana Chance?"

"Yes, Lonnie's wife. You're Charmaine's friend from Dallas?"

"That's right. I feel almost like an intruder here, where you all seem to know one another so well, but people have been very kind and welcoming." The girl was sweet, and her hands were cool. "That feels marvelous, what you're doing. Where did you learn it?"

"I don't know. Lonnie says it's a special gift."

"I'm sure it is."

"He's so wonderful to me. I never would've believed . . ." Her voice trailed off, and her movements slowed. After a moment, she said, "Sorry. I do that all the time. I guess I'm just still not used to being so lucky."

"How did you meet him?"

"I was typing my way through college, and I went to work in his publishing house. I used to see him walking through . . ." Her voice turned dreamy, and the pressure on her fingers lightened. "He was so . . . charismatic, is what people say, and they're right. I mean, every time I heard his voice, I just died. Have you met Lonnie?"

"Not yet," Dorrie said. "I saw you chanting together on the patio earlier."

"Oh, yes, we do that every day. It's for the baby, you know; we're pregnant. Lonnie says it will be a boy, the soul that was his brother in his Roman incarnation. I feel so fortunate."

"It's nice to have children."

"I mean, to be able to bring them together again. Lonnie's crazy about our little girl—you know, she's just a year old—but he can't wait for this baby boy."

"You've had a sonogram?"

"No, it's too early. Lonnie just knows."

She gave Dorrie's cheek a soft pat and took her hands away, and Dorrie stood up.

"How does that feel?" Liana asked.

"Much better, thank you." What would Liana do if she produced another girl? Dorrie wanted to take the poor starstruck child in her arms to protect her. "I hope everything goes well for you," she said.

"Liana?" a man's voice called. "Where are you?"

"That's my husband," Liana said. "Here, love," she called. "I was just massaging this lady's head. She was so tense . . . Honey, this is Dorrie Greene, Charmaine's friend."

"Nice to meet you," he said. "Better now?"

"Yes, thank you. Your wife helped me more than I thought possible."

"That's a good girl," he said. "Walter wants to talk to us, Liana. Come on in now."

Dorrie watched them cross the patio, Liana's white dress gleaming iridescently in the light of the colored lanterns, and looked at her watch. Ten o'clock — midnight, Dallas time. No wonder she was tired. She let herself into her room and went to bed.

Dorrie and Charmaine have cut class to go to the circus. It is in a large field in tents. They wander down the midway listening to a German-accented barker. Passing the sideshow tent, Dorrie stops to look at the garish paintings of Leslie the Hermaphrodite, half man, half woman; the Serpent Man, drawn with a man's blond head on a coiled serpent's body; the Siamese Twins, joined at the breast; the grinning Fat Man, his flesh rippling as the breeze catches the canvas.

The smell of sawdust and the rank odor of wild animals fill Dorrie's head, and she sneezes. Great clouds of gray matter come out

*of her nose, and her head becomes a bright
yellow balloon rising above the crowd. Charmaine jumps for the balloon, catches it, and
ties it securely to Dorrie's shoulders. They
pass a small tent decorated with pictures from
Charmaine's cards, where an old Gypsy
woman stares into a crystal ball. "Come in,"
the Gypsy calls hoarsely. "I see all, know all,
tell all . . ."*

*"Come on," Charmaine urges, tugging at
Dorrie's hand. "We're missing the show."*

*At the gate, a stocky man with masses of
curly gray hair stops them. He is wearing a
scarlet coat with brass buttons, and he bars
their way with a whip.*

*"You can't come in here," he says. "You
haven't paid."*

*Charmaine reaches into her pocket and pro-
duces two golden tickets. The man examines
them closely and then bites Dorrie's to see if
it's real.*

*"What are you bringing her for?" he asks
Charmaine. "She doesn't belong here."*

*"She's with me," Charmaine says. She takes
Dorrie's elbow and pushes past the man into
the big top. A tall clown in blackface takes
Dorrie's other hand and pulls them both to
front-row seats by the center ring.*

"What took you so long?" he asks. "We've

been waiting for you!" He hugs her and says something in her ear, but the calliope has begun to play and Dorrie can't hear him.

Twenty-one

Dorrie woke at eight the next morning and dressed in a crisp, white, pleated skirt, a sapphire silk-batiste blouse, and flat-heeled sandals. Remembering Jon's ministrations at her pre-Christmas makeover, she carefully applied foundation, blusher, lipstick, and eye makeup to her face and then brushed out her hair. By the time she was ready to wander into the main body of the house for breakfast, she felt something close to pretty.

She found Hermes Mason seated in lonely splendor in the dining room. The sideboard was set up buffet style with silverware wrapped in pastel napkins, bright stoneware, and juice glasses next to a large pitcher of freshly squeezed orange juice. Next to that was a coffee urn and cups. Platters of sliced melons, bowls of strawberries and pale green kiwi fruit, and a plate of orange sections and halved pink grape-fruits were artfully arranged on the rest of the table. At the end was a bell of cut crystal.

"Good morning," she said.

"Good morning, Dorrie. You look refreshed. You slept well?"

"Like the dead," she confessed. "Now I'm starved down to a nubbin."

"Help yourself," Hermes said, nodding at the sideboard. "If you'll ring that bell, Maria will come in and take your breakfast order: ham, eggs, oatmeal, pancakes or waffles, hash browns, anything you like. I recommend the waffles."

"Thanks." Dorrie rang and asked for a waffle with bacon and eggs. She poured coffee for her-self, refilled Hermes's cup, filled a plate with fruit to nibble on while she waited for the real food, and took a seat across the table from him.

"Where is everybody?" she asked.

"Sleeping, I suspect. They're not known for early rising, this bunch. I really expected to spend the morning alone."

"I didn't mean to intrude," Dorrie said. "I noticed Abbot has quite a library. I'll just go find something to read as soon as I've eaten."

Hermes laughed. "Please don't. I'm really glad to have your company."

She blushed, feeling inept. "Thank you," she said.

Maria brought her breakfast, and Dorrie could feel Hermes's eyes on her as she ate.

"It certainly is pretty here," she said. "Not just the house, though I've never seen anything like it before — not for a private residence, at least. But the area: the hills and the canyons. Everything in bloom, all these exotic plants, birds of paradise and pepper trees . . . and the ocean. I do so love the ocean." She looked up and gave Hermes her brightest smile. "Everything's so bright and colorful." She was rattling, sounding like a tourist. Like somebody who'd never been anywhere. He must think she was a complete idiot.

"It is beautiful," he agreed. "Have you had a chance to see any of the sights yet?"

"No. We just arrived yesterday. I'm hoping Charmaine will take me around during the week."

"I have a better idea," Hermes said. "Nobody's going to be awake here for hours, and it's such a beautiful morning . . . why waste it? Let's go for a ride, just you and me. I can take you into town or to the beach — even to the mountains — and still be back in time for dinner."

"Wouldn't that be a little rude? I mean, they're expecting us to be here, aren't they?"

He smiled. "They'll miss us like a nail in their shoe. Honestly, nothing's planned until this evening — just let me steal you for the day. Nobody will mind."

It would give Charmaine a little time alone with her friends, Dorrie thought, and glanced out the front window at the fog-shrouded ocean below. The sun would burn off the fog soon, leaving a clear vista from the house, but it wasn't the same as going down where you could actually smell the salt, hear the waves pound, feel the mist on your skin. She really would like to see the ocean up close again. It'd been years and years since she'd walked on the beach, and that was only the Gulf at Galveston.

"I don't want to worry Charmaine," she said.

"We'll leave her a note. Maria will give it to her. Come on, Dorrie, let's go. I'm excited about it now. I can't wait to show you around."

Dorrie smiled. He did seem excited. It was flattering, seeing a man excited at the prospect of a few hours in a car with her.

"All right," she said.

"Aren't we going away from the ocean instead of toward it?" she asked a half-hour later. Hermes had handed her a scarf to hold her hair down, and its end was whipping in front of her. She brushed it back and turned her face up to the sun as the scarlet Fiat convertible purred its way up the mountainside. They were on a winding road, but meeting little traffic—too early, she supposed, or maybe nobody really lived up here. Narrow streets and driveways kept leaving the road and winding into carefully landscaped, wooded lots, but almost no houses were visible.

"We're taking the scenic route," Hermes said. Assuming the voice of a tour guide, he added, "You are now seeing famous Mulholland Drive, home of the stars—and the obscenely rich." He grinned across the seat at her. "It'll take us through the Santa Monica Mountains, and we'll catch one of the canyon roads down to the beach. We're making a big loop."

"All right," Dorrie said. Not that it mattered. Having allowed herself to be kidnapped in the first place, she saw little point in arguing with the kidnapper about the getaway route. Anyhow, it was gorgeous. So different from home, this steep road. She might as well be on another planet.

Hermes pulled off the road onto a lookout site protected by a hip-high guard rail and stopped the car. He got out, walked around the car, and opened the door.

"Come and look," he said. "You're not afraid of heights, I hope."

"No. I've always loved high places." Jumping-off places, George had always called them. He'd hated heights. She looked across the canyon at glass-and-redwood houses that seemed to float

222

on air, with only their rear edges touching the earth. Most had wide decks, many with spas steaming on them. The canyon below was wild and deep.

"The houses are all on stilts," she said. "Isn't that sort of a precarious way to live? It's a long way down."

"Don't tell them. You're in Never-Never Land, Dorrie. Houses never-never fall, hillsides never-never slide, and fires never-never burn these hills. Ask anybody."

She turned to him, one eyebrow raised.

"You're referring to the mudslides and forest fires I never-never see on television?"

"The same," Hermes said. "Those are just Hollywood movies to fool the rest of the country, make them think we live dangerously out here. Dorrie, these people are *rich* rich! They know absolutely, beyond any question, that they're immune to disaster." He smiled. "If they didn't know that, you see, they might have to move."

"I see." Dorrie thought about that for a moment. "It follows, then, that earthquakes aren't permitted here either."

"Certainly not. Only out in the Valley, among the suffering middle class. This area is protected by magic. Can't you feel it?"

"Is that what I feel?" Dorrie took a deep breath, enjoying the warmth of a balmy, pine-scented breeze on her face. "How very nice." She smiled, nearly hypnotized with pleasure. "Nobody ever explained the power of money to me in just that way before, Hermes. It's very comforting."

He laughed. "You have to understand, these people are all busily creating their own reality with every stray thought that passes through their minds. They don't believe in disaster."

"Ah. Well, of course. That explains everything."

They got back into the car, and for the next twenty minutes or so Dorrie gave herself up to the luxury of fresh air, sunshine, and the sweet smell of the woods. At last they started to wind downhill through the dense but somehow civilized-seeming forest toward the Pacific Coast Highway. As they rounded the last bend, Dorrie saw the silvery ocean spreading away to infinity.

"Oh!" she gasped. "Hermes, it *is* magic!"

Three small boats with square sails as brilliant as a parrot's wings tacked across the bay. Farther out, a white yacht bobbed at anchor on the swelling sea. Gulls called, sailing overhead, and one perched on the guard rail at the bottom of the hill.

"These are all public beaches along here, one right after another," Hermes said. "We're in a National Recreation Area about twenty miles long, all the way from the Pacific Palisades, where Abbot's house is, to Point Magu. Would you like to stop?"

"Oh, yes! Can we walk on the beach?"

"Sure." He looked at her legs. "If I may recommend it, Dorrie, you might want to take off your stockings. I don't know about you, but to my taste barefoot's the only way to walk on the beach. Don't worry; the sand is warm." He pulled into a parking space facing into the guard rail, turned off the motor, and pulled off his shoes and socks.

He must walk the beach a good deal, Dorrie thought. His feet were as tan as his face and arms.

Hermes leaned over the seat and removed a blanket from its zippered plastic bag.

"I'll wait for you outside," he said. He got out of the car and stood with his back to her, one foot propped on the guard rail, while Dorrie wiggled out of her pantyhose and stuffed them into her purse. The idea of being barelegged in public felt uncomfortably strange, but it was the beach, she told herself; it was deserted, and this was California. Hermes surely must know the rules here.

When she joined him, he offered his hand to help her over the rail and onto the sand. It was warm, as he'd promised, and it felt good under her feet.

She smiled shyly. "I feel like a little girl," she

said. Grownups didn't do things like this.

"You look like one, Dorrie. What a lovely smile you have!" He put his hand companionably on her shoulder. "It's not every woman who's willing to walk barefoot on the beach, you know. They're afraid they'll get their feet dirty or step on some kelp. I could tell you would, though. You don't put on an act. You're just yourself."

"Who else could I be?" Dorrie said. She laughed softly. "I didn't know I had a choice."

"You don't, of course. Nobody does, but some people try."

He led her to the water's edge and stood beside her. Dorrie watched the waves run up the beach, saying *hush, hush, hush,* and felt tension she hadn't been aware of draining out the soles of her feet. She turned to Hermes and saw that he was watching her face instead of the sea. It embarrassed her.

"I'm glad you brought me here. It's even nicer than I'd hoped." A wave rushed up and covered her feet, icy cold, and she jumped backward, laughing. "But I'm not that hardy!" she said, and took a few steps back up the beach.

"Look," Hermes said, "kelp." The long string of gray-green seaweed had washed up on the sand at their feet. "Pop the bubbles with your feet, Dorrie. It's fun!"

226

He stepped on a bubble, and made a loud "plop."

"Come on," he said. "Play with me!" He grabbed her hand and pulled her down the seaweed string to the next bubble. "Pop it, Dorrie. Stomp on it!"

Feeling a little foolish, she lifted her foot and brought it down hard on the bubble. It felt slimy and resistant under her foot, but the wet-crisp sound of its breaking was satisfying. Fun. Laughing, she popped the next one, and the next.

"That's the way!" Hermes said, laughing with her. "Don't be shy. Do them all!"

He spread the blanket on the pale sand and sat on it, patting a place next to him, and Dorrie sat beside him.

"I haven't acted like this since I was a kid," she said. "I wish it were summer, so we could go in."

"If it were summer, we couldn't get near it," Hermes said. "I like it better with just you and me."

"You don't like crowds?"

"No. Small groups are better. How could I get to know you in a crowd of people?"

Why would he want to? Dorrie wondered. After this week, he'd never see her again. But his interest was nice.

Hermes peeled off his shirt and lay back on

the sand to stare up at the sky. The morning fog had burned off early, and a handful of clouds floated lazily overhead, changing shapes at will. His chest was brown and muscular.

"Look," he said, pointing. "A camel. See the hump, and the curve of its neck?"

Dorrie lay back, careful not to touch him, and looked up.

"Uh-huh," she said. "And there's a griffin: eagle's head, lion's body." She smiled. "Only in California."

They lazed on the beach for a long time talking of nothing in particular, looking up at the sky and making occasional comments on the clouds, soaking up the sun's warmth, cooled by a slight breeze. Dorrie tried without success to remember ever feeling so relaxed. How could she feel this relaxed, lying on the sand with a strange man? And a man who had expressed some interest in her, too.

Of course, it couldn't be *that* kind of interest—he was just being friendly, taking over a little of Abbot's hosting chore. She was long past exciting that kind of interest in a man. Though he was as old as she, and probably older; he was white-haired, after all. Still, he was very distinguished looking—almost handsome, except for the nose—and a long way from destitute, and he claimed intriguing special powers . . . She wondered if he could tell what she was thinking, but when she looked over his eyes were closed and his face peaceful. Wonderful physical condition, too, she thought. Meat enough to cover his bones, but not an ounce of fat. His chest looked as rich and smooth as slipper satin, inviting to the touch. Dorrie felt her face warm and realized that she was blushing.

"Don't you think it's time we started back?" she said.

"Must we? We were having such a good time." He looked at his watch. "I'll tell you what: it's almost time to eat. Suppose we drive into Malibu and have lunch there. I know a wonderful little restaurant right on the water where we can get a great sandwich, or a salad if you'd rather. Do you like avocados? Sprouts?"

She nodded.

"Great. And you can call Charmaine from there if you want, and let her know you're still in one piece."

Dorrie was quiet over lunch. She'd called Charmaine while they were waiting for their food, and Charmaine had seemed completely unconcerned.

"He's a good guy," she'd said, or maybe it was "good guide"; Dorrie wasn't sure. "Have fun. See you at suppertime." Dorrie didn't know what she'd expected: Charmaine wasn't her mother, after all. But Charmaine's easy acquiescence made her feel almost rebellious, as if she had to show somebody—what? It unsettled her, and she felt foolish for thinking anyone might have worried.

They walked along the beachfront road afterward and looked in the shops, including Lonnie Chance's. It was called "Rainbow Trail" and was full of books, posters, and New Age tapes and T-shirts. Shelves held all sorts of exotic gear, from crystals to stereo players and headsets for listening to the subliminal self-improvement tapes they had on sale. Hermes bought her a sky-blue, long-sleeved sweatshirt with a big rainbow across the breast, brushing off her refusal.

"It'll get chilly later," he said, "and you didn't bring a jacket. Anyway, it's my pleasure. Think of it as a souvenir of a lovely day." He looked closely into her eyes and then smiled. "You are having a lovely day, aren't you?"

"Yes, of course."

"Well, then." He paid for the shirt and draped it over her shoulders.

"You're not in a hurry to get back, are you?" he asked as they got into the car again.

"No. I'm accounted for, and they're not expecting us until evening."

"Good. If you don't mind, I'd like to stop by my place and check my messages and mail. It's not far."

Once past the town, he took a side road that

230

seemed to go straight up and wound around to a small house on a bluff overlooking the ocean. The side facing the road was windowless except for a small square of glass set in the door. Taking her hand, Hermes led Dorrie around the side of the house to some steps and up to a deck that wrapped around the ocean side of the house. The entire back was of plate glass in floor-to-ceiling panels, interrupted in the center by a door. A table and chairs occupied one end of the deck and a long-padded glider stood next to a raised spa at the other.

"Come on in," he said, opening the door and pulling her in behind him. He let go her hand and gestured to a long, low couch set at an angle to the window. "Have a seat. I'll just be a minute."

Dorrie seated herself and kicked off her sandals. She was used to standing in the store, but walking the beach and concrete sidewalks was another matter: her feet hurt. Sighing luxuriously, she slumped back against the couch, slid her hips forward, stretched out her legs, and wiggled her toes. Her stockings were still in her purse; she had not bothered to put them back on.

What a supremely odd day this had been, she thought. Alone with Hermes all day long . . . He hadn't said or done a single thing that was out of line, but still she felt . . . just antsy, she guessed, along with this strange lassitude, this "what-the-hell" feeling like nothing she'd ever felt before. Letting him steal her away like that, taking off the stockings that were her second skin and going barelegged . . . George would be appalled. But Hermes was right: she was in Never-Never Land. The rules she knew simply did not apply. She'd seen a girl with lavender hair, for pity's sake! What were bare legs, next to lavender hair?

She pulled herself up to a more ladylike position just as Hermes came back into the room.

"Getting a nice rest?" he asked. "You must be tired, after all that walking. Let me pour you a glass of wine."

Dorrie almost never drank wine. She looked at her watch. It wasn't even half-past two.

"It's a little early, isn't it?"

"It's only wine." He set her glass on the coffee table in front of her. "I know what you need," he said, sitting at the other end of the couch. "Put your feet up here, and I'll give them a massage."

Why not? she thought, swinging her legs up onto the couch. Bare legs. Lavender hair. A strange man massaging her feet. What did it matter? He took her right foot in his hands, placed his thumbs in her arch, and began kneading. It felt heavenly. Dorrie felt a sigh escape her.

"This has been such a strange day," she said. "Lovely, but strange. I'm trying to figure out how I came to be on this couch in this house, with my bare feet in the hands of a man I never met until yesterday."

Hermes laughed. "One of the very nicest things about being a thousand miles from home is that you can do things here you'd never think of doing there," he said. "God knows what kind of trouble I'd get myself into in Dallas. But you're not in any trouble here, Dorrie. You're just having a foot massage."

She picked up the wineglass and took a sip. It was nice, she thought, not too sweet and just cold enough.

"Nobody's ever rubbed my feet in my whole life," she said. "It seems the sort of thing you might pay someone to do. It's hard to believe you'd massage my feet just out of the goodness of your heart."

"They're perfectly nice, clean-enough feet, and it's my fault they're worn out. Just relax and enjoy it, Dorrie."

His hands worked the ball of her foot for a few minutes and then, one by one, her toes. She was so relaxed she could hardly keep her eyes open, even though her stomach felt funny and her inner thighs were unusually warm. There was one place on the inside of her toe . . . She shivered. Every time he touched it, she felt a tingle all the way up to the top of her leg. Must be hitting a nerve, but it didn't hurt. Actually, it felt kind of good . . . Behind Hermes, through the glass, she could see lacy little waves rolling up on the beach and chasing themselves back out, and she remembered the ocean's *hush, hush, hush.*

"You're making me sleepy," she said.

He laid her right foot down and picked up the left.

"You can take a nap if you like," he said. "The whole idea is to relax." He was breathing at exactly the same speed as she, Dorrie noticed: *in . . . out . . . in . . . out . . .* A nap would be nice. He touched the spot again, and a little shudder went up her spine.

"Thanks, but no. If I sleep now, I won't sleep tonight." She sat up straighter and put her feet on the floor. "That was wonderful. Thank you, Hermes."

"Here," he said, "turn away from me." He moved closer and put his hands on her shoulders. "Your shoulders are all tensed up. Hard as iron. Let me loosen you up a little." He smelled good, she noticed. Not like cologne, just good: the trustworthy smell of clean, healthy flesh.

His hands began moving down her back, and Dorrie felt a little flutter of nervousness below her belly. She could not be mistaken, she thought: the man was making a pass at her. It was absurd, of course: California was swarming with gorgeous, experienced, under-forty beauties with flat bellies and long legs; why would he make a pass at *her?* Her own husband, the man who'd loved her all those years, had almost never made a pass at her, and he was entitled! But there could be no other explanation for what was happening here. His hands moved slowly down her upper back, thumbs rubbing deep circles outward from her spine, and rested just below her waist. It was all Dorrie could do to remain upright. She took another sip of wine.

You can do things here you'd never think of doing there, he'd said. She could. Even this, maybe. The idea was shocking, but it intrigued her. If she wanted to, she could dance naked on the sands and no one would ever know. If she could only muster the courage, throw off all the "don'ts" that had been imposed on her all her life . . . Why not? Even if she made an utter and absolute fool of herself with this man, she would never have to see his face again. Nothing was real here anyway. She could just go back to Dallas and act as if it had never happened, as if she'd imagined the whole thing.

His firm hands encased her ribs, applying pressure with his thumbs and fingertips, moving, moving, warming her skin, relaxing her muscles. What would it be like? All those sexy novels, the movies she'd seen on cable when George was asleep upstairs . . . He wouldn't even watch the damned movies with her, let alone lay a hand on her in love. It had made her angry when she let herself think about it, which had been seldom. But she was thinking about it now. She'd wondered for a long time how it would feel to make love to a man who liked it.

This man liked it. She was willing to lay down money on that. He had pulled her shirt-tail out, and she could tell by the way his hands slid so gently, so firmly, so smoothly across the skin of her back just how much he must like it. No question: Hermes Mason would know exactly what to do with a naked lady if he found one on his couch.

She felt his lips touching the back of her neck, his warm breath under her ear.

"Feel good?" he murmured.

"Are you doing what I think you're doing?" Dorrie asked. Her voice sounded strange to her own ears, low and thick.

"Probably," he said. He sounded a little amused. "What do you think I'm doing?"

"Seducing me?" The words were whispered. If she were wrong, she would be mortified.

"Is that such a strange idea?"

"Beyond imagining," she said. "I don't know if I can do it, Hermes. I can't even imagine taking my clothes off in front of any man but

George. Isn't it awfully silly to do that with your clothes on?"

"Clothes are not the question," Hermes said. His hands slid around to the front of her body and cupped her breasts, and Dorrie gasped. Her belly felt hot and quivery, and her panties were damp. He unhooked the clasp of her bra and slid his hands inside it. "Clothes are easy. The question is, do you want to?"

Her head fell back on his shoulder and turned toward his face, and his mouth found hers. The kiss started out softly, an experiment on her part, but as she turned into it, his tongue tasted her lips and pushed her teeth apart and Dorrie felt her bones melt. She was trembling, and she could not catch her breath. One of his hands dropped down to her stomach and started a circular motion, moving lower and lower, heating as it went. She felt so warm. Like a nervous pony, her skin rippled under his touch.

With great effort, she broke the kiss and turned to him. Dropping her forehead against his neck, she murmured, "I believe I do."

"Good," he said. "I've wanted to ever since last night." He started undoing the buttons down the front of her shirt, and she held her breath.

"Just one thing," she said. "Please don't hurry."

*   *   *

He hadn't, she thought on the way back to Abbot's house. Not a bit. What George used to complete in five minutes—ten, tops—had taken Hermes two solid hours, and that was *before* the hot tub. Exploring, teasing, teaching. Astounding. She had not known her body could give such pleasure, not just to her but to him too—could exhaust her with one explosion after another, each a little larger than the last, until the final Fourth-of-July extravaganza: sparklers, skyrockets, Catherine wheels. The sight of his smooth hands resting lightly on the steering wheel gave her gooseflesh all over again.

"Hermes?"

"What?"

"This is going to sound stupid . . ."

"Never mind. Tell me."

"I just . . . I don't know the rules. What do I do now? How do we act toward one another?"

"Just the same, Dorrie. Nobody needs to know unless you want them to." He concentrated briefly on a series of short, sharp turns in the road before saying, "I did tell you I'm going to South America, didn't I?"

"Yes. It's not that. I'm going back to Dallas anyway." The sun was going down, and the air was becoming chilly. She reached into the back seat for the sweatshirt he'd bought earlier in the day and pulled it on over her head.

238

"What, then?" he asked.

"I never did anything like that before. I don't know how to think about it."

He laughed softly and reached across the seat to take her hand.

"You don't have to think about it at all, Dorrie. Get out of your head and enjoy your body. You felt it, and judging by your reactions, it felt really good. Isn't that enough?"

"I suppose." She was lying. She'd lived in her head for as long as she could remember. It was the only safe place she knew. But he wouldn't tell, and she didn't have to either. No one but her would understand. They would think he'd taken advantage of her, but he hadn't. He'd given her a gift.

Dorrie folded the memory into a tidy little packet and stashed it in a special place in the back of her mind where it would be accessible but could not intrude when she didn't want it. No one would ever know. She would treat it like one of her dreams.

Twenty-two

The next morning, Charmaine borrowed Abbot's car and took Dorrie shopping.

"There's a bookstore I always visit when I'm out here," she said. "Let's drop in."

The store occupied a narrow slot in a block-long white stucco building. Over the door, pink neon script fluttered "Orion Books." The window displayed a picture of Walter Friml, his dark eyes commanding the passerby, and a collection of his books. As they entered, a bell tinkled overhead and the man at the back raised his head.

"Charmaine!" He hopped down from his high stool and came around the counter, arms extended.

"Hello, Soon Ling," Charmaine said, taking his hands. "I'm real glad to see you again."

The inside of the store reminded Dorrie of the basement stacks of the library at Stofford: row after row of white-painted wooden shelves stood so close together that there was barely room for one person to squeeze past another. Subject titles were handwritten in wax pencil on the shelves: Acupuncture, Astral Travel, Astrology, Buddhism, Cartomancy, Clairvoyance. . . . Hermes had said he was clairvoyant. Dorrie pulled a book from the shelf and glanced through it. The pages were brittle and brown, and the frontispiece pictured a man in a high, starched collar wearing round spectacles. It read like Thackeray, with long, perfectly constructed and punctuated sentences and paragraphs that went on for pages, its tone formal and its language rich. Dorrie closed the book and replaced it on the shelf. George would think she'd lost her mind.

"Dorrie?" Charmaine called. "Where has that girl got to! Dorrie, come and meet Soon Ling!"

Dorrie stepped around the end of the stack and offered her hand. "How do you do?" she asked.

"Happy to meet you." Soon Ling's hand was small and firm. "Are you enjoying your visit to California?"

"Very much. Charmaine's friends are such interesting people."

Soon Ling studied her face for a moment and then smiled. "But they are no different from you," he said.

Dorrie shook her head, smiling denial. "We're

241

all human, of course, but these seem to be a very special class of humans."

"They are no different from you," Soon Ling repeated. "You will see."

After lunch, she stretched out on a chaise longue in the lacy shade of a pepper tree to read, but she couldn't concentrate. The sky was too blue, the clouds too white, the flowers too brilliant, and the scent of the air too strange. Snatches of conversation she'd overheard last night and today rolled around and around in her brain.

". . . and his aura turned this terrible muddy red . . ."

". . . working on my reality . . ."

"They'd had this past-life relationship, see . . ."

"They are no different from you."

No, she thought. We all have two arms, two legs, one head . . . but what goes on inside the head!

"Good afternoon. May I join you?"

The voice was rich and deep. Dorrie turned to see a tall man the color of polished teak with a heavily lined, nearly flat face. His sparse and wiry beard was patched with silver. Above it were large, deep-set, caramel eyes. Dressed like a gardener, the man carried himself like a king.

"Please," she said.

Sitting opposite her, the man leaned forward

and offered a long, broad hand. "Jedediah Peebles," he said.

"I'm Dorrie Greene. How do you do?"

"Very well, thank you. What are you reading?"

"I'm not, not really." Dorrie removed her glasses and put them in their case. "I went into mental overload about twenty-four hours ago." She put her hand on top of her head, as if to steady it.

Jedediah laughed, showing large, even teeth. "Head swimming?" he asked. "You should see the lights swirling over it. Like a swarm of bees!"

"You see lights?"

He nodded. "Your aura."

"What do they look like?"

"You've been through a very dark time, but your aura's clearing now; the muddy colors are dissipating, brightening. Things are getting clearer to you. Someone died . . . your husband?" Dorrie nodded. Her widowhood was no secret. ". . . and you were feeling lost . . . purposeless. But now someone's come into your life to get you back on the track."

"That would be Zada, I suppose, my store manager. Certainly not Charmaine—I've never known anybody who could derail me as quickly as Charmaine!"

"Different tracks lead to different destinations. You're at a decision point with several ways open to you. Until now, you've always been confined by others' expectations, unable to go your own way for fear of letting them down. Now the others—your parents, your husband—are gone, and you're on your own. Perhaps Charmaine thinks you were derailed back then, and she's trying to get you back on your original path."

Honestly, Dorrie thought, these people do say the most personal things! It never even occurs to them that they might offend somebody. She shook her head.

"I don't think so. I love Charmaine to death—always have—but she's always been . . . strange. Like a vacation from real life, you know? I couldn't live like she does."

Jedediah was still watching Dorrie closely, and it made her squirm. She rubbed the back of her neck.

"Life with my husband was very orderly," she said.

Jedediah smiled again. "Too orderly, perhaps. A pain in the neck sometimes? I take it he saw Charmaine as a threat."

Dorrie put her hands back in her lap and stared at the emeralds in her engagement ring. "They didn't get along. All the years we were married I hardly saw Charmaine unless he was away."

"But she was always there when you needed her, even if it meant coming from thousands of miles away. Your miscarriage. Your mother's death."

"You're right." How had he known? At her age, her parents' death was an easy guess, but how had he known about Charmaine? Those things had happened so long ago . . . why would Charmaine have mentioned them to him, and when? "I told George once, it was positively uncanny." Her hand went unbidden to her neck again. "George never did understand what I saw in her . . . We're so different."

"You've been together before," Jedediah said. "I get a sense of pre-birth agreement: you chose to work out some pretty heavy karma, and she was to support you while you did it."

"I see," Dorrie said.

Jedediah laughed. "No, you don't," he said, "but you will. And, by the way: if you get an invitation to Arizona, be sure and go. There's some real interesting stuff for you there."

Sure I will, Dorrie thought. And you're the King of Prussia.

Two's call came in the middle of the afternoon. One of the maids brought the phone to the front porch where Dorrie was sitting alone to rest and admire the view. Two sounded anxious.

"Mother? What's going on out there?"

"I can't begin to tell you! Is anything wrong?"

"No. I just wanted to be sure you're all right."

"I'm fine, thank you. Charmaine's taking good care of me, and it's beautiful here. The house overlooks the ocean. I was just sitting and watching it."

"How're you getting along? She keeping you out of mischief?"

"Charmaine looks downright sedate next to this bunch. I feel as if I've run off with the circus!" She laughed. "She's calling me 'Kewpie Doll'—says I just wander around all day with big round eyes and a cute little smile on my face. But I'm as safe as in my own bed, honey. It's just more interesting here."

"Well, you know how Dad always felt about her. I'll be glad when you're back home where I can keep an eye on you." He cleared his throat. "You're sure everything's all right?"

Dorrie felt her jaw tighten.

"Two, it's kind of you to care, but really! What kind of mischief do you expect me to get into: immoral, illegal, or both? I'd appreciate it if you'd trust me to act like a grownup!"

"It has nothing to do with being grown up, Mother." Two's voice took on the patient, explanatory tone she'd heard him use with Trey and Wendy, the one that always set her teeth on edge. "It's a matter of worldly experience. You're very naive, and I don't want anybody to take advantage of you. I'm just trying to keep you safe."

Dorrie counted her fingers before answering.

"And how does one gain 'worldly experience' with someone like you to guard her from it?"

"You don't need any! You've gotten along fine without it for more than fifty years."

Dorrie sighed.

"Two, you really are the limit! I do appreciate your concern, but did it ever occur to you that a reasonably bright woman in middle age might be able to decide for herself what she wants? God willing, I have a long life ahead of me. I don't intend to live it in purdah!"

"I'm just trying to take care of you the way Dad did. He gave you a real good life, Mother," Two said. He sounded injured. "You don't have anything to complain of."

"You haven't lived my life, Two. You don't know what complaints I might have, but that's beside the point. Your dad's gone now. That life has ended, and I need to start another. I'd appreciate it if you'd stop breathing down my neck while I do."

"Well! Don't concern yourself over *my* feelings, Mother! All I'm trying to do is help, but you just go ahead and do it your own sweet way! Don't mind me!"

"Thank you, Two. As I said, I appreciate your concern."

Dorrie's hand shook as she hung up the phone. She couldn't believe she'd just been so ugly to her own son. But George's "protection" had been frustration enough; she would not suffer it from her son.

Dorrie joined Charmaine in the loft later. Hermes was there, his face brightening as she entered the room, and the gray-robed runemaster, along with the Chances, Darius Fogg, and Dovie. Elizabeth Van Hartesveldt sat apart from the group talking with a beautiful Oriental girl Dorrie had not seen before.

"Sit down, Dorrie," Charmaine said. "We were just talking about Lonnie's new seminar. He's about to introduce one that's right up your alley: 'The Spiritual Quest.' "

Liana patted the spot next to her, and Dorrie smiled at her and sat down.

"Since you're all here," Lonnie said, "let me try out the guided fantasy on you. You, too, Dorrie. It's part of the seminar, and I especially want your reaction."

Do I look that green? she wondered.

"What do we do?" she asked.

"Just shut your eyes, relax, and listen," Lonnie said. "Use your imagination, and when it's over I'll ask you about your experience. Not just you, of course; everybody."

"All right," someone said, "let's get on with it."

Dorrie shut her eyes, and Liana reached over to squeeze her hand.

"Breathe . . . deeply, now," Lonnie intoned. "Lean back in your chair and relax. If you'll feel more comfortable lying on the floor, feel free to do so." He paused. Nobody moved. "I'm going to count down from ten to one now, and with each number I want you to relax more deeply. Ten . . . nine . . ." Dorrie made a conscientious effort to loosen her muscles and slow her breathing.

"Now imagine you're in a forest," Lonnie said. "Look around you. Notice the types of trees and plants you see. Are there animals? Insects? How does it smell, sound? *Be* in this forest."

Dorrie saw a little apple tree in bud and watched the patterns the sunlight made as a light breeze ruffled its leaves. A bee buzzed near it, frustrated that its flowers had not yet opened.

"Now you see a path. Look at the path and start following it."

Dorrie could see no path in the wide, flower-strewn meadow ahead of her. In her mind, she began to walk straight ahead.

"You're deep in the forest now," Lonnie said. Dorrie was glad that he, at least, couldn't see inside her mind. ". . . and suddenly, as you round a bend, you see a dragon!" Lonnie's voice rose dramatically.

Really! Dorrie thought, half-amused, I can't even conjure up a forest! A strange, loose, sparkly shape floated before her, but try as she might she could not make a dragon of it.

"What do you do?" Lonnie demanded. Dorrie nodded politely to the shape. It bobbed in front of her for a moment as it approached, and her arm tingled as it passed.

"As you continue down the path, you find a key. What does the key look like?"

Dorrie looked all around, but no key appeared. Why had she let herself get dragged into this stupid game anyhow? she wondered. She hated games!

"Now there's a lake ahead of you," Lonnie said. "On the other side is the house you're going to. How do you get across the lake?"

Dorrie stood at the shore, listening to the water lap at her feet. She took a deep breath and found herself on the other side.

"The house is surrounded by a high fence. How do you get through it?" Lonnie's voice was urgent; he sounded almost as if his mystical dragon were guarding the place. She stepped through the open gate before her, but no house was there. She saw only a meadow carpeted with flowers, walled by aspens, and roofed by a shimmering blue sky.

Lonnie paused for a long moment.

"All right," he said. "Now I'm going to count you back up from one to ten, and with each number you'll feel more alert and rested. When I reach the number ten, you'll feel as refreshed as if you'd had a long nap, and you'll be eager to tell me your experiences. One, two, three . . ."

Dorrie roused and looked around at the others, who all stared expectantly at Lonnie.

"We'll start with you, Dorrie," he said. "Tell me, what did you see?"

"I've never been very good at games," she said. "I don't think I did it right."

"There's no right or wrong; everybody sees something different."

"Come on, Dorrie," Liana said, squeezing her hand. "Don't be shy."

"Well . . . The best I could do for a forest was one little apple tree."

"That's interesting," Lonnie said. "The forest represents the problems of life. Apparently your problems are few, and they produce nourishing fruit." Wouldn't that be nice, Dorrie thought. "What about the road?" he asked.

"There wasn't any road. I just started walking." Lonnie's eyebrow lifted, and she said, "I did try; I just couldn't see any road. I could go anywhere I wanted; all I had to do was choose my direction."

"I see," Lonnie said. "Well, that's very unusual, but like I said, everybody sees it her own way. What about the dragon?"

Dorrie looked away. "There wasn't one of those, either," she confessed.

A slight edge came into Lonnie's voice.

"What did you see?"

"Just a sort of shape. I didn't know what it was, but certainly nothing like a dragon."

"That's wonderful, Dorrie!" Liana cried. "Isn't that wonderful, Lonnie? She's not afraid of anything!"

"It's an enviable state of mind," Lonnie said. Frown wrinkles appeared between his eyes, and his voice was taut. "What about the key? Did you see a key?"

"No," she said, "but I didn't really need one. Nothing was locked."

"Tell me, Dorrie," Lonnie said, his voice growing sharper, "how did you cross the lake? Did you swim or find a boat or walk around it or what?"

"I'm sorry. I don't know. I just did."

"But *how?*" he demanded.

"I just took a deep breath, and there I was."

The others were staring at her, and Charmaine looked as if she were about to burst. Dorrie knew she was spoiling the game. She wished he'd ask somebody else.

"And the house?"

"There was no house, either, just a meadow . . . I told you I didn't do it right! Liana, what did you see?"

"I already know what everything means," Liana said. Her eyes were wide. "It's not fair for me to answer."

Charmaine stood abruptly.

"Will you-all excuse us?" she said. "Dorrie, the zipper's jammed in my dinner dress. Come help me."

Charmaine could hardly contain herself until they got outdoors on the patio.

"Did you make all that up?" she demanded then. "You did, didn't you! You were pulling his leg!"

"What are you talking about?"

Charmaine exploded into laughter so rich it doubled her over and brought tears to her eyes.

"Oh, Dorrie!" she wailed, wiping them with the backs of her hands. "If you had seen Elizabeth's face!" She started howling again and collapsed onto a low wall. "Where in the world did you come up with those answers?"

"That's what I saw! Come on, Charmaine, I feel bad enough already. Don't laugh at me!"

"Oh! Oh!" Charmaine wrapped her arms around her middle and howled. "Oh, I'm gonna pee my pants!" she shrieked. Dorrie glared at her, and Charmaine struggled to pull herself together. It took several tries, punctuated by fits of cackling.

"My God, girl, don't you realize those folks in there think you're one of the Ascended Masters?" Charmaine said when she could speak. "I could start a cult around you this minute!" She started giggling again.

"But I didn't do anything! I didn't even play the game right!"

"That's just it! Old Lonnie thought he had a live one, somebody he could just lead right down the garden path, only you didn't go! Were you watching his face?"

"I could see he was upset, but I thought—"

"You always do." Charmaine took Dorrie's hands and looked up into her face. "Look, sweet thing, it's all right; you haven't done anything wrong. Just don't tell, okay?"

She stood up, grinning, and gave Dorrie a hug.

"Come on, let's go fix my dress. I haven't had a laugh like that in twenty years!"

Twenty-three

Sunday afternoon, as the party was breaking up, Dorrie went out to the front porch to sit in a big butterfly chair and escape the crowd. A green lawn stretched to the edge of the bluff; below, the beach hemmed a broad expanse of ocean that glittered like rumpled blue tinfoil.

A soft west wind carried the sea's low roar up the bluff, its sound as regular and relaxing as a heartbeat. A feathery pepper tree stood at the bottom of the lawn, its branches waving in the breeze. Beneath it a bird-of-paradise plant bloomed in violent shades of blue and orange against emerald leaves. At the verge of the canyon was an enormous white boulder shaped like an upturned hand in which Jedediah Peebles reclined, staring out to sea.

This weekend had been like a visit to Wonderland. Dorrie'd always thought of herself as fairly open-minded on the question of psychic phenomena, but these people took it to the limit. Sweet Dovie . . . The story of Dovie's "awakening" had disturbed her, but except for that, the woman herself had proved as ordinary as bread.

Yesterday's conversation with Jedediah had felt almost commonplace until she'd had time to think about it. Now she was having a delayed reaction: how in God's name could he know all that about her?

He'd been right about the way she'd been stifled by others' expectations, especially those of George and her father. She wasn't the only one; Dorrie was convinced that Daddy was the reason Barbara'd married as she did. Choosing a Beatnik knockabout was the surest way she'd known to get herself disowned and out from under their father's heavy hand. And Mama . . . Mama had quietly wrapped her car around a tree as soon as her children were safely married and gone. It had gone down as an accident, of course, but Dorrie'd always wondered. Mama had been so quiet for weeks, and just two days earlier she'd taken Dorrie into her bedroom and given her a big box of family relics: old photos and letters, a few pieces of jewelry that had been special to Dorrie's grandmothers, a comforter that Grandma

Rose had made from the wool of her father's sheep.

"You should keep these things, Mama!" Dorrie had protested.

"No, dear," Mama'd said. "It's time to pass them on now."

Mama had escaped, all right—and almost taken Dorrie's right to drive with her. From that day forward, George'd had a fit every time Dorrie suggested learning to drive a car; not until the children started school, when carpooling and the like had made his position impossible, had he finally, reluctantly, given in. Barbara'd come home for the funeral and had another set-to with Daddy, and nobody'd heard a word from her from that day to this. Dorrie had carried on alone, confined to the respectability her husband and father demanded. Sometimes she'd felt they were in cahoots against her.

There had been times, she remembered, when she'd wanted to bust loose—go crawl through the Mayan ruins or join a commune, like Charmaine—but she'd found that having chosen George and children excluded that.

Once, the October after Marcie'd gone away to school, she'd planned a vacation for herself—even rented a cabin at Lake Murray. Still in the Slough of Despond, she'd wanted to go alone, but George had been so upset she'd cancelled. She'd resented it for years. Her only comfort in losing him was the relief of not having to account for her every move, and she felt so guilty about the relief that she could hardly admit it even to herself.

As Jedediah rose and started toward the house, the air around Dorrie filled with the scent of sweat and Cashmere Bouquet. What? she thought, as she would have answered a voice.

"Someone's behind you," Jedediah said.

The front door opened, and Charmaine stuck her head through it.

"Come on, you two," she said. "Soup's on."

Still feeling bad about Two, she called Marcie later that afternoon. Kurt called Marcie to the second phone and stayed on the line.

"How're you doing out there, Mom?" he asked. "Having fun?"

"It's interesting. I was wondering, honey, have you-all heard from Two?"

"He called me at the office yesterday," Marcie said. "What in the world did you say to him? He's ready to have you committed!"

Dorrie sighed. "I was afraid of that. I'll probably end up having to apologize; I really was tacky. I lost my temper, that's all."

"What was he doing?"

"Well, he called to find out how I was doing and I ended up getting irritated at him. I spoke when I should have kept still."

"You don't have to be ashamed to stick up for yourself, Mom," Marcie said.

"I'm not very good at it; I have to get too mad first. Poor Two!"

"I expect he'll survive it," Kurt said.

"Well, I hurt his feelings. I felt bad afterward."

"Hurt his feelings! Mother, the man has the hide of a rhinoceros!" Dorrie could almost see her daughter's lip curl. "What you bruised was his sense of godlike power. I wouldn't worry about it too much!"

"I'm sure you wouldn't, Marcie, but I'm his mother. I do worry."

"Give her a break, Marcie," Kurt said. "There's no need to make your mother fight with both her kids."

"Sorry, Mom," Marcie said. "It's between you and him, of course. All I want to tell you is, don't let him bully you. I quit years ago; there's no need for you to put up with it. And you don't need to apologize for saying what's on your mind. I'm sure he asked for it."

"So tell us what you've been up to out there in Lala Land," Kurt said. "What's going on good?"

"I don't even know where to begin! Char-

259

maine has dropped me right into the middle of Oz out here: psychics and astrologers and I don't know what all. There's even a big-time guru."

"Sounds like quite a group. Are you having fun?"

"My eyes are on stalks, honey. I'm just trying to keep still and look like nothing surprises me. It's an education, I'll say that."

"As I remember," Marcie said, "all the adventure stories you ever told me about your girlhood starred Charmaine. Sounds like she's at it again."

Dorrie laughed. "Well, I think she's trying to get me to star in my own stories this time. I'm resisting, but you know Charmaine."

"Just have a good time, Mom," Kurt said. "Lord, if you haven't got sense enough by now to stay out of trouble, it's too late to worry about it!"

"That's essentially what I told Two," Dorrie said. "Shoot! I was too timid even to go through the middle-aged crazies! All my friends were dyeing their hair and dumping their husbands, starting boutiques and running off to become artists, and there I sat in a three-year state of depression, wondering where they found the courage. I'm not likely to disgrace the family now!"

"You took your angst out constructively,

Mom," Marcie reminded her. "You rebuilt the house!"

Dorrie felt a little better, hanging up the phone. It was nice to know somebody sensible had faith in her.

Dorrie was glad when everybody finally went home. The Chances stayed on, planning to return to Arizona at the end of the week, but she saw little of them except at mealtimes. Her nerves felt scraped raw, and what she really wanted was to go into hibernation for a month.

Even so, Dorrie's heart went out to Liana. Liana spoke often about her little girl, who was staying with the housekeeper while her parents attended to Lonnie's business in Los Angeles. It was clear that she wished she could have brought the baby along.

"Where are you going from here?" Liana asked Dorrie on Wednesday afternoon. They were sitting at a table in the patio drinking fruit concoctions.

"Home. I left the store to come here, and I feel like it's the only thing left holding me to earth. All this is so strange to me. It's like visiting another planet."

"But haven't you had a good time?" Liana seemed as anxious as if she alone were responsible for Dorrie's pleasure.

"Of course I have, and I've met some fascinating people. I just have the feeling that this isn't Real Life."

"Whatever you're living is 'real life,'" Lonnie said. He had walked up behind her as she was speaking, and his voice made her jump.

"I can't argue with that," she said as he sat down. "But it's nothing like any life I can ever remember; it feels more like dreaming."

Charmaine's book had recommended keeping a dream diary. At Soon Ling's shop, she'd picked up a "nothing book" bound in black calico for the purpose, but she hadn't remembered a dream since she bought it.

"Anyhow," she said, "this is a far cry from running a jewelry store in Dallas. I've got to get back pretty soon."

"I know what!" Liana said, clapping her hands together. "We're going home to Arizona Friday, and it's on your way: you could come with us, and I could show you my baby! Dorrie, it's so beautiful there, the red earth and the rocks and canyons — it's not like anyplace else in the world! You've got to see it!"

"See what?" Charmaine crossed the patio and sat with them, a tall glass of something pink in her hand. "What're you-all talking about?"

"Sedona," Liana said. "We've just invited

Dorrie and you to visit our place this weekend. Oh, please make her come!"

"I went there once," Charmaine said. "Years ago, before anybody but the Indians knew about it. I'd love to go back."

"Dorrie, the most miraculous things happen there!" Liana said. "You wouldn't believe—the earth forces, the magnetism. It's like a chakra for the whole earth! Healings, dreams, past-life memories . . . People find their spirit guides and everything!"

"It sounds exciting," Dorrie said. A spirit guide—an ancient Navajo crone, say, or some turbaned Oriental—was just what she needed to complete this trip. She could go into business like La Van Hartesveldt, advising everybody else how to live their lives when she hadn't yet figured out her own.

Charmaine grinned. "We'll talk about it," she promised Liana.

Later, in a Malibu coffee shop, Dorrie and Charmaine argued.

"I want to go home," Dorrie said. "I've been in a surrealist's heaven for a week already, and it's wearing me out. Miracles are all I need!"

"It'll be good for you. A Taurus with all that Libra and Aquarius? Earth and air, solidity and spirit in one. It's just the thing!"

Dorrie shook her head.

"What are you afraid of?" Charmaine demanded. "It's just this really beautiful place southwest of Flagstaff in the National Forest — red rock country. There's an artists' colony, and metaphysical people have started hanging out there over the past few years. It's like a little Santa Fe. We'll stay in the Chances' house and hike through the rocks, that's all. We can still be back on Monday."

"Charmaine, please don't do this to me. If you knew how frazzled I feel . . ."

"Well, think about it," Charmaine said. "It's only two days."

Twenty-four

The air had been bumpy over the San Bernadino Mountains, but it smoothed out over the desert. Seated with Charmaine in the back of Lonnie's corporate plane, Dorrie looked down upon the barren floor of the Mojave. It was flat as a griddle. How had the pioneers ever made it to the coast? she wondered. Down there, you'd think there wasn't another thing in the world but sand. You had to get up in the air to see the desert's end.

"So what do you think?" Charmaine asked.

"I've stopped dreaming." Dorrie turned away from the window to look at her friend. "I haven't dreamed since the night we got there."

"Maybe you've just stopped remembering. People do sometimes when they're working something through. God knows you've had a lot to take in. Your mind does it without you, sort of — keeps you in the dark till you've got things figured out."

"Like George?" Dorrie said.

Charmaine laughed. "Touché!"

"Well," Dorrie said, "I wish I'd get it all figured out and let myself know what's going on. I miss my dreams. They weren't always fun, but they were interesting."

"You will. I'm really glad you decided to come along on this trip. You'll love where we're going now!"

"Uh-huh."

"Really! There's this pretty little village with an unpronounceable name, all Spanish Colonial—really a showplace, you know?—with art galleries and craftsmen and all. We can go shopping."

"I hate shopping."

"Maybe you can find something for the store. Jewelry, or ceramics. Take it on consignment."

"Maybe." Dorrie stared out the window. More mountains appeared beneath them: the tail of the Sierra Madres, she supposed. Tall firs and redwoods grew like patchy whiskers between the timberline and the point where the mountains rose out of the sandy desert floor. At this height, it was not hard to think of the world as the single organism Charmaine's books called it, all parts together making up a whole . . . which might itself be part of a larger whole. If the individual cells of her body could think, Dorrie supposed, some of the really smart ones might

266

figure out that together they made up a hair or a tooth, even a whole organ. But how could they ever understand that all together they made up Dorrie Greene?

"What's driving me crazy," she said, "is that they keep telling me I'm psychic." She shook her head. "I'm about as psychic as your left hind foot."

"Everybody's psychic. They just don't pay attention."

"So I've been told. Look, Charmaine, I've got a nice, safe, boring life. I know what to expect. God save me from miracles!"

Charmaine laughed.

"Come on, Dorrie, aren't you the least bit curious, even? Wouldn't you like to know what you're capable of? You're at a place in your life where you can do anything you want. All your 'duties' are done; now it's time to play. What are you scared of?"

"I'm not scared. I just don't want to mess with it. I don't want my life disrupted anymore."

"It never can go back the way it was before; you might as well make it interesting. Anyhow, it's always seemed to me that a good, stiff dose of disruption was just what you needed."

"Thanks a heap. I've always known I could count on your sympathy."

"Any time," Charmaine said, grinning.

* * *

The sun shone brightly when they landed at the little airport outside Flagstaff. A copper-skinned man with shoulder-length black hair and an aquiline nose waited beside a van into which he helped Lonnie load their bags. It was half-past eleven.

"Rafael says lunch will be ready when we get home," Liana told Dorrie. "It'll take almost an hour to get there, but it'll be worth it. Luz is such a good cook! She and Rafael are Yavapais. They live on the place."

The drive through the mountains in the national forest was worth the whole trip, Dorrie decided before they arrived. The narrow road, full of switchbacks, offered one spectacular view after another. After miles of forest, the land changed abruptly at Oak Creek Canyon.

From there on, every turn displayed rust-colored mountainsides sparsely covered with shaggy evergreens. The brilliant blue sky formed a backdrop for enormous, layered rocks carved by the wind into mythic shapes: giant statues of men and animals, rugged obelisks, a great fist with one finger pointed at the sky. They looked like the scattered toys of a titan's children.

When they arrived, Dorrie and Charmaine followed Liana across the courtyard of the tan, Spanish-style, adobe house toward a glass door. Inside it, her nose mashed against the glass, was a toddler in a blue dress. Liana opened the door and scooped up the baby, who immediately started to wail.

"It's all right now," Liana hushed her. "Look, sweetheart, Daddy's coming! Don't cry now!" The baby snuffled herself into silence as Liana showed the women to their rooms.

Lunch was served in the breakfast room on a table laid with a peach-colored cloth and set with terra-cotta dishes whose inside surfaces were glazed turquoise. Three walls of the room were covered with bone-white plaster, and its entire east end was walled with glass, offering a view down yet another canyon. In the distance, across a narrow strip of road, the canyon walls framed a bell-shaped rock as tall as a four-story building.

Luz had prepared a thick, spicy stew with cornbread and a salad of tropical fruit. Over lunch, Lonnie described the Sedona area.

"The Indians say it's where the Great Spirit gives birth to rainbows," he said. "It's one of four places on the earth's surface—not counting the poles, of course—where a compass goes out of control: the site of the Pyramids in Egypt, the island of Kauai, the Bermuda Triangle, and Sedona. But what makes Sedona so special is, there are four vortexes here: two electrical, one magnetic, and one electromagnetic."

"What does that mean?" Dorrie asked. "How does it affect people?"

Lonnie pointed out the window. "That's Bell Rock, right out there," he said. "Bell Rock and Airport Mesa, the electrical vortexes, are yang: positive, masculine energy. They give people a physical and mental charge. I don't know how many times I've seen somebody go in with the flu or strained muscles or worse things, and come back without them."

"The magnetic one, Cathedral Rock, is yin," Liana's soft voice added. "That's feminine energy. It works on the spirit, and people have past-life memories and visions, or they get into channeling. Automatic writing works better there than anywhere. Even people who've never been able to get any results with it before are successful there."

Dorrie made a mental note to read up on automatic writing. Channelling she'd already seen, and she wanted no part of it.

"And the electromagnetic vortex combines them?" Charmaine said.

Lonnie nodded. "It creates a perfect balance of yin and yang, positive and negative energy. In Boynton Canyon, you get the best of both."

"How come I didn't know all this stuff when I was here before?" Charmaine said. "Shoot, I'd never have left!"

"Maybe you weren't ready," Lonnie told her.

"Well, I can't wait to get out into the vortexes," Charmaine said. She grinned. "I guess me and Dorrie'll have our own private seminar, won't we. That's real big of you, Lonnie."

During the afternoon, as Lonnie told stories about the miraculous vortex occurrences he'd seen or heard of, Dorrie felt progressively more anxious. What had started as a lark now loomed before her as a test, and one for which she was not prepared. Charmaine and Liana, she knew, held expectations for her that she could not fulfill; the only result she could now imagine was disappointing them and feeling like a failure.

Charmaine and Lonnie entered into a discussion of brain waves and mental states, and Dorrie tuned out until she heard Charmaine say, "What do we need to look out for?"

"Well," Lonnie answered, "the rattlesnakes are in hibernation. That's one danger we don't need to consider, though of course, there are still the scorpions. And it's rugged country; be careful you don't fall or turn an ankle. The only other thing is, if you hear voices, use your own judgment about whether to do what they tell you. There are evil spirits as well as good ones out there."

He meant it, Dorrie saw. In this day and age, the man was seriously discussing the danger of encountering an evil spirit!

"One other thing," he added. "It's against the law to take anything out of the canyons, especially plants or artifacts." He turned to Charmaine. "If you see a crystal or a bit of rock you want, ask the spirits. If they give permission, it's all right."

Dorrie wondered how much of this Charmaine was buying. Interesting If Proved, indeed! she thought. Give me a break!

"If you-all will excuse me," she said, "I think I'll go outdoors and take a walk around the place. I've been sitting too long."

Outdoors, the sun was dropping like a huge, molten marble through apricot jelly. The air felt crisp and cool. A light breeze lifted Dorrie's hair, and she pulled her sweater closer around her shoulders. Pines and cedars surrounded the hilltop house, and their scent prickled her nose. Underfoot, dry needles formed a carpet so soft that her footsteps were inaudible; she could hear only the wind rustling the branches.

Dorrie, she heard, and she caught a whiff of her grandmother's scent. She whirled around, seeking the source of the voice, but saw nothing.

"What?" she said aloud.

I am with you, she heard. *Don't let the vor-*

texes frighten you. Whatever happens, I will be there.

Oh, please! Dorrie thought. She sat heavily on a flat, red rock. It was still warm from the day's sun, and she laid her hand against its smooth surface. I'm so tired, she thought. This is too much.

Rest, she heard. *Relax. Look; the stars are coming out. Turn to your left, and watch the moon rise.*

A full moon, bright as a spotlight, floated over the ridge across from her. Its face was silvery pale, but Dorrie could see every detail of the mountains and valleys etched upon it. She remembered a British play she'd seen, in which an astronomy professor's wife went mad because men had landed on the moon and destroyed its mystery. No, she thought. Footprints fade, but the mystery remains. The fact that men could name the minerals that made up the moon, that they knew its weight and density, made it no less beautiful or poetic. It remained a miracle.

It's the same with mankind, she heard. *You have always known there is more to man than can be touched or measured.*

This is nothing that couldn't come out of my own subconscious mind, Dorrie told herself firmly. I've already thought all these thoughts; I'm just making it up. It's all this hoorah I've been through. It's making me crazy.

You are not crazy, and I am not a figment of your imagination, the voice said sharply. *Really, Dorrie, sometimes you make me tired! Must I prove myself, at last? All right. Here is something you don't know: you and Liana are kin. She is the great-granddaughter of my first cousin Aurelia Blossom. Check that out, and then tell me you've made me up!*

"I'm sorry," Dorrie said meekly, but Rose was gone. Dorrie picked herself up and went back inside the house.

Twenty-five

Dorrie slept a deep and dreamless sleep and woke before the sun. She showered and dressed in heavy twill pants, tucking them into the boots Marcie'd talked her into buying before she'd left Dallas — in a former life, she thought ruefully — and pulled a thick, bottle-green sweater over her head.

She found Charmaine and Lonnie in the breakfast room. Lemon-colored sunshine flooded through the windows, lighting the blond ash table on which Luz was piling bowls of fruit and bread, platters of meats and scrambled eggs, and plates piled high with cornmeal pancakes. A large glass of freshly squeezed orange juice sat by each place.

"Hey, slugabed!" Charmaine greeted her. "There you are! What do you think of this sunrise?"

"It's gorgeous," Dorrie said, standing at the window. "I've never seen anything like it before.

275

The colors are so beautiful. . . . The light is completely different here."

Liana entered the room with her baby in her arms.

"Look at the sunrise, Crystal!" she crooned. "Look at all the pretty colors in the sky!"

Crystal crowed and waved to Dorrie, who smiled and reached for her.

"I love sunrise," Liana confided, depositing the baby in Dorrie's lap. She removed the tray from the high chair and pulled it up to the table. "When I was little, I always woke up real early. My great-grandma would be the only one up, and we'd watch the sun come up together." She took the baby back and put her in the chair. "I sure did love my Granny 'Relia. The sunrise always makes me think of her."

"Relia?" Dorrie said. "What an unusual name."

"Aurelia Blossom was her maiden name. I've always thought it was real pretty. We gave it to Crystal; her whole name is 'Crystal Aurelia Chance.' " Liana bent to kiss her baby's head and looked out the window again. "Look how the sun hits Bell Rock, almost like a spotlight. Isn't that just an amazing sight?"

Dorrie repressed an urge to return to her room and write "I believe" a thousand times.

"You must enjoy being able to see the vortex right out your own window," she said.

"Especially that one," Lonnie said. "It's what they call a beacon rock; the energy goes straight out the top, just like a radio signal. We've seen UFOs hovering over it a dozen times or more."

"How exciting!" A UFO sighting would really make this trip complete, Dorrie thought. She wouldn't even need to go home then; Charmaine could pack her straight into Terrell State Hospital, and she could spend the rest of her life stringing beads.

As soon as it was late enough, while the others were getting ready to go out, Dorrie called the store. Zada's gravelly voice was reassuringly down-to-earth.

"You'll be back Monday?" she asked.

"Yes. I'm in Arizona now. We're going to a crafts village this afternoon, and I thought I might pick up some pottery or jewelry on consignment and bring it back. What do you think?"

"Well . . . I don't know. The rage for Southwestern is beginning to fade . . ." Dorrie waited. "It's not that I don't trust your judgment, of course, but you're not very experienced. I wish I were there with you."

"I do, too, but that'll have to wait for another trip."

"The thing is," Zada said, "I hate to think

about you buying from just anybody. Mr. Greene only bought from established manufacturers." She cleared her throat. "Of course, it's your store, Dorrie. Whatever you think . . ."

Dorrie shoulders slumped. Zada would never say no to her boss, but Dorrie knew her "it's your store." If the stuff didn't sell, she'd never hear the end of it.

"I guess you're right," she said.

"Are you having a good trip, Dorrie?"

"Tons of fun. It's amazing." She grinned, thinking of Zada confronting Gasm El Cid. What a clash that would be!

"Well, enjoy yourself. Everything's under control here. Nothing to worry about. Oh, by the way, Travis Burton said to tell you hello."

"All right, Zada. Thanks. See you Monday."

It was still chilly when they left the house. At the highway, Lonnie turned west.

"We'll go to Airport Mesa first," he said. "It's the other electrical vortex, easier to get at than Bell Rock. I've seen people so energized by this place that they only want about an hour's sleep a night."

He turned off the highway and drove about a half-mile toward the large table rock ahead, stopping near a sign that said "Rainbow Ray Focus." Whatever that might mean, Dorrie thought. They got out of the car, and Dorrie followed Lonnie, Liana, and Charmaine up a short hill. When she got to the top, she looked down the trail to a large, flat area that ended at the edge of a cliff. Charmaine was skipping down the trail like a teenager, and Dorrie laughed aloud.

"Come on down!" Charmaine called. "It's great!"

Dorrie half-ran down the hill to her. She felt as giddy as if she'd shed thirty years. The view was breathtaking. She sat on a rock to watch the others, but could not stay seated; she felt like turning handsprings instead.

"Remember *Cocoon?*" she said. "When those old men jumped into that swimming pool, how they all started to laugh and cut up?"

"Me too," Charmaine answered. "I'd like to build a house right here and never leave it!"

"Hello!" Dorrie called down the cliff. Her voice came back to her: "Oh! Oh! Oh!"

"I'm here!" she yelled, and the rocks bounced back, "Hear! Hear!" Dorrie giggled. "I'm acting like a fool!" she said.

"So who cares?"

Dorrie climbed a rock to see farther down the canyon. "Lord, it's beautiful!" she cried, jumping back down. "I don't believe I'm doing this. I'll be stiff as a goat tomorrow!"

"Nah," Charmaine said. "You're just feeling

frisky. You'll be okay."

They went back to the little village of Tlaquepaque and ate lunch in a health-foods store whose proprietors, a married couple, greeted the Chances like old friends. Afterward, since Lonnie had business in town, the women strolled around the shops for an hour or so while their food settled, admiring Navajo blankets and Zuñi pottery. Dorrie wished she had brought a second pair of shoes. Her new boots were rubbing the back of her right heel raw, and she could feel a bunion rising on her little toe. Well, no use complaining; she'd soak her feet when she got home.

One shop, called "The Crystal Vale," sold rock crystals and books about their metaphysical qualities. On a shelf near the back were lead-crystal balls on intricately carved stands of teak, ebony, and rosewood. Wouldn't Two have a fit if she brought one of those home! Maybe later, she thought. I'm too stirred up right now.

Lonnie was waiting on the sidewalk when they left the store. "Three o'clock," he informed them. "If we're going out to the canyon, we'd better get going."

They started back out the same road, and well past the Airport Mesa sign Lonnie turned right and drove several miles off the highway. The road forked, and they started climbing as he followed a sign to Boynton Pass. Dorrie had begun to wonder how high up the mountain he would take them when he turned off the road and stopped. They left the car and started walking up a narrow, dirt track.

Dorrie's right boot had begun to cripple her, and climbing was difficult. They rounded a bend and she stopped stock-still, forgetting her pain.

Ahead of her, off to her left, sheer red-rock walls rose a thousand feet and more into a cerulean sky. Far above, a hawk wheeled, its wings still. Dorrie felt herself strengthen and, impelled by awe, followed the others into the canyon. She could never look long enough at this sight, she thought. Her eyes could never take it all in.

"The Indians call this place the home of the Great Mother," Liana said. "It's my very favorite place in the world."

"That's not hard to understand," Dorrie said. The place took her breath away with its sense of benign but absolute power. She could imagine the massive, white-bearded God of her childhood sitting on the cliff opposite, scooping up red mud from the canyon below to make Adam.

"Can you two take care of yourselves for a few minutes?" Lonnie called. "We want to go meditate for a while."

"We'll be fine," Charmaine said. As they disappeared behind a red boulder, she turned to Dorrie.

"You okay?" she asked. "You're awful quiet."

"I'm fine. Just overcome." Dorrie's ears were humming, and she could see a bright cerise-and-yellow rainbow surrounding Charmaine's head and shoulders. She blinked her eyes, but it would not go away.

"Listen," she said, "if you'd like to go find a place to meditate, too, feel free. I'll be okay. I'm just going to get out of these boots and rest my poor, blistered feet."

Charlene studied her for a moment, and Dorrie stared back at the odd rainbow around Charmaine's shoulders.

"All right, then," Charmaine said. "If you really don't mind being alone . . . Just stick around here, and I'll come back for you."

"I won't move from this spot," Dorrie promised. She watched Charmaine wander off into the trees and turned to stare again at the sheer cliff opposite her. There was no wind, and the air had grown warm. Dorrie stripped off the jacket she'd been wearing and spread it on a flattish, knee-high bench of rock that projected from the hillside.

She could not stop staring. Every living thing she looked at had a multicolored halo: the trees, clumps of grass, even the jackrabbit that sat statuelike on its haunches at the edge of the canyon staring at her and the gray squirrel that chattered on a limb over her head. Dorrie felt overstimulated in a way that would normally irritate her, but now seemed invigorating. The golden light was like a solid substance, something she could stretch out her hands and touch. She wished she had worn sunglasses.

Dorrie sat on her coat and took off her boots. Her toe was pink and swollen, and a water blister the size of a quarter had formed on her right heel. They'll have to carry me back to the van, she thought. I'll never get my boots back on. She raised her eyes to the top of the rock face opposite her. Then, shutting her eyes against the sun, she relaxed and let her mind wander.

Dorrie looks to her right and finds George seated below her on the rusty earth, his knees drawn up and his head resting against them. She is afraid to touch him.

"George?"

He raises his head and looks at her as if she were a stranger.

"George, are you real? Why did you die? You weren't even sick! You could have stayed for years and years . . . seen Wendy and Trey grow up, traveled with me the way we always planned . . . George, I'm so alone!"

"You'll be all right," he says. "I was alone all my life, and I managed."

"You weren't alone! You had me. You had

the children."

"We're all alone, every one of us. I never had you; I only married you. All that about 'the two becoming one' . . . If I'd ever let you know me, you'd have left. You could never have loved me."

"I did love you — I do! I would never have left you."

"Perhaps not. I couldn't risk it." A wintry smile crosses his face. "I'm beginning to see things a little differently now. I was so sure . . . But you were a good wife. It wasn't your fault."

Dorrie's eyes burn, and her throat thickens. George reaches toward her without touching her.

"You're still young, Dorrie. Find someone else, a man who can accept what you always wanted to give."

"Oh, George, after thirty-five years? I don't want one!"

"You will," he says. He is fading from sight. "It's all right. You deserve it."

"George!" she cries, but he is gone. Dorrie's face is wet. She realizes that she is weeping and begins to sob uncontrollably. The tears of a life-time's frustration and sorrow for a man who could not be loved pour down her face and splatter upon the rock, leaving her throat raw and aching, her eyes shut.

Dorrie feels something smooth and muscular

wrap itself about her body. She opens her eyes to behold a crested serpent, its skin shining gold, its topaz eyes staring directly into her own, and she cannot look away. She is one with the serpent, its wise eyes tell her. I am you and you are me. We are of the same substance, the stuff of God.

She is exploding, dissolving. All the particles of her being separate and shoot out above the trees, over the earth, above the rock face opposite her like a million shards of light, shimmering into the void, mingling with the billions of particles that are "other" until she can no longer distinguish her self from anything else. We are all one, the voice of the serpent says. He is part of you yet. She feels her cells regrouping, coming back together to form hands, feet, body, breast, neck, head. Her hands and feet tingle even after she regains her sight and focuses upon the head of the golden serpent.

This is fantasy, she tells herself firmly. I am I. The serpent is not real.

The serpent smiles and its lidless eyes gleam, sucking her into the tunnel of itself. She feels her whole self gather to roll into the tip of its tail and back again, shoot out between the curved gate of its teeth, and come to rest on the branch where the squirrel still scolds. Hush, she tells it, and it falls silent, its shoebutton eyes expectant.

285

Below is a somehow comical sight; her body still wrapped in the serpent's golden coils. Birds call, and the squirrel flicks its tail and races to the tree trunk. Sitting on a limb and looking at herself, Dorrie feels as if she's been let in on a colossal joke.

Back in her body, she feels the laughter boiling up from her navel. It burbles out of her mouth and bounces off the rocks that surround her. The serpent nods its head—"Now you know," she understands it to say—and unwraps itself from around her body. Laughing still, Dorrie watches it slip into a cleft in the rock and disappear with a satisfied flick of its tail.

"Dorrie? Dorrie, are you okay? What happened?"

Dorrie turns, still laughing, toward Charmaine's voice. She cannot catch her breath to speak, and the muscles in her diaphragm start to ache as the laughter continues to erupt from her mouth.

"Dorrie! Stop it, now! You're hysterical!"

"Ah!" Dorrie cries. "Ah! I must be!" She sighs, beginning to breathe normally again.

"What the hell happened? What are you so tickled about?"

"Oh, Charmaine!" Dorrie started to laugh again. "You'd never believe it in a million years! It's just this place . . . I think it's making me crazy."

"Well, put your boots on. The lovebirds are coming, and the sun's going down. We've got to go back."

Dorrie pulled on her boots. She stood up and walked a few paces, and then went back and took off the right one to look at her foot. Her heel was as smooth and white as a baby's. There was no sign of a blister on it.

On her return to Dallas, Domino met Dorrie at the front door and scolded nonstop while she carried her bags upstairs to unpack.

"Poor old cat," she said. "Thought you'd been abandoned, didn't you." Jessie had dropped by every afternoon to put out his food and bring in the mail, but Domino had never had much use for strangers. He was Dorrie's cat.

"Prr-rrr-rou?" He jumped up on the bed and padded her pillow.

"It's not time for bed yet," she told him. "I've got to unpack first, anyhow. Give me a minute."

The cat jumped into her open suitcase and — with a peremptory "Myatt!" — sat determinedly upon her clothing.

Dorrie laughed.

"Oh, all right!" She sat down on the bed, and the cat immediately hopped out of the suitcase and padded over to her lap.

"I'm sorry," Dorrie said, stroking him slowly from brow to tailtip. "It's all right now. I'm home. Forgive me?"

Domino regarded her steadily for a moment before speaking. Then he turned toward her and placed his paws on her shoulders.

"Prr-rrr-rrow," he said on a descending note, and rubbed his face against her chin, first one side and then the other. Dorrie ran her hands down his sides, smoothing his thick, black hair as he padded her shoulders, his claws sheathed. The cat began to purr, his voice as deep and rolling as a well-tuned motor, as Dorrie continued to pet him. At last he butted his head against her chin and dropped gracefully into her lap where he curled himself into a circle.

Dorrie stroked his fur and rubbed behind his ears for several more minutes, speaking gentle nonsense. Finally she said, "Enough?"

Domino bumped his head against her hand one more time and jumped down.

Downstairs, she checked the plants in the orchid room, poking her finger into the pots to see how dry they were. She'd watered heavily before she left, and Susan had kept an eye on her plants while she was gone.

Dorrie picked up the mister and sprayed the orchids, which needed as much water through their leaves as through their roots. Bellefleur's bud sheath was half the length of her thumb, she noted with satisfaction. In a few more weeks, the buds would begin their long, slow job of flattening the sheath, which would finally split open under their pressure to let them emerge.

Dorrie is dressing for a date. She is young and full of joy, dancing around the bedroom of her teen years in a crinoline petticoat and a strapless lace bra. Standing before the mirror, she raises her arms and lets a flowered voile dress drop onto her body. It is halter-style, backless, with a three-tiered skirt whose hem is eight yards around. Smiling, she pirouettes to admire the flare of the skirt, the creamy skin of her shoulders. She pins a fresh gardenia in her light-brown curls, and its sweetness fills the room.

As she dabs on her new hot-pink lipstick, the doorbell rings downstairs. Dorrie hears the door open, hears her mother's voice invite him in, and dances down the stairs to meet her date.

It is Travis, and he has brought her chocolates.

Twenty-six

Returning to the store Monday morning was like entering a decompression chamber. The Hummel figurines, the patterned china, the silverware, the rings, and necklaces all seemed dull and static. Dorrie had to force herself to pay attention.

"We got along fine!" Zada told her, sounding surprised that Dorrie'd even bothered to ask. She'd only been gone a week, Dorrie thought, and already she was superfluous.

Travis dropped by the store Wednesday in time to take her to lunch. He drove her across town to a fancy tearoom in the European Crossroads.

"So how was your trip?" he asked after they'd ordered. "See anything exciting?"

"It was a whole nother world. We stayed in a place that would put the Taj Mahal to shame, and my friend dropped me, all unaware, smack into the middle of the New Age. Psychics, astrologers, this weird woman who channelled an ancient Egyptian who spoke King James English . . . I'd never seen anything like it."

"Sounds like a freak show. Are you glad to be back?"

"Yes and no. I mean, it's always good to be home. I've got a lot to sort out. But it was fascinating; I'd like to know more about what they're doing."

"What they're doing, sounds like to me, is playing with people's heads. It's all garbage, Dorrie, you know that. Astrology!"

"I know. I always felt that way too—that if you can't explain it logically, it must be false. But now I wonder. Maybe there's more than one kind of logic, just like there's more than one kind of physics."

"What do you mean, 'more than one kind of physics'? I only know of one."

Dorrie fiddled with her napkin as she answered.

"Anymore, I understand, there are two: one for everyday life, so to speak, and one for special occasions. I've been reading up on it: Einstein's theory of relativity blew Newton's laws to smithereens."

Travis was staring at her. How pretentious I must sound! she thought, and felt her face grow warm.

"Well," she finished, "it just makes you think,

is all. If things aren't what they seem, what are they?"

Travis shook his head. "I deal in facts and figures, Dorrie. This magical thinking is beyond me."

"I met this man," Dorrie said quietly, her gaze dropping to her hands. The emeralds in her ring looked dull and heavy. "He knew more about me than he had any way of knowing. I'm not talking about guesses or everyday intuition; I mean detailed knowledge. I don't mind telling you, it made me wonder."

"Your friend was with you. Didn't you say she'd known you all your life?"

Dorrie shook her head. "Charmaine wouldn't. Anyhow, some of it was stuff she didn't know." She looked up. "I watched him fish it out of thin air, Travis. He'd never laid eyes on me before, and he knew what was in my . . . heart."

Travis watched her as the waitress brought their food. When she lifted her fork, he spoke slowly. "Look, I know I'm your accountant, but I'm not just your accountant; I'm your friend too. And as your friend, I have to tell you: this is dangerous, Dorrie. You're extremely vulnerable now, newly widowed, trying to rebuild your life. A lot of these people prey on loneliness and grief." He looked hard at her, as if to emphasize his point, before asking, "Did any of them offer to put you in touch with George?"

292

"No." Dorrie could see that he meant well, but really! "It wouldn't be necessary anyway, Travis. I talk to George all the time."

He reached across the table and covered her hand with his own.

"After Janie passed away I used to think about her a lot too, things I wished I'd said or done while she was still with me. That's normal. But don't get carried away with it, Dorrie." His voice was gentle. "I know how much it hurts—God knows, I know that pain—but George is gone. You can't bring him back."

"I know." There was no point in going any farther with it, Dorrie thought. It would only worry him. "Well, anyway, it was a beautiful trip. We stopped by Arizona on the way home, and I've never seen anything like it."

She switched to a travelogue and then to business for the rest of the lunch hour, and Travis seemed relieved to be discussing solid reality again. After lunch, he drove her back to the store and came in for a few minutes.

"The books are in real good shape," he said, looking up at her from George's desk. "I'm really proud of the way you're taking hold here."

As he was leaving, Travis took both her hands and looked intently into her eyes.

"Dorrie," he said, "I must tell you, I've developed a lot of respect for you over these past few months. And, um . . . I've become fond of you.

293

I really like you, Dorrie. You're a fine woman. But you're so vulnerable right now . . ." He lowered his gaze, and then looked back up at her.

"What I mean is, any time you get to feeling lonesome—like you need a friend—you know where I am. I haven't wanted to rush you, but . . . well, you know where I am."

To Dorrie's utter amazement, he brushed her forehead with a kiss on his way out. Remembering the scene on her way to sleep that night, she could not help smiling. She had known Travis was kind, but his worry for her was a surprise. And the kiss, too . . . that had been sweet.

Dorrie is climbing a cliff. A pale, cold sun gives light without warming her, though she is sweating. She has been climbing for a long time, with little progress, and she can't hang on much longer. A gray sea pounds on sharp rocks beneath her, and gulls wheel, squawking, overhead. They are laughing at her, and no wonder: she climbs awkwardly, slipping back a foot for every two she gains, and time is running out. The cliff face is sheer and slippery, with handholds few and far apart: a stunted tree here, a narrow fissure there.

The rock is slimy with iridescent trails left by fat, pink slugs, some as long as her hand, that crawl blindly around her. The creatures fascinate at the same time they repel her. Slow, mindless, insistent, perhaps seeking only the warmth of her body, they continually bump against her. They do not hurt her, but their touch makes her shudder. They excrete a viscous substance as thick and pale as mucous: her hands, her legs, her body are covered with it, and she cannot hang on much longer.

I am too old for this, she thinks. My muscles are too slack, my back too weak. The smell of the slugs, like sour milk, fills her nose and mouth, and she wishes for a drink of ice-cold water to wash it away. Perhaps there is a fresh spring at the top, she thinks, reaching upward. The largest slug rubs itself against her cheek and she hangs her head, not understanding her shame.

Later that week, walking to lunch past the sporting goods store that had gone out of business in the fall, Dorrie saw shelves going up inside. The old sign over the shop had come down, and on her way back she watched the new one going up: "The Golden Serpent." It sounded almost Chinese, she thought, but the raw memory of her vision made her shiver. The following Monday, a bookstore opened under the new sign. That afternoon, Dorrie called Charmaine.

"You ought to come and visit my new neighbor," she said.

"Oh, yeah? Who's that?"

"I haven't been yet, but there's a new bookstore three doors down. Looks like your kind of place. Why don't you pick me up around half-past four, and we'll go down there before it closes. I've got a story to tell you, anyhow."

A tall woman with hair like drifted snow looked up from behind the counter when they entered the store. Fresh, smooth skin and pink cheeks belied the color of her hair; it must, Dorrie thought, be premature. The woman's round eyes, of an unusual violet shade, were surrounded by laugh wrinkles. Dorrie liked her on sight.

"Can I help you-all find anything?" the woman asked.

"Thanks, we'll just browse," Dorrie said. "I'm your neighbor, Dorrie Greene, from the jewelry store."

"Glad to meet you," the woman said. "Megan Lloyd. I've just come from Taos. How long have you been in business here?"

"My grandfather built the building in the Twenties, but I just took over this fall after my husband died. We've needed a bookstore. I'm glad you're here."

"Thanks. Feel free to look around. There's a little bit of everything here, but we're mainly into metaphysics and self-help."

Dorrie noticed a display of quartz crystals. She glanced through one of the books about them and put it back on the shelf.

"Where did you get the name for your store?" she asked.

"The serpent is an ancient symbol of wisdom," Megan answered. "And I just like 'golden'; it had a ring to it."

"You know what Freud had to say about snakes, don't you?" Charmaine said.

"Of course. But Freud only subverted the symbol a hundred years ago. The serpent has meant wisdom since before Adam and Eve; he offered Eve knowledge, not sex."

Dorrie grinned. "I always did think Eve got a bum rap," she said. "What's wrong with knowledge?"

"It made them like the gods, as I recall," Charmaine said. "I always thought that was interesting too: 'gods,' not 'God.' They were afraid that if Adam and Eve ate from the second tree they'd know they were immortal, and then the gods wouldn't have anything to hold over them. They couldn't have that!"

"Where in the world did you read that?" Dorrie asked. "I don't remember that part of the story!"

"It's in Genesis. The Bible's full of all kinds of amazing stories, if you just read for yourself.

297

I wonder they haven't banned it, for the violence if not the sex."

"Charmaine!" Dorrie said.

"Well, I carry Bibles, too," Megan said. "King James, Revised Standard, Jerusalem, New English, the Aquarian Gospel, the Gnostic Gospels, the Lost Books of the Bible . . . Like I said, a little bit of everything."

"So what's your story?" Charmaine asked Dorrie later that evening. Dorrie was standing at the stove mixing chunks of chicken into vegetables and sauce.

"I had a vision in Arizona," she said. "Scared me so bad I couldn't talk about it till now." She described her experience.

"I don't know what to tell you," Charmaine said at last. "How have you kept it to yourself all this time? My God, a thing like that . . ."

"I had to think about it," Dorrie said. "It was too . . . big."

"It must have shaken you clean down to your boots."

"Shaking *in* my boots is more like it! I didn't like all that crying and laughing. I was out of control, you know?"

"I know. But it didn't matter. You were by yourself, nobody but me to see and I don't mind. Everybody cries sometimes, Dorrie. It's okay to cry if you feel like it."

"I guess. Daddy used to send me away for crying, and George never could handle tears. I learned not to cry in front of him, it hurt him so. Made him feel helpless."

"Did it ever occur to you that that was George's problem? Hell, it's no wonder you've had sinus problems all these years!"

"You sound like Two," Dorrie said.

"Do I? Well, for once in his uptight life, maybe he's making sense!"

"I still don't know what to make of it, Charmaine. I really thought I'd lost it out there. Visions and dreams . . . I'm still wrestling with my grandmother, and here's George telling me I couldn't love him." Dorrie's eyes filled, and she wiped them with the backs of her hands. "See? It's still going on!"

"Well, of course, George never did like me; I always thought that was why he was so stand-offish. Do you mean he was like that with you too?"

"Not as much, but he was always kind of squirmy about intimacy. George was hard to get close to. But why come to me like that now, when he'd had all those years to tell me?"

"Maybe he wanted to comfort you — to let you off the hook, sort of. He was saying it wasn't your fault you couldn't get closer; there wasn't anything you could do about it."

Charmaine stood up and crossed the kitchen

to put her arms around Dorrie. "You were a good wife to him, Dorrie. The best. It's not your fault he was lonely or that he died."

The absolution went through Dorrie like a thousand volts. Every cell in her body tingled in response to it as she stood perfectly still, her tears wetting Charmaine's cheek. She felt her spine straighten and her shoulders lift as she stepped back, her eyes wide.

"I didn't know I thought it was," she said softly. "I thought I'd let it go." She sat down heavily, shaking her head.

"No telling what kind of baggage people are carrying around with them till they let it drop," Charmaine said. "Maybe now you can let it go and get on with your life."

It was time she did that, Dorrie thought later, wrapping the comforter snugly around her in bed. Poor George. Imagine believing nobody could love you! The relief of talking about it made her realize how much effort had gone into keeping the vision to herself. She could sleep for a week.

Walking along a beach, Dorrie hears the shush, shush, shush *of waves at her left and the shrieking of gulls overhead. The sun burns her,* and she moves toward the cliffs to seek shelter.

Squeezing through a narrow fissure in the rock, she finds herself in a tunnel that is like milk glass lit from behind. She follows its pearly walls to a small room where she finds a pedestal on which a mummy stands. Seeing a strip of winding hanging at its head, Dorrie knows she is here to unwrap the mummy.

It is slow work. The winding cloths are stuck together, some with resin but others with blood from the body's wounds. In a niche in the cave wall, she finds a jar of balm and slathers great handfuls of it on the mummy to soak the bandages so she can pull them away.

Dorrie uncovers the head first. It looks like a carving but feels like ancient leather. As she rubs balm into the skin, it begins to soften; the wrinkles fill in, the color is restored, and at last she recognizes her own face. Now she works more urgently to soak off the bandages. At first she is afraid to touch the worst wounds, some still raw and others suppurating sores, but the balm restores everything it touches to glowing health. Dorrie rubs it carefully into every nick and scratch, smoothing away old scars and healing the more recent wounds until the whole body has turned from dessicated leather to peachy, living flesh.

When, after many hours, Dorrie completes the job, the woman steps down off the pedestal and embraces her. Overcome with love and pity, Dorrie shuts her eyes. When she opens them again, the woman is gone.

Slowly, exhausted from her labors, Dorrie makes her way back through the tunnel, squeezes out its narrow entrance, and walks across the warm sands into the sea.

Twenty-seven

Soon after her return from California, Dorrie received a brochure in the mail listing Continuing Education classes at the community college she passed every time she went to Two's house. It might be fun, she thought; get her out of the house at least one night a week on her own. She could do with something intellectually respectable but still mind-expanding, to balance California and Charmaine's books. There, she thought, her finger resting on the class "Women Novelists in the Twentieth Century." That would do. During her lunch break the next day, she drove out to the school and signed up.

Dorrie was expecting a roomful of twenty-year-olds, but the class was made up principally of women in their thirties and forties. The professor was a fuzzy-haired woman with a sweet, fluting voice and an abstracted manner who insisted that the students call her "Elizabeth" instead of "Professor" or "Ms. Gardena." She was several years older than Dorrie, wearing a frilly peach blouse under a severely tailored navy suit.

Elizabeth passed out a sheaf of handouts, including a two-page course description and two lists of books: one to be read and discussed in class, and another to be read for fun. Dorrie looked at the authors: Maya Angelou, Margaret Drabble, Doris Lessing, Alison Lurie, Mary McCarthy, Tillie Olsen, Grace Paley, Alice Walker, Fay Weldon. The list included a book of short stories called *Bitches and Sad Ladies,* and one of the novels was named *The Life and Loves of a She-Devil.*

What was she getting herself into? Maybe she should just take the lists home and forget the class, curl up in the privacy of the orchid room with Domino in her lap, and read herself blind. She'd been out of school too long.

Once the preliminaries were over, the first class period was taken up with a "get acquainted" exercise in which each woman told her name and why she had chosen to take the class.

"I'm Millie Crutcher," said the little woman seated next to Dorrie. "I'm here because my daughter made me come. She wants my 'feminist consciousness' raised. She thinks I'm a wimp."

Dorrie joined in the sympathetic laughter. "I suspect mine does too," she said, "but at least I chose the class myself. I'm just trying to find out what's out there. I think I'm looking for balance, but mostly I'm just groping in the dark."

"A lot of women are," Elizabeth said. "You're not alone in that."

At break, a slender, graying, leather-skinned woman dressed in tan pleated chinos and a flowered silk blouse approached Dorrie. Her midwinter tan and jewelry spoke of money. She was not wearing a wedding ring.

"I'm Lavonne Christy," she said. "Want some coffee or a soda?"

"I'd love some. Where is it?"

"The machines are down this hall. Come on, I'll show you. You haven't been here before, Dorrie?"

"I haven't been in a classroom in thirty-five years. Talk about a fish out of water!"

"Well, don't feel like the Lone Ranger," Lavonne said. "The local colleges are full of widows and divorcees; we probably keep these night classes in business. Besides giving us something beyond ourselves to think about, it's a good place to meet people—men, too, though not in this class."

"That's okay. I'm not looking for one of those. Only lost the one I had about six months ago, and I'm just now getting used to being alone."

They turned a corner and entered a small lounge with metal-and-plastic couches, a few long tables with folding chairs set around them, and food and drink machines. Half a dozen other members of the class had arrived ahead of them and were bunched around the Coke machine.

"Hi, Vonnie," one of them said. She was plump, with falsely golden hair knotted loosely above a cheerful face. "Catch a new one?"

Lavonne laughed. "This is Dorrie Greene. It's her first class. I'm just showing her the ropes."

"Welcome to the club, Dorrie," the woman said. "I'm Marva Chiles. How do you like it so far?"

"It was a little intimidating until I met you-all," Dorrie said, "I saw my last classroom in 1956. But I think I'm going to like it. Have you been coming here long?"

"Two or three years. I take two classes each time, one serious and one just for fun."

Dorrie was afraid to ask. "Which one is this?"

Marva laughed, a rich, warm sound. "I hope it's going to be both," she said. "However seriously you take it, it's great to be among women who've lived a while in this world and talk about how things work. And when you're reading this stuff, you can hardly think about anything else, much less talk of it."

Dorrie hoped she was right.

The next day, she carried her book list to Megan's at lunchtime. Charmaine was there, sharing a brown-bag lunch.

"Hi," Dorrie said. "I didn't expect to find you here."

"Hey, Dorrie! Megan and I were just talking. Turns out we've got mutual friends in San Jose and Taos. What're you up to?"

"I just brought this book list in. Megan's got a little feminist fiction section in the back, and I hoped maybe I could buy some of these from her."

"Let me see," Megan said, reaching for the list. She raked her eyes down it and smiled. "Good stuff. You'll like the Paley. I laughed right out loud, all alone in my bed. What did you do, join a class?"

Dorrie nodded. "Continuing ed, out at Brookhaven."

"Well, I think I can help you out with most of it. Some you'll have to get at the college bookstore, used. So how do you like the class?"

"I think it's going to be interesting. It's all women, like Stofford, so I felt right at home that way. The teacher's a little on the goosey side—wide-eyed and frizzy-haired. Somebody asked her toward the end of the class what you have to do to get an *A,* and she gave us ten minutes on the evils of competition. It turns out it's pass/fail; all you have to do is show up."

"In continuing ed, the idea is to learn it for itself, not for a grade," Charmaine said. "It's all discussion. You won't even have to turn in any papers."

"No, just read the books. We're starting with the short stories. *Bitches and Sad Ladies.* What a name for a book!"

"I've read it," Megan said. "It's got some good stuff in it. The 'bitches' are independent women, and the 'sad ladies' are the ones who can't stand up for themselves."

"Well," Dorrie said, "if that's the choice before me, I guess I'll have to take 'bitch.' I will say, though, it's not a name I ever wanted to be called!"

"Don't you take Thursdays off?" Travis asked over lunch the following Monday.

"Yes." They were eating at a Chinese restaurant four blocks from the store. The walls were covered with bright red fabric. Huge flowered urns stood at the entrance to the dining room, and golden chandeliers gave dim light from above.

"I've got a good idea: I have to go to San Antonio this Thursday to sign some papers. It's only about a half-hour flight, so I'll be home the same night. Why don't you come with me for the day?"

She would have to miss the garden club, but it would be such a nice break . . . and he looked so hopeful.

"Just for the day?"

"Sure. We can have lunch at this wonderful Mexican restaurant and traipse around the Riverwalk eating ice cream in the afternoon, and we can go see the HemisFair—you know, they turned that whole park into the most wonderful museum. They call it the Institute of Texan Cultures. Sounds pretentious, but it's really just an amazing collection of all the Native American and European and African sources Texans came from. There's even ethnic food."

"It sounds like fun, Travis, and I could use the break." She laughed, a little embarrassed. "When things are this quiet, Zada gets on my nerves a little. I feel like she's breathing down my neck."

"Great!" he said. "Can you be ready by half-past seven?"

"What do you think, George?" she asked that evening. She'd carried his picture to the kitchen and set it on the counter while she broiled a piece of chicken and cooked rice and vegetables to go with it. "He's been so kind, and he's never said or done a disrespectful thing."

George had told her—if it was George, there in the canyon at Sedona—to find another man. Though all Travis had asked her for was companionship, she wondered if he wanted more.

"I don't know what to think, though—does he just want to be a better friend, or something else? I got married too young, George; I never had a chance to learn to read the signals."

She thought of Hermes Mason and the day at his house. That had been another matter entirely. Travis was . . . different. He'd never been pushy, even told her he didn't want to

310

push. Dorrie laughed. What made her think he'd make a pass at her in the first place? At what point had she turned from a plump, moderately pretty, middle-aged widow into a Sex Goddess? She was just being silly.

"Prr-rr-owt?" Domino asked.

"Okay," she said. "Just a minute." She poured food into his bowl and gave him a pat.

It would be all right, she thought, quieting the flutter in her stomach. No sense in getting worked up over nothing.

Twenty-eight

Travis arrived at seven-thirty on the dot. Dorrie met him at the door in turquoise linen slacks, a peach-and-azure print shirt, and a teal sweater. She wore flat-heeled shoes.

"Perfect," Travis said admiringly. "We can stop at the pancake house by the airport for breakfast and be on the plane in an hour."

When they arrived at Love Field, they didn't go through the terminal. Instead, Travis parked his car near a northside hangar and they went directly inside.

"Morning, Mr. Burton," a man in coveralls said. "She's all ready for you."

"Thanks, Jim. Let's get these doors open." The men rolled up the huge metal door, and the sun struck the white wings of the little plane as a third man rolled steps up to its side.

"Okay, Dorrie, let's go." Travis climbed the

steps ahead of her and pulled open the plane's door.

"Where's the pilot?" Dorrie asked.

"You're looking at him." He placed his hand at her waist to usher her inside, and Dorrie felt her skin tighten under his touch. Don't be so silly, she told herself, hoping he hadn't felt her stiffen.

"You're flying it?" she said. "You never told me you could fly an airplane!"

"It never came up. Come on, you can sit in the copilot's seat next to me. The view's better, and we can talk."

As they rose over the city and flew south over the countryside, Dorrie was so enraptured she forgot to be scared. She'd never flown in a small plane before, and from there everything was visible: freeways like the spokes of a wheel converging on the city, the traffic reminding her of a cartoon about blood circulation she'd seen in high school; blocks of houses and stores with patches of open land between, looking as if they'd been dropped by a giant hand.

Farther out were toy farms with miniature cows and horses, toothpick fences, and dollhouses facing the roads, which lay like tan yarn between them. Rivers and creeks formed shining ribbons through the brown-and-green earth below.

"When did you learn to fly?" Dorrie asked, somewhere below Waxahachie.

"After Janie was gone, I needed something to occupy my spare time," he said. "I'd always wanted to fly, and the business gave me an excuse. It had grown then, and I had a lot of out-of-town clients. I love it."

"I can see why," Dorrie said. "What an adventure!"

They landed at a private airport in San Antonio, where a car was waiting, and drove into town. Travis took her past the site of the HemisFair that had taken place in the Sixties and, a block away, the Alamo, where palm trees swayed in a walled park.

"We'll go there after my meeting," he said. "I'll only be about a half-hour. Did you bring a book?"

Dorrie patted her large purse.

"Short stories for my class," she said. "Last night was the second meeting."

Travis installed her in a coffee shop in the front of the office building where he would be conducting his business, and a pretty young waitress with bright green ribbons in her hair and brighter black eyes brought her a glass of freshly squeezed orange juice. Instead of reading, Dorrie gazed out the window.

He couldn't have picked a prettier day, she thought. The sun shone down from a brilliantly blue sky, and the air had been growing balmy by the time they arrived; it would be flat warm by this afternoon. She'd been a little uncomfortable driving through the tacky streets around this district, but the district itself was as clean and bright as a house expecting visitors.

The town seemed to have been built in three phases. The first, Spanish Colonial, consisted of the Alamo and other nineteenth century buildings of whitewashed adobe at the center. Frame houses covered in gingerbread had grown up around them at the turn of the century. Stores of tan brick with white trim had been added in the Thirties, when the WPA had come in and dredged the river; the one across the street from her had "1932" inscribed above the door. The most recent additions were sparkling white stucco boxes, mostly hotels with regularly spaced, square windows rising as high as twenty stories above the streets. Somehow the three distinct forms of architecture came together in a pleasing, if eclectic, whole. Flower boxes along the street held scarlet and pink geraniums and dark green elephant's ear.

A bright red trolley passed twice while she sat in the window, picking up and dropping off housewives and waitresses and businesspeople and tourists—not many, at this time of year—dressed in as wide a range of styles as

315

the buildings that surrounded them. Dorrie could tell the people who were heading for work in nearby hotels and restaurants. Most were young, and the women wore brightly colored, flounced skirts with lacy blouses, the men somber black slacks with brilliant white shirts.

"Are you ready?"

She turned to see Travis slip into the seat opposite her.

Dorrie laughed. "What happened? Weren't they there? You haven't been gone but a minute."

He checked his watch.

"Forty-three minutes, but we're all done now. I take it you haven't been bored."

"No. I think I could sit here another hour just watching the people."

"Let's go out among them instead." Travis looked at his watch. "It's half-past ten; the Alamo should be open by now. Let's walk, okay?"

They had the entire Alamo almost to themselves, and Dorrie listened with real interest to the tales of the museum guides. It felt like a church; a sign near the door said, "Gentlemen remove hats." Cases of relics lined the interior walls: swords, bits of children's clothing, uniforms, guns, letters and other documents. Over them was a plaque saying "Be silent, friend, here heroes died to blaze a trail for other men."

Dorrie had grown up in Texas without ever seeing this shrine to its early settlers' heroism, and the thought of their privations and their courage in facing the dangers touched her. She stood for several minutes reading a letter home to Tennessee, written just before the Alamo had fallen. "Whatever happens here," its beautiful, spidery writing said, "remember always that your husband and father will carry you in his heart forever, even after death if it should be." It made her eyes wet.

When they left, they sat out front on a bench until one of the red trolleys came along, and they rode it about a mile to El Mercado, an enormous, mall-like structure that occupied at least a full city block and spilled over into the Farmer's Market next door. Dorrie was fascinated with its shops: souvenir stands; pottery shops; a little art gallery; a drugstore that sold — along with aspirin and cough syrups — herbal remedies and "magical" candles. They passed a leather-goods store and clothing stores full of the brightly colored, heavily embroidered costumes she'd seen on the streets.

"They pay some poor woman in Oaxaca fifty cents an hour to put her eyes out over these and then charge fifty dollars apiece for them," she said. "I wish I could buy from the woman herself."

"You'd look marvelous in one of these," Travis said, holding up a hot pink, peasant-style dress with a heavily embroidered, ruffled collar. "If you're not planning a trip to Oaxaca any time soon, this is the place to pay that poor woman for her work."

"Travis, they're for teenagers," she said. But they were lovely. She found a yellow one with bright red and green birds worked into a geometric design for Wendy.

"Now I'll have to find something for Trey," she said. Not only that, but she'd have to explain what she'd been doing in San Antonio. That would be an evening's entertainment in itself. Well, she thought, in for a penny, in for a pound. At the shop next door, she bought Marcie a Toltec god.

Several entrepreneurs had set up shop in the central gallery, offering everything from tapes of Mexican music to oil-on-velvet bullfighters and dancing girls.

"Oh, look, there's Elvis!" Dorrie said, laughing. "I didn't expect to spot him here!"

"You'll have to contact the *Star*," Travis said. "They'll want to speak to the artist."

At a T-shirt shop, Dorrie found Trey's gift: a shirt portraying an angry armadillo and the legend, "My grandmother went all the way to

San Antonio, and all she brought me back was this!" Next door, she found a big, black, high-crowned hat with feathers in the band to go with it.

After they'd wandered El Mercado from one end to the other, Travis took her back to a restaurant called "Mi Tierra."

"We're lucky to beat the lunch crowd," he said. "They stand in line hundreds deep to eat here." The lobby contained a baked-goods case as long as Dorrie's store was deep, and full of delicious-looking pastries. A hostess seated them at a dark wooden table near the window and brought a menu as big as a book.

"I'll have the *cabrito*," Travis said without opening his. "How about you?"

Dorrie stared at the long lists of foods, recognizing few of their names, and at last decided on the Number Three combination: a chili relleno, two soft cheese tacos, and a crisp meat taco with guacamole.

"What's *cabrito?*" she asked when the waiter had gone away.

"Kid. Baby goat. They barbecue it."

To each his own, she thought, wondering if piglet or lamb would make her feel as queasy.

After lunch, Travis handed her up into the trolley and they rode back to the Riverwalk — *El Paseo del Rio,* the signs said. More than a mile long, with gorgeously decorative bridges arching over the narrow green river — really hardly more than a creek, Dorrie thought — it looped through the tourist district. A block away were the Alamo and the site of the HemisFair grounds, now a park with museums and art galleries. Major hotels were spotted along the *Paseo,* with souvenir shops and restaurants and ice-cream stores between. Ancient, dark cypresses lined the riverbanks, leaning over to see themselves in the slow-moving water. At one end was an outdoor stage, the bank opposite in deep, stone-faced terraces, where Travis said shows were put on in good weather.

"Maybe this summer I can bring you back here," he said. "They perform native Mexican dances in gorgeous costumes every night for a month, and afterward we could go down to the Landing and listen to Dixieland jazz."

"It sounds like fun," Dorrie murmured, unwilling to look that far ahead with him.

In the museum shop, she found an ocarina in the shape of a lizard for Kurt and a handsomely illustrated book about the history of Texas for Two. They went back to the Riverwalk for ice cream cones then and walked most of its length in companionable quiet, stopping frequently to peer into shop windows and commenting to one another on the other tourists.

A churchbell chimed the hour of four.

"It's getting late," Dorrie said. "When did you plan to go back?"

"Pretty soon. We'll catch a cab. If we wait much longer, though, the traffic will be murder."

"I've just got one more gift to buy," Dorrie said. "I haven't found anything for Susan yet, and I can't leave her out."

"What sort of thing would she like?"

"I think I'm looking at it," Dorrie said. "Come on, let's go in here."

She reached for his hand and pulled him into a shop whose window was full of lace. Pinned up on the wall were dozens of mantillas, and she found a white lace triangle a yard wide. Susan could wear it to church, she thought. She would love its daintiness. As the clerk was folding it into a tissue-lined box, Dorrie realized that Travis was still holding her hand.

"Excuse me," she said, embarrassed, and released her hold. When she had paid the clerk and taken the box, Travis took the package in one hand and Dorrie's hand in the other. His hand was short and broad—a mechanic's hand—and strong. The gesture felt possessive, and the public display made her uncomfortable. George had never held her hand, let alone in public.

"Ready?" he said. They left the shop on the street side and found a cab stand. "Got everything?" he asked as he handed her into the back seat.

"I think so," she said, grateful to be let go.

Travis got in beside her and gave the airport address to the cabbie. Dorrie was busily checking her packages and folding them all into the big museum bag.

"What's the matter, Dorrie?" he said. "You seem nervous. Was it something I did?"

"I'm sorry," she said. "I'm just not used to . . . I didn't expect . . ."

"What? I was joking!"

Dorrie blushed and looked down at her packages, still putting little bags inside of bigger ones.

"I'm being silly," she said, keeping her head down. "I just didn't expect you to . . . I'm not used to holding hands, I guess."

He didn't answer for a moment, and she could feel his eyes on her. At last he said, "I'm sorry. I didn't mean to embarrass you."

Had she offended him? Dorrie looked up from her package-arranging, but Travis had turned away and was looking out the window. When they got to the airport, he followed her up the plane's steps and seated her as if nothing had happened, but his mood had shifted: he seemed more thoughtful and less inclined to joke. All the way home, they watched shadows lengthen beneath them as the sun gilded the undersides of the clouds on the western horizon. When they touched down in Dallas, the sun was a salmon-colored half-circle in a purpling sky.

"May I take you to supper somewhere?" he asked as they left the airport.

"It's been a long day, Travis. I'm starting to run down."

"I know. Me, too, but we have to eat. I'll take you home right afterward."

They were only a mile or two from her house. Should she invite him in and fix something? She felt a vague need to make up, though no hard words had been spoken. No. She'd had enough of his company for today, and if he were in her house she'd have to send him home and risk hurting his feelings again.

"All right, but no place fancy. We're not dressed."

They stopped at a JoJo's and had Monte Cristos and decaf. Toward the end of the meal, Dorrie yawned.

"Excuse me," she said. "What time is it, anyhow?"

"Only about seven."

"It's all the excitement," she apologized, "and the walking. I can hardly keep my eyes open."

He smiled across the table. "I'll have you home in thirty minutes, and you can kick your shoes off and collapse on the couch. Have you had a good time, Dorrie?"

"Oh, yes! It was a lovely day, Travis." She yawned again. "Thank you so much for thinking of me."

"Always," Travis said quietly. Dorrie did not answer. She didn't want to know what he meant.

Twenty-nine

On Sunday, Dorrie invited the children to dinner and passed out the gifts.

"What were you doing in San Antonio?" Marcie asked. "I didn't know you'd gone down there!"

"A friend was going for the day and invited me to come along," Dorrie said. "It made a nice break from the store, and the weather was just beautiful. We walked and walked; did the Riverwalk and the Alamo and the Museum of the Americas — you really ought to take the children there some time, Two. And my friend said that in the summer, they have shows at an outdoor stage there. Maybe I'll go back for that sometime."

"What friend?" Two asked. "Was it Charmaine?"

As Dorrie hesitated, Kurt picked up his ocarina and tooted a few sweet notes.

"I want to try," Wendy said. To Dorrie's relief, Two turned his attention to Kurt's efforts to teach her "Pop Goes the Weasel." Saved again, she thought. With any luck, by the time Two got around to wondering about that question again he'd be at home.

February had come and gone, taking the worst of the cold weather with it. One morning Dorrie saw the forsythia on the south side of her house budding. In a week it would make clouds of buttery blooms, to be followed by the brilliant anemones planted in front of it, and she'd have flowers to cut for the house. Winter was nearly done.

"Listen," Charmaine said at lunch that day, "I'm working Megan's booth at the psychic fair Saturday. Want to go?"

"What's a psychic fair?" Dorrie asked.

"I've joined the Psychic Association—Megan's a member—and three or four times a year they put on a fair to raise money. People come and have their fortunes told or listen to lectures or buy stuff: crystals, cards, books. It's fun."

"I can imagine," Dorrie said. It would be a zoo, even weirder than California, with nuts right off the street. "You've joined the psychics now? How psychic are you, Charmaine?"

"About that much." Charmaine held her thumb and finger up about an inch apart. "You don't have to be psychic to join, just interested. Anyhow, don't change the subject. You don't have anything else to do, and there's all kinds of good stuff to look at. We can go for dinner after."

"They all look like housewives and bookkeepers!" Dorrie said. She'd found Charmaine and they were helping Megan set up her bookstall at the fair.

"What did you expect? Turbans?" Megan laughed. "Most of them *are* housewives, and a couple are even bookkeepers. We also have two college professors, a clinical psychologist, and a minister!"

The psychic fair took up an entire ballroom at the Holiday Inn on Central Expressway. Outside the double doors was a ticket seller who gave them identification cards. Inside, tables had been set up around the periphery for the readers, and more tables formed a rectangle in the middle of the room for vendors. Megan had the end nearest the door. Behind her on the left was a man selling unmounted semiprecious stones; on the right was a woman selling reproductions of ancient Egyptian artifacts.

"You know these people?" she asked Megan.

"A lot of them. I joined when I lived in Taos. That's one reason I chose Dallas when I got tired of the desert."

"What are they like?"

"Like anybody, more or less, except for their special talents. Of course, some of them have pretty fancy egos, but I guess that's true of any group with special talents. Musicians are no different, and God knows actors and artists aren't."

"I suppose not," Dorrie said. "I just wonder . . . well, you know that old saying: 'If you're so smart, why ain't you rich?' I don't mean money, necessarily, but it seems that somebody who could foresee the future would be able to avoid a lot of problems the rest of us run into: car trouble, food poisoning, unhappy marriages . . ."

Megan laughed. "Well, you'd think so, wouldn't you. But there's a vast difference between knowing and doing. I don't need to be psychic to know that fats and sugar are bad for me, but I'm still a sucker for a hot fudge sundae."

Dorrie had not expected the large number of people who came in once the doors were opened. Dozens rubbernecked around, looking at the psychics' signs and the vendors' displays, and more sat having their cards or their palms

328

read. She saw a white-haired woman in tears as the young blond reader across from her held her hands and talked earnestly. Another reader cupped his hands around a highly polished obsidian ball and talked in low tones to the scruffy teenaged boy whose fate he was reading.

In her own wanderings, Dorrie approached the table behind Megan's. A small basket held egg-shaped pieces of polished rose quartz; others held uncut carnelians, amethysts, turquoise, and pale green, cloudy aventurines. Next to a box of moss agates was a display of clear quartz crystals ranging from near slivers to six or eight inches long. Some of the smaller ones were attached to the ends of copper tubes, with silver or gold wire wound around the tubing.

"What are those for?" Dorrie asked the man who sold them. Leaning forward, she read his name tag: "John Falconer: The Crystal Wand."

"They're wands," he said.

"As in 'magic wands'?"

He smiled. "Some people think so. Crystals are amplifiers, you know; connecting them that way just makes them stronger. What's interesting to me is the way certain stones seem to have an affinity for certain people. Some people say a crystal calls them."

"Really! How does it do that?"

The man laughed. "Look here," he said, moving a tray of clear stones toward her. "Hold your hand over the tray. Move it slowly back and forth till you feel an impulse to stop, or until one of the stones seems especially attractive to you."

Feeling foolish, Dorrie did as she was bid. As she looked at the stones, she saw a face formed by fractures inside one and picked it up to look more closely.

"There," the man said. "You see? Now hold it loosely in your hand and relax. Relax, now . . . What do you feel?"

"It's warm!" Dorrie said.

"Can you feel its vibration?"

She stared at the stone, intrigued by the face in it; slits of eyes; a long, crooked, high-ridged nose; thin lips, slightly parted as if it were about to speak; a long, narrow beard. Her hand started to tingle.

"That's only your suggestion! It can't be the stone itself!"

He laughed with pleasure at her amazement. "It's yours; it belongs to you."

"Well, I don't know about that, but its face certainly is interesting. What do you want for it?"

"Give me a dollar, just to feel like you paid for it. The stone has found its owner; I can't accept more."

"I can't let you . . . What will I do with it?"

"Put it inside your pillowcase. It'll make your dreams more vivid."

Dorrie smiled. "I'm not sure I want to do that. Half the time, I try hard to forget them!"

She saw a customer approaching.

"Well, thanks for the crystal," she said. She laid a dollar in his hand and slipped the stone into her pocket, pleased as a child with a new play-pretty. Her thumb rubbed its smooth sides and sharp edges, the rough end and the pointed one, over and over as she looked around the room.

Dorrie wandered around the hall looking at the other vendors' displays and picking up bits and snatches of the conversations going on around her.

"Don't trust him," she heard a reader say. "He's real smooth and polite on the outside, but see here?" He pointed to a card with several large swords on it. "That's a stab in the back."

"In the next week," she heard another say. "By mail."

"You'll have to cut that out if you want this thing to go anywhere," an Oriental man said to the frizzy-haired, overdressed woman across from him. "You ruffle his feathers one time too often, and he'll be out of there."

She stopped to look at a display of Tarot cards, amazed at their variety of designs. There was the deck Charmaine had used; Dorrie recognized some of the cards. But the others . . . one was in Spanish, and another was trimmed in gilt. One deck was full of softly romantic pictures that reminded her of the Rackham illustrations in the King Arthur book she'd given Trey. They were pretty enough to mount and frame. She checked the price and went away shaking her head. Not this week, she thought, returning to her table.

Back at Megan's bookstall, Dorrie's eyes strayed across the hall to a tall man with spun-silver hair and deep-set, pale eyes. He didn't seem to need cards or a crystal ball; the man simply looked at his questioner for a long minute, leaned back in his chair, shut his eyes, and started talking. She glanced at him again, fascinated by those eyes, and he caught her looking and smiled. She smiled back and quickly looked away.

"He's something, isn't he?" Charmaine said. "All that talent, and good-looking besides. I picked up his brochure earlier while I was on break. Name's Galen Williams, all the way from Nebraska."

"He doesn't look much like a farm lad to me," Dorrie said. "There can't be that many psychics in Nebraska."

"Well, not that admit it. I reckon there's about as many there as anywhere." Charmaine put a strip of tickets into Dorrie's hands. "He's free for the next fifteen-minute segment. Why don't you go talk to him?"

"What about?"

"Shit, about anything!" Charmaine said. "Your life's in such good order you don't have any questions?"

"I don't know that he could answer them," Dorrie said. "I don't know that anybody could."

"It won't cost you anything; I'm buying. Go talk to him, Dorrie."

Dorrie took the strip and left the booth. The sign over Galen Williams's table said, "Life Readings." He was still talking to someone, so she signed her name on his sheet and backed off several paces to give them privacy. After a few minutes the client stood up, shook Galen's hand, and thanked him. Galen glanced over at Dorrie and down at his sign-up sheet.

"You're Dorrie Greene?"

She nodded, her mouth suddenly dry.

"I've been watching you. Glad you finally decided to drop over. Sit down, Dorrie."

She sat opposite him in a straight-backed chair.

"Give me your hands," he said. She held them out, palms up, and he covered them with

333

his own so that his fingertips rested on her wrists and hers supported the heels of his hands. Broad as a farmer's his short hands were white and smooth. Galen's eyes closed and rolled back under their lids. After a moment, he opened them again.

"How long since your husband died?" he asked.

"Nearly six months."

"I see a lot of gems, jewelry. You were his treasure?"

Dorrie smiled. "In a manner of speaking, I suppose."

Galen laughed softly.

"Oh, I see—it's literal too: a jewelry store. Yours, now."

She nodded.

"You're doing all right, running it, but it's not as exciting as you expected. You've always wanted more excitement in your life, but that's not it."

"It started out exciting," Dorrie said. "A big challenge. But ever since Christmas . . . well, they don't really need me there. They get along fine without me."

"But you feel obligated to do it. What makes it your duty? Why didn't you sell?"

The question surprised her.

"I needed something to do, and I suppose I needed to prove—just to myself, you understand—that I could do that. It's not a duty. I don't think it is."

Galen studied her for a moment. "Business is not your business," he said. "You've done that. It's not what you're here for."

"What am I here for?"

He smiled again. "The same thing we're all here for, I suppose: to learn and to love. But we all come in with specific lessons in mind, and I don't think that's yours."

Dorrie remembered the recurring lost-classroom dream she'd had in her thirties, and had had again just before Charmaine came back.

"How do I find out what mine is?" she asked.

"Keep looking. It will be whatever you feel best doing, what engrosses you most. If you're bored or struggling or you can't make it work, and you're not comfortable with it, it's the wrong thing."

Dorrie shook her head. "You couldn't be more specific? My life's more than half over; if I don't find it soon, I won't have time to learn it."

"You'll have all the time you need," Galen said. "I see a lot of years ahead of you, and you're a natural student. Money's not going to be an issue: I don't see you going hungry, not ever."

He looked up, his eyes pale as a December

sky, and Dorrie remembered the hypnotic gaze of the serpent.

"Just don't let anybody—friends, family, people like me—don't let anybody tell you that you've got to do or not do anything in particular. Find your own way. Choice is what it's all about; don't let anybody interfere with your choices. That's happened too much in the past."

"All right," Dorrie said. "Thank you."

Galen looked at his watch. "We still have a few minutes. Is there anything else you'd like to ask?"

Dorrie looked at his sign.

"I'd like to know if I had some past connection with my husband, but I don't want to talk about it here. Can a person find out that sort of thing for herself?"

"Sure." He reached under the table and brought forth a pad of paper on which he wrote a name.

"See if you can find this book. It may even be in the stall where you're working; it's fairly popular. There's a technique in it that you can use on your own."

"Thanks," Dorrie said.

Megan did have the book.

"May I borrow this for a few minutes?" she asked.

"Go ahead," Megan said. "It'll be almost an

hour before we shut down here. Why don't you go sit in the lounge and read it while you wait?"

She pointed out the room.

"If anybody bothers you, just tell them you're with me," she said.

Dorrie entered the lounge and found it empty. She took a table under an overhead light and opened the book. The technique, once she found it, seemed fairly straightforward, a sort of self-induced waking dream. Why wait? she asked herself. I can do it right here.

In a dim area at the back of the lounge stood a deeply upholstered couch. She made herself comfortable on it, reread the instructions until she felt sure of them, and closed the book. Well, here goes, she thought. Her palms were moist. She wiped them on her skirt, took the crystal out of her pocket, stared at its face for a moment, and shut her eyes.

She is standing outside her front door, focusing on a nick in the paint on the window's crossbar. She turns, sweeping her glance past the end of the porch to the street, walks eight paces to the steps, and descends— one, two, three, four—to the walk, aware of the change from wood to concrete underfoot.

Now she walks to the street where she turns back to face the house.

Dorrie takes a deep breath and feels herself rising, rising, until she is looking down at the roof. It needs a patch over the back bedroom, she notes, and the wooden fence behind the house is beginning to sag.

She turns north and soars over blocks of houses, over a park, faster and faster, over the freeway that circles the city and on over the countryside, so fast that the land below becomes a blur. Soon, she tells herself, she will land in another time and place, a place she has been before, in another body, with George.

Her flight slows, and she looks down upon the British Isles lying like emeralds set in a silver sea. Northeast she flies, over Ireland to a narrow spot north of England where the seas cut deeply into the island on either side. She begins her descent toward a city on the eastern coast, noting its location in order to find it on a map later, when she returns from this journey.

The city is cold and gray, full of stone. Its streets are full of men and women in early Victorian dress, horse-drawn wagons whose iron wheels clatter on the cobblestones. There are few gardens. Dark smoke rolls out of the chimneys, laying a pall over the cold city. She glides into a narrow street of tall houses with many-gabled, slate-tiled roofs and enters the richest one.

There she sees a woman, not young but hugely pregnant, weeping inconsolably. The woman's husband has been killed by highwaymen on his return from London where he has been on business. A young boy—it is George—clings to her, saying, "Don't cry, Mama. Please don't cry."

The woman goes into labor, gives birth to a girl child, and soon dies. The child, Dorrie knows, is herself.

Now the scene changes. Years have passed. The baby is a young woman: slight, dressed all in gray, with smooth black hair pulled severely back into twin chignons behind her ears. She is standing with her back to the fireplace in which a meager fire glows. Her head is bowed, her hands behind her. George, now in his thirties, sits stiffly on a dark horsehair sofa, lecturing her.

"I would sooner go to my grave than send an innocent woman into the suffering of childbirth," he says. "I shall never marry, and I have refused all suitors for your hand as well. So long as I live, I shall protect you from that dreadful fate."

"Hugh is as good a man as ever lived," the girl says. "Surely he can protect me! And as to the dangers of childbed, I am willing to face

339

them. The world is full of women who have dared and lived to see their children grow."

"No," George repeats. "Not while I live."

Now Dorrie sees a series of later scenes from that life, in which the young woman has all the privileges of the mistress of a fine house but is never allowed a husband. Her brother rejects suitor after suitor until they stop asking. Her beauty fades. She manages his household, arranges his meager social life, distributes his alms, and sits silently in the evenings as they read, side by side, near the fire; she gives her love to the children of the poor, dies a virgin at eighty-four, and is laid away in a cold and narrow grave.

Dorrie withdraws from the empty house to rest above the clouds. She is sad, but her sorrow cannot outweigh her outrage at the unfairness of what she has seen. The rage explodes, blowing her across the oceans and the earth with a power she has never felt before. She lands with a thud on her own front porch and opens her eyes to find herself on the battered couch at the psychic fair.

Breathing hard, Dorrie felt the blood pounding in her ears, the anger coursing through her veins. Her fists were clenched, her whole body taut with rage.

How dare he! she thought. Who did he think he was, God Himself, to steal her life that way? By what right had he imprisoned her in that cold stone house for all those years?

You could have eloped, a voice within her said. *You didn't have to accept his decision.*

Oh, shut up! she told it. I never had a chance! Hell's bells, he *raised* me to be his servant!

And what about this time? You chose it this time.

They chose it! George and my father set me up while I was away at school, and I was too dumb to know any better. I *trusted* them!

You let it happen, the voice said. *It was not a shotgun wedding, Dorrie; you could have said no. When are you going to take responsibility for your own life?*

Fury blazed through her once more, a fine rage that reddened her face and set her mind afire.

"Right now!" she said aloud. "This very minute!" Dorrie lifted her wrist to check the time, and her rings caught her eye. The emeralds were dull and lifeless, dirty looking. She pulled the rings off and dropped them into her purse.

There could be no way to check its facts, she thought, but her "memory" had felt true as the world. She never had understood why, when all her friends were marrying for romantic love, she'd chosen George. It wasn't just to please Daddy, though it had pleased him; it had been some recognition in herself that it was intended, the right thing to do.

In forty years of knowing George, she'd never had a romantic thought about him, and sex had ended almost before it began. After George's vasectomy, except for occasional lapses, they *had* lived like brother and sister. And she had worried and stewed and wept salt tears because George didn't want her anymore, thinking all the time it was her fault . . . *Damn* his eyes!

The flood of memories made her so furious she started to shake. Orphan be damned! He'd never had it in him to love her like a husband! He'd cheated her of that love not once, but twice, left her to wonder what was wrong with her to deserve such unnatural treatment . . .

Dorrie's fists clenched. And I chose it, I chose it, *I chose it!* she told herself, pounding her fist upon her leg. What kind of ninny would choose a life like that? And whatever had possessed her to let it continue?

Well, blast him to perdition! Next time he could just pick somebody else to cure him of his fears. Dorrie wasn't about to put herself through that again, not for anybody!

Just before they shut down for the afternoon, a woman approached Megan's table. Dorrie was relieving Charmaine, taking a brief turn as bookseller.

"Excuse me," the woman said, "but don't I know you? I'm Alicia Talbott."

Dorrie looked up. The woman was tall and thin, thirty years past coltishness but still as angular as a worn fence. Her face was long and narrow, the eyes large and bruised looking, the mouth turned down at the corners. Looking at her, the phrase "walking wounded" popped into Dorrie's mind.

"I'm sorry," Dorrie said. "I don't think so. I have one of those faces; I look like everybody's old friend's sister." She smiled. "May I help you find anything? What subjects are you interested in?"

"I like spiritual writing. Inspiration," the woman said. She picked up Walter Friml's latest book and turned it over in her hands. "What do you think of this one?"

"I haven't read it. I met him in California recently."

"Did you really? What's he like? I'd love to meet him!"

Dorrie smiled. "He's very . . . positive. He was talking about the book, but I didn't hear; somebody else was talking to me. I've read other works of his, though. He's a serious writer, no sensationalist."

"Well," the woman said, "his approach is a little overintellectual for me. He sounds more like a professor of logic than somebody talking about the life of the soul." As she said "soul," her eyes widened and she sighed.

"You like a more poetic approach?" Dorrie said.

"Did you read Bach's *The Bridge Across Forever* and *One?* I loved those! And Rod McKuen . . . he writes so movingly about love. After all, love is what it's all about, isn't it?"

The woman laid Walter's book down and picked up a small book of verse bound in lavender cloth. Opening it, she read aloud:

"When all is said between us, dear,
Just this remains: love casts out fear.
Let us exchange, then, heart for heart,
And Death itself cannot us part."

She looked up from the page and sighed again. "My dear husband made his passage several years ago," she said, "but now I understand—he isn't dead; he's just gone on ahead to wait for me." She patted the book. "Thoughts like these help me not to miss him so terribly."

"Have you read this?" Dorrie asked, holding up another book. "I lost my own husband recently, and a friend gave it to me for Christmas. It was written by a medical doctor who got his patients to tell him about their near-death experiences. Many people think it's as close as we can come to proof of life after death. It's only anecdotal evidence, of course, but it's been a comfort."

"I can't bear to read about death," the woman said. "The subject is so harsh. I prefer to take comfort in my poetry."

Alicia Talbott paid for her comforting book and left Dorrie more depressed than she had felt since before Christmas. Dear God, she thought, is that what I'm doing? Just killing time while I wait to join my dear departed, a man who's wrecked two lives for me already? Rose, where are you now? she wondered, but there was no answer. She must have imagined that too.

This was what Travis had warned her about: becoming that poor, sad, foolish woman, enshrouding herself in sentimental doggerel to shield herself from loneliness. Dorrie shuddered.

She was quiet as she helped pack up Megan's stock and remained nearly silent all the way home in the car.

"How about supper?" Charmaine asked.

"I'm too tired," Dorrie said. "You two go ahead without me. I'm just going to have a bowl of soup and go to bed."

It was half-past six when she let herself into the empty house. George stared at her from the mantelpiece, a mute question on his face. She picked up the picture and turned it face down on the mantel.

"I'm too angry to talk to you right now," she said. "Some other day, George. I've got to figure out a way to forgive you and let you go, but first I have to forgive myself."

She kicked off her shoes and padded around the kitchen, warming a can of Campbell's Soup for One and toasting an English muffin, too restless to sit and too tired to stand.

Travis was right. She had to quit this, let it go and get on with her life. It wasn't healthy, all this messing around in the unknowable past. When she'd set out to discover who she was, she'd never dreamed she'd find such a wimp! Well, that made two things she couldn't be anymore: George's wife, and a dishrag. Here she'd thought she was doing so well, and now look at her! She just felt so worn out. Even tears were too much effort, and what good were they anyway?

When her food was ready, Dorrie sat at the kitchen table and dug in her purse for her address book. Pulling down the telephone, she dialed Travis's number.

Thirty

"Dorrie!" Travis said. "What a nice surprise!"

"I'm not interrupting you, am I?"

"Not a bit. I was just watching a rerun of a show I didn't care about the first time. Are you all right?"

"I guess so. I just — You said to call if I got lonesome. I guess I'm lonesome."

"Have you eaten?"

"I'm eating now. Soup. I was too tired to fuss."

"Put it in the fridge, and I'll bring you Chinese. What do you like? Sweet and sour? Almond chicken? Fried rice?"

"You don't have to do that. I just wanted somebody halfway sensible to talk to."

Travis laughed. "I'd really like to come over if it's no imposition. Just wait for me, okay? About half an hour."

"I'm not going anywhere."

His enthusiasm was a bit more than Dorrie'd bargained for. She took a quick shower and blew her hair dry, suppressing the tinge of anxiety that rose within her. You're being ridiculous, she told her reflection. He's just coming over to sit with the widow lady, that's all. But all the same, she took extra care with her hair and makeup. No need to look any worse than she had to, she thought.

Dorrie had just tied the sash on the azure silk lounging pajamas she'd bought in California when the doorbell rang. She ran down the stairs to answer it.

"Come in," she said, taking the white paper sacks out of his hands. "Travis, this smells wonderful! You really didn't need to . . ."

"It was no trouble. The restaurant's just around the corner from my place, and I hadn't eaten yet either."

He came into the kitchen to help her dish it up. It made her uncomfortable. George had never set foot in the kitchen for anything more complicated than a glass of water. Dorrie set the table, watching out of the corner of her eye as Travis found the serving dishes and emptied the paper boxes into them.

"Janie never did like to cook much," he said. "I learned out of sheer self-defense, but then I loved it. She used to sit at the table and read the paper to me while I worked."

"That must have been nice. It sounds so . . . companionable."

"It was. That was before it was the fashion for a man to bring home the bacon and cook it too, but she did her share." He laughed. "My Janie was

348

one devil of a mechanic. I never had to fix a lawn mower in eighteen years."

After supper, he rinsed the dishes and put them in the dishwasher while Dorrie put the leftovers away. Then he followed her into the living room and picked up the *TV Guide*.

"What's on?" she asked. They settled on a "Live From Lincoln Center" salute to George Gershwin, and the rich chords of the "American in Paris" suite filled the room. Dorrie found a forgotten bottle of white wine in the back of the refrigerator and poured them each a glass, but she could not sit still to drink it. Every time she settled, she thought of another task that needed doing and jumped up to do it.

The fourth time she rose from the couch, Travis took hold of her wrist.

"What now?" he asked.

"My plants. I forgot to mist them."

"They'll live through the night, Dorrie. For pity's sake, sit down. Rest yourself." He continued to hold her hand as Dorrie sat stiffly beside him on the pillow-backed couch. When the Gershwin program shifted to show tunes, Travis stood up.

"Dance with me, Dorrie," he said.

She felt her body loosen as they danced to the sweet old songs: "Embraceable You," "How Long Has This Been Going On?" and, at last, "I've Got a Crush on You." Travis was a much better dancer than George had been, more supple and rhythmic, easier to follow. His hand at the small of her back gave firm but subtle signals, guiding her gently through the steps. Dancing was such an intimate act, Dorrie thought. She had never been comfortable dancing with strange men, adapting to their rhythms, accommodating herself to their bodies . . . but Travis was not a stranger. Hadn't he said he was fond of her?

"I haven't danced in years," she said.

"You're very good. It's nice to dance with a woman who remembers the old songs, the old steps."

When the concert ended, he switched off the television.

"What did you do today?" he asked.

"My new friend—the one who owns the bookstore—had a stall at a psychic fair. Charmaine and I helped her out."

"A psychic fair? That must have been interesting."

"It wasn't what I expected, though I don't know just what I did expect. They all seemed so ordinary. You think, Gypsy ladies and men with long robes and turbans . . . but it wasn't like that. There was a black man there in one of those whattayoucallits, a dashiki, but most of them looked just like anybody. And an awful lot of people came through—more than I would have believed."

"Did something happen to upset you? You didn't sound like yourself on the phone."

"Nothing, really. Right at the end, I was talking to this poor woman. I just felt so sorry for her.

She broke my heart."

"What was the matter?"

"Well, she'd been widowed for several years, and it seemed like she couldn't let go of him, like she was just waiting for the time she could join him." She glanced down. She'd forgotten to put her rings back on, and her hand looked naked. "It was just so sad."

"Yes. But she isn't you, Dorrie. You're doing real well. George has been gone less than six months, and look at you: you're running the store, you've been on a vacation with your friend . . . and now you're sitting here with me." He laid his hand against her cheek. "I think you're doing real well."

Tears filled her eyes. "I hope so," she said. "I can't bear the thought of ending up like that."

Travis pulled her to his chest and folded his arms loosely around her.

"You won't," he said. "That's nothing for you to fear." He rubbed her shoulder and let her cry for a minute. "I used to miss Janie so bad I thought I'd die, but it gets easier after awhile. I promise it does."

Dorrie pulled away and reached for a tissue. "I'm getting tearstains all over your shirt," she said. "Honestly, Travis, this isn't what I called you for."

"I know," he said. "It's okay." He put his arms around her again, laid her head into his neck, and stroked her hair. She could feel his pulse in her

351

temple, and its regular *ka-thud, ka-thud* calmed her. His body felt solid as an oak. Travis rubbed her back and shoulders with loose, rhythmic strokes, and she could feel herself softening under his hands.

"Dorrie?" he said.

"Mmmmm?"

He lifted her chin and looked into her eyes. "I'd like to kiss you. May I do that?"

She looked at him for a long moment. Saying no had never been easy, she thought, even when she wanted to, and he was being so kind . . .

"All right."

The kiss, gentle and searching, surprised her. She hadn't had a kiss like that since she was a girl, and it stirred long-lost memories in her body.

"Mercy!" she breathed, and he laughed softly. "You're some kisser, you are!"

He gave her another, this one more intense. A flutter of guilt arose in the back of her mind, and she put it down. Accepting Travis's kisses would do no harm. Responding to an unexpected hunger, she took a third, and then another. His hand slid down her back and pulled her closer. Dorrie felt like a block of ice set out in a tropic sun.

Travis laid his mouth against her ear. "Dorrie? Let's take it upstairs."

He stood up and pulled her into his arms for another ravishing kiss. Dorrie's legs would hardly hold her. She took his hand and led him silently up the stairs.

She woke early in the morning, her legs tangled in the puffy comforter, one foot icy cold, aware before she opened her eyes of the warm, stocky body behind her, the heavy arm over her waist. Not George, she thought, and then remembered. She was naked.

Gently, she lifted the arm and moved out from under it, praying Travis would not wake before she had her clothes on. Leaving George's robe on the bedpost for her guest, she stepped into the closet, slipped into her own robe, and silently gathered clothing to take down the hall to the bathroom. Travis slept like a stone. She could hardly even hear him breathe.

Well, she thought, standing under the hot shower, it wasn't quite what she'd had in mind, but she wasn't sorry. Embarrassed . . . she was that, but she'd live through embarrassment. Please, God, she thought, let him be as sweet this morning as he was last night!

She blushed. Three times, at their ages! The first so feverish, so wild to get at each other that they hadn't even turned on the light, but made love by the streetlight shining through the window. Nothing had mattered except to bare each other's flesh, to touch and taste and make that connection. Dorrie had read about such heat, but had never felt it before. And then, the second slow buildup: she had been amazed at his second erection growing against her thigh, and he'd grinned and said, "I can't help it. You make me feel like a twenty-year-old kid!" That time he had stroked and petted her, kissed her in places that shocked her, done things for her pleasure that she had never even imagined until she'd had a series of orgasms that left her shaken and exhausted. They had slept then, but woke again before dawn to find themselves at it again, sweet and sleepy.

"I hope you won't expect this of me every time," Travis had said, smiling, afterward. "I couldn't live up to it. I can't believe that happened."

"Me either," Dorrie said. "Travis, we're too old for this! We need to get some sleep!"

"Tell him," he said placing her hand on his dormant penis. She felt it stir and lifted her hand.

"Now, cut that out!" she'd scolded, laughing. Travis had curled himself around her and held her breast in his hand as they drifted off to sleep again.

Dorrie cut off the water and stepped out of the shower to find Travis waiting with a heated towel. He wrapped it around her and then hugged her.

"Morning, beautiful," he greeted her.

"Good morning," Dorrie said, flustered. "I hope I left enough hot water for you. You were sleeping so soundly . . ."

Travis laughed. "Judging by last night, a cold shower won't do me a bit of harm!"

She turned her back as he dropped George's

robe over the toilet lid and stepped behind the shower curtain. Drying herself quickly, Dorrie put her robe back on and carried her clothes back to the bedroom to dress.

By the time Travis came downstairs, the table was set and she had french toast browning on the griddle. Bacon sizzled on the stove, the coffee was made, and she'd poured herself a cup. She dished up the breakfast, handed Travis his plate, and sat across from him.

"How do you feel?" he asked.

"Surprisingly well," she confessed. A little stiff, but he didn't need to know that. "Yourself?"

"Great. Slept like a top."

"I should think you would!" Looking at him was difficult, and she didn't know how long she could keep up the banter.

"It was a lovely night, Dorrie," Travis said softly. "Lovely in every way."

"For me, too. I just . . . well, I hadn't planned on it."

"I know. I didn't either, but I'm real glad it happened."

"Yes. I just need a little time to think about it, that's all." She looked away from him. "I'd never been with anybody but George. I didn't know what to do."

"You did fine. You were wonderful." Travis took a sip of coffee, eyeing her over the rim of his cup. "Never?"

Dorrie blushed as the memory of her day with Hermes surfaced. That had been a dream, she told herself sternly. She didn't need to confess her dreams to Travis.

"Well, there was a little fumbling around in 1947 Chevys but . . . no. Not that."

"That's amazing." Travis took another sip and set his cup down. "How does that happen in this day and age?"

"It didn't happen in this day and age; it happened almost forty years ago. Nice girls didn't then. And then I married George, and that was that. I never felt especially virtuous about it; that was just how it was."

"And George . . . you don't have to answer if you don't want to, but I take it George wasn't very . . . uh . . . experimental?"

"He wouldn't put in cable for the longest time because it carried sexy movies late at night. I finally talked him into it for the arts channel."

Travis grinned. "Did you ever see any of those movies?"

Dorrie blushed again. "One or two, after he died. They were interesting, but I finally had to turn them off. I don't think I'm cut out for voyeurism."

He laughed. "Never mind. I've always felt people learn better by doing anyway."

Dorrie heard a thump at the front door.

"Paper's here," she said, rising. "I'll go get it."

He'd gone home around noon, and she'd spent the rest of the day and night trembling on the brink of an anxiety attack and avoiding the front room where George's picture still lay face-down on the mantelpiece. What would Travis think of her now? What would sleeping together do to their business relationship? Would he think he owned her now, like a husband? What if it didn't work out — would she have to find another accountant? Where had he learned to do all those wonderful things, and would he want to do them again?

"Are you all right, Dorrie?" Zada asked her the next day. "You seem distracted."

"Something on my mind," Dorrie said, embarrassed. "I'll straighten myself out during lunch."

She'd gone home at noon, fixed a bowl of soup and some toast, and sat down in the orchid room to pull herself together. Bellefleur's sheath had pushed itself out to the length of her thumb, and it was beginning to fatten at the bottom with buds to come. Dorrie envisioned the flowers: stiff, crystalline, white petals and sepals tipped with pink, a ruffled carnelian lip. She wondered how many there would be on the stem.

Zada greeted her on her return to the store.

"You just missed Mr. Burton. He left something on your desk. Said to call it to your attention."

Controlling her urge to dance, Dorrie sped

back to the office to find a wrapped giftbox. Inside was a box of chocolates with a poem, copied out in Travis's careful hand, taped to the top:

Oh, what unutterable bliss
I felt, receiving your first kiss!
And, my lascivious touch returned,
Ah! how my soul and body burned—
The very marrow of my bones
Made merry by your fullblown moans!

Inventive beyond all comprehension,
We found a mythic fourth dimension
And stayed until the morning's light
In that sweet wonderland of night.
Sweet Dorrie, a blessing undisguised
Are you, and one most highly prized!

(If this seems a fool's exaggeration,
Know you have caused this wild elation.
Forgive my tripping, stumbling tongue;
That's how it is when old's made young!)

                                                    Travis

Thirty-one

Charmaine dropped by the store on Wednesday in her "I'm from Big D" outfit: faded bluejeans, a sheepskin-lined denim jacket, and a huge black Stetson hat with a whopping yellow silk rose and feathers stuck in the hatband. She had accessorized this fetching getup with alligator boots, a silver concho belt, and Navajo necklace and earrings: huge chunks of turquoise set in handworked silver.

"Hey, girl, what you been up to?" she greeted Dorrie.

"Does it show?" Dorrie was only half kidding. She'd felt unlike herself all week, obsessing on Travis and sex and starting over and George and how much to tell the kids, and Travis and sex and starting over . . . The thoughts whirled in her mind without end, exhausting her, making it impossible to concentrate on anything else. She couldn't even read her homework. Having gone through the poem word by word times beyond number, looking for clues to its meaning, she had it firmly committed to memory by now—but she'd put a hundred interpretations on it and why he'd sent it. Her favorite was that the verse was the true outpouring of joy it pretended to be. The worst was that he was turning the experience into a joke, or simply gloating.

"What? You look just the same to me." Charmaine looked at her more closely. "Well, sort of. Something worrying you?"

"I'll work it out."

"Want to go to lunch? I've just been down at Megan's and thought I'd stop by. It's almost noon."

"Sure," Dorrie said. She walked to the back, got her sweater, and told Zada she was leaving. "Can I bring you anything?"

"Just a sandwich, if you go somewhere they have them. Ham and swiss on whole wheat would be nice."

At lunch, Charmaine pulled a sheet of lavender paper from her purse. "I got just the thing to take your mind off your troubles," she said, pushing it across the table. "Take a look at this."

The paper said "Dallas Psychic Association" at the top, and below was a list of courses with their meeting times and tuition costs.

"Good lord, Charmaine, what are you doing

with this?"

"Got it from Megan just now. Look here, there's one called 'Developing Your Psychic Potential.' Don't you think that would be fun?"

"Just what I need. I don't have enough on my hands with all that stuff that happened in Sedona and the store and my class and . . . Sure, Charmaine, sign me up."

"Don't be such a poop. Come on, Dorrie, it'll be fun."

"That's what you said the last time, and I thought I'd lost my mind. I'm still not sure I haven't."

"You're saner than anybody I ever knew; your only problem is, you don't believe it yourself." She grinned. "Remember when you said you'd always wanted to do something adventurous? And I said I'd find something, didn't I? Well, girl, this is it: I'm calling in my chit. You're going exploring in unknown territory."

Psychic development's not a patch on the exploring I've gotten into, Dorrie thought. It should be a snap. She knew better than to argue any further. She never had been able to get around Charmaine once her mind was made up.

That evening, Travis took her to the movies. He held her hand through the show, and his thumb rubbed absently against her fingers and explored her palm in a way that was at once companionable and unsettling. When the hero folded the heroine in his arms and they fell into bed, Travis squeezed her hand. She felt like a teenaged girl in a middle-aged body.

Afterward, he drove her home and parked his car at the back of the driveway.

"Would you like to come in?" she asked. "I could make some coffee."

"Sure." He followed her into the kitchen and sat at the table. "Is something wrong, Dorrie? You're awfully quiet this evening."

"Just thinking." She laughed softly, embarrassed. "I can't stop thinking."

"Me either. It's wonderful."

"Wonderful and terrible. I can't think about anything else, just what happened and what of it."

"What of it?"

"Well, aside from everything else—the kids, our business relationship, George . . . the moral aspects of it—I just wasn't ready, Travis. I always have to think about things before I do them; been that way all my life. It was . . ." she smiled ruefully and shook her head, "well, it was a shock to my system. Several systems."

Travis chuckled. "You seem to be recovering nicely. And what happened wasn't so terrible. It wasn't like 'straight sex,' for its own sake, you know; I thought it was real sweet and friendly." He took her hand again. "Neither of us is married, Dorrie, we like each other a lot, and we're not hurting anybody. There's no reason for it to change what goes on at the store—we can be as discreet as you like there. George is gone, and at the moment it's none of the kids' business. The world has changed, Dorrie. Nobody cares anymore who sleeps with whom."

"I know, but that's other people. I just never imagined myself in bed with a man I wasn't married to, or even talking about it. Not that I want to talk about it! We hardly even know each other when you think about it."

"Well, we'll just have to work on that. I want to know you, Dorrie, and in a much deeper sense than the Biblical."

"Maybe that's what scares me," she said. "I don't know that George ever did."

Dorrie's life fell into a new routine: classes on Wednesday nights, weekends hacking around with Travis, occasional Sunday dinners with Marcie or Two, and work through the week. Business lunches with Travis became more frequent, and she would soon be starting classes with Charmaine. When she attended the March meeting of the garden club, Grace Imbry chided her for her absence the previous month.

"We've worried about you," she said. "I tried to call a few times, but you weren't there."

"Dorrie's busy as a bug these days," Jessie said. "Lord, coming and going at all hours, you never saw the like! There's this nice-looking man in a black Lincoln, keeps coming over—who is that, Dorrie?"

"He's my accountant," Dorrie said. She'd forgotten how Jessie watched the street. What must she think? "He's teaching me to keep my books."

"Uh-huh," Jessie said. "Well, he's the best looking accountant I ever laid eyes on, I'll give him that. And he dresses like a million dollars. Married?"

"I haven't asked," Dorrie said. "Who's our speaker today?"

She would have to caution Travis; it was no use talking to Jessie about it. Use her own car more, and come in the back door. Even Jessie couldn't see through a wooden fence.

"What do you think about it?" she asked Domino later. "Here I haven't even told my own kids, and the whole garden club is talking!"

She'd been reading *The Color Purple* and had laid it down to rest from the awfulness of that poor woman's life. There were worse things, she thought, than being ignored; Celie would have been delighted to be ignored. Her situation was so painful that Dorrie could only take it in little bits. Now the book lay face down over the arm of the pink couch, and the cat had jumped into her lap.

"I'm going to have to say something pretty soon," she told him. "It's not fair. Kurt will be tickled silly, and Marcie won't mind, but Two . . . I really can't deal with Two right now."

"Pff-ffft," Domino said. He patted her cheek with his paw, jumped to the back of the couch, and batted at Bellefleur.

"Leave that plant alone!" Dorrie said. She stood up to stop the pot's swaying and stuck her finger over the edge into the tree bark it was planted in. Almost time to water again, she thought, but a good misting would do for today. The sheath had fattened. She could see the outlines of three buds.

"Trr-rrow?" Domino called. He was on his way to the kitchen.

"I'm coming. Lord, you're worse than a kid!"

Dorrie is in an airport where Travis has come to meet her plane. She has been traveling with George, but he went on and sent her back home alone. Now Travis is helping her to collect her luggage.

They have a hard time getting out of the airport, getting separated in the crowd, reuniting, then losing first their way and then the car; but at last he turns on the engine and prepares to drive her home. Dorrie is leaning over the back seat, counting her bags.

"I'm missing one," she says, "I've lost the camera bag." The bag is George's, full of special lenses and filters.

"You'll never find it now," he says. "It's lost. You might even have left it behind in Europe."

"Well, it's a shame," Dorrie says. "It had a lot of valuable equipment in it."

"You can afford to replace it now," Travis tells her.

He is right, Dorrie thinks. She'd like to have it for old times' sake, but the camera was badly out-of-date. It's time for a new one, and George's old lenses and filters won't fit a new camera.

On Sunday, Two and the family picked Dorrie up on their way home from church. Over dinner, he asked her about the store.

"I guess I'm doing all right," she said. "Sales are back up after the post-Christmas slump, and of course we're heading into weddings and graduations. Travis told me at lunch last week that we're doing better than we have for several years."

"Travis?" Two said.

"You remember Travis Burton, Dad's accountant."

Two frowned. "You had lunch with him?"

"Mm-hmm."

366

"Dad never had lunch with him."

"I don't know whether he did or not. I enjoy it."

"I don't like it," Two said. "I've heard about those two-martini lunches. Never did believe you could do any serious business at one." He shook his head, frowning his disapproval. "The books are at the store. How can you talk about them in a restaurant?"

"Martinis! Really, Two!" How could anybody so thick maintain a medical practice? "Not that it's any of your business, but we usually have soup and a sandwich. He comes by the store to check the books."

"Usually? *Usually,* did you say? You mean, now that he knows exactly what you're worth, he's started taking you to lunch? Really, Mother, I thought you had better sense!"

Dorrie stiffened. "Only God knows exactly what I'm worth," she said. "Travis just knows my financial situation."

Two shook his head, irritated.

"You know what I mean. I just don't want anyone to take advantage of you."

"Bull."

Two's jaw dropped. Susan went pale, Wendy's eyes widened, and Trey didn't even try to hide his grin. Dorrie laid her hands in her lap and started counting her fingers. When she spoke, her voice was low and firm.

"I've told you this before, Two, and I wish

you'd listen. I am not a ninny. I am an adult, no-longer-married woman with sense enough to operate a business at a profit. Despite your apparent opinion to the contrary, I can operate my private life as well. And you might as well know: it's not just lunch. I'm seeing him in the evenings too."

Two drew breath to protest, but she raised her palm to stop him.

"And that, my dear son, is the end of this discussion."

Surprised at her own satisfaction over the modest victory, she turned to her grandson. Trey's grin was as wide as his face.

"So. How did you like the King Arthur I brought you, Trey? It was my father's book, you know. I always loved the illustrations, did you?"

After dinner, she helped clean the kitchen, grateful that for once Susan didn't shoo her out.

"He really does worry about you, Mother," Susan said timidly, studying the pot she was scrubbing. "He doesn't mean any disrespect."

"I know," Dorrie said. "It's just that George always kept me wrapped in cotton batting, all our lives together, and I let him get away with it. He was my husband, and he was older, and he needed the feeling of taking care of me. But Two is my *son!*" Bending to stack plates on edge in the dishwasher, Dorrie looked up at her daughter-in-law.

"George did his level best to keep me a child," she said, "and he almost succeeded. When he died, I didn't even know who I was without him to tell me. I couldn't do one thing but cook and keep house, and I didn't have anybody left to do that for. I'd never made a major decision alone in my life, just told him what I wanted and let him decide." She stood upright and looked into Susan's shocked face.

"He thought he was doing right by me, honey, but when he was gone I felt like one of those ancient Chinese women with bound feet. I could hardly take a step on my own."

She lifted Susan's chin and looked into her eyes.

"Don't let that happen to you, Susan. I see Two treating you just like his father treated me; it's all he knows, all he ever saw growing up. But don't let him cripple you. Start planning now. Your children will be grown in ten years — what will you do then?"

Susan's eyes were wide. "I don't know," she said.

"Think of something," Dorrie told her, snapping the dishwasher shut. "And don't let it be a surprise. Start talking about it now, to pave the way."

"Mom, he'd have a fit! Last year when he was sick, I offered to do my own checkbook one time and he called me 'Marcie' and stomped off to sulk!"

"It's fear, honey, plain old fear. He's like his dad that way—thinks the only way he can be safe is to control every little thing in his world—and you're part of his world, just like the kids are. But you see, it's not possible; the burden of responsibility is too great. Trying only leads to ulcers and heart failure. If he won't give you any control over your own life, you'll just have to take some—for his sake as well as your own."

"What can I do?"

"Do as you like, at least part of the time!" Dorrie took hold of Susan's shoulders and looked straight into her eyes. "Honey, you were on the dean's list—you don't get there on a pretty face! Why shouldn't you be in charge of your own checkbook? Anybody with fourth-grade math can keep a checkbook!"

"Mom, he'd think I didn't love him any more. He *needs* to be in control!"

"He doesn't need to keep you in rompers." Dorrie let her daughter-in-law go and turned to wipe the countertop. "I love him, too, darling, but you're not doing him any favor by cultivating his neuroses. Two's got to learn that the world doesn't stop spinning just because he took his hand off it for a minute or let somebody else take a whirl. I promise you, you'll both live longer."

"Well, they do say stress is hard on a man . . ."

"It's not doing you any good either, Susan."

Dorrie cleared her throat and turned away. "Just one more thing while I'm at it," she said. "I won't be so crude as to ask about your sex life; I really don't want to know. Only this: if it's not to your satisfaction, the modern world is full of therapists. Do something about it now, while he's young enough to change. Don't live with it. And if you do, don't blame your husband."

She laughed, a short and unconvincing bark. "I've been so careful not to be an interfering mother-in-law, dear—this may be the only advice I ever give you. Pay attention to it."

Thirty-two

A few days later, Dorrie was standing behind the costume counter at the store when a smartly dressed, fortyish, red-headed woman came in carrying a briefcase.

"Excuse me," she said. "Are you Ms. Greene?"

Dorrie nodded. "What can I do for you?"

"I'm Marian Thalberg, Membership Chair of the UPBW, United Professional and Business Women. Do you know our organization?"

Dorrie confessed her ignorance, and Ms. Thalberg filled her in.

"So you see," she concluded, "in addition to our many charitable works, we serve as a mutual support organization: a sort of old girls' network. I came in today to offer you the opportunity to join us."

"Thank you very much," Dorrie said. She was stunned. Yes, she owned the store. Yes, she did the best she could at operating it with Zada's help. But she still didn't feel like a "businesswoman," and clearly not in the same league with this aggressively businesslike person.

"I, ah . . . I've never been much of a club-woman," she said. "I've only been working in the store since September, Ms. Thalberg. Perhaps my manager, Zada Strait, would be a better candidate for membership. She's been a responsible member of our staff for twenty-five years, and managing the store since my husband's death last fall. Ms. Strait is the true businesswoman here."

"Your manager's a woman? Why, that's wonderful! There aren't that many stores of this quality owned and operated by women, you know. We'd be delighted if you'd both consider membership in the UPBW."

"I really don't have the time to take on a new commitment right now," Dorrie told her, "but I'd be glad to call Zada to talk to you. She might be interested."

When the woman had left the store, Zada came to Dorrie with her eyes sparkling. Dorrie had never seen her so excited.

"Thanks, Dorrie," she said. "I've wanted to join that group for ten years, but they wouldn't have me until now. What did you say to them?"

"Only that you're managing the store. I'm glad they invited you to join at last."

It seemed snobbish to Dorrie. Zada was the same person, doing the same job she'd been doing all this time. The mere fact of the title shouldn't make the difference in whether the group would welcome her. But if Zada was happy, that was what counted.

It first surprised and then amused her that they wanted Ms. Greene of Hunter & Greene as a member. Little did they know, she thought. She wasn't a "professional woman." She grinned to herself. She had to admit that, even misplaced, the respect was nice.

Dorrie never did tell Travis about the blowup with Two. He might think she was asking for some kind of commitment, and she didn't want one. Sleeping with him was enough for now. Imagine! she thought. Waiting till you're a plump, middle-aged widow to find out about that!

"You look different," Charmaine told her. "Shiny like. What's up, Dorrie?"

Dorrie smiled. "I guess I can tell you." She straightened her face and made her voice sober. "I've finally done something adventurous, Charmaine."

"Is that what's been making you so weird for the past couple of weeks?" Charmaine studied

Dorrie's face. "I could tell you've been worried. Come on, Dorrie. Tell!"

Dorrie remembered when they were sixteen years old, holding those terribly serious, all-night discussions about whether it was all right to kiss a boy on the first date, or if he'd think you were a chippy and never respect you any more. Travis's kisses melted her bones. His touch made her fluttery, distracted her so that she could not even think. The very sight of his hands could give her gooseflesh. She couldn't hold it in another minute.

"I'm sleeping with Travis Burton!" she sang. "Oh, Charmaine, I never imagined!" She blushed. "It's just begun. I'm still getting used to the idea, and nobody knows yet. I only told Two I was having lunch with him, and he like to had a fit."

"What did you do?"

"Told him it was none of his business, essentially; that I'm a big girl now."

"Good for you!" Charmaine laughed. "God, old Two must've shit a brick!"

Dorrie laughed. "Well, not quite, but he was straining."

"Dorrie, this is great!" Charmaine cried. She threw her arms around Dorrie and wrapped her in a choking hug. Then, drawing back, she looked into Dorrie's face. "So how do you feel?"

"Confused. Thrilled out of my gourd. Scared to death. Astounded. All these years I didn't know what all those heaving bosoms and throbbing other parts in Susan's books were about—thought they were the silliest sort of wild exaggerations—and now, suddenly, I do! Full of the most amazing yearnings . . . I want to spend the next six months with him on a desert isle." Dorrie laughed. "I feel like every romantic song or story you ever heard, and then some. Even, 'Why Don't We Do It in the Road?' "

Charmaine laughed and hugged her again. "Congratulations, Dorrie. Honey, the worst I ever had wasn't bad, but there's nothing to beat good sex!"

"I'm finding that out. Jiminy! But I'm feeling real strange about it, Charmaine. I don't think I'm even in love with him, but . . . well, it must be rutting season or something. Lord, I can't keep my hands off him, nor he me!" She laughed, embarrassed but too excited to stop. "Ah, sweet mystery of life, at last I've found you!"

"Oh, Dorrie, I'm so glad for you! After all these years! So do you think it'll go on?"

Dorrie nodded. "It doesn't show any signs of cooling down, though I guess it's got to sooner or later. It's not like we were in love, and even if we were . . . well, it wouldn't be possible to

376

keep up this pace. Not that we're not fond of each other. That's real; it's genuine. Only . . ." Dorrie stared off into space for a moment and then collected herself with a small shake.

"I guess I don't even know what 'in love' is. I remember how I felt about Mickey Spires when we were sixteen: the rocks in my stomach when I didn't see him and the butterflies when I did. I always thought there must be a little of that for 'in love,' but I've never felt it since."

"But you married George—you never felt that way about him?"

"It wasn't that kind of love. And of course, that kind's for youngsters; I don't expect to find it now."

"Don't kid yourself, Dorrie. My grandma fell ass over teakettle in love at seventy-three, and him too; they got married and lived together till they flat wore each other out!" She gave Dorrie a searching look. "No butterflies with Travis?"

Dorrie smiled.

"Oh, yes, butterflies enough. No rocks. When he's gone, I think at least as much about 'it' as him—probably more."

"Well, that's no surprise, considering you never knew about 'it' before! Dorrie, I know you're about to jump out of your skin with this, but I promise you'll calm down some after a while. He's just brought a new part of you to life, and you're not used to it."

"I guess," Dorrie said doubtfully. She laughed softly. "You'd think, though, that I could appreciate the giver as much as the gift. It's just so . . . much. I feel real strange about it. He's a lovely man. Did I tell you he brings me poems?"

"No!"

"It's sweet. And flowers and little inexpensive pretties . . ." She blushed, thinking of the red silk teddy he'd brought his Scarlet Woman. It had come with a Robert Graves poem that started out,

"Down, Wanton, down! Have you no
    shame
That at the whisper of Love's name,
Or Beauty's, presto! Up you raise
Your angry head and start to gaze?"

She hadn't been able to help laughing. "And he's funny," she added, "and terribly sentimental in his own way. Not at all like George."

"So why aren't you in love with him?"

Dorrie shrugged.

"What can I tell you? Maybe it's just too soon."

The truth was, Dorrie realized later, that for all Travis's desire for intimacy, there were certain things she couldn't talk to him about. Every time he found one of her "spook books," Travis went all tight-lipped on her. He seemed almost jealous, as if with him around, she shouldn't need that.

"This is such garbage!" he'd exploded on Sunday. He'd come downstairs in the morning to find her reading *Seth Speaks,* and had taken it from her to read the jacket notes. "Come on, Dorrie, you're an intelligent woman—you *know* it's garbage!"

"Some of it may be," she'd agreed. "But some of it makes real sense."

"Like what!"

"I've seen ESP at work, even experienced some; I know there is such a thing. Channeling . . . well, I don't know: what I saw was a crock, but parts of this make sense. I do think there's something to reincarnation. It explains more than anything else I've ever heard."

"Dorrie, it's bullshit! It's wishful thinking, wanting everything to be fair when everybody knows it's not! Airplanes blow up, earthquakes level whole cities, children starve, painful illnesses strike the good, and the wicked die easy! Life is *not* fair! The kindest fate would be for death to be final. Maybe it's not—I don't know—but the last thing you'll find on the other side of death's door is another life! This is all self-delusion!"

Dorrie took the book from him, puzzled by his outburst. "I'm only indulging my curiosity, Travis. What are you so upset about?"

"I just hate to see you wasting a fine mind on that trash when you could be doing something useful." He turned away and plunked down on the couch to fume.

Like what? she'd wondered. What did he want from her? But there was no point in going on with it. She'd shelved the offending book and gone into the kitchen to make coffee.

The conversation was still bothering her when she went to bed that night. Why did he seem so threatened? He didn't have to believe in what she was doing, she thought — just let her alone to do it. It didn't have anything to do with him. Maybe that was why it made him so angry. You'd think a man who'd cooked the meals and let his wife fix the lawnmower would be willing to let a woman use her mind whatever way she wanted to! Well, she'd been told what to do all her life; she'd be damned if she'd be told what to think besides. She put it firmly out of her mind and went to sleep.

Dorrie is driving down a country road she

has been down before. She enters a stretch where the road is under repair. Ahead of her is a DETOUR sign on a diagonally striped barrier. Its arrow points into a little roadside park.

Oh, she thinks, I remember this place! The trees, which had been sheared off flat in her earlier visit, are now growing. Tall, straight, pale green shoots point straight up from their tops; they are too new even to have leaves yet, but growing vigorously. She notes that many of the trees are fruit bearers — cherries, apples, peaches, a little plum. Two new ones — a pecan and a spreading hazel bush — have been transplanted into the area behind the little old man's hut.

Dorrie follows the walk around behind the hut where she finds an open window. She taps on the glass. The old man looks up from the massive tome he is reading, smiles, and beckons her to come in. He meets her at the door and takes her hands in his, spreading her arms wide.

"Let me look at you," he says. "I'm so glad you came! You're looking wonderful!"

Dorrie looks down at her body and realizes that she's a girl again. She recalls Danny Kaye in Hans Christian Andersen, *telling the children about the Ugly Duckling. "A swan? Aw, go on! Say, I* am *a swan!" It makes her laugh, but she feels beautiful in the old man's eyes.*

"I was just about to have some lunch," he says. "Won't you join me?" He asks how she's getting along, and she says well, but he knows already. He just wants to hear her say it.

"I'm so happy to see the trees growing again," she says.

"Yes, they're doing very well." He grins. "I planted the nut trees just for you." Dorrie remembers how serious she's been since George's death. She hasn't played or cut up for so long she's almost forgotten how.

The next time she comes here, she knows, the trees will have borne fruit.

"Look what I found at the college bookstore," Dorrie told Travis that weekend.

He took the blue-bound, oversized paperback from her hand. Its large "USED" sticker nearly covered the title, *modern poems*.

"This is great," he said, looking through it. "Hopkins's 'Glory be to God for dappled things . . .' I always loved that one. And look here, there's a whole section of Dylan Thomas . . . and Matthew Arnold: 'Ah, Love, let us be true to one another!' "

"I know. I've been reading it for three solid days." She sat beside him and they browsed through the book, reading favorite bits and pieces to one another. He picked a Roethke poem.

I knew a woman lovely in her bones,
When small birds sighed, she would
  sigh back at them . . .

"I haven't read poetry since I was a girl," Dorrie said. "I'd forgotten how much I love it. Listen to this: it's from Yeats's 'Prayer for My Daughter.'

"In courtesy I'd have her chiefly learned.
Hearts are not had as gifts, but hearts are
  earned
By those that are not entirely
  beautiful . . ."

"It sounds good on paper," Travis said, "but I don't believe it for a minute. You can't earn anybody's heart, no matter how hard you try; they have to give it freely or not at all. If love's not 'no matter what,' it's not love; it's barter."

"You think so? My mother used to recite that to me, and I always believed it. I mean, you've *got* to be good to be loved! If you're mean and hateful, if you're a liar or a thief, how could anybody love you?"

Travis laughed. "Lord, Dorrie, read the papers! Look at the world's literature! It's full of stories about charming and adored villains, abusive husbands whose wives won't press charges — and good, kind people who deserve love and don't get it. Nobody's all that good, anyhow, except in spurts. I'd hate to think we had to earn love! Deep down, none of us really deserves it."

He paused and reached to touch her cheek, and Dorrie felt her skin warm.

"Except you, of course. You do."

Dorrie laughed, embarrassed. "Maybe we all deserve it, just for being alive," she said. "I'll have to think about that."

Thirty-three

"I'm glad to see you-all. Thanks for coming."

Dorrie, Charmaine, and ten strangers sat around a long table at the Psychic Association's headquarters in northern Dallas, at the first meeting of the new class. The instructor, a pretty, plump, thirtyish woman named Velma Suiter, wore faded bluejeans and a purple T-shirt that bore the slogan, "What do you think I am, psychic?" With her round, ruddy cheeks, circular blue eyes, and sunny little smile, she lacked only red hair to be a living Campbell's Soup Kid. Velma Suiter seemed almost as appropriate to her role, Dorrie thought, as Donna Reed cast as Mata Hari.

And if they were in this for the money, as Travis had suggested, they weren't making it. The headquarters, housed in a vacant storefront, consisted of a small reception area and a large central room with one large and two small classrooms arranged around it. At the front were two small, closed offices. The little classroom they were in had bare walls the color of aged newsprint, a mud-brown tile floor, and an eight-foot folding table surrounded by tan metal folding chairs. A bookcase at the rear held the Association's library—about three dozen dog-eared volumes with titles ranging from *A Handbook of Parapsychology* to *Atlantis: The Antedeluvian World*. Dorrie, in a plum wool skirt and flowered cotton blouse, was the best-dressed person in the room.

Her classmates ranged from a pair of lovestruck teenagers who sat side by side, their hands and eyes locked, to a large, white-haired man in jeans and a sweatshirt at the far end of the table. As they introduced themselves, Dorrie discovered four students, two housewives, a psychologist interested in "alternate means of communication," a high-school music teacher, a men's clothing salesman, and a man who wrote computer software.

"What we're going to do tonight and each night for the next six weeks," Velma said, "is just experiment. Think of it as play. Everybody's results will be different, and 'different' isn't wrong. In what we're doing, there's no such thing as 'wrong.' We're all individuals, and nothing's more individual than our psyches." She paused and gazed around the table.

So anything goes, Dorrie thought. Another

freak show. Hooray! Bless Charmaine's peaked little head, she's done it again!

"Another important point," Velma went on, "is, this is not a contest. We're here to support each other, not to compete.

"Now: whether they admit it or not, everybody on the face of the earth has had some kind of psychic experience at some time or other. They've had premonitions or 'dreamed true,' or they've had poltergeists, or they've run into ghosts." Little does she know, Dorrie thought. "They've known the phone was about to ring and who'd be calling or the exact words that were about to leave somebody's mouth. Every one of you has had something like that happen, so let's talk about that now."

The stories that went around the table seemed fairly ordinary: the teenaged boy's predictive dream about a football score; the man who'd changed his ticket at the last minute and avoided a plane crash; even the long and complex tale of a woman who'd felt compelled to go to the hospital, only to meet the ambulance carrying her daughter in from a wreck, and the "near-death experience" of the old man. They were the kind of vaguely unsettling stories of which one's seatmate might unburden herself on a plane, knowing she'd never see you again; the kind about which people would say, "Well, isn't that unusual!" and then, too disturbed to put any stock in them, shrug off.

Dorrie's own experience had taught her that sometimes events outwit all known laws of nature; she accepted the stories. What surprised her was, first, that these people would share them with people they planned to see every week; and, second, the aura of intimacy that rapidly enveloped the group as they spoke. It was as if they were relieved to get the stories off their chests among people who might not think they were completely off their trollies. Almost half of them began, "Well, I've never told this to anybody before, but . . ."

She noticed that the women told their tales more easily than the men. The men seemed to find either their fingernails or the upper corners of the room of immense interest the moment they started talking; their attitudes ranged from wonder to irritation, and their reticence varied in relation to their ages: greatest at the center, and least at the extremes. The women spoke quietly, claiming neither credit nor blame for the events, simply offering them up for consideration.

Charmaine presented an experience from the Indian ashram, and Dorrie told of her mother's death.

"One day more than twenty years ago, I was having coffee with Charmaine, here, sitting in the breakfast room with the sun shining in, talking about our moms, when I started to get this antsy feeling. I look up at the clock—it was two forty-seven — and said, 'Something's wrong.' I didn't know what, but the feeling built up almost into a panic, and I knew I had to find out about my mother. I called and called, and when nobody answered, I started calling hospitals. Finally one of them admitted she was there, but they wouldn't tell me anything about her. I was getting dressed to go down there when my father called to tell me she'd wrecked her car. She'd died in that hospital at two forty-seven."

It was not the sort of story she normally told to strangers — even George had scoffed — but Charmaine was there to verify it. Nobody at the table turned a hair in response; they all just nodded sympathetically, and the next person took her turn. I could have made up anything, she thought, and they'd have swallowed it whole. But wasn't she swallowing theirs? And why not? What did any of them have to gain by lying?

Still, the whole idea of baring one's soul to a group of strangers went against her grain. Approach/Retreat, she thought, remembering her freshman psychology professor's classification of internal conflicts. The events fascinated her, but she was sorely out of practice at this sort — any sort — of intimacy. It made her feel creepy.

When all the stories had been told, the class took a short break.

"Lots of energy in that room," Charmaine said.

"I keep hearing that word, Charmaine, but I don't know what people mean by it. They all mean something different. It's like 'vibes,' some kind of insider's language that has no meaning outside the group."

"I beg your pardon. When did you become a semanticist?"

Dorrie sighed. "You're only sarcastic when you know I'm right. Just spare me the jargon, please."

"You're a little testy tonight, Dorrie. What's the matter?"

"Sorry. It's just getting to me for some reason."

"You scared somebody's going to read your mind and tell your secrets?"

Dorrie laughed. "Don't be silly, Charmaine. Come on, they're going back in."

The second half was taken up with exercises. In one, they drew names for partners and moved their chairs to sit two by two. Then Velma had them rub their hands briskly together to "rub up their auras" and hold their hands, palms out, about a half-inch from the partner's.

"You're going to exchange information," Velma said. "Remember, this is a game. Turn off your intellect and work through intuition: just open your mouth and listen to what comes out. And when one person's speaking, the other can't say anything but 'yes' or 'no.' "

Dorrie surprised herself. Her partner was a girl of about twenty-two, slender and sharp-faced, with drab blond hair hanging to her shoulders and hiding much of her face.

"You've just applied for a job?" Dorrie's mouth said. What in the world had made her ask that?

The girl nodded.

"You're going to get it, but not right away. They'll call you back for two more interviews. Somebody there wants the job for a friend, and she'll try to keep you from getting it, but they'll choose you in the end." Oh, dear! She was giving false hope to this poor, bedraggled child! Well, it was only a game. She hoped the girl wouldn't put too much stock in it.

"When?" the girl asked.

Dorrie shook her head. "I don't know." She paused, waiting, fascinated at the information that was flooding into her mind, but distrusting it. She didn't doubt that some people were psychic—just not her, she kept insisting to herself. All she was was observant. So how had she known about the job?

"What else?" the girl asked.

There was no point in being afraid of it. It was a harmless experiment, a *game,* she repeated to herself, and she'd never have to do it again if she didn't want to. She turned off her inner critic and opened her mouth.

"You have a brother living near here, but

391

your mother's a long way away, and she worries about you. She wants your brother to look out for you, but you-all don't get along well enough." The girl nodded, her eyes big. "And you just broke up with your boyfriend." Dorrie shuddered unexplainably. "It's a good thing. Don't go back to him."

"You're right!" the girl said. "My mom's in California, and my brother's so wrapped up in this girl he's dating that he doesn't have time for me. And I *did* just break up with this complete jerk, and I wouldn't go back to him if he were the last man on earth!"

"Good," Dorrie said. How had she known? She caught a whiff of Cashmere Bouquet and shook her head: No. She hadn't been aware of Rose since she came home from Sedona, and those had been special circumstances. Not here. Not now. A picture of Dovie Freebird flashed behind her eyes. Please, God, she prayed, don't make me like that!

At the end of the class period, Velma asked them all to hold hands around the table.

"Anybody who gets an impression," she said, "just say it. If it belongs to anybody here, they can claim it."

Dorrie sat tensely, waiting for visions of a drugged girl in a dumpster to surface, but no such image appeared.

"Has anybody here been to Arizona?" the

392

woman across the table from her asked. "I just keep seeing these high, red cliffs."

That Saturday, she went to the park at White Rock Lake with Travis. He brought a wicker basket with a folding lid.

"You can't look till we get there," he said. "It's a surprise. And you'd better like it; I was up all night preparing it!"

The basket held cold roasted chicken, home-made potato salad with dill and mustard, sliced ham, three kinds of bread, dill and sweet pickles, black olives, celery and carrot sticks, and two types of cheese, along with a bottle of rosé wine and real china, crystal, and silverware. He'd even packed linen napkins.

"Lord, Travis," Dorrie said, laughing, "I was so proud of losing fifteen pounds—now I'll put it all back on in an hour!"

"Eat," he commanded. "I'll watch your figure. You don't need to worry about it."

Later, they dropped by his house to put the basket away. He lived in a small, stuccoed house in Highland Park, the one he'd shared with Janie. They entered through the arched entrance of a covered porch into a foyer with a curving staircase. To Dorrie's right a wide, rounded arch opened into a formal living room done in shades of rose and aqua. On the wall was a large chalk drawing of an Indian woman gazing down at the baby she held in her arms.

"That's a lovely drawing," Dorrie said. "Where did you find it?"

"Janie did it one year when we'd been to New Mexico. I've always loved it. That was a nice vacation."

She followed him down a long hall hung with black-and-white photos of nature scenes: high and rugged mountains, their peaks capped with snow; a stand of trees with a shaft of sunlight shining through, reminding Dorrie of a cathedral; a patch of wild violets with dandelions blooming behind. Their gray tones added a touch of mystery to the otherwise commonplace subjects, as if they were being seen by moonlight.

"She took those too," Travis said.

"She must have been quite an artist," Dorrie said.

"She was. Never did settle on one kind of art, though. She did everything from ceramics to poetry."

Dorrie's artistic endeavors had never exceeded embroidering Marcie's dresses and making quilt tops. She had half a dozen patchwork tops of her own designs folded on a closet shelf, and never had even got around to quilting them; working out the designs had been fun, but quilting was work. Every time she opened her closet door, they shamed her.

"Now we're in my territory," Travis said, leading her into the kitchen. "Sit down. I'll make us some coffee while I put these things away."

"Can I help you?"

"No, just sit and talk."

"I'm not Janie, Travis." Dorrie's voice had a slight edge. "I know my way around a kitchen, and I never could sit and watch somebody else work. I wasn't brought up that way."

"All right, then, help if you'd rather." He set the basket on the table and turned to wrap his arms around her. "I don't want you to be Janie, any more than I want to be George. They're other people, Dorrie. We've got to make our own relationship."

While Travis put the leftovers in the refrigerator, Dorrie put their dishes in the sink and ran water over them. They finished tidying up in silence, and then ambled together into his living room. Travis dropped on the teal blue velvet couch opposite the television set, picked up the *TV Guide,* and patted the seat beside him.

"There's a Fred Astaire movie on television," he said then. "Want to watch it?"

"Okay. Which one?"

"Follow the Fleet. It's got 'Dancing in the Dark' in it."

"Sounds good to me. You know, he always played those suave, devil-may-care, 'don't tie me down' characters, and he wasn't a bit like that. They say he was really shy. He stayed married to the same woman forever, and after she died he waited a long time to marry again, and they were together till he died."

"I know. Took him years and years before he'd even kiss a woman on screen. It wasn't necessary; the romance was there without it. Old Fred was smarter than his directors and screenwriters; he knew what his audiences wanted. He left the mystery in it, left something to the imagination."

"Well, I'm afraid those days are gone," Dorrie said. "You should see what I'm reading for this class I'm in: women falling in and out of beds, describing every last tickle and touch while they're there." She blushed. "And my lord, the anger! Man-bashing seems to be the order of the day. They all seem to need somebody to blame. Romance may be so dead we'll never revive it!"

"We'll revive it," Travis said. "You and me, all by our ownsomes."

"Tell me something you've never told anybody before," Travis murmured later that night. He'd brought her home after the movie, and they'd made love. Now they were curled together, spoon fashion, his breath lifting the hair behind her ears.

A lifetime of guilts and pain washed through Dorrie's mind, and she sighed. After a moment, she reached into the drawer in her night table and brought out a packet. She handed it to Travis.

"What's this?"

He opened the envelope and dumped out travel brochures and an airline ticket.

"My escape hatch," Dorrie said. "I was going to leave him. I've kept it hidden for fifteen years."

"Maracaibo. It's a long way."

Dorrie's eyes filled, but she smiled. "I wanted someplace warm," she said. "And someplace they didn't speak English, so nobody would bother me."

"You never went."

"I couldn't. I had responsibilities here. But I thought about it a lot. There were times that ticket was all that stood between me and despair." She laughed bitterly. "It probably wasn't even valid after the first six months, but I clung to it like a life raft."

"Poor darling." He laid the papers aside. "Well, you won't need it now. Maybe we'll go together some time."

"I just never realized," she said, snuggling back into the curve of his body. "I thought all men were like George, so cold, so afraid of closeness. I never in my wildest dreams imagined a man who'd want me to tell him my secrets. For the longest time, I worried about Marcie's husband; he's so open-hearted and affectionate, I thought maybe he wasn't a 'real man.' "

Travis laughed, and the sound rumbled comfortably in her ear.

"The world's full of different kinds of men. Men are as different from each other as women are, and God knows women are! That's the fun of it, Dorrie. Everyone is different."

"Are you suggesting I do a little more experimenting? Explore the field?"

His hold on her tightened gently. "Far from it. I've still got a lot to show you, and you've got things to teach me too. We're not done with each other—not by a long shot!"

"What could I possibly teach you, Travis?"

"Ah, Dorrie, you're a whole new world to explore." His hand slid across her belly. "I haven't even learned this geography yet, let alone the Inner Woman. I spent twenty-five years with a woman as different from you as a woman could be, and I loved almost all of them—never contemplated Maracaibo, anyhow. But I'm loving my time with you now."

"Well, you make me feel like a girl again. It's silly, almost. Here I was, this nicely settled matron, and an accountant starts sending me poetry! What next?"

"Wonders never cease, that much I know. And it surely is a wonder that a wonder like you came into my life."

Thirty-four

Dorrie felt more alive than she'd felt for years. Her orderly routine gave her a degree of safety, but leading a double life was high adventure. Unready to discuss Travis with the children, Dorrie hugged her secrets to her and let her mind whirl, confiding only in Charmaine.

"It's ridiculous," she told Charmaine. "At my age! I never imagined this kind of . . . heat. Next to the way I feel, Chinese mustard is mild as mayonnaise!"

"Congratulations! What's ridiculous isn't finding it now; it's never having found it until now. A true case of 'better late than never.' "

"I'm not sure I have the strength for it," Dorrie joked darkly. "What's tons of fun at twenty can kill you past fifty."

"I can see the headlines now." Charmaine drew her hand in a broad arc, framing them. " 'CPA FUCKS CLIENT TO DEATH: 55-Year-Old

Widow Dies Smiling.' Do you know how many people's fantasy it is to die that way?"

Dorrie laughed. "Well, I can't die till I've learned my lesson, and I don't think that's it. Not all of it, anyhow." She took a sip of coffee. "It's about independence, I know, but I wonder what it is exactly. That man at the psychic fair said business isn't it, and I think he's right; if the store were it, I'd be more interested. Honestly, Charmaine, there are days it's all I can do to drag myself down there. I think I'm going to read myself blind."

Always a careful housekeeper, Dorrie now had books stacked on every surface in the house: the end tables in the den, the breakfast table, her night table. Books lay face down, opened to the place she'd quit reading, on the kitchen counter and on top of the television set. *The Summer Before the Dark* lay next to *Messages From Michael* on her night table; *The Accidental Tourist* and *Seth Speaks* shared the coffee table in the orchid room; *Supermind* lay over the side of the bathtub, *Memoirs of a Catholic Girlhood* in the rack next to the commode, and *Fear of Flying* on the arm of her chair. *The Power of Myth* lay on the dining room table next to the *I Ching,* and several translations of the Bible were scattered through the house for reference. *The Joy of Sex* was on her night table — Travis had brought it, and she'd overcome her shyness enough to look at it

400

with him—and *How to Make Love to a Man* (Amazing! Travis delighted in what it taught her; George would have thrown her out of bed!) was hidden at the back of the top drawer in the kitchen desk. She studied as seriously as a Ph.D. candidate and resented the time she had to spend on other things, even occasionally grudging her nights with Travis.

My twin obsessions, she thought: sex and the spirit, the famous mind/body question. Sometimes she worried about her sanity, but no Dr. Wisemann could solve her problems—not even if she could bring herself to tell him. She'd rather sort them out herself.

One problem, she saw now, was that she'd denied her body for so many years she'd almost forgotten she had one. Letting George end their sex life had only been the beginning. She'd learned to shy away from human touch, afraid it would remind her of what was lacking in her life. Read only nonfiction for years—history, travel, nutrition—avoiding emotional content altogether, and then spent another ten or fifteen years on psychology and anthropology, intellectualizing the emotions. Worn her clothes to rags because adorning herself had seemed a waste of time. The only physical luxury she'd allowed herself was having her hair washed and set every week, and that only because she didn't want to fool with it herself and because it pleased him to support his neighborhood merchants.

Giving in on sex had caused troubles she'd shut her eyes to for years, though even now she didn't know what she should have done differently. Had an affair? Even if she'd had the self-confidence, the idea offended her; if she couldn't make love with her husband, she'd as soon do without. As she had, she thought bitterly. Leave him? She'd thought long and hard about that and stayed for all the wrong reasons—security, stability, simple inertia—even knowing they were the wrong reasons.

Life with George had been less "bad" than just "not so good." He never did drink. He hadn't beaten or berated her. He hadn't stayed out nights with the boys—there'd never been any boys. God knew, he'd never fooled around. His was a passive abuse: denying her the intimacy and comfort of his touch. It had been a punishment, she realized now, though she still didn't know what she'd done to deserve it—except have her own ideas and desires instead of those he wished on her. He'd been coldest toward her when she'd dared to disagree. But even that was not deliberate. His fears had simply been too great to overcome.

As a result, she'd consciously shut down her desire, put it on ice when Marcie was a baby and poured all her energies into child-rearing and homemaking. It had been like cutting off the heat in just one room: after a while the nearby rooms cooled off, and then, imperceptibly, the whole house. She'd piled on sweaters and gone on about her life, never thinking that her children could be frozen by the same cold. Finally, she'd become so inured to it that she'd forgotten what warmth was. The simple touch of a human hand could scald her.

She should have demanded that George respect her feelings, but until Dr. Wisemann, nobody'd ever told her they had a right to respect. A woman models her expectations about men on her father, and Dorrie's father had never believed feelings were respectable; he respected only intellect. So instead of insisting on her right to her emotions, she'd denied them and grown "calluses of the heart." It had taken her a long time to understand the dark side of that defense, that the same calluses that protect you from pain protect you just as efficiently from pleasure. If sandpaper can't hurt you, she thought, you'll never feel silk at all.

Once she figured that out, she'd made a conscious effort to allow herself more vulnerability, but she'd been closed so tightly for so long that even now, being made aware of her own feelings sometimes came as a shock. Other people's feelings were easier, but she still missed them sometimes. Look at poor Marcie and the *Books of Knowledge*. She should have known, should have recognized her daughter's lack, especially having suffered the same lack herself for so long, but she'd missed it. Every parent makes mistakes, she told herself, but one that big was hard to forgive herself.

And now Travis had come into her house and turned the heat up, reminding her what wonderful things warmth and feelings could be. She would have to discover for herself the line between thawing out and getting burned.

Dorrie is in a cold white place. The ground is covered with snow, and the air is a white fog so thick she cannot see beyond the stretch of her arm; it feels like walking through ice-cold milk. She is shivering, and her bones ache. Somewhere up ahead, she knows, there is a warm house full of people who are waiting for her, but she's not sure she can find it in the fog.

A voice calls out to her: "Dorrie!" The fog muffles it, and she cannot tell where it is coming from. "Dorrie! Dorrie! This way!"

She stumbles blindly ahead, coatless, her feet bound in rags, until a warm pair of arms folds around her. It is Travis.

"I'm so cold," she says. "So cold . . . Do you have a blanket to wrap me in?"

"Will this do?" he asks. He is holding out a mink coat lined in scarlet satin. In his other hand are a fur hat and muff, warm woolen socks, and high boots of black leather. He helps her into them and then takes her arm.

"Come," he says. "They're waiting. The stew

*has been on the fire all day long just waiting for
you to come and eat."*

Susan dropped into the store on Friday and
invited Dorrie to lunch. The day was bright and
cool, and they strolled three blocks to a little
tearoom that offered pretty salads, "crois-
sandwiches," and herb teas. Susan was wearing
a fitted navy suit, and her blond hair was in a
classic French twist. The pearls George had presented her at her engagement party hung
around her neck over a soft, collarless, pink
blouse.

"You certainly do look smart today, Susan,"
Dorrie said. "I'm so glad ladylike clothes are
making a comeback."

"Thanks, Mom. You've upgraded your own
wardrobe considerably over the past few
months. I love that sweater. The blue is so
pretty with your eyes."

Dorrie laughed. "Thank Charmaine for that.
She put all my clothes in garbage bags and took
them to a shelter in December. It was buy new
clothes or go naked!"

Susan's eyes widened. "Weren't you mad?"

"At Charmaine? Might as well be mad at the
weather. No, honey, it was the right thing to do.
I needed a jolt. It was cheaper than psychother-
apy, and probably more effective."

They arrived at the tearoom, where a multicolored floral tablecloth accented by bright, solid-colored napkins invited them to a table by the window. The tableware was silverplate, and the waitress brought them ruby goblets of icewater.

"So what brings you into this neighborhood, all the way from Carrollton?" Dorrie asked when they were settled.

"I'm out begging," Susan laughed. "My sorority alumnae group's having an auction, and I'm trying to get merchants to donate things for it."

"How're you doing?"

"They're being very generous. I've got everything from professional haircuts and perms to framed paintings and fancy bedspreads promised." She looked away shyly for a moment, and then met Dorrie's eyes. "What can I count on from you, Mom?"

Dorrie laughed. "How about a Waterford bowl?" She had one that had been collecting dust in the store for nearly a year. People seemed to be spending their money on more practical things these days, with the country in a recession.

"Wonderful!" Susan bent to retrieve a pen and notebook from her purse and entered the bowl on a long list.

"I didn't know you belonged to the alumnae group. When did that happen?"

"I just decided I needed to get out of the house more, and it was something George would accept. Actually, I'm having a good time. We meet during the day, and one day a month we go to the Shrine Children's Hospital and play with the kids—read or tell stories or do art projects." She smiled self-consciously. "They've got me chairing this auction. I was really surprised."

"Susan, that's wonderful! Tell me!"

As Susan talked, her voice took on an intensity and excitement that Dorrie hadn't heard for a long time. Susan had organized the entire project, formed a committee to carry it out, and assigned duties to its members. She had rented the space, arranged for its decoration, contacted the newspapers and radio and TV stations to announce the event, and was now out collecting donations from area merchants.

"It's going to be almost as big as the Channel 13 auction!" she bragged. "Mom, it's been the most exciting thing!"

"Honey, I'm so glad to see you using your talents this way! And it's plain to see how much you're enjoying it."

"Oh, I do, Mom. The social contacts—I didn't realize how much I'd isolated myself when the children were young. You know, Wendy'll be in middle school next year. They're really growing up. What with music lessons and soccer practice and Girl Scouts and church group activities, it seems I hardly even see them anymore. A weekend at home with everybody there has become a rarity. I had to do something."

"Tell me about it," Dorrie said, smiling. "Of course you needed something to do. I'm just glad you've found something productive, something that uses the best of you. You really are wonderfully efficient, Susan—a talented organizer. Look at what you've accomplished!"

"Oh, Mom!"

Dorrie grinned. Susan sounded just like Marcie used to in her teens.

"It's not like I've done it alone, you know. Everybody helped. It was just a matter of deciding what needed to be done, and seeing that it got done. Anybody could do that with the help I've had."

"You show a becoming modesty, dear, but not much respect for what you've done. How many women are willing to devote the amount of time you've given to this project? How many would have known what needed to be done, let alone been able to organize the job? How many could have seen it through as you're doing? Give yourself some credit, Susan. You deserve it."

Susan laughed, surprised. "Maybe I do, a little," she said. "Thanks, Mom."

Thirty-five

"I'm sorry that class is over." Dorrie set her mug on the red vinyl tabletop and smiled across the booth at Charmaine. They were at Kip's Big Boy, sharing a late snack after their last session of the Psychic Development class. "I felt pretty silly doing some of that stuff, but it was fun. Do you want to take another one?"

"Sure. I picked up the new class list on the way out tonight. What's your pleasure?"

"I don't know, Charmaine. How about this one on dreams?" She frowned. "Oh, I can't. It meets Wednesdays." Dorrie studied the list, and then looked up with a grin. "The rest of it doesn't seem too promising: Atlantis is ancient history, if it's history at all. Astrology's full of numbers, and I hate them. You already do Tarot. 'Finding your Soulmate'?"

"I've found three already. Think I'll give that a rest."

Dorrie laughed. "Well, you never know. Look at me! I don't know that Travis and I are soulmates, but we sure are having a good time."

"Give me that thing," Charmaine said. "There's got to be something better. Here's 'Programming Prosperity,' taught by good ole Tommy Teeterbaugh. I think we can skip that one—have you seen the heap of junk that old boy drives?" She paused, staring at the course list. "Well, will you look at that! 'The Shaman in You . . .' and guess who's teaching it!"

"I'll bite," Dorrie said.

"Olivia Barnes! And she's not even letting them charge for it!"

"Who's Olivia Barnes?"

"She teaches anthropology and comparative religion at the university. Ain't it amazing who you find on the membership list of the Psychic Association! I took a course in myth from her years ago, back when I thought going back to school might distract me enough to stand being married to Max. Best class I ever took. She's a marvelous teacher and a real interesting person. She teaches by the Socratic method: all questions, no answers. We talked about it one time, and she says she refuses to 'rob people of their challenges.' But she presents some wonderful questions, and not just about the class material either."

"What do you suppose she's doing teaching at the Psychic Association?"

"God knows. Maybe coming out of the closet, at long last. But I will say this: whatever Livvy Barnes is teaching, I want to learn."

"Sounds all right to me," Dorrie said. "When does it begin?"

Expecting a tall, imposing, professional woman, Dorrie was surprised the next week. Olivia Barnes's tiny frame, snowy hair, and pixyish face made Dorrie think of Estelle Winwood as the Fairy Godmother. But after listening for two hours, watching Livvy draw out the shy and shut down the bombastic, Dorrie saw that Livvy was beyond comparison. After the class ended, Dorrie hung back and approached her.

"I just wanted to thank you," she said. "I was surprised it was over. Two hours felt like twenty minutes."

Livvy laughed.

"Well, thanks! I guess that just demonstrates the relativity of time, doesn't it!" She smiled warmly. "I'm glad you've come. You'll be back next week?"

"Nothing could keep me away."

"Good. We'll be doing a guided meditation. It'll be interesting."

Oh, Lord, Dorrie thought. Another one of those! Well, she'd survived Lonny Chance. She guessed she could survive Olivia Barnes.

411

* * *

Dorrie was spending less and less time at the store. Zada's efficiency was such that anything Dorrie could do, Zada could do better, and giving up responsibility to a novice made her nervous. Dorrie no longer asked for time off when she wanted it; she simply told Zada she was going to be gone. Zada seldom objected, and then only mildly. Though Zada was always properly respectful, Dorrie felt that Zada was usually glad to see the back of her. By the end of March, Dorrie found herself working part time.

"I seem to be turning into an absentee owner," she told Kurt one day. He'd dropped by the store to pick her up for lunch, and she'd told him he was lucky to find her there.

"How come?"

"Well, business is slow this month. I don't want to lay anybody off or cut hours when they're all meeting mortgages." She studied her hands for a moment before going on. "And then, I guess I thought it would be a lot more interesting than it is. I used to envy them so— my dad and George had this challenge game where one would name a supplier and the other'd have to give his address and phone, or one would say a customer's name and the other would have to tell what the customer'd bought last . . . They'd play it over the dinner table, and I used to feel so left out. All I knew was how many tablespoons in a cup, or how to sub-

412

stitute soda and cream of tarter for commercial baking powder. The store seemed so exciting, and George just lived and breathed business . . ."

She sighed, remembering, and gave a slight shrug.

"But it's not like that for me. Zada took me to the china market in February, and I felt like a tourist. All those lovely things, and I was bored silly before the first day ended. I mean, how many china patterns can you look at before your eyes cross?"

"You don't sound real happy with it."

"I guess not. Zada doesn't need me. She gets along fine all by herself, and I think having me around just gets on her nerves." Dorrie frowned, and then shrugged again. "I don't blame her: she thinks I'm not serious, and she may be right. I work Mondays because it's her day off, but most of the time I go in late and leave early, just say hello and fool with the books a little, wait on an occasional customer. I do enjoy the customers, but a high-school kid could do what I do. Zada does all the real work. She loves it, just eats up all those tacky little details. I know how important they all are, but they bore me stiff."

"Are you listening to yourself, Mom? You don't have to do this, you know. Even if you don't want to sell the store, you don't have to work in it."

"I know. That is, now I know. But I had to do it last fall. I did have to, then."

"Why did you?"

"Well, of course I felt closer to George there than anywhere. But more than that, I think I needed to prove that I could. The only reason my dad didn't include me when I was young was that I was a girl; he just naturally assumed that girls can't handle business and I'd marry somebody who would. And George . . . well, George was of another generation, one that believed that a 'real man' could provide well enough for his wife that she'd never have to earn money. He was ashamed to have me working in the store. But instead of making me feel like a princess, the way they meant it to, it made me feel like a dummy." She laughed softly, embarrassed. "I guess I just had to prove I wasn't a dummy."

Kurt smiled and reached across the table to cover her hand with his own. "You didn't have to go to all that trouble, Mom. I could have told you that."

That Sunday afternoon, after Travis left, Dorrie went out in the backyard to divide and transplant the perennial daisies she'd planted three years ago. The weather had been warm, and it had rained two days earlier. The soil was moist but not sodden, and easy to dig. She was half-entranced with the feel of the warm earth on her hands and its sweet, fertile scent, imagining the flowers in their summer bloom, when Jessie startled her, calling from the gap in the hedge.

"How you doing this fine day, Dorrie?" She crossed the yard with two big glasses of iced tea. "Thought you might like a drink."

"Thanks, Jess, I would." Dorrie sat back on the grass, and Jessie plopped down beside her and handed her the glass. She was biting her tongue, Dorrie saw, curious as a magpie. Well, she'd just wait.

It didn't take long. After a few minutes of small talk, Jessie put her hand on Dorrie's arm. "I know it isn't any of my business, and you don't have to tell if you really don't want to, but I wouldn't ask if I didn't care: Dorrie, what's going on with that man? I know you said he's your accountant, but I never yet knew an accountant who made house calls!"

Dorrie laughed. "Caught again," she said. "I'm not ready to tell the world about it yet, but we've been seeing a lot of each other socially. 'Boyfriend' is a ridiculous term at our ages, but 'gentleman friend' is even sillier."

"Do the kids know?"

"Sort of." She told Jessie about the confrontation with Two. "I talked to Marcie and Kurt later, and they're okay with it. Two thinks he's a fortune hunter, out for George's money."

"Well, you know Two. And it's only natural, I guess, for a son to worry about his mother. I

415

know my boys'd be worse than Reese was with the girls when they were dating. They'd be setting up interviews and meeting men at the door with baseball bats!"

Dorrie laughed. "Two would if I'd let him, I guess. He has no idea how much time Travis and I are spending together."

"He's good to you?"

"Wonderful, Jessie. It's a revelation."

Jessie looked at her closely, assessing the answer, and then smiled. "Good," she said. "You do what makes you happy, Dorrie. It's high time — past time — you did."

"Let's take a shower," Travis rumbled that Saturday night after they'd made love. "We're sweaty as a pair of hogs." He ran his finger down her breastbone and belly and dripped the sweat into her navel. "See there?"

Dorrie smiled and stretched. "I don't know that I can walk all that way," she said. "You've worn me out."

"I'll get a wheelchair. Roll you down the hall and slide you into the tub."

She laughed aloud as she sat up. "I'm not ready for that quite yet. All right, I'm coming."

Travis draped her robe around her shoulders, and they sauntered down the hall with their arms around each other's waists. In the bathroom, he turned on the shower, stepped into the tub, and offered Dorrie his hand.

The warm water drizzling down over her body felt like a piece of heaven. Dorrie turned and tipped her face up into it as Travis poured liquid soap into his hands and lathered her back, her bottom, and her legs. As his hands slid up her inner thighs, she turned and bent to soap his shoulders. Travis held her bottom and leaned his cheek into her belly.

"Wash your hair?" Dorrie murmured.

"Sure. Why not."

It was thinning at the crown, and gray was invading its once-rich brown. The back of his head was round as the earth.

"You have a lovely head," Dorrie said. "So well-shaped. My mother used to say you could tell a lot about a person from the shape of his head, though I never did find out what." She stepped around him, out of the stream. "Stand up now. Rinse."

As Travis stood, she admired his sturdy frame: his broad back, square butt, and thick legs looked as strong as some primitive wood carving. She never stopped being surprised at the differences between Travis's thick body and George's long, narrow boniness.

"Can it tell if you ought to marry someone?"

"What?" Dorrie felt as if she'd missed part of the conversation.

"The shape of the head. Does it tell whether

somebody'd make a good husband?"

"I don't think so. What are you talking about, Travis?"

"Marriage." He turned and put his arms around her, and the warm water ran down over them both. "I want to marry you, Dorrie. We've been working together for six months, sleeping together for almost three—it's not like we'd just met. And I love you."

"Oh, my," Dorrie said. She stepped back and looked at him again from more distance. "I don't know, Travis. I suppose it's foolish, but I hadn't thought that far ahead." She shook her head. "I hadn't thought ahead at all."

"Think now." He bent to kiss her, but Dorrie stepped out of the tub and wrapped herself in a rose-colored bath sheet.

"The children don't even know; they think we're just sharing an occasional lunch or an evening out. It would be a shock. Two . . . my son is extremely protective. Bad as a Victorian father."

"Never mind the kids. Mine don't know either. We can deal with them later. Just tell me if you'll marry me." He left the shower and put his arms around Dorrie, and she leaned her forehead into the curve of his neck.

"I don't know. It's not you—you're wonderful, Travis," she said softly. "I just don't know if I want to be married again."

"You could keep all your assets separate, of

418

course. It's not your assets I'm after. It's you."

"Not my assets, but my ass?"

Travis laughed, delighted. "You see? I never do know what you'll say or do next! You make life exciting, Dorrie. I want to spend the rest of my life learning to know you." He hugged her close. "And as asses go, yours is sweet as a ripe peach. I want that, too."

"You've got it. Have had it for months. Oh, Travis, I don't know what to say!" She turned and stepped away from him. "I'm just now getting used to *not* being married!"

"You won't answer me, then." His voice sounded dead as a fallen leaf.

"I can't! Good night, Travis, this is a big decision!"

"But do you love me?"

"I . . . There's more to it than that."

"No, there isn't. If you love me, marry me. If you don't . . ."

"There *is* more! We're talking about our whole lives!" She turned back to look at him. His shoulders were slumped, and he turned away. "Please, Travis, don't let's quarrel about this. I don't want to quarrel with you."

Travis reached for a towel and wrapped it around himself. "I guess I'd better get my clothes on and go."

"You don't have to. It's past midnight. Just come on back to bed, and we can go to sleep."

"That's all right. You need time to think, and

you can do it better without me here." Travis brushed past her through the door, and Dorrie watched his stiff back move down the hall.

Blast! she thought. She'd hurt his feelings. She sighed, drying herself, and then put her robe back on and followed him.

By the time she got to the bedroom, he was fully dressed and tying his shoes.

"Travis, please," she said. "Don't go like this."

"It's all right. You think about it, think about what you want and whether I can be part of it. You know my number." He stood up and started through the door. "I'll be in on Tuesday to look at the books. No need to see me out. Sleep well."

She did not. Instead, she lay awake for hours alternating between guilt and indignation. It had been so nice—why did he have to spoil everything? All her life she'd been up to her neck in duty and responsibility—didn't she deserve a rest? Why couldn't she just be his dear and sexy friend? Good night, it had taken her fifty-five years to learn to be a sexpot: why did Travis have to make a wife of her at this late date?

When she finally did sleep, her dreams were a jumble of sorrows: leaning against a cyclone fence, her fingers wrapped around its wires, watching people dance outside; waiting to be punished for sassing the teacher, when all she'd done was ask a question; standing inside a diamond-paned window, weeping as her friends leave for a party to which she's not allowed to go.

She woke up too early, feeling a hundred years old. The morning paper was full of disaster-blaring headlines: a missing child, the rape of a young woman, murders, and political accusations of graft and corruption from here to Christmas. Even Dear Abby was appalling this morning: a vicious daughter asking Abby to agree that she should have her father committed because he refused to acknowledge her "proof" that her dead mother'd had an extramarital affair. Poor man, Dorrie thought. Poor woman! Imagine being so angry at the dead that you passed it down to the living!

She wandered into the living room and started tidying up. George's picture was dusty, and she wiped it with her shirt tail.

"So now what?" she asked him. "I know you said I ought to find a new man, George, but really! Don't you think it's a bit soon? I'm just now learning to take care of myself. I don't want to put my life in somebody else's hands all over again." She shook her head. "It was one thing when I was twenty years old and fresh out of school, moving from my daddy's house into my husband's. Begging your pardon, George, it wasn't all that different from living at home.

But I've changed; now I feel as if I take up more room, somehow. I know they've taken 'obey' out of the marriage vows, but I'd still feel crowded with a man in the house, having to step aside and make way. I'm afraid I'm not as good at sharing as I used to be. It feels like giving myself away these days."

Lord, this room looked musty! Strange how the life went out of a room when you stopped using it. Clean, vacuumed, in perfect order, it looked like a room in a model home: uninhabited, furnished just for show. She'd bought a second TV, a little one, for the orchid room, and when Travis was in the house they stayed in the kitchen or back there until it was time to go upstairs.

How would her house feel with Travis in it? Living in his house—Janie's house—was out of the question. She'd made this house her own ten years ago when she'd redesigned it. Even though she rattled around in it now, she didn't want to leave. But she still wasn't one bit sure she was ready to bring somebody else here to share it.

"Shoot!" Dorrie said. She spent the day in a fit of cleaning.

Thirty-six

When Travis dropped into the store on Tuesday, he was cool and businesslike. He didn't mention his proposal and did not kiss her goodbye when he left. The next day she asked him to lunch. After they'd ordered, she reached across the table and took his hand.

"We've got to talk, Travis."

"I thought everything had been said."

"Of course it hasn't. You're hurt, and I'm sorry. I feel bad when I see you so silent and cold. It isn't like you."

"You pulled the rug out from under me pretty sharply. I was so sure you'd say yes."

"I'm sorry. I really am, but look at it my way, will you? I was married at twenty, straight out of school. I went from a sheltered girlhood to a sheltered womanhood—you commented yourself on how closely George had guarded me. Being sheltered is all very well, but you know there's another side to that coin: 'sheltering' is what they do for children, the retarded, and the insane. It's so confining!"

She looked into his eyes, but saw no understanding there.

"Travis, the past six months have been scary. I've had a lot to learn, and I didn't think I'd make it. But it was the first time in my life I've been really free, with no one but myself to account to."

"Freedom can be a lonely place, Dorrie."

"I know. I've felt that, too—that, and a fear almost like agoraphobia, as if all the boundaries had disappeared and I couldn't tell where safety lay. Even so, I like it. Maybe it's selfish, but I can do what I want when I want, and never have to explain myself to anyone. After a whole lifetime of explaining myself, I can't tell you how good that feels."

"So what do you want to do? What's so pressing, so private that you can't share it?"

The waitress came and set their plates down. Dorrie withdrew her hand, and Travis stared at the bowl of steaming vegetable soup and the BLT on his plate while they waited for the waitress to leave.

"That's just it. I don't know for sure." Dorrie looked down at the table. "What I'd like right now," she said quietly, "is to go on like we were a little longer while I figure it out. I'm going to

424

be around for a long time yet, God willing, and I want to consider all my choices before I decide."

"And how long will that take? A week? A month? A year? Five?"

"I don't know. Not before September, anyway. Two would never get over it if I remarried before his father had been dead a year. It will be shock enough that I'm considering marriage at all."

"Are you? Considering marriage?"

"Of course I am! But I'm considering the alternatives, too, and I don't want to be rushed." She reached across the table and took his hand again. "Just please give me time."

"What if I won't? What if I can't take maybe for an answer?"

Dorrie sighed. He had seemed so patient with her, right up to this moment. She hoped it would last just a little longer, but she wasn't about to be blackmailed. If he wouldn't, he wouldn't.

"In that case, Travis," she said, "the answer would have to be no. 'Maybe' is the best I can do right now."

Travis shook his head, exasperated disappointment on his face.

"Well, I guess it's time I got you back to the store, then. We can talk about it some more this weekend, if you like."

"What's the matter, Mom?" Marcie asked that

425

evening. She had picked Dorrie up on her way home, where Kurt was preparing another lovely dinner. "You're awful quiet tonight. Tired?"

Dorrie laughed softly. "You wouldn't believe it if I told you."

"Try me."

"Well, the truth is, I'm thinking about marriage. My own in particular, and marriage in general."

"Are you! Why?"

She was sorry she'd said anything, sorry she hadn't just pasted on a happy face and kept her thoughts to herself.

"It just came up, that's all."

"Come on, Mom, I didn't just fall off a turnip truck. People don't just think about marriage for no reason. What brought it up?"

She might as well tell her and get it over with, Dorrie thought. She was going to have to say something sooner or later, and Marcie'd be a lot easier to start on than Two.

"You know I've been seeing Travis Burton—I told you that."

Marcie grinned. "Two's fit to be tied, practically frothing at the mouth."

Dorrie smiled. "I'm glad you're not taking it as hard as he did. The thing is, Travis wants to make an honest woman of me." She grinned, watching Marcie's eyebrows shoot into her hairline. "He's asked me to marry him."

"You're kidding! When did all this happen?"

426

"It's been happening for several months. We started out with lunches, and then we had a few dates, and now I guess we're what you call 'an item.' The first time we went out together in the evening was in January, but it didn't really get . . ." she blushed, "serious until after I came home from California."

"So do you love him?"

Dorrie smiled. Marcie could deny it till she was blue in the face, but she was like George in so many ways. No chitchat — get straight to the point.

"I don't know. I mean, he's wonderful to me. I never saw anybody be so sweet to a woman except your Kurt. And he's kind and generous and thoughtful and all those good things . . . and romantic! Travis is so romantic it sometimes scares me! I'd marry him in a minute, if . . ." Her voice trailed off into embarrassed silence.

"What's stopping you, Mom? Is it just too soon, or have you got something against marriage, or what?"

"I don't know, honey," she said. "This is the first time in my life I've ever had a chance to look at marriage from the outside, so to speak, when I haven't either been married myself or living with married parents. I'm studying the question from a new perspective."

"I used to watch how things were with you and Dad," Marcie said. "Whatever he wanted was what you did, no matter how you felt about it. You'd take up for me or Two once in a while, but you never did take up for yourself. Let me tell you, Kurt had some tough talking to do when he wanted us to get married!"

"I'm sorry for that, honey. I'm sorry for a lot of things, but especially the way I let your dad ignore you kids." She sighed. "Watching the way other marriages work, I think maybe I never did get over being a little bit afraid of him; at least, of displeasing him. That's just the way I was brought up. The husband was master in his own house."

Marcie snorted. "And what did that make the rest of us?"

"It just never occurred to me to take up for myself—even that I'd need to. I wasn't raised to stand up to a man, only to stand by one. The husband made the decisions because the world held him responsible for the household; I asked once, and my mama said it wouldn't be fair to give him the responsibility without the power. That's just how things were done."

Dorrie looked down at her hands and then back up at Marcie's face, and sighed. Things were so different for women now. How could she make her daughter understand?

"The 'sexual revolution' and the 'empowerment of women' didn't come along till I'd been married twenty years," she said, "and my children were almost grown by then. There didn't seem to be any reason to change."

"Yes, there was. It's called 'slavery,' Mom."

Dorrie smiled. "Well, that's a little strong. 'Voluntary servitude' is closer, but even that . . . I did cooperate in it, honey. I might have felt rebellious once in a while, but I never did rebel."

"Why not? God, I could never live like that!"

"You're of another generation, though I will say your brother's doing his best to duplicate his parents' marriage."

"And why not? He's male! He's found himself a nice, docile, decorative little bride to fulfill his every whim — why should he change?"

"Susan cooperates in it, just like I did, though I spoke pretty strongly to her about that a few weeks ago." She was still surprised at the things she'd said to Susan. Maybe Susan would act on them sooner or later, and maybe she'd let them lie forever. A lot was at stake — more than Susan even knew. Start tinkering with a marriage at just one corner and the whole thing might collapse — or it might get to working better than you'd ever dreamed. It was a gamble, and Susan was no gambler.

"You have to understand the bargain, Marcie," Dorrie said. "First of all, of course, they really do love each other. But leaving that aside, he provides all her needs — food, clothing, social position, a nice house — and frees her from all serious decision-making. If anything major goes wrong, he's responsible. In return, she keeps herself and his house pretty, cooks his meals, bears and rears their children, coordinates his social life, and is always available for sex. She has no responsibilities at all outside the house and no final ones inside it; he oversees all her decisions. It's a tradeoff: she gives service and fidelity in exchange for an endless childhood, and he gives financial support and protection in return for absolute power. They're both getting what they want, even if it kills them."

"Endless childhood! What's the use of living?"

Dorrie laughed.

"You never could wait to be grown up, could you? You chafed under the restraints of childhood when you were four years old, but some people prefer them. It goes back to what my mother said: if you're not free, if you have no real power, you're not responsible. You can't be blamed when things go wrong. It just depends on who you are."

"So who are you, Mom?"

"I wish I knew," Dorrie said ruefully. "I didn't really begin to grow up till this year—didn't even know I hadn't. Here I am, looking at my fifty-sixth birthday and just now going through adolescence!"

At class Thursday night, Dorrie was still distracted. Compelling as Livvie's discussion of self-direction was, Dorrie could hardly keep her mind on it. When the topic moved to Inner Guidance, she was almost ready to leave the room. Inner guidance wasn't any more reliable than any other kind, she thought, and sometimes less—look at the mess it had got her into!

"Everyone has a guardian," Livvie said. "It doesn't matter what you call it: angel, spirit guide, 'God in you,' or even superconsciousness, we all have a system of guidance available to us all the time. But many people don't know how to access it for advice or instruction. One way is through meditation, and anyone can meditate. It doesn't require formal methods and steps— Joseph Campbell said all of life is a meditation, most of it unconscious and, I might add, most of it on the wrong things: which hairstyle suits you best or whether to buy the Ford or the Chevy. What I propose is to teach you a failproof method of going inside yourself to find your own truth."

If she had a choice, Dorrie thought, she'd take "superconsciousness." "God in you" still sounded arrogant, if not downright pretentious, and a spirit guide seemed a bit much, even after Rose.

"Shut your eyes," Livvie instructed. "Take a deep breath, and as you inhale, roll your eyes back as if to look out the top of your head. Now exhale slowly, and let your eyes roll back down to their natural level. That puts you in alpha. Now just breathe deeply a few times,

431

deeply enough that your belly expands on the inhalation, and relax." She paused, waiting, and then went on.

"Imagine yourself in front of a door. Take the first door you see, no matter what it looks like; the first door is the right one. And now open your door and step through it into the most beautiful and comfortable place you've ever imagined. Go ahead, now. Go on in and look around."

Dorrie found a heavy, industrial steel door. As she watched, it melted, leaving only a doorway ringed in light: no walls, no door, only the frame. She stepped through and found herself in a clearing in a wood with the ground rising before her. She walked up the grassy slope, found herself at the edge of a bluff overlooking a deep blue lake, and sat herself down on a fallen log.

"This is your own place. You can come here to rest whenever you want to, and here you can meet your guidance," Livvy's voice told her. "If you ask now, guidance will come."

Now what? Dorrie thought. A whirling column of mist at her left caught her eye, and she turned toward it. When it cleared, she was looking at the Old Man of the Wood: silvery, hooded cloak; beard halfway to his knees; walking stick carved with runic symbols; eyes shining with mischief under bushy white eyebrows. The whole picture was so overdone she wanted to laugh.

Give me a break! she thought. The old man laughed and shape-shifted into a plump, apple-faced old woman in a cotton housedress like those Rose had always worn. She seemed to be laughing, too, and as Dorrie stared, the old woman turned into a turbaned Oriental man in a white Nehru jacket.

Oh, cut it out! This is no time for that! Dorrie glanced away for a moment, and when she looked back, her dream friend was in the others' place. Her friend looked as tickled as a four-year-old with a private joke.

It's you! Dorrie thought. *What was that all about?*

I was just looking for a form you'd take as seriously as you've been taking yourself recently.

Olivia's voice cut short Dorrie's indignant response.

"Ask your guide anything you like. That's what guides are for."

Do you have a name? What can I call you?

How do you like 'Aurora'?

It's very pretty. Is that your name?

It'll do. Do you have any questions for me?

I don't know what I'm supposed to do. Travis wants to marry me. Should I marry him?

Do you want to marry Travis?

I don't think so. At least, not now. I'd feel like a coward.

433

Why?

Wouldn't it be sort of like running home to daddy?

Would it? Or would it be more like running away?

Running away! From what?

Aurora smiled, and Dorrie became uncomfortably aware of hiding something from herself.

"You're supposed to guide me, not pick on me! Dorrie thought. *If you can't be any more help than that, go away!*

Aurora faded slowly, like the Cheshire cat, and Dorrie's last sight of her was the patient amusement on her face. Dorrie felt as guilty as if she'd snapped at her grandma, and cross as well. She hadn't come here to be made guilty. She had a son for that and a lover. Aurora was supposed to make her happy.

"Your guardian's main job is to tell you the truth," Olivia said. "If the truth about your life makes you happy, your guardian will make you happy. If you're not doing what you set out to do, it will only make you examine your life until you find a way to shape up. Don't expect a pat on the back when you deserve a kick in the butt."

Thanks a lot, Dorrie thought. So much for "inner guidance." It's just the same as the outer: no use at all!

434

"Well, who came when you called?" Charmaine asked later over hot chocolate at the café.

Dorrie described her experience.

"She was playing with me!" she said. "Of all the guides in the universe, I get one that makes fun of me!"

Charmaine laughed. "Maybe that's what she thought you needed. You do tend to take yourself pretty seriously sometimes."

"I never have been flippant, if that's what you mean," Dorrie said. "But I didn't realize I was as self-absorbed as all that. I do have a sense of humor, Charmaine."

"I know you do, a great one. Now use it on yourself, sweet thing. Look, I know you've got problems — but I know of a thousand people who'd swap problems with you any day of the week. Quit worrying, will you?"

"You're almost as much help as Aurora. How did I get mixed up in all this foolishness, anyhow? Spirit guides! I'm no shaman!"

"You as much as any," Charmaine said. "Look, the point is just to listen to 'God in you' — by whatever name you call it — and do what seems right. Only you know what's right for you; nobody else can tell you or ought to try."

"Shoot! Maybe Travis is right. Maybe I ought to junk all this, become a wife again, and let

435

somebody else make the decisions. It sure is easier that way."

"He's asked?" Charmaine said. Dorrie nodded. "What did you say?"

"That he'll have to wait till I know what I want. But I don't want to have to answer to anybody, that's the big thing. I want to live according to my own lights, not somebody else's."

"Times have changed, girl. Anymore, being a wife doesn't have to mean you lose your decision power. Wives are equal partners now, or hadn't you heard?"

"My daughter is. My son's wife isn't. I guess it all depends on whom you marry."

"And who you are," Charmaine said. "But there's no way around it: if you want the marriage to work, being a wife is being half a whole. There's a lot to be said for it when it works, but independence has its advantages too. I couldn't have done half the things I've done if I'd been married."

"You *were* married, Charmaine. Three times."

Charmaine laughed.

"See? But I meant in between and since. If I were married right now, I'd be in California, not here. I don't want to be joined at the hip with anybody ever again. It makes me antsy. I guess the real question here is whether you want to play onesies or twosies."

"Travis hates it that I'm studying all this

stuff," Dorrie said. "Every time he finds one of my books, he goes all tight-jawed on me. He can hardly stand it."

"That's what I'm talking about," Charmaine said. "Look, Dorrie, you're not me; the same things aren't important to you. I'm real big on personal freedom, always have been, and you've always been able to put up with restrictions. And we all know my track record's nothing to brag on. But I will say this: I sure would think twice about marrying somebody who wouldn't let me follow my own nose."

Charmaine had the whole vocabulary down pat, Dorrie thought: personal freedom, restrictions, "God in you." Her and Livvy and Jedediah Peebles . . . even Aurora! It was a conspiracy!

"The problem is," she said, "I'm in trouble either way. If I say 'yes,' Two will be horrified; if I say 'no,' Travis will be hurt—he already is, and all I said was 'not right now.' I even thought about asking him just to live with me—people do it all the time now. But even leaving Two's opinion aside, I don't think he'd go for it. He wants to be married. And my feeling is, if the commitment's there we might as well marry, and if it's not, what are we doing?"

"Screwing around?" Charmaine said.

Dorrie laughed. "It's an inelegant description, but I suppose so."

"There's nothing wrong with that, you know.

437

The world's full of unmarried people who live together, and they're not all kids. You're as human as the next guy."

"I know: 'Old enough to know better and young enough not to care.' " Dorrie stared down at her naked hands. "I wish he'd never asked."

"How times have changed!" Charmaine said dryly.

Dorrie laughed. "You're right. My worst problem is whether or not to marry a thoroughly nice man who's also a wonderful lover. We should all be so unlucky! Well, I guess I'll sleep on it. Again."

Dorrie is in the garden on her hands and knees in the mud. The air is cool and the sky cloudy, and the soil smells rich and fertile from the rot of past years' growth. She is digging up clumps of iris and dividing the Shasta daisies she planted several years ago. They stay alive but do not bloom. Maybe if she moves them to a sunnier spot . . .

The lilies that used to give her such pleasure have all but taken over the garden, and she's tired of them. Their sweet odor seems cloying, and their pale colors lifeless. Susan likes them, Dorrie thinks. She will give them to Susan and plant poppies in their place. She sees clumps of papery, scarlet blooms with black centers, ferny leaves in place of the lilies' straplike foliage.

Yes. And in front of them, brilliant gaillardia, golden coreopsis, royal blue salvia: hardy, bright flowers that thrive in heat or cold, impervious to drought and pests.

On the warm side of the house, she sees buds on the Peace rose, her favorite. She lifts a bud in her hand and watches as it slowly opens, yellow blushing to pink, into full bloom. The fragrance rising from its petals fills her head and makes her smile.

Thirty-seven

When Travis came on Saturday, he brought Dorrie a bouquet of pink and white carnations, painted daisies, and blue iris. Thanking him, she touched his cheek briefly with her own and carried the flowers to the kitchen.

"They're lovely, Travis," she said, reaching up over the refrigerator for a vase. "I do like fresh flowers."

"I've been acting like an ass. I'm sorry, Dorrie."

She glanced up, startled. He looked miserable.

"I'm sorry I hurt you," she said. "You do understand, though?"

"Sure. I won't mention it again. Just let me know when you're ready to talk about it, okay?"

But all through the evening, Dorrie felt as if she were on tiptoe. The issue lay between them like a sleeping bear, demanding a wide and silent space. Travis drank more than usual, insisted on watching a movie that didn't begin till midnight, and then fell asleep on the couch while it was playing.

Like George, Dorrie thought, hurt. George had always gone to sleep before bedtime so there could be no question of making love to her. *I work so hard for you,* the act had said. *Worry myself to exhaustion. How can you ask me to make love to you besides?* Well, let him sleep on the couch then, Dorrie thought. When the movie ended, she covered him with a light blanket and went upstairs alone.

In bed, she lay and thought about the man downstairs who wanted to marry her. A good man, over all. A kind one and, next to George, a miracle of sensitivity. Except, of course, for this one lapse, and that was partly her fault; she'd hurt him . . . But if she married him . . . then what? Would he retreat like George behind a newspaper while she fixed his dinner, washed his socks, made up his bed? *Her* bed!

That was another question: where would they live? Not here. Her very flesh shrank at the thought of bringing another man into her house, but this house was the only solid and unchanging thing in her topsy-turvy life. Her mooring. To leave it would be to sail off into the great unknown like a balloon at the mercy of the world's winds. No telling where she'd come down, or if she ever would come down at all.

Still, she thought, her life so far hadn't been such a glowing success. She had strayed from her purpose like a lost sheep. The picture of The Good Shepherd that had hung in Rose's parlor for so many years formed in her mind: sweet, long-haired young man, lamb wrapped around his neck . . . She shook herself. Turning Travis into The Good Shepherd would not avail. If she'd learned anything at all in the past months, it was that she was responsible for her own salvation.

But marriage did have its points. It was safe, for one thing, a nice, safe, conventional thing to do. A second chance too. If she could just do it right once—create a really happy, loving, intimate marriage, a true union . . . but of course there was no guarantee of that, not with the best will in the world, and if she failed . . .

Dorrie sighed. It might be nice, though, someone beside her for the rest of her life. Somebody to talk to, who would talk back. A warm and affectionate body beside her in the night . . . Travis loved to cuddle, loved the sweet shared jokes and intimate talk she'd always yearned for as much as he loved the act itself. He liked to be naked with her and unashamed. He loved her nakedness with all its flaws. With Travis she felt desirable, even sometimes beautiful, after all those years of feeling plain and dumpy with a man who despised sex and let her think it was her fault. And she didn't have to play a role with him. Whatever she truly was seemed to be okay with Travis, at least most of the time. A woman could do worse.

What had Aurora meant about marriage being like running away? Dorrie wondered impatiently. Running from what? *Yourself,* some part of her whispered. *If you concentrate on being half, you can avoid learning to be whole.*

Shoot! Dorrie thought, flopping over on her other side. Why couldn't she have both: her love and her life? Greed, that was her problem. She'd started to enjoy her time alone. She was, she realized with a small shock, less lonely with George gone than she'd been with him there.

Lord, what a puzzle! The hard choices of her life had always yielded to list-making: drawbacks on the left, benefits on the right, matched up point for point. Not this. With this, the factors kept changing character every time she looked at them. Onesies or twosies, Charmaine had said. Dorrie pulled the pillow over her head and willed herself to sleep.

Dorrie is in an airport again, trying to find the right gate. The gates are out of sequence, and some have letters instead of numbers. She keeps referring to her ticket envelope, but the numbers on it change each time she looks.

She is overloaded with old baggage. Awkward, heavy, the bags and bundles keep falling out of her arms, but she stubbornly keeps bending over to pick them up. A man steps on her hand and doesn't even say "excuse me"; he gives her a scornful look instead, as if she'd put her hand under his foot on purpose. The airport is so crowded she can hardly make her way, and as she drops her bags they begin to disappear. She is not sorry. She'll miss them, but they were too heavy to carry anymore, and the things in them were worn and out of date. She will replace them when she arrives, if she can only find the plane.

"Flight 231 now boarding for . . ." The rest of the message is garbled, but that is her flight number. She looks up at a TV monitor that held flight information a moment ago, but now it is showing a Roadrunner cartoon: Wylie Coyote runs off the edge of a cliff, looks down, realizes he is not on solid ground, and plummets off the screen.

Bodies press in on her from every side, and she cannot get her breath. She lets go of the last of her old baggage and starts elbowing people out of the way. If she doesn't find the gate soon, the plane will go without her and she will be left alone again, with her business finished and nothing to do. She is nearly frantic, searching for the gate.

* * *

Dorrie woke to the smells of bacon and coffee. Downstairs, she found Travis preparing a breakfast tray.

"Good morning," she said. "You certainly look busy!"

"I was just bringing you breakfast in bed."

"I appreciate the thought, but I'm up now. Can I do anything?"

"It's almost done. Just sit."

Travis dropped bread in the toaster, poured the coffee, and brought the breakfast to the table.

"Sleep well?" he asked, sitting opposite her. "I'm sorry I crapped out on you like that."

"I guess it's been a rougher week for you than I realized."

"Well, it won't happen again."

"Relax, Travis." A hint of sharpness edged her voice. "You don't have to make love to me every time we're together, you know. Only when you want to."

Travis gave her a long look, assessing her intent.

"I did want to," he said. "I just passed out before I got to it." He shook his head, as if in wonder. "You're something, Dorrie. I've never known anybody just like you."

She smiled. "That's good?"

"It's wonderful."

"So being different is okay? Or do I have to be different in just the right way?"

"What do you mean?" Travis shrugged. "I love you as you are. I guess I'd hate it if you painted your face green and shaved your head, but I'd still love you." He stared at her, aware that his answer hadn't satisfied. "What are you after, Dorrie? What is it?"

"My 'spook books.' My classes at the Psychic Association. Do they paint my face green?"

"Oh, that." He sighed and looked away. "I don't understand why you do it. You're too smart to be taken in by that sort of nonsense."

"I'm just trying to sort the wheat from the chaff." She saw him draw breath to argue, but cut him short. "There is wheat, Travis. If I hadn't had . . . unusual experiences of my own, I never would have read word one about it, but I have."

"What experiences are you talking about?"

Dorrie laughed wryly. "Oh, just little stuff. Visions. Instantaneous healings. Visitations from the dead. Picking up information out of thin air. Your normal, run-of-the-mill psychic stuff."

"God damn," Tarvis said, his voice flat. "I guess you'd better tell me, Dorrie."

"Where shall I start?"

"The visitations will do. George?"

446

"My grandmother, first. She died about thirty years ago. She came to me when she died."

"I see." He stared at the tabletop with a determined patience that irritated her and then looked up. "You want to tell me about it?"

She did, briefly and without emotion.

"What else?" he asked.

"I had another . . . encounter with her in California, in January, and she still comes to me once in a while. The other things . . . well, they're hard to describe and impossible to explain."

"And George? Does he come to you too?"

Dorrie didn't like his tone of voice, but she was determined to stay calm. "Not any more. I haven't been much aware of him for months now." If she knew Travis another fifty years, she would never tell him about Sedona.

Travis shook his head. "What happens when your grandmother comes to you?"

"Nothing special. It's like talking with her. She always says she loves me."

Travis looked up at her, his face full of frustration. "Dorrie, *I* love you! She's dead! Your grandmother's dead, and George is dead, and Janie's dead! I'm real; I'm here; I *exist!* Why can't you accept love from the living and let the dead lie?"

"It's not like that. I'm not holding séances, for pity's sake! I don't have any control over it!"

He reached across the table and took her hand. "That's what worries me. Dorrie, they're gone! Let them go! This is morbid. Find something healthy to occupy your mind. This scares the hell out of me!"

Dorrie shook her head, her jaw set. "Neither my sanity nor my immortal soul is in danger, Travis. I've just got to figure things out the best I can, and I'm looking for answers wherever I can find them. The old answers just won't do anymore." She paused for a moment, and then looked straight into his troubled eyes.

"I'm sorry if it worries you, Travis, but this is my life and my mind. I have to use it my way. If we're going to be friends, you'll just have to trust me."

"Who does he think he is?" she asked Domino later, after Travis had left. "That was the very thing I was afraid of: here I've been fighting off Two for months, and Travis no more than asks me to marry him before he starts trying to take over my life! Do you think if I said yes, he'd present me with a list of forbidden books?"

"Yow," the cat said. He jumped into her lap and rubbed his head against her shoulder.

"I guess I've grown up some, though," she said. "If that'd been George, I would have said 'yes, dear,' and hidden the books away forever so he'd never see what I was reading again. At least I told him."

Domino jumped to the back of the pink velvet couch and batted aimlessly at the tassel that hung from the bottom of Bellefleur's hanging basket.

"Cut it out," Dorrie told him. "You knock that down and you're a dead cat."

He grinned at her—there was no other word for it—and leaped to the floor. Dorrie looked at her plant and saw that the bud sheath had at last opened. It contained three tight buds, pointed at each end like pale green bombs. They were about as big as her thumb, and a new lead had begun to grow from the front of the plant. It would flower again when these were gone.

On Monday, Travis called and invited her to dinner at his house. The peace between them still seemed fragile, and she was careful not to mention any sore subjects while they ate. While they were cleaning up afterward, he put his hand on her arm to get her attention.

"There's something I have to tell you," he said. "About last Sunday: I was wrong, Dorrie. You're an intelligent woman and a sensible one. If that's what you're interested in, you have a perfect right to read it till your eyes fall out. I still think it's weird, but that's not your problem: it's mine, and I'll just have to live with it."

Dorrie stood stock still, too amazed to respond. In her whole life, she could never remember her husband—or her father, for that matter—making such a concession.

Thirty-eight

The following day when Charmaine came to Dorrie's for supper and the evening, she seemed unable to sit still for two minutes at a stretch. Her mind was far away.

"What in the world is the matter with you?" Dorrie asked her at last. "You've been pacing this house like a caged beast all night!"

"Guess my feet are getting itchy again," Charmaine said. "Do you realize I've been home for more than half a year? That's the longest I've stayed in one place forever!"

"Where do you want to go?"

"Can't make up my mind. China. Egypt, see the Pyramids. England, maybe, to Stonehenge and around there. They've been doing a lot of archeological digs in England the past few years. Do you know, they think they might have found Camelot?"

"Camelot! That's a myth!"

451

"Maybe not. There's a guy thinks he knows who Arthur was, and they've found remains . . . castle walls and things. I'd kind of like to go and have a look-see."

"England," Dorrie said softly. "To me, England is Jane Austen and the Brontës. Flower gardens. I've always had this yen to taste strawberries and Devonshire cream. If reincarnation's a fact, I think I must have been happy there."

"Think so? It'd be fun to go and see how much at home you felt. And there's London, of course . . . I could spend a month just looking around London."

"All the places you've been, and you've never been to England?"

Charmaine shook her head. "I've missed all of Europe, somehow. Hey, you know what I'd like?"

"What's that?"

"I'd like to take a year or so and go around the world. Eastern Europe's open now and Russia and China . . . How'd you like to go to China, Dorrie? See the Great Wall, go to where they dug up all those statues of soldiers?"

"I can hardly imagine it. That trip to Los Angeles was about as far from Dallas as I've ever been."

"You're kidding me."

"No. There just never was any reason to go. George took me on business trips sometimes, but they were no sightseeing tours. I stayed in hotels playing George Greene's Lovely Wife."

"Blaah! Give me shelter!"

Dorrie laughed. "It wasn't that bad! It's just that all I ever saw was the insides of fancy ballrooms and convention centers where jewelry was being shown. It wasn't fun, but of course we didn't go for fun." She grinned. "I've come to the recent conclusion that George didn't believe in fun."

"Shoot, I could have told you that thirty years ago! Go with me, Dorrie — I'll show you fun! We'll fly to London, take a train down to Somerset, spend a month in an eighteenth century manor house that's been converted to bed and breakfast. We can rent a car . . . Come on, Dorrie, it'll be great!"

"Like when?"

"Hell, next week! Tomorrow!"

"Charmaine, give me a break! I can't just go kiting off to England with you like that! I have a store to run, a garden to catch up with, a man wanting to marry me . . . I can't go anywhere now!"

"Give it a rest, girl. Zada runs the business for you, and you can hire a gardener. Travis will live; it'll get him off your back, give you time to think. You just never have been able to handle spontaneous action, that's your problem. Come on, take a chance; for once in your life, do something you haven't thought to death first!"

She was probably right, Dorrie thought, but all the same . . .

"You're not talking about some weekend in Los Angeles, Charmaine. You said a month, and that's just to start. Lord only knows where you'll want to go after England, but I'll lay down money it won't be home!"

"Okay. Not tomorrow. Not even next week, but soon. Think how wonderful it would be, getting away by ourselves, leaving your troubles behind, seeing someplace you've never, ever been in your whole life . . . Will you just do that? Will you just think about it?"

A picture flashed across the screen of Dorrie's mind: a small, stone house roofed in thatch, set like a topaz in an emerald lawn and surrounded by beds of brilliant delphiniums and pinks, roses blooming by the wide front door—the homiest house on earth, with a soft, white-haired woman smiling by the door, her arms outstretched.

"Oh, Charmaine, don't tempt me!"

"If I don't, who the hell will? It's my job!"

Dorrie grinned. "All right, I'll think about it. I really will, but will you do me one favor? Don't push me, will you?"

"Tell you what: I've got some business of my own to wind up before I take off again. It'll only take a few weeks if everything goes all right—take you a month to get a passport anyway."

She crossed the room and looked at a calendar hanging on the wall.

"I'll make reservations for us to fly out June 20—that's a Friday—and I'll set up our accommodations. That gives you six whole weeks to make up your mind, Dorrie, and I promise I won't bug you more'n once a week between now and then. Now, I ask you, does that sound fair? Is that a generous offer?"

Dorrie shook her head. "Coming from you, it's more than fair. All right, it's a deal."

"She's doing it again, Domino," Dorrie said when Charmaine had gone home. She was reading late again, and when her eyes had begun to feel sandy, she'd laid the book down. Domino lay beside her on the bed, purring. "Now she's gone off to collect travel brochures and start making plans for me that I don't even know about. It's only been two hours, and it's already too late to say no! Charmaine's been that way all our lives, like a force of nature. I always get mad at myself afterward, but I'd as soon go up against a tornado as argue with Charmaine."

She stroked his black-and-white fur, and the cat stretched beneath her hand. Charmaine was one of the few strangers he allowed to touch him, and he came to meet her at the door. Sometimes she said hello to the cat before she greeted Dorrie.

"You can't help loving her, she's been so good to us," Dorrie said. "I've always loved her anyway, even when I didn't approve one bit of what she was doing." It reminded her of the "hearts as gifts" discussion with Travis. "I guess Charmaine's the one who taught me you can love somebody you don't approve of. I just thought she was a special case." She scratched in front of Domino's tail, and he raised his back the better to enjoy it. "I only wish she wouldn't be so quick to shanghai me into her fits of whimsy."

"Meee-yat?" the cat asked.

"Like California. I don't know yet how she talked me into that — just bowled me over, and the next thing I knew, there I was on an airplane to L.A., and then in the wink of an eye to the canyons of Arizona. I never even had a chance to catch my breath. I don't suppose it did me any permanent harm, but it's just so . . . unsettling!"

She'd stopped petting him as she spoke. Domino fitted his head into the curve of her palm and pushed.

"All right," she said, and scratched behind his ears. England! It was so far away, farther than she'd ever been before. But she had to admit Charmaine was right: the store didn't need her, and the garden had just been an excuse. Even Travis . . .

She felt as whipped up and spun around by what was happening with Travis as she'd ever felt with Charmaine, but Travis was different; he didn't operate on whims. Travis was offering her permanence in a world so fast-changing that she could hardly keep up with it, where all

Charmaine ever offered was disruption.

Dorrie grinned. Not that Charmaine's disruptions weren't interesting; only that they were always so strange and sudden. She'd complained one time, and Charmaine had told her it kept the blood moving through her veins — that without Charmaine, Dorrie would get so stodgy her veins would clog, and she'd die of simple boredom. But there was no likelihood that her blood would turn to jelly in her veins with Travis. Just the opposite: she could feel it pumping every time she thought of him.

Why couldn't they both just leave her in peace, let her make up her mind in her own time? She hated change!

Dorrie reached for the light, and the cat jumped off her bed. Still, for all the disruptions they'd caused in her life, she wouldn't give back a minute of the time she'd spent with either one of them this year. It was a matter of control, she decided. All she wanted was to be in control of her own life and not answering to other people's demands. Was that so much to ask?

Sunday, after breakfast, as Dorrie and Travis sat at the table reading snippets out of the newspaper to one another, they heard the front door open and shut. Travis turned toward the sound.

"What's that?" he said. "Are you expecting anybody?"

"Mom?" Two's voice called. "Mom!"

"In the kitchen," she answered. She smiled helplessly across the table, feeling like a schoolgirl caught necking on the couch. "My son," she whispered.

"I just dropped in to—" Two said, pushing open the dining-room door. The sight of Travis stopped him as abruptly as a glass wall. Dorrie saw his eyes widen and his face darken.

"Good morning, Two," she said. "You remember Travis Burton."

Travis stood and extended his hand across the table.

"I haven't seen you since you graduated med school, George. Your father was very proud of you."

"Your accountant?" Two stared at the hand as if it were floating disembodied in the air, shook his head sharply, and looked up at Dorrie.

"May I speak to you privately, Mother?"

"What is it?"

"Please, Mother. Alone."

"Excuse us, Travis," she said. "I won't be a moment." Dorrie rose and followed Two's rigid back into the living room.

"May I ask what that man is doing here at this hour on a Sunday morning?" he demanded. "What's going on here, Mother?"

"Use your eyes, Two. He's reading the paper. What are you doing here?"

"I went out for doughnuts and stopped by to

see if you'd go to church with the family." He snorted. "Looks like you could use it."

Dorrie stiffened. "No, thanks. If I thought your church had anything to offer me, I'd go without an invitation." Her lips felt as stiff as if glue had dried on them, and she was hunched like a turtle in its shell. She squared her shoulders. "Wasn't it Jesus who said, 'Judge not, lest ye be judged'? It seems to me you're leaping to a slanderous conclusion, Two. Where is it written that I can't have a guest to Sunday morning brunch?"

Two turned away from her and started pacing the room. "He looked awful damn comfortable sitting at your kitchen table in his stocking feet with his shirt open. For God's sake, Mother, his hair's wet!"

Dorrie had to laugh. "Is that what's bothering you? Wet hair? Good night, Two, I thought it was something serious!"

"This is serious! My God, Mother!"

Dorrie sat down on the end of the couch. She laid her bare hands in her lap and stared at them for a moment, sighed, and looked up at her son.

"I suppose you're right: it is serious. Here I am, coming up fifty-six years old, raised two children, widowed nine months, and the very child I raised thinks it's his duty to run my life. Son, I apologize. I don't know what I'm doing wrong. Try as I may, I can't seem to make you understand that I'm a full-grown human being, entitled to make my own decisions."

Two's face was approaching purple, she noted, and his eyes were nearly popping out of his head. Better get his blood pressure checked before he had a stroke of his own. She'd suggest that later, but now Dorrie felt the power of righteous indignation flowing through her veins, forcing itself out in ice-hot words.

"I'm really getting tired of telling you this, Two, but let me try it one more time. If I went out tomorrow, draped myself in satins and furs, took a twenty-two-year-old lover, and flew to Monte Carlo to play my life away at baccarat, it would be my choice and you'd have no right to interfere. For the last time, this is *my life!* From here on out I intend to live it my way. If I want your opinion, I'll ask for it. Is that perfectly clear?"

Two looked absolutely poleaxed, she saw with some satisfaction. He stared at her for a full minute before gathering himself to nod.

"Good. Thank you for dropping by, then, and I'm afraid I'll have to decline your kind invitation. Is there anything else?"

Two, still red and now beginning to sputter, looked toward the kitchen, turned back toward his mother, and shook his head.

"Then you'd better get those doughnuts home. You don't want to be late to church."

Still shaking his head, Two drifted toward the front door. Dorrie turned smartly and marched back to the kitchen.

"Well?' Travis said.

Dorrie smiled broadly and sat down.

"I really do that very well," she said. "I had no idea. Should have started years ago."

"Do what?"

She laughed. "That's the first time I can ever remember standing up on my hind legs and saying, 'You can't do this to me.' It's astounding! He rolled right over!"

"Good for you," Travis said uncertainly. "I guess that means you're all right?"

"All right! Travis, I'm the Queen of the World!"

Thirty-nine

The letter from Bijoux arrived at the store the last week of April.

Dear Ms. Greene,

Last November, Bijoux made an offer to purchase Hunter & Greene Jewelers. To our regret, that offer was rejected.

We have looked for other properties in the University section of Dallas, but have found nothing suitable for our purpose. Therefore we would like you to consider another proposal for the sale of your store.

Our representative, Mr. Fred Savage, will be in Dallas May 7 and will call for an appointment. We have increased our offer significantly and hope you will reconsider at that time . . .

"What do you think?" Dorrie asked, handing it to Travis over lunch.

Travis's eyebrow rose as he read the letter.

"Well, it looks like you've got a decision to make. May 7—that's less than two weeks away! What do you want to do?"

"I'm not sure; I might take them up on it. It can't hurt to listen, anyhow." Dorrie grinned. "They offered me the world last time; I guess they're fixing to throw in the moon and stars now."

"Do you want me to meet with the two of you when he comes?"

"Of course. I'm a lot more savvy than I was last fall, but you're the professional. It's only natural to include my accountant, don't you think?"

"Better get Walt Longstreet in on it, too, if you're serious." He looked closely at her. "You are serious, aren't you. You're going to sell this time."

"I think so. It's . . ." She hesitated. "I know this is going to sound frivolous, but it's just not fun. Travis, I'm fifty-five years old and I've got enough money to last the rest of my life. I shouldn't have to do anything I don't enjoy, and frankly, the store bores me to distraction. The first little while, I felt like I was finally playing with the big kids, but now . . ." She laughed, surprised at herself. "I guess now I am one of the big kids!"

"All right!" Travis said. "It's about time you figured that out!

* * *

That afternoon she cut a bouquet of airy, long-stemmed, pink and purple pincushion flowers, Shasta daisies, and her special, collectors-item bearded iris and carried it through the hedge to Jessie.

"I'm celebrating," she told her. "I think I'm going to sell the store."

"Are you! I wondered how long it would take. It was good for you for a while—took your mind off your troubles, I expect—but you were never really cut out for that."

"I know. I think I just had to hang onto my little blue blankie for a while longer. They made the offer last fall, but I felt as if everything were being taken away at once; I turned them down. Now I'm ready, and I can let go of it on my terms."

"Well, sit down, Dorrie, and we'll have a glass of tea to celebrate." Jessie got down glasses and opened the refrigerator door. Over her shoulder, she said, "What will you do now?"

"I'll keep busy. My garden's gone straight to the devil this spring—I'll spend some time out there. Study . . . I have to clear a path through all the books to get from the front door to the back." She took a swallow of tea. "Travis wants me to marry him, but I haven't been able to make up my mind to it."

"Marry you! My goodness, Dorrie, I had no idea!"

Dorrie laughed. "Well, there, you see? You can't learn everything by looking out of windows!"

"But tell me about it! How come you can't make up your mind to it? What's wrong with him?"

"There's nothing wrong with Travis. He's a prince among men if I ever met one. It's just . . . I don't know, Jessie. I've known since the day I married George that he'd die before me, but I didn't expect it to be like this. I thought I'd be older, maybe in my sixties." She laughed softly. "You know how old that looks to a twenty-year-old girl! I thought I'd be an old woman and that I'd just dress in black and live the rest of my life alone. I've never minded being alone. And even when I got up into my thirties and forties, I still never thought I'd marry again. I mean, I was doing then what I thought marriage was about: rearing children and keeping house, and there was no reason to do it all over again.

"I even wondered why older people bothered to marry at all, what with the sexual revolution and all, and people of all ages living together right and left without benefit of clergy. Why marry? It only messes up your finances! But now I don't know. Travis wants marriage; he wants permanence and commitment and a lifelong companionship. I ought to want marriage. It's the expected thing in a society built for two. I'm lucky to have found anyone at my age, let alone

465

anyone like Travis. You'd think I'd want to hang onto him!" She smiled. "I even want to want marriage. I just haven't talked myself into it yet."

Jessie reached across the table and patted her hand. "Well, goodness knows there's something to be said for lifelong companionship, even if it does get in the way from time to time. That old bed can get awful cold, too, without a man to warm it, and I've always thought one was better than a bunch. You can get comfortable with just one, where a different one every time would be an awful strain." She grinned. "Not to mention the difficulty of finding them at our age. Look, I know it's a cliché, Dorrie, but sayings only become clichés because they're true: listen to your heart. You don't want to go repenting in leisure."

Dorrie smiled. Jessie always had been so open with her feelings; never felt the need to hide a thing, just laid it out for the world to see. Dorrie'd always envied her that. Half the time, she didn't even know her own feelings.

"I don't want to repent at all. That's why I'm not in any hurry to make up my mind." Dorrie shook her head. "He's being really patient, but I'm going to have to decide something pretty soon."

She stirred her tea idly, listening to the ice clink. "Charmaine wants me to go to England with her. I might do that just to get away, avoid the decision for a while. Maybe I'll see it clearer from six thousand miles away."

"England! Oh, Dorrie, how exciting! When?"

"It's not for sure, but late June. She wants to stay a month, she says, but you know Charmaine: it could be a year."

"So what's stopping you? God Almighty, I'd be on the first plane out of here!"

"Well, there's Travis . . ." she said. "I've put him off, but he won't wait forever. And the store; I've got to get that cleared up. And of course, there's Two. Two's ready to have me committed." She told Jessie about their confrontation, and Jessie hee-hawed like a donkey, wheezing to catch her breath.

"Good for you, Dorrie!" She reached across the table and grasped Dorrie's wrist. "So now where's the twenty-two-year-old lover? And does he have a friend?"

"You've got to be kidding! The only way I'd take a kid that age is fried!"

Jessie laughed. "Oh, I don't know, it depends on what you want to do with him. You might have a real good time!"

"Give me a break, Jessie! What do I know about Twisted Sister and the Grateful Dead? The Velvet Fog is more my speed!" She grinned. "But I'll tell you what, as mad as I was, if I'd known a boy that age, I'd have fitted him out with a tux and taken him to the Starlight Ballroom just for spite. Let Two chew on that for a while!"

"I take it you haven't straightened it out with him yet."

"Not yet. We will, of course, but I'm letting him think about it. Maybe by next fall, if I do decide to marry Travis, he'll be relieved that somebody's keeping me out of worse trouble."

"Do you think you will?"

"I don't know, I really don't. I just don't know if I want to do it again."

"Well, of course it wouldn't be the same. I mean, you're older—your kids are grown now, and you must've learned something in the first marriage. And he's not George . . . Is he like George?"

"Not a bit. Different as night and day. But I just have this feeling Travis wants us to walk arm in arm forever down the rest of life's road, and I don't want to walk arm in arm with anybody—not even somebody I love. I'm willing to consider side by side, but only on condition that if one of us finds an appealing detour that doesn't interest the other, we can meet back up at the junction."

Jessie laughed. "Have you told him how you feel?"

"I didn't know until just this minute when I heard myself say it." Dorrie smiled. "Isn't it surprising what you hear coming out of your own mouth!"

"It's true, George," she told him later. It was harder and harder to feel his presence anymore. The living room felt as empty as a warehouse.

"That's the problem, I think: I just don't want anybody interfering with my newfound freedom. Is that selfish?"

She didn't think so. It was just that she was feeling like a sixteen-year-old kid with his first driver's license: she wanted to get out and go. Maybe later she'd settle down, be more willing to accept trade-offs, do somebody else's thing instead of insisting on doing her own. But right now, the feeling was too new. She wanted to enjoy it.

Dorrie stands at the top of a tall, round tower, peering between its crenellations at a terrifying scene below. People scream as flames lick the tower walls and spurt out the windows; on the ground, large black dogs snarl and slaver, attacking those who try to escape through the door. A hooded man, robed all in black and mounted on a black horse, stands guard. Someone falls headlong, wailing, from a window, and the dogs leap up to tear his flesh. Thunder rolls, shaking the tower, and Dorrie sees a great bolt of lightning strike the top of a distant hill. Where it touches, the earth splits. The crack runs toward her like a freight train, widening as it comes, and Dorrie watches it swallow the trees and buildings in its path.

She stares in growing horror at the destruction around her, and then thinks, "This is not real.

This is a dream." She is less alarmed, but still not willing to stay where she is; the crack is nearly upon her. She climbs to the highest point she can reach and looks down. Heights have always petrified her.

"Jump!" someone calls. Dorrie performs a perfect swan dive toward the ground, spreading her arms like a bird. Halfway down, she lifts her head and her body follows. She is flying! She flaps her hands and finds she can steer—up and down with her head, side to side with her hands. Swooping and diving, gliding on the air like a gull, Dorrie is ready to jump out of her skin with astounded joy. I'm free! she thinks. Look at me! I can fly!

The earth splits, and the tower collapses into it. Dust rises to obscure her vision of the people below. All she can hear, soaring far above them, is the thunderous fall of the tower and the people's wailing.

Marcie called her the next evening.

"Your birthday's next Friday," she said. "Kurt and I thought we could have a party: Two and his, Charmaine, Jessie and Reese Buynum, Travis Burton. It's about time we got acquainted with Travis, don't you think?"

Dorrie laughed. "Thanks, honey. It's a lovely idea, but I do wonder about the wisdom of putting Two in the same room with Travis and Charmaine." She hadn't seen Reese since last fall, either, and that could be interesting. Surely he wouldn't embarrass her in front of Jessie. "I don't know that we could keep the lid on with just one of them!"

"I'll speak to Susan beforehand. You know her horror of 'unpleasantness.' We'll keep him in line."

"Knowing your tact, dear, I'm sure there won't be any trouble."

Marcie laughed. "Don't forget, Mom, Kurt will be there. He'll keep me in line."

"Well, it's an interesting idea."

"So how's it going with Travis? You've been awfully quiet."

"I'm still thinking, honey. He asked, and I said, 'Not now,' and he said, 'When?' and I said, 'I don't know,' and that's where it stands. You know I never was one for snap decisions."

"Will he wait?"

"He'll have to. I'm not going to be rushed into a decision that'll affect the rest of my life, and I think that deep down, he respects that. Travis doesn't leap without looking either." She laughed. "It's just, he thinks he's looked long enough, and he can't understand why I haven't. We'll work it out, honey. That is, if he survives the birthday party!"

Travis picked her up at the store Friday afternoon, and they went for an early supper at the Chinese restaurant a few blocks from his house. He'd been out of town on business for more than a week, and she'd missed him.

"How did it go?" she asked in the car. "Did you have a good time?"

"Well, I missed you, of course," Travis said. He reached for her hand and laid it on his thigh. "But other than that, it was all right. I visited a half-dozen clients out in West Texas and Albuquerque, and then made a quick trip up to Santa Fe to visit my daughter." He paused. "I didn't quite know what to say about us, just told her I'd met a woman I was interested in and a little about you. Have you thought any more about marrying me?"

Dorrie laughed. "If you must know, I've thought about little else. Travis, I do love you; how could I not? That's not the problem. I just . . . Maybe it's just too soon. And there's so much else going on right now."

"The store? We've got that meeting with Savage on Tuesday. Did you call Longstreet?"

She had. George's lawyer was even older than George; he'd been her father's lawyer, too, in the style of the Victorian "old retainer." Dorrie had known him a long time, but never well; his frosty demeanor kept people at arms' length. Except for a few special clients of many years' standing, he'd retired several years ago.

"I don't know how much help he's going to

be," Dorrie said. "I invited him along for the meeting, and he wasn't real enthusiastic about going. Though I do think he'll be relieved to be out of it. I'd like to find a new lawyer, but once this is over I don't expect to have much use for one. If I wait long enough—"

"You'll need a new will. Do you want him to handle that?"

"He can handle a simple will, Travis, and it will be simple: a few charitable bequests, and everything else to be divided equally between the two children. I'm not one of those people who go around leaving the spring to young lovers."

He laughed. "They can't have it, Dorrie; we're still using it." He reached down and squeezed her hand. "But of course, every day is spring with you."

"Travis, you silver-tongued devil, you!" Dorrie laughed. "Where do you get all these things?"

"From a fertile mind, my dear. You can't read poetry for fifty years without picking up a few turns of phrase. The problem is, finding somebody to use them on. You're the perfect object, Dorrie: everything I ever heard or read about love applies to you."

"You're embarrassing me," she said. "I never knew anybody so extravagant with praise. Sometimes I think you must be making fun of me."

"Never. It's a new kind of love, Dorrie, apples and oranges. Not even oranges: bananas! I can't even speak of it in the same breath with the first one. Youthful marriages are for growing up to-gether, having and rearing children, building up an estate. They start out romantic, but when the first infant's cry is heard in the house, the ro-mance begins to go. However much the couple may adore each other, they're involved in as much a business relationship as a love match.

"But at our age, all that's over. We've pretty well done whatever we're going to do profession-ally, and our kids are grown and gone. If all's gone well, there's not much more we can do for them, either, except keep on loving them and ad-vise them if they ask. The hard part's over for us. We can look forward to all the time alone we want, to travel and rest and read books and talk about them, take up hobbies, join a little theater group, anything we want to do—together. They don't call them 'The Golden Years' for nothing, Dorrie, and those are the years I want to spend with you."

"It's a magnificent offer, Travis, it truly is. I'm probably an utter fool not to jump at it. But give me time, please. I'm just not ready."

They turned into the restaurant's parking lot, and Travis parked and cut off the motor.

"Just promise to tell me when, sweetheart. I'll be ready."

Forty

It was raining hard when Travis picked Dorrie up for the party.

"We're under a tornado watch," she told him. "That'll be interesting on the twentieth floor of a glass building."

"It'll be a good show, anyhow. You're not worried, are you?"

Dorrie laughed shortly. "I'm a lot more worried about a tornado inside."

"We're all grown-up people," Travis said. "I know my last meeting with your son didn't work out real well, but maybe we can do better this time."

When they arrived, Two and his family were already there. Two stood glowering out the window with a drink in his hand as Marcie and the children greeted Dorrie. She'd just finished introducing Travis when the doorbell rang and Charmaine and the Bynums came in.

"Charmaine, you look wonderful!" Marcie said. "How many years has it been? You haven't changed a hair!" She turned to Jessie. "Lord, Jessie, I haven't seen you and Reese in a month of Sundays! How are you?"

"Doin' fine," Reese rumbled. He stared at Dorrie. "Your mom's made some changes in the past few months. I see her workin' out in the yard and hardly know her." He laid his heavy hand on Dorrie's shoulder. "You're lookin' good, Dorrie."

"Hi, Jessie. Hello, Reese," Dorrie said. She shrugged off his hand and slipped her arm through Travis's. "I'd like you to meet my friend Travis Burton. Travis, Jessie and Reese have lived next door to me forever."

The men sized one another up, shaking hands.

"Glad to meet you, Travis," Jessie said. "I've seen a lot of you, just never said hello."

Two crossed the room and put his arm around Dorrie. "Hello, Mother," he said. "Happy birthday." He dropped a dutiful kiss on the top of her head. "Charmaine. Burton. Jessie and Reese, how are you?"

"Doin' fine, boy," Reese said. "How's business in the doctoring profession these days?"

As Two reached to shake Reese's hand, Dorrie slipped from under his arm.

"Where are Susan and Kurt?" she asked.

"Where do you suppose?" Marcie said. "Last time I checked, he was showing her a better way to handle puff pastries!"

Dorrie left Marcie to complete the greetings and escaped to the kitchen. Travis would have to take care of himself; she was feeling too nervous and crowded.

"Happy birthday!" Kurt greeted her, sliding a cookie sheet into the oven. He stood up and bent to kiss her cheek, holding his hands behind him like outstretched wings. "Can't touch you — I'm covered with flour. One second while I clean up."

"Happy birthday, Mother," Susan echoed. "Is everybody here?"

"We all came in together. The rest are in the other room."

"Guess I'd better go say hello," Susan said. "George might be needing me."

Kurt wiped his hands and hung up the dishtowel, and then dropped an arm around Dorrie.

"How's it cookin', Mom?"

"I didn't stick around long enough to see. Travis and Reese Buynum are squaring off like a couple of roosters. Charmaine looks like the Gypsy Queen, and Two looks like he's been sucking lemons."

"When doesn't he?" Kurt gave her a squeeze. "Come on, you can't hide in the kitchen all night. You're the guest of honor!"

When they returned to the living room, Charmaine, Travis, and Marcie were standing at the window with the children, watching a lightning display to the southwest.

"Nothing I love better'n a good thunderstorm,"

Dorrie heard Charmaine say. "Will you look at that? It's better than Fourth of July at the Cotton Bowl!"

"I've never been there," Wendy said. "My daddy won't take us to Fair Park. He says it's not safe."

"Crossing the street's not safe," Charmaine said. "Some things are worth taking a chance."

"The question is," Travis said, "does a child have the judgment to know which things those are? Seems to me she's better off accepting her father's judgment until she's developed some of her own."

"Judgment's like muscles," Charmaine said. "You can't develop what you're not allowed to use."

Dorrie laid a restraining hand on Charmaine's arm.

"Let's don't preach rebellion right here and now," she said. "You don't have time to do any good."

Charmaine laughed. "You're right." She dropped a hand on Wendy's shoulder. "You ask your daddy what's an anarchist, honey. I been one all my life. It's fun, but that has its dangers too."

A clap of thunder rattled the glass, and a tree split in the park below. Dorrie took an involuntary step backward. Travis took her arm.

"Come away from the window," he said. "That was a bit close."

Yes, Dorrie thought. Insulating Travis from Charmaine would give her something else to worry about, besides evading Reese Buynum and keeping Two from making an ass of himself with her oldest and newest friends.

"What would you like to drink, Mother?" Two said. "There's all kinds of sodas, and I've made up a batch of Bloody Marys."

"A Bloody Mary sounds just right, thanks. Charmaine? How about you?"

"Yes, thanks."

"Well, Charmaine," Two said, handing them drinks, "how have you been? It must be ten years since we'd heard anything of you till last Thanksgiving."

He was trying, Dorrie thought, even if his tone did suggest that another ten wouldn't have hurt his feelings.

"Well, you know what a rolling stone I've always been," Charmaine said. "I been scrubbing off moss all my life."

"Charmaine just commented to me the other night that this is the longest she's stayed in one place for years," Dorrie said. "She's going to England soon."

"Is that so!" Travis said. "I've always wanted to go there. How long a trip do you plan?"

"Oh, about a month to start, I guess. I've invited Dorrie to go with me."

Dorrie felt Travis stiffen at her side. "Nothing's decided," she started to say, but Two interrupted.

"To England? That's a long way from home!"

"Do her good," Charmaine said. "Your mom's been stuck in this old town her whole life. It's high time she looked around a little."

"The United States is a big country," Two said. "Maybe she'd like to look around here first."

"I've always dreamed of England," Dorrie said. "I haven't said I'd go yet, but it sounds awfully tempting."

"You never told me that," Travis said. "When did all this come up?"

"Just a couple of weeks ago," Dorrie told him. "I've hardly seen you." His tone irritated her. He'd been gone for more than a week. Anyway, where was it written that she had to tell him her every thought?

"I been going through brochures like crazy," Charmaine said. "Dorrie, I know I said a month, but we could spend a month in London alone and not see everything!"

Dorrie laughed. "What then, Charmaine? Paris? Rome? Why not a tour of the Continent and the Holy Land?"

"Mother, you're not serious! Think of the terrorists! You could get hijacked!'

"No, of course," Dorrie started to say, but Charmaine interrupted.

"What an adventure! You'd really have something to tell your grandchildren then!"

Two went white, and Travis turned away and stared out the window. A flash of lightning sil-

480

houetted his rigid form against the city skyline so that he loomed like one of the skyscrapers.

"I never heard anything so irresponsible in my life!" Two protested. "Mother, you can't seriously be planning to travel with this woman!"

Charmaine laughed.

"Honestly, Two," Dorrie said, trying to laugh with her. "Loosen up! Can't you tell when somebody's joking?"

"It's not a joking matter," Two mumbled.

"Come and get it!" Kurt called. "Dinner's on the table."

When they sat down, Dorrie was grateful to see that the main combatants were separated. She'd been given the place of honor at the head of the table, with Two and Marcie at her left and right. Charmaine was between Reese and Kurt; Travis sat between Marcie and Jessie. The hand-lettered pink place cards had balloons and streamers painted on them, and a bouquet of pink, white, and lavender balloons floated overhead. Jessie and Marcie took turns grilling Travis, each in her own style, and Charmaine talked across the table to Trey about recent archeological discoveries supporting the probable location of Camelot near Salisbury. Dorrie let down the guard she'd been keeping up since this explosion in the making had collected at the front door, and began to relax. Maybe it would be all right after all, she thought. I was nervous over nothing. They're all getting along just fine.

"You-all have outdone yourselves," she told Susan. "I don't believe I've ever had such a beautiful dinner." The puffed pastries Kurt had been teaching Susan were filled with lobster thermidor. They were accompanied by glazed baby carrots and chunks of pink-skinned new potatoes mixed with young peas still in their shells.

"I'm glad you like it. Kurt cooked; I only made the cake and did the decorating. I've been thinking about going into catering some day." She smiled. "Took me some time to figure out the seating."

"You did it just right, honey."

"This day is full of surprises," Two said. "What are you talking about, 'going into catering'?"

"After the children are grown," Susan said. "I'm just thinking ahead to what I'll do when they're gone."

"Why, you'll take care of me!"

"I thought I'd taught you to take care of yourself," Dorrie said. "Don't get excited, son. If there's any fault here, it's mine: I'm the one who told Susan to start thinking about what she'll do when the kids leave home. I was bored to distraction after you kids left!"

"Anyway," Susan said, "there's no need to get worked up about it now. It's ten years away."

"Christ almighty!" Two said. "My mother wants to get herself hijacked, my wife wants to go into business for herself—what do you suppose

482

my daughter'll want, a career in a punk rock band?"

"Well, her uncle has contacts in the music business," Marcie said, grinning across the table. "If that's what Wendy wants, I'm sure he'll be happy to help."

"Over my dead body!"

"That can be arranged," Marcie said. "You'll take care of it yourself if you don't loosen up a little. My God, Two, your face looks like a tomato!"

"Stop it, you two," Dorrie said. "For pity's sake, this is a birthday party, not a barroom brawl! Behave yourselves!"

Still laughing, Marcie pushed her chair back and stood up.

"Keep your seats, you-all," she said, standing. "It's time for the *pièce de résistance*."

Wendy helped her clear, and the two returned carrying a two-tiered cake decorated with candied violets and purple ribbons. Pink candles blazed around the lower tier, and a fresh, lavender rose was centered on top.

"Happy birthday to you . . ." they all sang, Travis's voice rumbling and Charmaine's croaking off-key. "Happy birthday, dear Dorrie, happy birthday to you." Wendy set the cake carefully before her grandmother.

"Make a wish," she said. "You have to blow out the candles and make a wish now, Grandma."

Dorrie shut her eyes and thought, *courage,* as she blew.

"Presents!" Wendy cried. "Get the presents, Aunt Marcie!" She hugged Dorrie. "I can't wait till you see mine. I been working on it for months!"

"Well, then, I'll just open yours first."

Wendy pulled a flat package from the middle of the stack and presented it to Dorrie, who carefully removed its bright ribbon bow and paper to uncover a framed cross-stitch sampler.

Dorrie could see the learning process at work: with each color of thread, the stitches grew more even. The colors themselves were bright enough to put her eyes out. At the top, a golden sun rose over violet mountains. Brilliant green leaves and flowers of every color twined down the sides to frame words worked in scarlet: "Today is the first day of the rest of your life."

"Wendy, it's beautiful," Dorrie said. "My goodness, the work that's gone into it!"

"Do you like the colors? The colors in the magazine were real dull, so I changed them. And I like what it says—isn't that a nice thing to think about, every day new?"

"It is, darling, and I love the colors." She kissed Wendy. "Thank you. I'll hang it in my bedroom. It'll be the first thing I see every morning."

Dorrie opened the other gifts, saving Travis's for last. Trey used his pocket knife to cut the heavy box's sealing tape, and Dorrie lifted its flaps. Inside, she found a bronze reproduction of Rodin's statue, "The Lovers." Two's face was a study. Fortunately, Dorrie thought, he looked too stunned to speak.

"My gawd!" Reese burst out. "The damn thing's indecent!"

"Oh, my!" Dorrie said. "Travis, it's beautiful! I don't know what to say!"

"I think the gift says a lot," Charmaine said. Her voice was sober, but her eyes were full of mischief. "You might want to respond in private."

"Don't start, Charmaine," Dorrie warned. She looked around the table and found all eyes on her.

"Well," she said, gathering her courage, "as long as I'm at the center of attention, I might as well make my announcement."

Marcie grinned in anticipation, and her hands clapped beneath her chin. Charmaine smiled benignly, as if at a favorite child: God only knew what she was expecting, Dorrie thought. Two's head snapped up, and he fixed his mother with a suspicious glare.

"What now?" he demanded.

"I've decided to sell the store."

"Oh!" Marcie looked disappointed.

"Without even consulting us?" Two said.

"I consulted you last fall. Have you changed your opinion?"

"Of course not! I'm just glad you've come to your senses!"

"Thank you, Two," Dorrie said dryly. "I'm so glad you approve."

"What will you do now, Mom?" Kurt asked.

"Everything I ever wanted to, if I'm lucky. Rest, to start. Travel some: the world's wide open, and I feel like I've never been anywhere. Study. I went over to SMU and picked up a catalogue last week, and there's about a hundred hours I'd love to take just for the information." She paused. "I'm starting all over again, just hoping it's not too late."

"Of course it's not!" Charmaine said. "Congratulations, Dorrie! I think it's great!"

Driving home, Travis was quiet.

"You and Marcie seemed to hit it off pretty well," Dorrie said.

"She's a bright girl. Pretty, too. I enjoyed talking with her."

"I'm glad. I could tell she liked you too. Actually, the evening wasn't quite as bad as I'd feared. We managed to avoid any actual bloodshed, at least."

"You sure did put the whammy on me before dinner, about going to England. When was that decision made?"

"It hasn't been, not completely. I haven't said I'll go." She paused. "I did apply for a passport, though, just in case."

"Applying for a passport doesn't sound like

486

'just in case' to me. It sounds like you're going."

Dorrie's body stiffened at his accusing tone. She'd put off telling him for just this reason, knowing he'd try to talk her out of going. *He's not George,* a voice inside her said. *He's not your father. He can't stop you unless you let him.* She took a deep breath to calm herself.

"If I sell the store, there's nothing to stop me going. I'll have the time and the money, and I'm entitled, aren't I?"

"What do you mean, 'nothing'! What am I, chopped liver? You didn't even tell me about it!"

"I tried, Travis; I just never quite managed to get it said. I'm telling you now. I always did want to travel—you know that—and George never would. Charmaine's my oldest friend in the world, and I may never get another chance like this."

"Hell, Dorrie, *I'll* take you to England! We can honeymoon in China, if that's your desire! I'll take you anywhere you want to go—just ask!"

"I didn't ask Charmaine; it just sort of happened, the way things always do happen around her. We were talking one day, and it just sounded like so much fun. I've always wanted to go to England, and I've been thinking about how much fun it would be to travel with Charmaine for years. The only time we ever had a chance was last winter when we went to California." She was babbling. Why couldn't she make him see?

"Charmaine's been planning out the itinerary,

making all the reservations and everything, and she's so excited. She'd be disappointed if I backed out now." Dorrie paused, and then added, "Besides, I don't want to."

"But you'll be perfectly happy half a world away from me for a month."

Travis pulled into her driveway, slammed on the brakes, and cut off the motor.

"God dammit, Dorrie, you can't just sail away like this! I want to marry you! *I* want to travel with you!"

"Nobody said you couldn't; just not this time. This time, I'm going with Charmaine." Dorrie opened her door and stepped out onto the drive, her decision made final. "It's not like I wasn't ever coming back. It's only for a month, Travis. I'll be back."

Travis slammed his car door and followed her toward the house. He caught up with her on the porch where she was feeling in her bag for her keys.

"I don't want you to go, dammit!"

Dorrie opened the door and, taking a deep breath to steady herself, turned to face him.

"You've made that clear. Are you coming in?"

Travis barged through the door and slammed it behind him.

"What's come over you?" he demanded. "You're not like this, Dorrie. Don't you even care how I feel? We've always cared how the other one felt!"

Always! she thought. Four months of dating, and he was saying "always"! And now he was going to pile guilt on her. Well, two could play that game! She sighed.

"Of course I care. I wish you could be happy for me! Instead, I'm planning the vacation of a lifetime and you're angry. It sort of takes the shine off, you know?"

She started to walk away, but Travis grabbed her arm and jerked her back.

"Dorrie, I want to make you happy. Stay with me!"

"Don't do this, Travis," she said quietly, her face set. She shook off his arm and started for the kitchen. Passing the living-room arch, she turned back and looked directly into his eyes.

"You can't make me happy. Nobody can make anybody else happy. That's something we have to do for ourselves." George's photograph stared at her from the mantelpiece, and she stared back at it for a moment before going on. "I'm going to England with Charmaine for my own pleasure. I can't remember the last time I did something entirely for myself, and I deserve it. You can be mad because I went without you or glad I'm having a good time or completely indifferent—it's your choice." She turned and stalked back to the kitchen.

Travis followed, shaking his head. "Dorrie, we *can* make each other happy! I want us to be together forever, doing everything we can to make

489

each other happy. What's wrong with that?"

Dorrie crossed to the refrigerator, her back to him, filled two glasses with ice and tea, and handed him one.

"It's a lovely idea, Travis, but it just doesn't work that way." She sat at the table and gestured him to the chair across from her. "I used to try so hard to make George happy, and I never could. I spent thirty-five years wondering where I'd failed, and didn't realize until he was gone that George simply wouldn't have it. He thought he didn't deserve to be happy, so he refused to be. Joy, if you'll pardon my language, scared the living hell out of him."

She looked across the table, her face hot, her eyes pleading with him to understand.

"Travis, please, if you care for me the way you say you do, be happy that I'm doing something wonderful!"

Travis stared at her as he drank his tea. At last he shook his head. "This is pointless. You're determined to go? Your mind's made up?"

Dorrie nodded.

"What about marrying me? Will you answer before you go?"

"We can talk about it when I come home if you want to," she said quietly. "Maybe I'll know what I want by then."

He set his glass down hard on the table and stood up. "I see. Did it ever occur to you that I might want something else by then?"

Dorrie shook her head. Really! she thought. Threats, now! It was too much.

"If you do, we'd better know it before than after," she said. "It's best to wait."

Travis looked around the kitchen as if he'd lost something, and then collected himself. "Well, I guess I'll go then."

"I thought you were spending the night."

Travis laughed harshly. "I don't think so. If I have to find my own happiness, I reckon I'll have to look someplace else. It's not in this house. Not tonight."

Dorrie watched him go, half sick with a mixture of anger and guilt. Fighting always had that effect on her. Usually, she just got quieter and quieter when she was angry until she turned into a slab of frozen stone. If she did get mad enough to say anything at all, she always said too much, hurt feelings, and ended up close to tears, wondering if she'd ever see the person again.

She locked the door behind him, wandered into the den, and switched on the TV. Grace Kelly, all skin and bone in a white tunic, lay beside a swimming pool and pushed a model sailboat out on the water while Bing Crosby sang: "I give to you and you give to me/ True Love, True Love . . ."

Good luck, Dorrie thought, and changed the channel.

Forty-one

Selling the store was an enormous relief. The day the papers were signed, Dorrie drove straight to the new car agency where she traded in George's 1979 Olds oceanliner for a silvery little sedan just her size with plush seats, automatic everything, and a polite voice that reminded her to fasten her seat belt, fill her tank, turn off the lights, and take the keys with her. She wrote them a check, and they prepped the car while she waited. On the way home, she felt for the first time as if she were driving the car instead of the car driving her.

That evening, she picked up Charmaine and drove her halfway to Denton for a catfish dinner on Lake Lewisville. Driving up the interstate, she opened up the sun roof and stuck her hand out into the air.

"I feel like a teenager!" she said, and Charmaine laughed.

"It's about time—you never did act like one, even forty years ago! Look, I know I promised not to bug you more'n once a week about the trip, but we've been so busy I'm two weeks behind. How about it? Our flight's less than five weeks away, you know."

Dorrie smiled. "All right, Charmaine. You've been a real good girl. Now you can tell me: what plans have you been making behind my back?"

"London, to start. I'll drag you through the historical district during the day and to the theaters at night, but just for two days. After that . . . you'll never guess!"

"I'm already worn out! What next?"

"There's this tour—what a find! You won't believe!"

Charmaine was loving this, Dorrie thought fondly. She should have been a suspense novelist—better yet a dramatist so she could star in her own stuff. Then all she'd need to add was producing and directing, and she'd be in hog heaven. Dorrie grinned at the thought. She would not want to be an actor in Charmaine's play.

"Come on, let me have it."

" 'A Woman's Tour of Ancient Britain!' We'll take the train—I ordered us a month's train pass—to Tintagel, where Arthur was born, and visit Glastonbury and Stonehenge and Avebury . . . Be at Stonehenge on Midsummer's Eve!" Charmaine was all but dancing in her seat. "And we'll stay in a fifteenth century castle by the sea in Wales and learn about the Druids and the Norns, and go to the Welsh Folk Museum . . . and there's even an add-on trip to Ireland!" She said it with such a flourish that Dorrie could almost hear the trumpet fanfare.

"We can see the Waterford glass factory, and of course we can't miss the Spode works; they're right there where we'll be."

"Sounds exciting," Dorrie said, but the words were tumbling out of Charmaine's mouth so fast she didn't really need prompting.

"And I knew you'd be interested in Edinburgh, so I've reserved a bed-and-breakfast there for a few days — even rented a car for side trips — and as long as we're there, we might as well see the Loch Ness and those northern islands: the Isle of Skye, or Shetland for a sweater. And then back to London by way of the English Lake District Wordsworth and all those guys were so crazy about, and Stratford-on-Avon for Shakespeare and the college towns and Windsor and then back to London and really see the town!"

Dorrie crossed three lanes to get to the Hickory Creek exit and slowed as she left the highway.

"You've got us covering a whole lot of territory there," she said. The restaurant was a block ahead on the right. She smiled at Charmaine. "Think I'm up to it?"

"Shoot, you'll be so full of sass you won't know

what hit you! Anyhow, it's not as far as it sounds. The whole of England's not much more than a day's trip long, and everything's so close together there's a new sight to see every time you lift your eyes." She grabbed Dorrie's hand and shook it, grinning. "Think of it, Dorrie: Midsummer's Eve at Stonehenge!"

Pulling up to a stop sign, Dorrie threw her arms up in mock self-protection.

"All right! All right!" She laughed. "I don't suppose you'd like to go shopping with me? I'll need a new raincoat and some walking shoes, anyhow!"

"Buy it there, is my advice. I'll take you to Harrod's the first day out. And for God's sake, carry expandable luggage! If you're anything like me, you'll come back with four times what you took along."

Maybe she would, Dorrie thought that night, waltzing around her bedroom as she prepared for bed. She pulled the lovely blue nightgown Travis had given her from the hook on her closet door and slid it over her head. It made her a little sad: except for business dealings, during which he'd been distinctly cool, she hadn't seen him since their fight. She lifted her chin determinedly. For once in her overdisciplined life, she might just indulge herself. After all, Charmaine Stubbs wasn't the only woman in the world entitled to a whim. Dorrie'd been saving them up for years!

* * *

The next day, Dorrie went to the store to announce the sale. She arrived a half-hour before opening, and Zada was already there.

"We need to talk," Dorrie said.

"You've sold the store." Zada's voice sounded like the knell of doom.

"Yes. But I had your job written into the contract, Zada. You can stay at your present salary or better till you're ready to retire, and they promised to honor your pension."

"I saw it coming," Zada said. "I knew all along you'd get tired of it. You were never cut out for this."

"I'm afraid you're right. Still, I didn't do too badly while I was doing it, did I?"

"No," Zada conceded. Her expression was bleak. "It's going to be an awful change. I don't know if I can deal with it."

"Zada, you can deal with anything. I've watched you." She put her hand on Zada's arm and looked into her face. "And I want you to know, I've appreciated your help and loyalty all these years, especially since George's death."

Dorrie looked around the store. "I'm going to miss it," she said. "It's always been part of my life. I used to come here when I was only four years old and talk to the crew, and when I was older, at Christmas, Daddy'd let me come in after school and do all the gift-wrapping. Paid me fifty cents an hour, and I thought I was rich." She smiled, remembering.

"We had a fine-jewelry salesman named Si. You wouldn't remember Si — he retired before you came on staff — but he was like an uncle to me, used to drill me on French verbs when I was in high school." Dorrie's voice softened. "You've all been like family over the years."

"You and Mr. Greene . . . you've been good bosses," Zada said. Her voice was thick, and she turned away. After a moment she said, "He would've hated this. Mr. Greene thought chain stores were a blight on the business community, the ruination of the small merchant. The only time I ever heard him swear was about the big malls opening at North Park and Valley View. He said he hoped they'd choke each other out and leave the neighborhood merchants alone."

"I know," Dorrie said. "But the sale was his idea; he's the one who started all this in motion. This store has survived thirty years longer than most. I think he finally just gave up."

"And now you're giving up."

"No, just facing up — to reality. I'm not a merchant, Zada. I thought this was where I belonged, but it's not. You are, and you do belong here, and you deserve to work with people who understand and appreciate what you're doing. In the long run, I think we're both better off."

"What about Willis?"

"He can stay too. They'll remodel, of course—these fixtures are almost old enough to classify as antiques—and enlarge, take over the storefront next door when its lease runs out in July. That's why they were in a hurry. You'll get a long, paid vacation while that's going on and come back to a brand-new store."

"I like it the way it is." Zada's voice was thick with emotion, and she was hunched like a turtle withdrawing into its shell.

Dorrie smiled. "I liked the way my life was, too, but change isn't always a bad thing. Give the new owners a chance, Zada. They're reasonable people. They might even be able to teach you something worth knowing. Bijoux's famous for its training programs. And if you can't stand it, your pension fund will mature in a year."

"We'll see." Zada turned away and blew her nose. Then Dorrie saw the ramrod going up her back again, and the manager turned back with her shoulders squared.

"Well," she said briskly, "the day's about to begin. I guess we'd better get to work."

Dorrie went to the back to clean out her desk, but except for the small photos of George and the children in their silver frames, there was nothing there she wanted to take home with her. It would be a clean break. There was nothing left to hold her here.

* * *

She felt restless all that evening. Like a balloon set loose from its moorings, she could find no place to light. The pink couch felt lumpy. It was beginning to break down; she would have to have it reupholstered soon. Perhaps while she was gone, she thought. She laid down her book and switched irritably from channel to channel on the television, wishing there were something to watch or that Travis were there to talk to.

Travis wasn't the first man to give her the silent treatment. She could take it. It was just so sad. Two weeks without a word. She missed him — not just the lovemaking, but *him* — but if letting him rule was to be the cost of the relationship, she'd just have to learn to get along without him.

It just went to show: they all wanted submissive females, even a man as apparently liberated as Travis. She wanted a loving companion, but he wanted a subordinate. Well, tough. Travis wasn't the only man in the world. Maybe she didn't want a man at all.

You know better than that, her inner voice said. *Don't be dumb.*

Oh, hush! she told it. Go to sleep!

Dorrie is a soldier somewhere in Eastern Europe, camped with the others on a broad plain ringed by mountains. It is nighttime, dark and cold. Icy winds rattle her tent flaps and make her shiver. Her tan uniform has shiny brass buttons and red epaulets, and she is cleaning an automatic rifle. A battle is about to begin.

She is in a war of independence in which her people have revolted against the nation's government. Her people have lived quietly in this high valley, isolated from the world for many years, but recently the rulers have started to encroach upon them. They want to supervise the education of the valley's children, tell Dorrie's people what crops to plant and when, conscript their young men for their army. It is time to fight.

The enemy will come over the mountains, through the pass, and her army will be waiting. The coming battle will not be an easy one, and it may only be the first of many, but she has faith in her troops; whatever their losses, they will carry the day. Dorrie polishes her rifle and waits for morning.

On Monday, Dorrie drove to Highland Park and bought soft-sided luggage. She called Walt Longstreet, made the new provisions in her will, and arranged to sign the papers before she left. Then she bought travelers' checks and arranged for an American Express card in her very own name. George had hated bank cards. The only

500

credit cards she'd ever had were from locally owned department stores.

"Wonderful!" Kurt said when she told them the news. "While you're in London, Mom, see if you can get tickets to the Glyndebourne festival. You'll love it."

"What a trip, traveling with Charmaine!" Marcie said. "Lord, I'll bet she'll keep you hopping!"

"I expect so," Dorrie said. "You should hear what-all she has planned: everything from Camelot to the Scottish Highlands with Midsummer's Eve at Stonehenge the centerpiece. But she seems to think I'll hold up all right."

"I can just see her poking around in all that Druidic stuff," Marcie said. "She'll come home in a white robe with oakleaves in her hair and her pockets full of runestones. Look out, Mom— she'll put a spell on you!"

Dorrie laughed. "Charmaine's had me under a spell since I was ten, honey, and I don't show any signs of getting over it. What more can she do?"

Even Two found a reason to congratulate her on the trip.

"At least it'll get you away from Travis Burton for a month," he said. "I still don't trust Charmaine Stubbs as far as I can see her, but she's a damned sight safer than a fortune-hunting accountant!"

"I suppose that depends on where you think the danger lies," Dorrie said. "I know the pleasure it gives you to worry about me, dear, and I wouldn't interfere for the world, but I'm afraid I can't share your gloom. I'm fond of both of them, but Charmaine's more sheer fun than anybody I've ever known, and she's never done me a thing but good. She does get a little overenthusiastic sometimes, but I don't know how I'd have lived these last months without her. And as to Travis . . . well, don't worry about Travis. It's me he wants, not the fortune, but I think he's just about given up." She felt a surprising pang at the admission and shook it off.

"I sort of thought you-all might get married, Mother," Susan said softly. "I really liked him." Two glared at her, but she did not shrink.

"Travis thought so too, but I think he got over it. I guess we can sort it out when I get home, if he's still interested."

Aren't you brave! a voice within her jeered. *Little Miss Independence!* She hushed it. If she couldn't have both Travis and freedom, freedom would have to be her choice. The quarrel had shown her the strength of her hunger for autonomy: while she wasn't looking, it had grown past simple desire into a determination so fierce it sometimes frightened her. Whatever it cost, she would be her own mistress from this day forth.

Megan found Dorrie a clutch of travel guides

and lent her several coffee-table books: one about archeological discoveries concerning King Arthur, one about Celtic culture and its remaining artifacts, and several picture books about the British Isles. She also produced a lavishly illustrated *Mabinogion,* the book of Celtic kings and heroes. Dorrie shared them with Charmaine, who added new sites to their itinerary.

"This list gets longer and longer," Charmaine said, looking up from the *Mabinogion.* "What say we make it two months instead of one? I could spend a whole month in Wales alone!"

Dorrie laughed. "We'll see how it goes," she promised. "I can stay as long as I want to now. The store's gone, and it looks like Travis is too." It still hurt. Dorrie pushed it down and went on. "Just as long as we're out of there by winter. I hate cold weather."

"Winter! Now, that's the time to see Italy and Greece. Spain, maybe." Charmaine looked up, her eyes teasing. "You sure you don't want to make a world tour out of this? I've never been to Australia."

Forty-two

Charmaine was at the house a few days later when the deliveryman came. The women had been drinking Red Zinger tea and poring over travel brochures in the sunny back window of the kitchen. Dorrie carried the long, white box and the smaller, squarish one back to the kitchen and set them on the bar.

"My lord, flowers and chocolates too!" Charmaine said. "And there's an envelope—come on, Dorrie, open it!"

Dorrie opened the envelope and saw a verse written in Travis's neat hand:

> APOLOGY
> A man in love is helpless
> Heart and hormones combine
> To render him incapable
> Of leaving his love's shrine,

And you, my love, are shrine enough
To bring me to my knees
In abject rue of foolish words.
Will you forgive me, please?

T.

Below the lines, he'd added, "Do what you must, so long as you come back to me."

"Bless his heart," she murmured.

"What?" Charmaine asked.

"It's from Travis. We had a big fight after the birthday party. I thought I'd never see him again."

"How come?"

Dorrie told her.

"I just . . . I don't know, Charmaine, I'm not the same anymore." She took the tissue from around the flowers and smoothed it on the bar top for folding. "Maybe it's all that stuff I've been reading, or maybe it's just that it's always been men whose thumb I was under, but I'm too quick to feel crowded. He's been so patient, tried so hard not to push . . . Of course he was disappointed that I wanted to go away without him! What could I have expected?"

Charmaine laughed affectionately. "God, Dorrie, you're such a pushover! Let me tell you something, girl: when a man starts getting 'owny' with you, it's time you got yourself some breathing room. Don't tangle yourself up with a jealous man! You're free for the first time in your whole life. Enjoy it!"

It went all over Dorrie. Pushover! Well, she told herself, Charmaine didn't mean it. She was just overstating herself again, as usual. All the same, it rankled. She forced an answering laugh.

"You always did know what's best for me, didn't you, Charmaine? What I want to know is, who died and left you king?"

Charmaine snorted. "Well, excuse the hell outta me! I'm only trying to help! Come on, Dorrie, you've let men con you into living their way all your life. Show a little spunk, for God's sake!"

Dorrie looked up from her paper-folding and met Charmaine's eyes. "You always are trying to help and never asking if I need it. Been blowing in and out of my life like a tornado for forty years, having your fun and leaving me to clean up the wreckage." She smiled halfheartedly. "Stop helping, will you?"

"Have it your way, baby," Charmaine said. "Just don't come crying to me when he starts bossing you around, because he will — I promise he will. You beg for it, Dorrie; just bat those baby-blues and look helpless every time you run up against something you don't want to deal with. You were the same way as a kid — nobody ever could wait to help poor, sweet, little Dorrie." Her voice dropped into a bitterly ironic tone. "Never mind Charmaine — she can take care of

506

herself!"

Dorrie was shocked. Charmaine, angry that nobody'd volunteered to take care of her? It was like hearing a lioness tell you she was a rabbit at heart. As if I could help it! she thought.

"You sound like Custard the Dragon, crying for a nice, safe cage." Dorrie's voice was cool. "I never noticed you listening to any advice, even when people tried to give it to you. Everybody knew Charmaine Stubbs always did it her way, and the rest of the world had better, too."

Charmaine stood up and fixed her with a hard look.

"You're a fine one to talk, from your 'nice, safe cage'! Put up with a man for thirty-five years who wouldn't let you blow your nose without explaining why—that's taking care of yourself, all right! Just give your life away? Stick it out and wait for your troubles to go away by themselves? I've got news for you, Dorrie: they don't. Sticking it out's not the only answer. Sometimes *getting* out's the way."

Dorrie kept the bar between them as she squared her shoulders to answer.

"How would you know? You never stuck around long enough to find out!" Her stomach hurt, and her eyes stung. "At least I tried. Maybe I didn't do the right thing every time, but I stayed. I raised my own children. I didn't walk away from my responsibilities, just say

507

'Okay, everybody, you can fend for yourselves now; Mama's got better things to do'!"

Dorrie couldn't believe she'd said anything so awful. She felt sick. What in the world was wrong with her?

Charmaine's eyes narrowed, and she took a step forward. Dorrie could feel herself cringe, and she deliberately straightened herself.

"God damn you, Dorrie Hunter, how dare you say that to me? You'll never knew what that cost me! Don't you think I wanted to raise those boys?" Charmaine slammed her hand on the bar top. It rang like a rifle shot, and Dorrie jumped backward. "I'd been taking up for you since we were children, but you wimped out on me the only chance you ever had. I didn't hear you testifying in that damned kangaroo court what a wonderful mother I was!"

Dorrie's eyes filled. I will be double-damned, she thought, if I'll let her see me cry about this. She turned away and blinked back the tears before she answered. Her fists were clenched, and her throat was tight with pain and anger.

"As I remember," she said coldly, "you'd just run through a half-dozen lovers and were 'getting back to the earth' on a commune. What should I have said? 'She's the most stable person I ever know?' Right! Don't blame me, Charmaine. You did it to yourself!"

Charmaine glared. "Don't you dare patronize

me, Miss Priss!" She leaned across the bar, her face inches from Dorrie's and her eyes glittering. "And don't you ever piss and moan to me again about how oppressed you've been! All you ever had to do was stand up *one time* and no 'No more,' and old George would've gone belly-up. But you couldn't do that—oh, no, not Dorrie! Dorrie's a *lady!*" Her face was red, and she was breathing hard and fast. The scorn in her voice cut like a butcher's knife.

"A *lady* doesn't insist; a *lady* doesn't demand—God, I heard enough of that crap at Miss Pickerel's to choke a horse!" She minced across the kitchen waving Dorrie's favorite antique Limoges teacup, her little finger elegantly crooked. "A *lady* will keep her mouth shut and swallow her own vomit before she'll complain or call attention to herself. Just take it and die, that's what a *lady* does! Well, go ahead and be a lady if that's what suits you, but count me out!"

Charmaine drew back her arm and hurled the cup past Dorrie's head. It shattered, and the Red Zinger spread down the wall like a bloodstain.

Dorrie gasped and stared at the stain. After a moment's silence, she forced a brief, humorless laugh. "Ladies don't throw china, either, Charmaine. But don't worry about that: nobody's ever mistaken you for a lady. Not with that mouth!"

Charmaine whirled to face her, and Dorrie took an involuntary step back. The women stared at each other for a long, silent minute. When Charmaine spoke again, her voice was dangerously low.

"Now you sound just like my mama: 'Watch your mouth, girl; you sound like a truck driver. Din't you learn nothin' at Miss Pickerel's? Why caint' you be more like that sweet little Dorrie Hunter?' " She glared through slitted eyes. "Little Miss Prim and Proper, that was you. Little Mary Sunshine, drowning in shit while she tells you what a pretty shade of brown it is! Sweet little Dorrie! All the backbone of a garden slug—all the yen for adventure of an ant!"

Dorrie felt as if their mouths had taken on lives of their own to spew out poisons stored up for forty years. Every muscle in her body was taut. She could feel the blood throbbing in her throat, hear it inside her head.

"If I was the ant, you've been the grasshopper," she said. Her voice sounded like somebody else's, some vicious harridan with ice in her veins. "Adventure's one thing, Charmaine, but responsibility's another. I had things to do: a home to make, children to raise. You can't know the number of times I wished I were anywhere but here, but I stuck it out; I did my duty. You never could stand George, but he was my husband and he did the best he knew how by me. So I didn't give up. I kept my vows."

Charmaine folded into the banquette and

dropped her head into her hands.

"Bullshit, Dorrie," she said wearily. "You put your life in his hands and let him run it because you were too damned scared or lazy to run it for yourself. That's not 'keeping your vows,' that's just being a wimp." She looked up. "It's *your life,* Dorrie! If you don't live it, it's wasted!"

Dorrie turned away and wiped impatiently at her eyes. Her stomach felt like a knotted rope in a game of tug of war. She wanted this demolition party to end, but she couldn't stop it.

"I have lived it. I just haven't lived it your way. And if self-determination's the point, what's the good of doing it your way instead of George's — or Travis's, for that matter? At least Travis would stay with me if we hit a bump in the road. You'd fly out of the car so fast it would make my head swim!"

"So now I'm undependable, am I?" Charmaine impaled her with a look. "A fly-by-night? I suppose you think I'm selfish, too. Go on, Dorrie, say it! You think I'm selfish!"

Dorrie shook her head, her eyes swimming. "I don't know what you are, Charmaine. Maybe not selfish, maybe just willful. You've always been that. Sometimes I admired your courage, but I wasn't you. I had to do it my way, and my way was to tough it out and look for the good in things. I might have left George, but I could never have left my children for somebody else to bring up."

"You cut deep when you finally sharpen the knife," Charmaine said. Her voice was hard as steel. "Well, let me tell you something, girl: if there's one thing I've always known when to do, it's cut my losses. It takes a real stubborn masochist to live with a man who'll never speak his love, and I've just never been into self-punishment. If it don't work, fix it or throw it out; that's my way."

"And you're welcome to it," Dorrie said. She wasn't sure how much longer she could stand up. Her knees were wobbly, and she felt all-over sick. She rounded the end of the bar, crossed the space between them, and gathered up the travel brochures from the table. Holding them out to Charmaine, she said, "Maybe you'd better plan on going to England by yourself. You don't want to travel with a *lady!* It might spoil your fun."

"Suit yourself," Charmaine said, standing. "Don't bother to show me out. I know the way."

"You always have," Dorrie said.

She watched Charmaine walk down the hall and out the door, and then folded into a chair. How could they have said such hateful things to each other after all these years? She remembered Charmaine telling her once that there was nothing like a good fight to set your blood to racing. Charmaine always felt invigorated after a fight.

512

Not Dorrie. Dorrie felt as if she'd been beaten with a board. She folded her arms on the table and laid her head on them, too shocked to cry.

All afternoon she wandered through the house like a lost soul, unable to concentrate on the simplest tasks long enough to get them done. She stuffed Travis's flowers into a tall crystal vase, but forgot to throw away the box. She sponged the tea stain off the wall, but failed to pick up the pieces of the cup. She loaded the dishwasher and forgot to run it. She opened the laundry chute and pulled the clothes out on the floor, but her mind wandered off in the middle of sorting them, and she left them lying in heaps in front of the washer.

All the while, her memories of the good times of their girlhoods alternated with Charmaine's scornful "lady" and her accusation of betrayal. George had been horrified at the very idea she might be called upon to testify in court. He'd wanted her to go to San Francisco with him the week of the trial. The only chance she'd ever had for a vacation, she thought bitterly, and she'd turned him down to stand by Charmaine in a cause that was lost before it ever started. But she'd been under oath! What could she have said that she didn't say to change the outcome? Nothing! She'd known Charmaine was hurt, but she'd been helpless. Things had never been the same between them since.

When the phone rang several hours later, she was sitting at the kitchen table staring at Travis's flowers.

"Oh, hi," she said, hearing his voice. She sounded like a ghost.

Travis hesitated. "Um . . . Did you get the flowers?"

"I'm looking at them now. They're beautiful, Travis. Thank you."

"What's wrong, Dorrie? You sound as if you'd lost your best friend!"

Dorrie started to laugh, but she wound up crying. "I have," she sobbed. "Oh, Travis, I have!"

Travis was silent for a long moment, and then she heard him clear his throat.

"Sit tight," he said. "I'm on my way. Twenty minutes, Dorrie. I'll be there."

She hung up the phone, sat at the table, and let the tears come.

When Travis came in, he found her at the sink, splashing cold water on her mottled face. Without a word, he picked up a tea towel and blotted her face dry, put his arms around her, and pulled her head down into the curve of his neck. She leaned gratefully on his shoulder for several minutes, and then straightened up.

"I'm better now," she said. "Got my crying done before you came; at least I won't inflict that on you." She sniffled. "I'll be all right now."

"It's okay, Dorrie. You can cry if you need to.

Care to tell me about it?"

Dorrie shrugged. "Charmaine and I had a fight. Oh, Travis, it was awful! The things we said to each other!" Her eyes filled again, and she wiped them with the backs of her hands.

"What was it about?"

"I don't really know. I mean, it started out over you, but that was just the start. It was really about us, her and me. Forty-years worth, all in one big blowout, clear back to the Year One." She shook her head, still shocked by its venom, and tried to laugh. "It was spectacular, Travis. We should have sold tickets."

Her voice broke.

"Well, you'll be happy about one thing, anyhow. The trip's off."

Travis cupped her jaw in his hand and looked into her eyes. "I'm sorry, Dorrie. I truly am. I didn't want it that way, didn't want you hurt." He put his arms around her again, and she stood in their safe circle and laid her head on his shoulder. After a moment, she looked up with brimming eyes.

"The flowers are lovely, Travis, and the poem . . . Thank you."

"I'm forgiven, then?"

"No, I'm just standing here in your arms because there's no place else to go. Of course you are!" She took a step back and looked up at him.

"I felt almost as bad about that fight as about

515

this one, if you want to know. I just took a stubborn streak and couldn't tell you." Her eyes filled again. "It hurt, but not the way this one did. It was . . . cleaner. This fight . . . we said terrible things to each other, Travis, things we can never take back. I don't know if we can ever be friends again."

Travis held her at arms' length and looked searchingly into her face.

"Who can't forgive whom?" he asked.

"I don't know," she confessed. "We both said cruel, hurtful things. I was like a woman possessed, said things I didn't even mean." She shuddered, and her eyes brimmed again. "We were so *angry!*"

"She didn't mean it either, Dorrie." He handed her the tea towel. "I can tell you're not used to fighting. Look, sweetheart, here's how it goes: people lose their tempers and say things to hurt. Then they get over it, and they forgive each other and go on. That's it!" He bent to touch his forehead to hers. "You and I are making up right now, aren't we? Give it a little time. Let the wounds heal over. You'll be friends again."

"I hope you're right," she said, but she had no faith in his words. All her life she'd been taught to guard her tongue, never to say anything she'd want to take back later. "You're not responsible for what other people do," she'd told her children, "but you are responsible for what you say

516

and do." Part of her anger, part of her pain, was for letting herself be goaded into dropping that guard.

"Once you've said it," her father had told her, "it's said. People might understand. They might even forgive, but once the words have been said, you can never unsay them."

She'd never been allowed to raise her voice in anger, and she'd learned never to say unforgivable words except to someone she hoped never to see again. In her entire life, Dorrie had never fought so openly with someone she loved. If Charmaine forgave her, she thought, it would be a gift, and one she didn't deserve.

"Get dressed, Dorrie," Travis said, hugging her. "Charmaine or no Charmaine, trip or no trip, you and I have something to celebrate tonight. I made reservations at La Mansion, and we're going dancing after. Come on. Forget your troubles, and let's get happy."

She did her best, even invited him to spend the night with her to make up for their weeks-long separation and took comfort in the loving, but long after Travis was asleep Dorrie lay staring at the ceiling. She kept going over the fight, trying to figure out at what point it had gone from "kidding on the square" to a vicious battle. Precisely when, she wondered, had she lost control? It was so unlike her. And Charmaine . . . how long had Charmaine carried around that scorn? Surely she hadn't hated Dorrie since they were children, the way she made it sound! Charmaine had been present at nearly every crisis in Dorrie's life; she wouldn't do that for somebody she hated. Dorrie had always taken her lead . . . maybe it was something as simple as that, that Dorrie'd dared to disagree. No. Charmaine was a strong personality, a take-charge girl if there ever was one, but she was no bully . . .

She could not get comfortable. Her pillow was hot, her feet cold. She flopped around so much that she was surprised Travis didn't waken and complain. The last time Dorrie glanced at the clock, it said 3:11 A.M.

Dorrie is at a funeral. The chapel is full of white lilies, and their too-sweet odor makes her queasy. Someone is weeping behind her in great, shuddering sobs. Her own eyes grow wet and her throat thick in sympathy.

She joins the line that is filing past the open casket, wondering who is in it. The other mourners are a disparate lot: a small Oriental man all in white, with a turban; a couple of oilfield roughnecks in bluejeans, boots, and plaid shirts; a woman in furs with a man in an Italian silk suit; a Peruvian peasant woman. The line moves slowly. Dorrie finally arrives at the casket and

518

looks inside.

Charmaine lies in the satin-lined box, her arms crossed over her chest and a lily in her hands. Her face is as white as library paste, her lips painted a garish red.

"Get up!" Dorrie tells her. "This isn't funny, Charmaine. Look how all these people are crying!"

Charmaine's eyes remain closed, but her hands pull back the burial gown to show a gaping hole in her chest.

"Who did this to you?" Dorrie cries. She is horrified and furiously angry.

"You might at least have come to visit me," Charmaine whispers. "This is not a journey I wanted to make alone."

Dorrie is overcome with grief. She had not even known that Charmaine was ill.

"Dorrie! Dorrie, you're dreaming!" Travis shook her awake. Her pillow was wet.

Forty-three

"I'm real sorry about your trip, Mom," Kurt said. "I know how much you were looking forward to it."

He'd picked her up for lunch, and they had carried take-out fried chicken to the Arboretum for a picnic. There were few other visitors on this weekday afternoon, and Dorrie was enjoying the great beds of delphiniums, roses, and iris. She couldn't keep delphiniums alive in her yard—the heat killed them. She wondered what the secret was.

"I'm a lot more upset about Charmaine than about the trip," she told him. "We've been irritated with each other before—you can't love somebody that long and never be irritated—but never like this. This was . . . devastating. I'm still not over it after a week."

"Have you tried to call her?"

"Several times. She didn't answer, just her machine. I hung up."

They walked in silence for a few minutes and stopped before a bed of mixed bluebonnets, pink and white and brilliant blue.

"It's probably silly, but I'm worried about her. I have this bad feeling."

"Like what, Mom?"

"I don't know. I just feel like something's wrong." She laughed softly, embarrassed. "I dreamed she'd died."

"Dreams are almost never about what they seem to be. Maybe it meant the friendship, not Charmaine herself."

"Maybe," Dorrie said, "but it doesn't feel like that." She remembered her nervous dread all the day of her mother's death. "I'm just afraid there's something wrong with her. I feel as if she needs me." She shook off the feeling with a little laugh. "Knowing Charmaine, she's probably in Ulan Bator or the Sudan by now. I'm worrying myself into an early grave while she's whooping it up in Outer Mongolia."

But the worry would not go away. She probed it every hour, the way one touches a sore tooth with one's tongue to see if it's better or worse. It made her angry: she'd felt sorrow after the fight with Travis, but not this nagging fear for him. Sometimes it would go away for hours at a time, only to surprise her at a quiet moment.

"You're awfully quiet," Travis remarked after supper.

"I know. I'm sorry." Talking only made it worse. She sighed. "I'll get over it." She switched on the TV and shoved a cassette into the VCR.

"Wait till you see what I found," she said, forcing enthusiasm into her voice. *"Kiss Me, Kate.* Howard Keel with a goatee and red tights." If Howard Keel couldn't take her mind off her troubles, she was troubled indeed. "Boy, was he something!"

But even Howard could not distract her completely. She pushed the worry firmly to the back of her mind. Charmaine was all right. She was tough as an old boot, certainly not suffering the effects of whatever Dorrie'd said to her. God knew, Charmaine had given as good as she got.

"Where is the life that once I led?" Howard sang in his rich, roguish baritone. "Totally gone. Utterly dead."

He was not alone in that, Dorrie thought, and a good thing, too. She sighed again and laid her head on Travis's shoulder. It would be all right. It had to.

That night and the next, her dreams were disturbed again. She could hear Charmaine calling to her, moaning "Dorrie! Do-or-rie!" but search as she might, she could not find her. She saw Charmaine in the grasp of a giant crab, fighting for her life. She tripped over Charmaine's headstone in a graveyard. Even when she dreamed of

522

other things, she was aware of Charmaine weeping in the background. Waking, she tried to call Charmaine, but all she could get was the answering machine.

"I'm sorry," she told it on the third try, feeling foolish. "I'm sorry about everything. I'll forgive you if you'll forgive me." She hung up, despairing. For all she knew, Charmaine might be in Timbuktu. She never had been one to stick around and work things out. She'd said so herself.

In midafternoon, when the phone rang, she ran to it.

"Dorrie?" Charmaine's voice sounded half-strangled. "Can I come over?"

"Of course you can! Charmaine, what is it?"

She heard a snuffle, and Charmaine took a deep, shuddery breath. Something must be terribly wrong. Dorrie had never known Charmaine to cry.

"Stay where you are," Dorrie told her. If Charmaine was that upset, she had no business driving. "Are you at home? I'll come to you."

In ten minutes, she was there. Charmaine must have been watching out the window because the door opened as Dorrie was running up the walk.

"What is it?" she asked, and stopped short. Charmaine's hair, always neatly braided, was undone and tangled around her shoulders. Her skin was splotchy and her eyes puffy and red. She was wearing an old chenille robe over a cotton nightgown at two o'clock in the afternoon.

"What!" Dorrie demanded.

Charmaine drew herself erect and cleared her throat. "I'm sorry," she said. "I shouldn't have called like that. I didn't mean to scare you."

"Never mind that. I'm here now. Charmaine, what in the world is going on?"

Charmaine drew another deep breath and tried to speak, but the words would not leave her mouth. She gulped and turned away to collect herself. Dorrie grabbed her shoulders and turned her back again.

"Charmaine Stubbs, if you don't tell me this instant what's wrong, I'm going to shake you till your teeth rattle!"

"Oh, Dorrie!" Charmaine wailed. "I think I've got cancer!"

"Cancer!" I knew, I knew! Dorrie thought. Oh, why was I so stupid? I should have hunted her down! Her arms reached out to embrace her friend and hold her close. After a moment, she reached up to stroke Charmaine's hair. She let her cry for a moment before leading her to the couch in the living room. Then, sitting beside her, she took Charmaine's hands.

"Tell me," she said quietly.

"I've had this lump in my breast, been telling it to go away for weeks, and I finally went and had a mammogram, and it's as big as a walnut and 'hot,' and I have to go to the hospital and have it out." Charmaine hiccuped. "They're talking about a mastectomy." She dropped her head on Dorrie's shoulder, and Dorrie held her.

"When?"

"Friday." Charmaine looked up through tear-filled eyes. "Oh, Dorrie, I'm so scared! I never have been able to stand hospitals!" She hiccuped. "Hospitals are where people go to die!"

"Baloney!" Dorrie said. "Hospitals are where they go to get well! But of course you're scared. Anybody would be." Anybody but Charmaine, she thought. She'd never imagined Charmaine scared of anything. "Charmaine, I'll stay with you. I'll be right with you all the time."

Charmaine sat up straight and shook herself. "I hate being scared! It makes me mad!"

Dorrie laughed. "That's the spirit! Listen, it's okay to be scared, even for an old toughie like you." She gave Charmaine's hands a little shake. "At least you're not alone. You've got me."

"Do I, Dorrie?"

Dorrie nodded. "Of course. What did you think?"

Charmaine sighed. "I thought I'd torn it for good and all, if you must know. Thanks, Dorrie. I'm sorry. I'm so sorry."

"Me, too. I'm just glad it's over." She sat beside Charmaine in silence. There seemed nothing more to say. Their hands, clutched together, said all that was needed.

Later, hesitating, Dorrie asked, "Have you told

your boys?"

Charmaine shook her head. "Hunh-uh. Not going to, either, unless they tell me I'm going to die, and then I'll put it off as long as I can."

"I see." Dorrie looked at Charmaine's hands, lying limp in her own, and shook her head. "No, I don't see. Why not? I'd tell mine."

"I don't want to worry them. Didn't want to worry you, either. I just couldn't help myself."

"Don't you think they have a right to know?"

Charmaine shook her head stubbornly. "I can't. Time enough for that if it turns out bad. You stayed with yours all their lives, Dorrie. They'd stick by you, want to take care of you. They love you. You're their mother." Charmaine's voice broke again. "Mine love me more like an aunt, and a distant one at that. They'd feel obligated, and I don't want obligation. I want love."

Dorrie was silent for a moment.

"How long since you told your kids you loved them, Charmaine?"

"I don't know." Her voice was thick. "Years. Not since they were little. I just . . . Max's wife made herself their mother; when she moved in, she took all their love. After a while they were just polite to me." She sighed. "Polite doesn't make it — not from your own kids. Not when that's all you get."

"She didn't take all their love, Charmaine. Love doesn't work that way."

526

"Yeah? When did you get to be such an expert?"

Dorrie grinned. This was more like the Charmaine she knew.

"I'm no expert. I only know it's not like a pie, that if you give more to one there's less left over for another. It's more like the magic cauldron in the fairy tales: the more you give, the more there is to give." She reached up to smooth Charmaine's hair off her forehead. "They used to miss you so badly, Charmaine. They'd come over to play with Two, and all they wanted was to sit in the kitchen and hear stories about you."

"You never told me. They didn't, either. They just clammed up the minute I walked in and sat there staring at me like I was some kind of freak. It like to killed me, Dorrie. All I wanted was to put my arms around them, and they were as stiff as a pair of brass andirons."

"They were in awe, Charmaine. They'd made you into such a romantic figure, it was like meeting a movie star." She paused, and then decided to go on. "And they never did understand the divorce and the custody thing. It made them angry. They felt abandoned, and Max encouraged it. He was bitter for a long time." She stared down at her hands. "I tried to tell them, but . . . Well, I wasn't you."

"Abandoned!" Charmaine's back straightened, her head came up, and her eyes glittered. "Christ almighty, Dorrie, you're sounding like my mother again: 'Threw it all away, girl, everything we gave you—the schooling, the beautiful wedding, that big house—threw it away like it was nothing!' Well, I *didn't* throw it away! It was *taken* away! I would've carried those boys to the ends of the earth, except for that damned, reactionary judge! I would *never* have left my boys—just their father, who was screwing every nurse in sight while I paid the damned bills!"

"You're preaching to the choir, Charmaine. Tell them. They're old enough to hear it now."

"I can't. It's too late."

"It's never too late to say 'I love you,' not if it's true. It might not heal everything in a minute, but it can't hurt." Dorrie was silent for a moment, and then added softly, "In my whole life, my father never said the words, 'I love you.' I would have given everything I've ever owned to hear them. Tell your boys, Charmaine. They need to know."

Dorrie got her dressed and packed a small bag for her, and around suppertime she took Charmaine back to her own house for the night. Charmaine had finally found a problem she couldn't run from, and for the next two days she needed all the support Dorrie could give her.

It was as if their fight had never happened, Dorrie thought. Charmaine's fear had driven their anger completely out of her mind. Only

Dorrie still felt bad about the things they'd said.

"Listen, Charmaine," she said the night before the surgery. "About the fight . . ."

"Forget it," Charmaine said. "I'm sorry I said those things. I didn't mean it, not any of it."

"Then—Excuse me, but where did it come from? You couldn't have made it up on the spot!"

Charmaine looked away. "Jealousy," she said. "Plain jealousy, I'm ashamed to say. My mama used to drive me crazy, telling me how wonderful you were. She said you were 'made of finer clay.' " She laughed bitterly. "Not that I didn't know—I just didn't like to hear her say it every five minutes."

She paused before looking up at Dorrie with pain in her eyes. "All our lives, you've had what I wanted: parents with clean hands who spoke decent English; a lasting marriage and a stable home; children who adored you. People respect you. You never," she smiled, "well, almost never lose your temper, and you don't go in for fits of high drama; you're always so serene. And you never give up. You never stop loving, no matter what."

Charmaine looked away. "God, but you're tough! You've always thought I was the brave one, Dorrie, but you're the one with real courage. I always wanted to be like you, but here I am: still a roughneck's daughter after all these years."

"Mercy!" Dorrie said. "Finer clay! I never

dreamed . . . Thank you. Nobody's ever said anything like that to me before."

"Well, for God's sake!" Charmaine said, laughing. "Don't you have anything to say to me now?"

"Well, let me see." Dorrie grinned. "There's a lot to be said for earthenware, you know. It's real colorful, and it can stand up to a lot of abuse. It may seem a little out of place at a formal banquet, but who gives those anymore? Earthenware is great for picnics, and I'm ready for a string of those!"

Charmaine's face crumpled. "You may have to take them without me," she said.

"What are you talking about? No cancer would *dare* to attack Charmaine Stubbs!" She put a hand on Charmaine's shoulder. "You're going to be just fine, Charmaine. You'll see. We'll board that plane on the twentieth, just like we planned, and be at Stonehenge on Midsummer's Eve. We'll have you dancing with the Druids in a week!"

She hoped it was true. The dream of Charmaine in her coffin, the hole in her chest, still haunted her.

She drove Charmaine to the hospital at six o'clock on Friday morning and stayed in the room with her while she was prepped for surgery.

"I'm sorry, you'll have to leave," an officious young woman told her. "Only the immediate family is allowed."

"We're sisters," Dorrie said.

She went out to breakfast after they wheeled Charmaine into surgery, but the food tasted like cardboard and she left most of it on the plate. In the car, she laid her head on the steering wheel and prayed: *Let it be benign. Grant her a long and happy life. Restore to her the awareness of her children's love.*

Charmaine had not told her sons. Dorrie waited alone until about half-past nine when Travis came in to sit with her.

"You didn't have to," she told him. "You hardly know Charmaine."

"I'm not doing it for Charmaine," he said.

"Well, thanks," she said. "I hope you will when this is over — know her, I mean. I hope you can be friends."

At half-past ten, a doctor in a green scrub suit came into the waiting room.

"Stubbs?" she said.

"Here. How is she?"

"She's in recovery. It was benign. We did a lumpectomy; all she'll have is a little white scar."

"How soon can she travel?"

The doctor looked surprised.

"As soon as she's well enough to go home, I suppose. I'd take it easy for a few days. We'll keep her under observation overnight, but she can go home in the morning."

"Do I need to do anything special for her?"

"I'll want to change the dressing in a day or

two. The stitches will fall out when they're ready. She'll be all right. Just love her."

That would be easy enough, Dorrie thought, smiling. She'd been practicing all her life. She took a deep breath, the first in days, and thought, *Thank you, God.*

"When can I see her?"

"They'll have her back in her room in a few minutes. We gave her a local, so she knows; she was conscious during the surgery. The grogginess is just from the tranquilizers. She'll be sleepy most of the day, but she's not in any danger."

She went back to sit with Travis, her face glowing with joy.

"She's all right?" he said.

"She'll be fine. It was just a cyst, not malignant." Her eyes filled, and she blinked back the tears.

Travis reached up to touch her face. "Don't cry now, silly," he said fondly. "There's no need now."

"I know." She swallowed hard and forced a smile. "They'll be bringing her back to her room in a few minutes. You don't have to stay if you have something else to do. I really appreciate your coming, Travis."

"De nada," he said. "It was bad enough you had to go through it at all, Dorrie. I couldn't let you go through it alone." He kissed her cheek. "Now that it's over, I'm just in the way. See if you can't get some rest, sweetheart. I'll call you tonight."

While she was waiting for Charmaine to be returned to her room, she found a pay phone and called her children, one by one: Two and Marcie at their offices, Susan and Kurt at home.

"I love you," she told them. "I just wanted to tell you one more time while I was thinking about it."

"Hey, Dorrie," Charmaine said when they'd returned her to her bed. She was groggy, but grinning. "Wanna go to England?"

Dorrie laughed. "Absolutely. I wouldn't cheat myself out of that for anything in the world." Her face was beginning to ache from so much smiling. "Doctor said you can travel in a day or two. Our plane doesn't take off for almost a week."

"Gimme that phone," Charmaine said. "I've got to call my boys. Maybe it's not too late, after all."

Dorrie is in a kitchen squeezing lemons for lemonade. Hearing voices, she finds herself in another room showing off her new house to her friends and family. She is proud of this house, designed and built with her own hands. It is beautiful and the most comfortable house she's ever been in. She takes Charmaine upstairs to show her the bedrooms. Her own room is white with big windows and the floor spatter-painted with brilliant spots of every color. The shelves are full of bright knicknacks that remind her of her life's best times.

"When did you do this?" Charmaine asks.

Dorrie laughs. "I think I must have done it in my sleep," she says.

Downstairs, her family wanders through the large living room, admiring its stone-faced fireplace, and into the sunlit dining room to take their places at the table. Travis enters, and Dorrie takes his hand and seats him next to her place. George hangs back, looking confused, and she gives him a hug before seating him at the end of the table.

In the kitchen, humming, she serves up the banquet: turtle soup and veal paprikash for Charmaine, sweet puddings for the children, a baked custard for Rose. Rose has always loved baked custard, Dorrie remembers, pouring caramel sauce over it. She dishes up hot, pungent chili for Travis and slices onions and jalapeños over the top. Kurt gets a large slice of chocolate cake, Marcie a cool gazpacho, Susan a delicate fruit salad. Dorrie fills plates with roast beef and potatoes for Two and George.

"You're sure there's enough?" George asks. "I've never been so hungry in my life!"

"Don't worry," Dorrie tells him, smiling. "There's plenty."

She serves her own dinner—turkey and dress-

ing, cranberry sauce, candied yams—and takes her place at the table. Dorrie eats slowly, savoring every mouthful. Then, her own hunger satisfied, she watches the others eat until they're ready to pop.

All the lines have gone out of their faces: the worry lines from George's forehead, the strain lines between Travis's eyebrows, the deep parentheses from around Two's mouth. She looks through the kitchen door and sees that all the dishes have refilled themselves. There will always be plenty to go around.

Forty-four

While Dorrie was worrying about Charmaine, Bellefleur had opened its three flowers, ripening to perfection just as she was about to leave town for a month. It was the most fragrant orchid she'd ever known, and the room was heavy with its scent. She hoped Jessie would enjoy it while she was plant-sitting and taking care of Domino. Dorrie would be back in time for the flowers that would bloom on the new lead; that would have to do.

She'd agreed to spend her last evening in town with Travis, though they'd made no firm plans. It would give her a chance to say a proper goodbye, she thought. He hadn't said another word about her off-again, on-again travel plans, hadn't even seemed surprised when she told him they were going after all, just wished them well and offered to drive them to the airport. Dorrie expected he'd want to spend the evening at home, so his request to dress up was a surprise.

"There's a good play at the Arts Center," he told her, "and one of my clients has just opened a new restaurant that sounds interesting. Sort of Mexican Yuppie Chic with live music."

After the show, they wandered through the West End looking for the restaurant. She took his arm as they crossed a street, and then dropped her hand to hold his as they walked.

"So how long will you be gone?" he asked.

"We've planned a month's stay, but I don't know . . . it could stretch. There's so much to see and do, and once you're over there it seems a shame not to go to the Continent."

"Will I ever see you again?"

Dorrie looked up to see if he were teasing and decided he wasn't.

"I'll come back, Travis. I just don't know when." She paused and looked at his pained face. "I'll miss you."

"Then why—?"

"The timing's all wrong, that's all. If somebody'd told me a year ago that I could care for a man as I do for you—even take him into my bed—without wanting a lifelong commitment, I'd have thought they had me mixed up with some other woman." She laughed softly. "But after all I've come through . . . well, I'll never say 'never' again, and 'forever' seems just as foolish. I just don't want to deny myself any choices until things settle down a bit." She smiled. "Think of it as a vacation, Travis. It may turn out to be a long one, but that's all it really is."

"Here we are," Travis said, pushing open a door. Jazz floated through it on the smells of grilled fajitas and chicken tacos; Dorrie could taste the charcoal. The owner greeted Travis and joked with Dorrie as he led them to a table near the dance floor. A five-piece band was playing a Beatles' love song whose words she could not remember. One chord progression in the middle of it had always given her the shivers. They played it just as she sat down.

"I hate that you're leaving," Travis said. "I'm trying real hard to be happy for you, and of course I'm glad Charmaine's okay, but I've got to confess: I hate it."

"I wish I could have it both ways," Dorrie told him, "be in two places at once, but my studies aren't that advanced yet." He looked startled, and she laughed. "I'm just playing with you, Travis. I don't think I'll ever get past serial time in this body."

"Just save some time for me, that's all."

"I will. I do love you, Travis. I want you to know that. And making love with you . . . well, I just never imagined." She watched a dancing couple separate and come back together several times. The last time, he spun her clear across the dance floor and made several turns of his own before she danced her way back.

"It's not 'goodbye forever,' love. I'm already looking forward to coming home to you." She reached for his hand. "But you do need to understand, Travis, this is how I am now: I'm going to be willful in my old age, think what I choose to think, go where I want to go, and do what I feel like doing. I've earned it, and I'm going to be stubborn about it. Nobody will ever interfere with my choices again. If you can't live with that . . ."

A young waiter in black pants, a white pleated shirt, and a bright red cummerbund brought them drinks, and they gave him their order. When he was gone, Dorrie looked down at their clasped hands and smiled.

"The thing is, I'm like a teenager just beginning to find myself. I've had an amazing adventure with you—more than just an adventure, of course—and I'm grateful for it. I know it's unusual to thank a man for that, but I do. You've been a revelation to me. And now I'm going off on an adventure with Charmaine that promises wonders beyond all telling. It might last a month and it might be six, but sooner or later it will end and I'll be back."

He stood and offered his hand, and they danced to a sweet old tune she hadn't heard since her teens.

"No other love have I, only my love for you. No other love will do," Travis sang softly as he led her in a tango.

"Will you write to me?" he asked as they resumed their seats.

"Of course! I want to share it with you. And I'll leave my itinerary so you can write too. I'll look forward to your letters."

"What if you meet someone else?"

"I'm not likely to land in one spot long enough for anything to stick. What's more likely is that you will if I'm gone too long."

"And then what?"

"Then I guess you'd have to choose." Dorrie smiled. "Just let me know what's going on, okay? I want full and complete descriptions of my competition." She leaned back to look in his face.

"Just one more thing I think you ought to know before you get in over your head," she said soberly. "My secret ambition is to become a salty old broad. It's going to be difficult to achieve: I almost never drink, I don't know how to swear properly, and I'm much too polite. Charmaine says she can't make a sow's ear out of a silk purse, but she's agreed to do the best she can."

Travis laughed. "We'll work on it together," he promised.

When they arrived back at Dorrie's house, he accepted her invitation to stay the night. His mood was sad and tender, and the loving sweet. Afterward, he went to sleep with one leg thrown possessively over both of hers, and he half-woke every time she stirred.

"It's okay," she said softly to his sleeping form. "I'm not going off the track altogether, just taking a little side trip. I'll be back."

Travis sighed heavily and turned over, as if some part of him had heard, and Dorrie stroked his back for a moment. Then she rolled over and shut her eyes.

England! She was really and truly leaving for England in the morning! Travis would wait if he thought she was worth it, and if he didn't . . . Well, then she was better off without him. She might never marry again, and then again she might . . . Time would tell, and she was in no hurry to find out. There was, she thought sleepily, too much else to think about just now.

Dorrie is high in the air, walking a wire cable less than half the width of her foot. She is tired, and the wire has worn through the bottoms of her crimson slippers, lacerated her soles, and left them bleeding. The height makes her dizzy. She teeters, balancing with her arms, and looks down.

Far below, Travis watches anxiously from the back of the store, where the stockroom has been converted to a boudoir. Waving, he calls, "You're too high, Dorrie! Come down! You're going to get hurt!"

Dorrie wobbles painfully along the cable and looks down at the beautiful, heart-shaped bed, inviting as a Valentine's chocolate box. Its coverlet is the same color as her slippers. If only it were not such a long drop . . . If she falls, she may never get up again. Straight ahead of her, on a platform at the end of the wire, Charmaine calls to her.

"Come on, Dorrie, you can make it! Just a few more steps, girl . . ."

It's not just a few steps, Dorrie thinks. It's miles and miles. I can't do it. But she has already passed the bed; if she falls now, she'll splatter like an overripe tomato. Should've turned back when I had the chance, she thinks, taking another grim step forward. If I'd had any idea . . . Her feet are killing her; she can see her life's blood draining from their soles, and the wire is slippery with it. If she doesn't get to the end soon, she is a dead woman.

"Come on, Dorrie, you're doing great!" Charmaine calls. "Look, I've got your prize!" She holds up something glittery, but Dorrie is too far away to see it clearly.

Now she gains her second wind. The pain is gone, and she is almost dancing toward her goal. She hears applause and looks down to see her mother and father, George, the children, and even Aurora below, clapping their hands and cheering. Rose is blowing kisses to encourage her. Dorrie straightens her spine and takes the last few steps along the tightwire. When she is within a body's length of the platform, she looks up.

Charmaine is holding out a golden pin in the shape of a chameleon. Dorrie wonders what is familiar about it, and then recognizes in its emerald eyes and diamond crown the stones from the rings she has put away forever.

DISCOVER DEANA JAMES!